Z

Z

A Novel of
Zelda Fitzgerald

THERESE ANNE FOWLER

ST. MARTIN'S PRESS ✿ NEW YORK

Z: A NOVEL OF ZELDA FITZGERALD. Copyright © 2013 by Therese Anne Fowler. All rights reserved. Printed in the United States of America. For information, address St. Martin's Press, 175 Fifth Avenue, New York, N.Y. 10010.

www.stmartins.com

Design by Steven Seighman

Library of Congress Cataloging-in-Publication Data

Fowler, Therese.
   Z: a novel of Zelda Fitzgerald / Therese Anne Fowler. — First edition.
     pages cm
  ISBN 978-1-250-02865-5 (hardcover)
  ISBN 978-1-250-02864-8 (e-book)
  1. Fitzgerald, Zelda, 1900–1948—Fiction.   2. Fitzgerald, F. Scott (Francis Scott), 1896–1940—Fiction.   3. Author's spouses—Fiction.
4. Authors—Fiction.   5. Nineteen twenties—Fiction.   I. Title.
  PS3606.O857Z23 2013
  813'.6—dc23

            2013003452

St. Martin's Press books may be purchased for educational, business, or promotional use. For information on bulk purchases, please contact Macmillan Corporate and Premium Sales Department at 1-800-221-7945 extension 5442 or write specialmarkets@macmilla.com

First Edition: April 2013

10 9 8 7 6 5 4 3 2

ONCE AGAIN
TO
ZELDA

Z

PROLOGUE

Montgomery, Alabama

December 20, 1940

Dear Scott,

The Love of the Last Tycoon is a great title for your novel. What does Max say?

I've been thinking that maybe I'll brave an airplane ride and come to see you for New Year's. Wire me the money, if you can. Won't we be quite the pair?—you with your bad heart, me with my bad head. Together, though, we might have something worthwhile. I'll bring you some of those cheese biscuits you always loved, and you can read me what you've written so far. I know it's going to be a wonderful novel, Scott, your best one yet.

This is short so I can send it before the post office closes today. Write me soon.

Devotedly,
Z-

If I could fit myself into this mail slot, here, I'd follow my letter all the way to Hollywood, all the way to Scott, right up to the door of our next future. We have always had a next one, after all, and there's no good reason we shouldn't start this one now. If only people could travel as easily as words. Wouldn't that be something? If only we could be so easily revised.

The postmaster comes, keys jingling, to lock up. "How are you, Miss Sayre?" he says, despite knowing that I've been Mrs. Fitzgerald since 1920. He is full-blood Alabama, Sam is; *Sayre* from him is *Say-yuh,* whereas I have come to pronounce those trailing soft consonants somewhat, after living away for so long.

I tuck my hands into my sweater's pockets and move toward the door. "I'm just about right as rain, Sam, thanks. I hope you are."

He holds the door for me. "Been worse. Have a good evenin', now."

I have been worse, too. Far worse, and Sam knows this. Everyone in Montgomery knows this. I see them staring at me when I'm at the market or the post office or church. People whisper about how I went crazy, how my brother went crazy, how sad it is to see Judge Sayre's children spoil his legacy. *It all comes from the mother's side,* they whisper, despite Mama, whose main crime is that she came from Kentucky, being as sound and sensible as any of them—which, now that I think of it, may not be saying much.

Outside, the sun has sunk below the horizon, tired of this day, tired of this year, as ready as I am to start anew. How long before Scott gets my letter? How long 'til I get his reply? I'd buy a plane ticket first thing tomorrow if I could. It's time I took care of him, for a change.

It's time.

That commodity, once so plentiful that we spent it on all-day hangovers and purposeless outings with people I've long forgotten, has become more precious than we ever imagined it could be. Too many of our dear ones are ruined now, or gone. Nothing except luck protects you from catastrophe. Not love. Not money. Not faith. Not a pure heart or good deeds—and not bad ones either, for that matter. We can, any of us, be laid low, cut down, diminished, destroyed.

Take me, for example. Until moving here to live with Mama this past April, I endured six years in a series of sanitariums in order to heal my broken brain and fractured spirit. Scott, meantime, straggled through a bunch of different hotels and inns and towns, always nearby me—until Hollywood beckoned again and I urged him to go. His luck hardly improved: for three years now, he's battled liquor and studio executives. He had a minor heart attack earlier this month.

Though I suspect he has someone out there, he writes to me all the time, and always ends his letters, *With dearest love* . . . My letters to him are signed, *Devotedly* . . . Even now, when we haven't shared an address in six years, when he's probably shining his light on some adoring girl who surely thinks she has saved him, we're both telling it true. This is what we've got at the moment, who we are. It's not nearly what we once had—the good, I mean—but it's also not what we once had, meaning the bad.

Mildred Jameson, who taught me sewing in junior high school, calls to me from her porch as I pass. "Say, Zelda, when's that fella of yours coming back for you?"

We're celebrities in this town, Scott and me. Folks here have followed our doings all along, clipping articles about us, claiming events and friendships that are as invented as any fiction Scott or I ever wrote. You can't stop the gossip or even combat it, hardly, so you learn to play along.

"He's writing a new movie script," I tell her, which is sexier than the truth: he's done with the studios—for-*ever,* he says—and is working only on the book.

Mildred moves to the porch rail. "You can't spend another Christmas apart!" Her gray hair is set in pins and covered by a filmy scarf. "Tell him to hurry up, for goodness' sake—and tell him to put that handsome Clark Gable in the picture. Oh, my, I do love Rhett Butler!"

I nod and say, "I'll tell him."

"Make certain you do. And tell him to be quick about it! We aren't any of us getting any younger."

"I'm sure he's working as fast as he can."

At a dinner we attended for James Joyce, in Paris back in '28, Scott lamented *Gatsby*'s lackluster sales and his slow start at writing a new book. Joyce told him that he, too, was making slow progress on a new novel, which he hoped to complete in three or four more years.

"Years," Scott kept saying afterward, never anticipating that nine strange and tumultuous ones would pass between *Gatsby* and his next. And now

again it's been six, but I am persuaded that he's going to finish this novel soon. After everything he's been through, every disappointment, every insult, this novel will restore him—not only to his readers but also to himself.

The other day, he wrote to me:

> I've found a title: <u>The Love of the Last Tycoon</u>. What do you think? Meanwhile, I finished Ernest's <u>For Whom the Bell Tolls</u>. It's not as good as his last, which explains why Hollywood's giving him over a hundred thousand for it. Together with the fifty grand he'll make for it being the first Book-of-the-Month selection, he's really rolling in it like we never were (though we did put on a good show). Quite a change from when all he could afford were those awful rooms over the sawmill in Paris, isn't it?

Ernest. Scott thinks we are all on an even keel nowadays, he and Hemingway and me. He said the new book came to him inscribed, *To Scott with affection and esteem.* He was so pleased. What I might have replied, but didn't, is that Hemingway can afford to be magnanimous; why wouldn't he tread the high road now that we are all in the places that, by his measure, we're supposed to be?

Scott went on,

> I just came across my Montgomery Country Club membership card from 1918, issued to Lt. F. S. Fitzgerald . . . do you remember that guy? Bold and dashing and romantic—poor soul. He was wildly in love with writing and life and a particular Montgomery debutante all the lesser fellows said was ungettable. His heart still hasn't fully recovered.
>
> I wonder if we're completely ruined, you and I. That's the prevailing opinion, but you've had eight pretty good months since you left the hospital, and my outlook's improving too. Haven't touched a drink since last winter, can you even imagine that?
>
> But Zelda, what wouldn't you give to go back to the beginning, to be those people again, the future so fresh and promising that it seems impossible not to get it right?

Lord help me, I miss him.

I wish I could tell everyone who thinks we're ruined, who thinks Scott's beyond washed-up and I'm about as sharp these days as a sack of wet mice, *Look closer.*

Look closer and you'll see something extraordinary, mystifying, something real and true. We have never been what we seemed.

PART I

If you aren't in over your head, how do you know how tall you are?

—T. S. Eliot

1

Picture a late-June morning in 1918, a time when Montgomery wore her prettiest spring dress and finest floral perfume—same as I would wear that evening. Our house, a roomy Victorian on Pleasant Avenue, was wrapped in the tiny white blooms of Confederate jasmine and the purple splendor of morning glories. It was a Saturday, and early yet, and cloudy. Birds had congregated in the big magnolia tree and were singing at top volume as if auditioning to be soloists in a Sunday choir.

From our back stairway's window I saw a slow horse pulling a rickety wagon. Behind it walked two colored women who called out the names of vegetables as they went. *Beets! Sweet peas! Turnips!* they sang, louder even than the birds.

"Hey, Katy," I said, coming into the kitchen. "Bess and Clara are out there, did you hear 'em?" On the wide wooden table was a platter covered by a dish towel. "Plain?" I asked hopefully, reaching beneath the towel for a biscuit.

"No, cheese—now, don't make that face," she said, opening the door to wave to her friends. "Nothin' today!" she shouted. Turning to me, she said, "You can't have peach preserves every day of your life."

"Old Aunt Julia said that was the only thing keepin' me sweet enough to evade the devil." I bit into the biscuit and said, mouth full, "Are the Lord and Lady still asleep?"

"They both in the parlor, which I 'spect you know since you used the back stairway."

I set my biscuit aside so as to roll my blue skirt's waistband one more turn, allowing another inch of skin to show above my bare ankles. "There."

"Maybe I best get you the preserves after all," Katy told me, shaking her head. "You mean to wear shoes, at least."

"It's too hot—and if it rains, they'll just get soaked and my toes'll prune up and the skin'll peel and then I'll *have* to go shoeless and I *can't*, I have my ballet solo tonight."

"My own mama would whip me if I's to go in public like that," Katy clucked.

"She would not, you're thirty years old."

"You think that matter to her?"

I thought of how my parents still counseled and lectured my three sisters and my brother, all at least seven years older than me, all full adults with children of their own—except for Rosalind. Tootsie, we call her. She and Newman, who was off fighting in France, same as our sister Tilde's husband, John, were taking their time about parenthood—or maybe it was taking its time about them. And I thought of how my grandmother Musidora, when she lived with us, couldn't help advising Daddy about everything from his haircuts to his rulings. The thing, then, was to get away from one's parents, and stay away.

"Anyway, never mind," I said as I went for the back door, sure that my escape was at hand. "Long as no one here sees me—"

"Baby!" I jumped at Mama's voice coming from the doorway behind us. "For heaven's sake," she said, "*where* are your stockings and shoes?"

"I'm just goin'—"

"—right back to your room to get dressed. You can't think you were walking to town that way!"

Katy said, "S'cuse me, I just remembered we low on turnips," and out she went.

"Not to town," I lied. "To the orchard. I'm goin' to practice for tonight."
I extended my arms and did a graceful plié.

Mama said, "Yes, lovely. I'm sure, however, that there's no time for practice; didn't you say the Red Cross meeting starts at nine?"

"What time is it?" I turned to see that the clock read twenty minutes 'til. I rushed past Mama and up the stairs, saying, "I better get my shoes and get out of here!"

"Please tell me you're wearing your corset," she called.

Tootsie was in the upstairs hallway still dressed in her nightgown, hair disheveled, sleep in her eyes. "What's all this?"

When Newman had gone off to France in the fall to fight with General Pershing, Tootsie came back home to live until he returned. "*If* he returns," she'd said glumly, earning a stern look from Daddy—who we all called the Judge, his being an associate Alabama Supreme Court justice. "Show some pride," he'd scolded Tootsie. "No matter the outcome, Newman's service honors the South." And she said, "Daddy, it's the twentieth century, for heaven's sake."

Now I told her, "I'm light a layer, according to Her Highness."

"Really, Baby, if you go out with no corset, men will think you're—"

"Immoral?"

"Yes."

"Maybe I don't care," I said. "Everything's different now anyway. The War Industries Board said not to wear corsets—"

"They said not to *buy* them. But that was a good try." She followed me into my bedroom. "Even if you don't care about social convention, have a thought for yourself; if the Judge knew you left the house half-naked, he would have your hide."

"I was *tryin'* to have a thought for myself," I said, stripping off my blouse, "and then all you people butted in."

Mama was still in the kitchen when I clattered back down the stairs. "That's better. Now the skirt," she said, pointing at my waist.

"Mama, no. It gets in my way when I run."

"Just fix it, please. I can't have you spoiling the Judge's good name just so you can get someplace faster."

"Nobody's out this early but the help, and anyway, when did you get so fussy?"

"It's a matter of what's appropriate. You're seventeen years old—"

"*Eight*een, in twenty-six more days."

"Yes, that's right, even *more* to the point," she said. "Too old to still be a tomboy."

"Call me a fashion plate, then. Hemlines are goin' up, I saw it in *McCall's*."

She pointed at my skirt. "Not as high as that."

I kissed her on her softening jawline. No cream or powder could hide Time's toll on Mama's features. She'd be fifty-seven on her next birthday, and all those years showed in her lined face, her upswept hairdo, her insistence on sticking with her Edwardian shirtwaists and floor-sweeping skirts. She outright refused to make anything new for herself. "There's a war going on," she'd say, as if that explained everything. Tootsie and I had been so proud when she gave up her bustle at New Year's.

I said, "So long, Mama—don't wait lunch for me, I'm goin' to the diner with the girls."

Then the second I was out of sight, I sat down in the grass and pulled off my shoes and stockings to free my toes. Too bad, I thought, that my own freedom couldn't be had so easily.

Thunder rumbled in the distance as I headed toward Dexter Avenue, the wide thoroughfare that runs right up to the domed, columned state capitol, the most impressive building I had ever seen. Humming "Dance of the Hours," the tune I'd perform to later, I skipped along amid the smell of clipped grass and wet moss and sweet, decaying catalpa blooms.

Ballet, just then, was my one true love, begun at age nine when Mama had enrolled me in Professor Weisner's School of Dance—a failed attempt to keep me out of the trees and off the roofs. In ballet's music and motion there was joy and drama and passion and romance, all the things I desired from life. There were costumes, stories, parts to play, chances to be more than just the littlest Sayre girl—last in line, forever wanting to be old enough to be *old enough.*

I was on Mildred Street just past where it intersected with Sayre—named for my family, yes—when a sprinkle hit my cheek, and then one hit my forehead, and then God turned the faucet on full. I ran for the nearest tree and stood beneath its branches, for what little good it did. The wind whipped the leaves and the rain all around me and I was soaked in no time. Since I couldn't get any wetter, I just went on my way, imagining the trees as a troupe of swaying dancers and me an escaped orphan freed, finally, from a powerful warlock's tyranny. I might be lost in the forest, but as in all the best ballets, a prince was sure to happen along shortly.

At the wide circular fountain where Court Street joined Dexter Avenue, I leaned against the railing and shook my unruly hair to get the water out. A few soggy automobiles motored up the boulevard and streetcars clanged past while I considered whether to just chuck my stockings and shoes into the fountain rather than wear them wet. Then I thought, *Eighteen, in twenty-six days,* and put the damn things back on.

Properly clothed, more or less, I went up the street toward the Red Cross's new office, set among the shops on the south side of Dexter. Though the rain was tapering off, the sidewalks were still mostly empty—few witnesses to my dishevelment, then, which would make Mama happy. *She worries about the oddest things,* I thought. *All the women do.* There were so many rules we girls were supposed to adhere to, so much emphasis on propriety. Straight backs. Gloved hands. Unpainted (and unkissed) lips. Pressed skirts, modest words, downturned eyes, chaste thoughts. A lot of nonsense, in my view. Boys liked me *because* I shot spitballs and *because* I told sassy jokes and *because* I let 'em kiss me if they smelled nice and I felt like it. My standards were based on good sense, not the logic of lemmings. *Sorry, Mama. You're better than most.*

Some twenty volunteers had gathered at the Red Cross, most of them friends of mine, who, when they saw me, barely raised an eyebrow at my state. Only my oldest sister, Marjorie, who was bustling round with pamphlets and pastries, made a fuss.

"Baby, what a fright you look! Did you not wear a hat?" She attempted to smooth my hair, then gave up, saying, "It's hopeless. Here." She handed me a dish towel. "Dry off. If we didn't need volunteers so badly, I'd send you home."

"Quit worryin'," I told her, rubbing the towel over my head.

She'd keep worrying anyway, I knew; she'd been fourteen when I was born, practically my second mother until she married and moved into a house two blocks away—and by then, of course, the habit was ingrained. I looped the towel around her neck, then went to find a seat.

Eleanor Browder, my best friend at the time, had saved me a spot across from her at a long row of tables. To my right was Sara Mayfield—Second Sara, we called her, Sara the First being our friend serene Sara Haardt, who now went to college in Baltimore. Second Sara was paired with Livye Hart, whose glossy, mahogany-colored hair was like my friend Tallulah Bankhead's. Tallu and *her* glossy dark hair won a *Picture-Play* beauty contest when we were fifteen, and now she was turning that win into a New York City acting career. She and her hair had a life of travel and glamour that I envied, despite my love for Montgomery; surely no one told Tallu how long her skirts should be.

Waiting for the meeting to start, we girls fanned ourselves in the airless room. Its high, apricot-colored walls were plastered with Red Cross posters. One showed a wicker basket overflowing with yarn and a pair of knitting needles; it exhorted readers, "Our boys need SOX. Knit your bit." Another featured a tremendous stark red cross, to the right of which was a nurse in flowing dress and robes that could not be a bit practical. The nurse's arms cradled an angled stretcher, on which a wounded soldier lay with a dark blanket wrapped around both the stretcher and him. The perspective was such that the nurse appeared to be a giantess—and the soldier appeared at risk of sliding from that stretcher, feet first, if the nurse didn't turn her distant gaze to the matter at hand. Below the image was this proclamation: "The Greatest Mother in the World."

I elbowed Sara and pointed to the poster. "What do you reckon? Is she supposed to be the Virgin Mother?"

Sara didn't get a chance to answer. There was a rapping of a cane on the wooden floor, and we all turned toward stout Mrs. Baker, in her steel-gray, belted suit. She was a formidable woman who'd come down from Boston to help instruct the volunteers, a woman who seemed as if she might be able to win the war single-handedly if only someone would put her on a boat to France.

"Good morning, everyone," she said in her drawl-less, nasal voice. "I see you've found our new location without undue effort. The war continues, and so we must continue—indeed, redouble—our efforts for membership and productivity."

Some of the girls cheered. They were the younger ones who'd only just been allowed to join.

Mrs. Baker nodded, which made her chin disappear into her neck briefly, and then she continued, "Now, some of you have done finger and arm bandages; the principle of the leg and body bandages is the same. However, there are some significant differences to which we must attend. For any who have not been so instructed, I will start the lesson from the beginning. We start, first, with sheets of unbleached calico . . ."

I squeezed rainwater from my hem while Mrs. Baker lectured about widths and lengths and tension and began a demonstration. She handed the end of a loose strip of fabric to the girl sitting nearest and said, "Stand up, my dear. One of you holds the bulk of the fabric and feeds it through as needed—that person is the roll*ee*. The roll*er*'s thumbs must be on the upper aspect of the fabric, the forefinger beneath, like so. As we proceed, the forefingers are kept firmly against the roll, thumbs advanced for maximum tautness. Everyone, up now and begin."

I took a loosely tied bundle of fabric from one of several baskets lined up along the floor behind me. The fabric was pure white at the moment, sure, but it would soon be blood-soaked and covering a man's whole middle, crusted with dirt and irresistible to flies. I'd seen photographs of Civil War soldiers suffering this way, in books that depicted what Daddy called "the atrocities done to us by the Union."

It was my brother, Tony, seven years older than me and now serving in France, who Daddy meant to educate with the books and the discussions. He never shooed me out of the parlor, though. He would wave me over from where I might be picking out a simple tune on the piano and let me perch on his knee.

"The Sayres have a proud history in Montgomery," he'd say, paging through one of the books. "Here. This is my uncle William's original residence, where he raised his younger brother Daniel, your grandfather. It became the first Confederate White House."

"So Sayre Street is named for *us*, Daddy?" I asked with all the wonder of my seven or eight years.

"It honors William and my father. The two of them made this town what it is, children."

Tony seemed to take the Sayre family history as a matter of course. I, however, was fascinated with all of these now-dead relatives and would continue to ask questions about which of them had done what, when. I wanted stories.

From Daddy, I got tales of how his father, Daniel Sayre, founded a Tuskegee paper, then returned to Montgomery to edit the *Montgomery Post,* becoming an influential voice in local politics. And Daddy told me about his mother's brother, "the great General John Tyler Morgan," who'd pummeled Union troops every chance he got, then later became a prominent U.S. Senator. From Mama I came to know her father, Willis Machen, the U.S. Senator from Kentucky, whose friendship with Senator Morgan was responsible for my parents' meeting at Senator Morgan's New Year's Eve ball in 1883. Grandfather Machen had once been a presidential candidate.

I wondered, that day at the Red Cross, if our family's history was burdensome to Tony, oppressive, maybe. And maybe that was why he'd married Edith, whose people were tenant farmers, and then left Montgomery to live and work in Mobile. To be the only surviving son in a family—and not the first son, not the son who'd been named after the grandfather upon whose shoulders so much of Montgomery's fate had apparently rested, not the son who'd died from meningitis at just eighteen months old—well, that was a heavy yoke.

Untying the calico bundle, I redirected my thoughts and handed Eleanor the fabric's loose end. "I had a letter yesterday from Arthur Brennan," I said. "Remember him, from our last trip to Atlanta?"

Eleanor frowned in concentration as she tried to form the start of the roll. "Was it thumbs under, or forefingers under?"

"Fingers. Arthur's people have been in cotton since before the Revolution. They've still got old slaves who never wanted to go, which Daddy says is proof that President Lincoln ruined the South for nothin'."

Eleanor made a few successful turns, then looked up. "Arthur's the boy with that green Dort car? The glossy one we rode in?"

"That's him. Wasn't it delicious? Arthur said Dorts cost twice what a Ford does—a thousand dollars, maybe more. The Judge would as soon dance naked in front of the courthouse as spend that kind of money on a car."

The notion amused me; as I continued feeding the fabric to Eleanor, I imagined a scene in which Daddy exited the streetcar in his pin-striped suit, umbrella furled, leather satchel in hand. Parked at the base of the broad, marble courthouse steps would be a green Dort, its hood sleek and gleaming in the sunshine, its varnished running boards aglow. A man in a top hat and tailcoat—some agent of the devil, he'd be—would beckon my father over to the car; there would be a conversation; Daddy would shake his head and frown and gesture with his umbrella; he would raise a finger as he pontificated about relative value and the ethics of overspending; the top-hatted man would shake his head firmly, leaving Daddy no choice but to disrobe on the spot, and dance.

In this vision I allowed my father the dignity of being at a distance from my vantage point, and facing away from me. In truth, I hadn't yet seen a man undressed—though I'd seen young boys, and Renaissance artwork, which I supposed were representational enough.

"Speaking of nakedness," Eleanor said, leaning across the table to take the end of the bandage from me, "last night at the movie house, an aviator—Captain Wendell Haskins, he said—asked me was the rumor true about you parading around the pool in a flesh-colored bathing suit. He was at the movies with May Steiner, and asking about you, isn't that sublime? May was at the concession just then, so she didn't hear him; that was gentlemanly, at least."

Sara said, "I sure wish I'd been at the pool that day, just to see the old ladies' faces."

"Were you at the dance last winter when Zelda pinned the mistletoe to the back of her skirt?" Livye said.

"You should've been down here with us on Wednesday," Eleanor told them. "Zelda commandeered our streetcar while the driver was on the corner finishing a smoke. We just left him there with his eyes bulging and went rolling on up Perry Street!"

"I swear, Zelda, you have all the fun," Sara said. "And you never get in trouble!"

Eleanor said, "Everyone's afraid of her daddy, so they just shake their finger at her and let her go."

I nodded. "Even my sisters are scared of him."

"But you're not," Livye said.

"He barks way more than he bites. So, El, what'd you tell Captain Haskins?"

"I said, 'Don't tell a soul, Captain, but there was *no bathing suit at all.*'"

Livye snorted, and I said, "See, El, that's what I like about you. Keep that up and all the matrons will be calling *you* wicked, too."

Eleanor reached for a pin from a bowl on the table, then secured the bandage's end. "He asked whether you had a favorite beau, who your people were, what your daddy did, and whether you had siblings—"

Sara said, "Might be he just wanted some excuse to make conversation with *you,* Eleanor."

"In which case he might have thought of one or two questions about *me.*" Eleanor smiled at Sara fondly. "No, he's most certainly fixated on Miss Zelda Sayre of 6 Pleasant Avenue, she of the toe shoes and angel's wings."

Livye said, "And devil's smile."

"And pure heart," Sara added. I pretended to retch.

"He said he's not serious about May," Eleanor said. "Also, he intends to phone you."

"He already has."

"But you haven't said yes yet."

"I'm booked up 'til fall," I said, and it was true; between the college boys who'd so far avoided military service and the flood of officers come to train at Montgomery's new military installations, I had more male attention than I knew what to do with.

Sara took my hand. "If you like him, you shouldn't wait. They might ship out any day, you know."

"Yes," Eleanor agreed. "It might be now or never."

I pulled my hand from Sara's and lifted another pile of fabric from the basket behind us. "There's a war, in case you haven't heard. It might end up being now *and then never*. So what's the use?"

Eleanor said, "That hasn't stopped you from seeing a military man before. He's awfully handsome. . . ."

"He is that. When he phones again, maybe I'll—"

"Chatter later, ladies," Mrs. Baker scolded as she strolled by, hands clasped behind her back, bosom straining forward like a warship's prow. "Important though your affairs may be, our brave young men would appreciate your giving their welfare more speed and attention."

When Mrs. Baker was past, I tilted my head and put my forearm to my eyes, mouthing, "Oh! The shame of it!" as if I were Mary Pickford herself.

2

===

That evening, the Montgomery Country Club's high-ceilinged ballroom was filled to capacity. Along with the young men and women from the town's top families were a handful of chaperones and dozens of uniformed officers who'd been given honorary memberships while assigned to nearby Camp Sheridan or Taylor Field. Those fellas would soon be joining their army and air corps brothers in the skies or on battlefields in places like Cantigny and Bois Belleau—but right now they were as youthful and happy and ready for romance as anyone there.

My ballet troupe readied itself behind a bank of curtains. Shoes snug, ribbons tied, skirts fastened and fluffed. Lipstick, rouge—though not one of us needed it, as warm and excited as we were. A final costume check. One more hamstring stretch, ankle flex, knuckle crack. Instructions to spit out our gum.

"Two minutes, ladies," Madame Katherine said. "Line up."

One of the younger girls, Marie, moved a curtain to peek out at the audience. She said, "Look at all those officers! I sure wish *I* had the solo."

Another replied, "If you were as good as Zelda, maybe you'd get one. Plus, you better quit eating so much cake."

"Hush," I said. "It's baby fat. Time and practice is all you need, Marie."

She sighed. "You look like a princess." Mama had pinned my wavy hair into as neat a bun as it would tolerate, then encircled it with a garland of tiny tea roses from her garden. The roses were the same deep pink as my costume's satin-trimmed bodice, and a shade darker than my diaphanous skirt. I *was* a princess, for right now anyway—and *right now* was all I ever cared about.

The orchestra began and I waited anxiously for my cue, glancing down once more to make sure my shoe ribbons were tied, that a bit of my skirt wasn't tucked into my stockings. Would I remember the one-more fouetté the professor had added last minute? Would the two new girls remember to split the line when I came upstage from behind them?

When I took the stage, though, all of that disappeared, and I felt so light that I wondered if I'd been specially charmed by one of our Creole laundresses. Or maybe the lightness owed to the fact that I was *finally* done with school. Maybe it was the energy of wartime, the sensation that all of time was faster now, and fleeting. Whatever the case, my body was supple and tireless. It seemed I'd hardly begun the dance when the orchestra played the final strains and the performance ended to cheers and applause.

While taking my bows, I noticed the officers at the front of the crowd. Like others I'd met, these fellas were a little older than my usual beaux. Their uniforms, with those serious brass buttons and knee-high leather boots, gave them sophistication that the local boys—even the ones in college—were lacking. The soldiers wore an air of impending adventure, the anticipation of travel and battles, of blood and bullets and, possibly, death, which made them more vibrant and alive.

A pair of tall boots paler than the others caught my eye. As I straightened, I followed the boots upward to olive-colored breeches, a fitted uniform tunic, and, above it, an angelic face with eyes as green and expressive as the Irish Sea, eyes that snagged and held me as surely as a bug sticks in a web, eyes that contained the entire world in their smiling depths, eyes like—

Something bumped my arm. "*Go,* Zelda," one of the young ballerinas said, and nudged me into line for our exit.

That officer was nowhere in sight when I returned to the ballroom after changing into my dress—corset included in the ensemble; shoes, too—and dabbing on Mama's own rose perfume. So I danced a tango with a boy I'd known my whole life, then followed it with a half-dozen more dances, a new fella for every new song. Sweaty brows, sweaty hands; sweat trickling down my back as I moved from one partner to the next, indulging no one of them more than another. They were useful accessories, these fellas were. Good dancers. Good company. Nothing more—though I wouldn't have said so to them. It was far more fun to let them think they had a chance.

Finally I took a break to catch my breath and get something to drink. As I stood near the doorway, cooling down and waiting for my latest partner to return with refreshments, here came the officer with the fawn-colored boots. Now I noticed the crisp white collar inside his tunic, his softly squared chin, the perfect almond shape of his eyes, and the long, feathery lashes that shadowed them. *Oh, my.*

He bowed. "Lieutenant Scott Fitzgerald, hoping to make your acquaintance." His voice was deeper than I'd expected, with no trace of Alabama or any place Southern.

I pretended to be shocked by his forwardness. "Without a proper introduction?"

"Life is potentially very short these days—*and* your latest partner might return at any moment." He leaned closer. "I'm wiser than I am impetuous or improper, rest assured."

"Well. General Pershing ought to be consulting you on strategy. I'm Zelda Sayre." I offered my hand.

"*Zelda?* That's unusual. A family name?"

"A Gypsy name, from a novel called *Zelda's Fortune.*"

He laughed. "A novel, really?"

"What, do you think my mother is illiterate? Southern women *can* read."

"No, of course. I'm impressed, is all. A Gypsy character—well, that's just terrific. I'm a writer, you see. In fact I've got a novel being read by Scribner's right now—they're a New York City publishing house."

I didn't know publishing houses from Adam. What I did know was that he held himself differently from the other boys—other *men,* I thought; he had to be in his twenties. And his speech had that dramatic flair you find in people accustomed to playacting in theater, as I was. When you'd spent so much time performing onstage, the habit bled into your life. Or, possibly, it was the other way around.

I said, "I thought you were an officer."

"My secondary occupation."

"There's not one bit of South in your voice, Lieutenant; where's home?"

"Princeton, before my commission," he said. "I did prep in New Jersey. My childhood was spent in Minnesota—St. Paul."

"A Yankee in every single way." I glanced beyond him; thirsty as I was, now I hoped my partner might forget to return.

"Yes—though I've developed quite an affection for the South since my assignment to Camp Sheridan. A growing affection, in fact." In those captivating eyes was what Mama would call "an intention." A spark, or sparkle; a glint or gleam. The fairy tales I'd read throughout my childhood were full of such words for such looks.

I said, "Well, that should make you more popular in these parts."

"I'm hopeful."

He smiled then, and I felt that smile like a vibration moving through me, the way you might feel if you walked through a ghost or it walked through you. "Hopeful," he repeated as the orchestra struck up a waltz, "and compelled to ask you for this dance."

"Well, I am waiting for that nice fella from Birmingham to get back with a whistle-wetter. It is so blazing *hot*. I don't know how you all can stand to wear all that"—I indicated his uniform—"and not want to just strip down and jump into some creek."

"I think it's because creeks are lacking somewhat in music and beautiful young women. Dancing, I've found, provides a good distraction from the discomfort of all this wool. Won't you help a fellow out?"

He offered his hand. How could I refuse? Why would I want to?

"I suppose it *would* be a service to my country," I said, just as the Birmingham boy returned with my drink. I took the glass from his hand, downed the punch, then returned the glass, saying, "Thank you *so* much," and let Scott lead me off into the ballroom.

He danced as well as any of my partners ever had—better, maybe. It seemed to me that the energy I was feeling that night had infused him, too; we glided through the waltz as if we'd been dancing together for years.

I liked his starched, woolly, cologned smell. His height, about five inches taller than my five feet four inches, was, I thought, the exact right height. His shoulders were the exact right width. His grip on my hand was somehow both formal and familiar, his hand on my waist both possessive and tentative. His blue-green eyes were clear, yet mysterious, and his lips curved just slightly upward.

The result of all this was that although we danced well together, I felt off-balance the entire time. I wasn't used to this feeling, but, my goodness, I liked it.

Two hours later, we stood facing each other in the pink glow of a driveway post lamp while the Club emptied out behind us. Any second now, Eleanor would come out, and then her daddy's driver would be there to ferry us home in the old phaeton I'd once decided to drive myself. I was twelve at the time, and the horses nearly ran away with me before the whole thing went sideways and I was flung into a hedge.

"Tell me more about this book business," I said. "I've never known anyone who could write more than a news article—well, Mama wrote a short play once, but that hardly counts 'cause it was a musical and it only ran some fourteen minutes—it was for a charity ball, we're always having charity balls here, do y'all do that, too, up North?"

He laughed. "Do you want to know about my novel, or St. Paul's society habits?"

"The novel! Both! Tell me every single thing about every single thing until El drags me off."

"How about this: I'll send you a chapter, and you can see for yourself what I'm about. Then you'll be able to say you were among the first to read F. Scott Fitzgerald's phenomenal first book."

"*F.* Scott?"

"Francis—after my cousin Francis Scott Key—*The Star-Spangled Banner*?"

"Not really!"

"Oh yes. Besides which, *F. Scott* sounds weightier, don't you agree? Authoritative."

"Absolutely." I nodded. "Why, I respect you more already and I haven't read a word. Imagine how much I'll admire you when I'm done. And then once it's an actual *book* . . ." I let the sentence hang like that, allowing his imagination to fill in the rest.

I wanted him to tell me more about how he'd done it, written a whole entire novel, and about what he liked to read, and I wanted to tell him what I liked to read, and then we could talk about things from those books. India, for instance; I'd been reading Kipling since forever. And Joseph Conrad's made-up Costaguana, from *Nostromo*—had he ever heard of it? Where exactly did he think it was? *Tarzan of the Apes*—had he read that one? Africa, now *that* was a place to talk about!

"The 'actual book' part may be a while, yet," he said. "Alas. I'll lend you something else in the meantime, though, if you like. Do you enjoy reading?"

"I'll read most anything. My friend Sara Haardt just sent me the strangest story, *Herland,* it was in a magazine, and it's about a society that's made only of women. I wouldn't like that much."

He grinned. "Good news, all."

None of the boys I knew had much interest in books. For them it was football and horses and hounds. I looked at Scott there in the rosy light, his hair and skin and eyes aglow with joy and ambition and enthusiasm, and was dazzled.

"*Here* she is," Eleanor said, slipping her arm around my waist. A linebacker-size fella was with her. "I thought maybe you'd snuck off like last time."

Scott said, "Snuck off? Had I but known—"

"To *smoke,*" El said the moment after I pinched her. "She'd snuck off to smoke with a couple of the older girls."

"Older than . . . ?"

"Seventeen," I told him. "I'm seventeen 'til July twenty-fourth, that's twenty-six—well, nearly twenty-five, really—days from now, given how it's closing in on midnight. Twenty-five days, and then I'm eighteen."

"After which time she'll be far less annoying, I hope. We don't smoke much," El assured him. "But it's good for preventing sore throats."

"It's good for making you *feel* good," I said, "which is why the law and my daddy have always been against women doing it."

"Who *are* you, by the way?" El asked Scott. She pointed at her companion and said, "This here new friend of mine, who is about to be on his way, is Wilson Crenshaw Whitney the Third."

"Scott Fitzgerald, the one and only," Scott told the two of them. Then, looking at me, he added, "Who very much wishes he didn't have to do the same."

"I purely hate that I have to go home," I told him. "If I wasn't a girl—"

"—I wouldn't insist you allow me to phone you tomorrow. All right?"

"There's my consolation, then," I said. The phaeton was rolling to a stop in front of us. I followed El to its door, adding, "Judge Anthony Sayre's residence. The operator will put you right through."

The morning's scattered clouds had, by afternoon, formed themselves into great towering columns with broad anvil tops while I lay on my bed, diary open, pencil in hand. I had one ear attuned to the thunder that might spoil my evening plans, and the other waiting for the telltale three short rings that indicated a telephone call for our residence. Scott still hadn't phoned, and now I was almost certain that he wouldn't. *He's all words, no substance,* I thought. *Writers are probably like that.*

Tootsie appeared at my bedroom door. "Teatime. Katy's got lemon pie, or tomato sandwiches—and *I* have gin."

"So Mama has gone out."

"Baby, I'm twenty-nine. Not exactly a schoolgirl, Lord."

"Yet you still wait 'til Mama's gone to pour a drink."

"I try to be considerate. Anyway, it's Daddy we need to worry about most . . . and God help me if he ever sees me smoking. I'm goin' to muddle up some mint and raspberries to go with that gin. Are you game?"

"Okay, sure." I glanced at my diary, where I'd been writing about the morning's Service League work. We volunteers had served doughnuts and coffee to soldiers at the train station canteen, and a married officer had taken an obvious shine to me. Though I knew I was supposed to discourage his interest, I flirted with him anyway. He was attractive and funny, and what harm was there in it? He was nothing more than a way to pass the time until we finished, until I could return home, until that charming lieutenant phoned.

I asked my sister, "Tootsie, how'd you know you were in love with Newman?"

"Oh-ho!" She sat down next to me. "Who is he? Tell!"

Katy called up the stairs, "Miz Rosalind, what'd you all decide?"

"What did we decide? Pie?"

I wrinkled my nose.

"The sandwiches," Tootsie yelled. "And rinse those berries for me, would you?"

"Yes'm."

Tootsie turned back to me. "Now tell."

"Nothin' *to* tell. I guess I ought to be aware of what to look for, is all. The signs of true love, I mean. Is it like in Shakespeare?" I sat up and took Tootsie's hands. "You know, is it all heaving bosoms and fluttering hearts and mistaken identities and madness?"

The sound of the phone ringing downstairs made my heart leap.

"*Yes,*" Tootsie said with wide eyes, holding tightly to my hand as I jumped up. "Yes, it is *exactly* like that. Gird yourself, little sister."

3

In mid-July, Sara Haardt and I were just leaving a Commerce Street hat shop when I heard a man call my name.

"Miss Sayre! Hello!"

Scott waved as he walked toward us through a throng of young women who turned to watch him. He tipped his hat and smiled at the women as he passed. Even dressed in civilian clothes—white shirt, blue sweater vest above crisp, cuffed brown pants—he seemed exotic, rare, desirable. I'd seen him twice since our first meeting, once when he brought me the typescript chapter from his novel, and then again after I'd read it. Both meetings had been too-brief exchanges of smiles and compliments enacted over cheese biscuits (Scott) and melon (me) at the diner, while Eleanor and Livye looked on from a booth nearby. Tempted as I was to clear my dance card and devote my weekends to this handsome Yankee interloper, as Tootsie called him, it was hard to know whether I should take his attentions seriously.

"How nice to run into you," I said when he reached us.

"Do I give too much away when I confess it's no coincidence? Your sister said I might find you here."

"Well, gosh, we're flattered, aren't we, Sara? Oh—Sara, meet Lieutenant Scott Fitzgerald of Princeton University. This is Miss Sara Haardt, of

Goucher College. Suddenly I feel undereducated—not that I have any use for college. I could hardly sit still long enough to finish high school."

"It's a pleasure to meet you, Miss Haardt."

"She's brilliant, don't let her fool you," Sara said.

I pointed to the store's window display. "Woman of the world that she is, Miss Haardt has been tryin' to educate me on what up-to-the-minute ladies are wearin' on their heads these days—which apparently is not these big feathered confectionaries you see here."

Scott said, "I'd have to agree. The New York City shops were all showing smaller, less ornate styles last time I was there."

"A fella who knows fashion!"

"I'm observant, that's all. Writers have to be."

Sara, tall and wiry and far plainer in appearance than in intellect, said, "Are you a writer, then?" She did this as innocently as you please, as if I hadn't already told her everything I knew about him.

"Since about the time I could hold a pencil."

"How fascinating," Sara said. "I do a little writing myself. Zelda and I were on our way to get lunch; why don't you join us, and you can tell us all about your work."

"I'd love to, truly, but I have to get back to Camp Sheridan." He turned to me. "Before I go, though, Miss Sayre— Zelda, if I may—I recall you saying a time or two that your birthday's next week. If you'll permit me, I'd like to arrange a little party at the Club in your honor."

"You would? I don't know what to say—"

"Say anything you like, except don't say no."

I laughed. "That narrows my options."

"Just as I intended. I've got to run." He grinned as he backed away. "I'll phone you with the details!"

As we watched him hurry up the street, Sara said, "What a lovely gesture—too bad you'll have to disappoint him."

"Too bad I'll have to disappoint Mama, you mean, when I tell her that her party is off—but I'll make sure Scott invites her and the Judge, and maybe she can still do the cake."

Upon hearing my news in the parlor after dessert that evening, Daddy said, "That boy obviously lacks good judgment. He hardly knows you. Where did you say he's from?"

I hadn't said, and wasn't about to. "He did three years at Princeton before leaving to join up, and now he's serving at Camp Sheridan."

Mama said, "He's enthusiastic, I'll give him that."

"He is," Tootsie agreed. She was working a needlepoint American flag; I'd teased her earlier about turning into Betsy Ross. She said, "When he phoned this morning and I told him Zelda was out, he insisted that he *had* to know her whereabouts. 'It's extremely urgent!' he said, as if his very life depended on it."

"Frivolous is what he is—probably too much money and not enough sense. You see that a lot in carpetbaggers. Don't be surprised if it comes out that his people are actually from the North."

I said, "*I* think he's terribly romantic, and it's *my* birthday after all."

Daddy reached for his cognac, the single drink he would allow himself, and only on Friday nights. "Be that as it may, your mother—"

"—understands the appeal of a handsome suitor," she said, and smiled fondly at Daddy, which was enough to persuade him to relent.

On the night of my birthday, the party took place in one of the Club's parlors, a high-ceilinged room lighted by a wide crystal chandelier overhead and smaller crystal sconces along the walls. For the occasion, I'd persuaded Mama to shorten a spring-green, scoop-necked silk dress so that the hemline would stop midcalf. I wore it with a new narrow-brimmed straw hat and a pair of sleek high heels like some I'd seen in *Picture-Play*. "Tell me more about this boy," Mama had said while pinning up the dress, but I put her off. "You just have to meet him," I said. "Then you'll see."

I loved the Club, it being the site of so many entertaining times, but the gaslights seemed a throwback now that electric lights were being used in all the modern buildings. Its elegantly shabby Oriental rugs and its creaking floorboards and its silent, colored staff were the antithesis of modern, too, and proudly so. This was my daddy's South, my daddy's club—not literally, but it might as well have been.

Now Scott stood in the center of the room, hands raised, and announced, "Ladies, gentlemen, welcome to Miss Zelda Sayre's eighteenth birthday fête! I'm Scott Fitzgerald, your host and Miss Sayre's most ardent admirer."

He looked distinguished in a nicely cut pearl-gray suit. His tie was pale blue with gray stripes. His eyes, grayish green in that light, reminded me of the rare icicle in Montgomery, or a pebbled creek's rushing stream in early spring. They revealed his intelligence in a way that made me want to dive inside his head and swim in its depths.

My friends cheered, and then Scott went on, "Jasper, our bartender, has created a drink in Zelda's honor. I described her to him, and this gin-and-soda-and-apricots concoction is the result. You've *got* to try it, it's outrageously good."

"How about all this?" Sara Mayfield whispered, watching Scott consult with Livye, who was at the piano. "He's wild about you, isn't he?"

"I guess he is." My chest was strangely tight.

"This must be costing his whole month's salary. Does he have family money?"

"I have no idea. He went to Princeton, so I suppose there's some."

"How old is he?"

"Twenty-one," I whispered. "He's a writer; he's already written a novel. I read part of it, and it's awfully good. He plans to be famous."

"There are worse things to plan on."

"The Judge says anyone who'd throw a party like this for a girl he just met must be frivolous."

Sara looked over at Daddy, whose stiff posture and expression said he was there under duress. She said, "There are worse things to be."

The music began, and then Scott joined Sara and me. "I've persuaded your friend Miss Hart at the piano, there, to play us a fox-trot. Shall we dance?"

"Seeing as you've gone to all this trouble, I s'pose I'd better say yes."

"Is she always this fresh?" Scott asked Sara.

"Hold on to your hat, mister," was Sara's reply.

A little while later, he told a story about a train trip he'd taken from Princeton, across the country through Chicago to St. Paul. In his telling, the land was blanketed in sparkling diamonds, his vivid fellow travelers were wise or funny or sad, the cities were cornucopias spilling over with ambition and industry.

He's so worldly, I thought. Whereas I was the opposite, having never been farther from home than the North Carolina mountains. *Worldly, but just as warm and eager as a golden retriever . . .*

I was about to ask him whether he didn't have golden retriever in his bloodline somewhere when Daddy pulled me aside.

"Baby, it's time you made your good-byes."

"It's early."

"Regardless. Mr. Fitzgerald asked us *three* times to have one of those cocktails. He might show a bit more restraint."

I thought the cocktail was well worth the attention Scott was giving it—not that I could let Daddy know this. I laughed and said, "No, I'm pretty sure he won't."

Daddy's eyes narrowed. "I'm certain you gave him your regrets as well."

"Yes, sir," I lied. "Well, I did have a *sip* of champagne—so's not to be rude to our host. I'd hate for anyone to think you didn't raise me right."

He wasn't fooled. "It's plain he's unsuitable; I won't have you wasting any more of your time with this boy."

Mama said, "Now, Judge, it's her birthday," and laid her hand on his arm.

"I'd really like to stay, Daddy," I said. "All my friends are here. How would it look if I left so soon?"

He thought this over, then sighed heavily, as if his being sixty meant invisible forces like time or gravity pressed harder on him nowadays. "*Tootsie* will escort you home, then," he said, eyeing Scott, who was now using empty champagne glasses to build a tower atop a table. "Are we clear about that?"

"Yes, Daddy—but he's a good person, you have to get to know him better is all. Things are different now than when you were our age."

Seeing my parents in the doorway, Scott left his tower to hurry over and shake Daddy's hand, then kiss Mama on the cheek. "Thank you both for being here. Zelda is fortunate to have such parents as yourselves. And what a fine job you've done with her!" he said, looping his arm around my waist. "She's remarkable."

"Hmph," Daddy said.

"Happy birthday again, Baby," Mama said, hugging me. "We're very proud of you. It's hard to imagine that you're all grown up now." Her eyes were misty. "*All* of my children are grown." She turned to my father. "Judge, you'll have to help me understand how this could have happened."

"The usual way," he said, taking her elbow. "Good night, Baby."

As soon as Mama and Daddy were out the door, Scott turned around, took my hand, and called over to Livye, "Dear girl, play us a tango!"

Daddy's space in our otherwise feminine house was the library, a small room lined with dark maple shelves full of books. He'd inherited a great lot of them from his own father, then added to them liberally. He read serious novels and biographies and philosophy and history books, all of which he said helped him better understand the plight of man, an understanding that, in turn, helped him be a better judge. A man with my daddy's intelligence and love of books should, I thought, be impressed with Scott's ambitions, so during supper a few days after my party, I mentioned Scott's novel.

"He's calling it *The Romantic Egoist,* and he hasn't got a publisher yet, but a good one—Scribner's—is considering it this very minute."

"Writing is a good pastime, a sign of an active mind—but it's no way to earn a living. What does he mean to do as a profession?"

"Writing books can be a profession," I said, even though I wasn't certain this was so. The only people I'd ever heard of doing it were very famous, and already dead. I said, "Charles Dickens—he did it. And Henry James."

Daddy's sour expression was his response.

Tootsie gave me a sympathetic smile. "Lieutenant Fitzgerald is a lively young man."

"Lively," our father said, "will not put food on a family's table either—and especially not when a great portion of whatever income he does receive goes to drink. His name—*Fitzgerald*—that's Irish, you know. And I'll suppose he's a Catholic. I'm a fair man, but there are good reasons those people have the reputations they do. Baby, you don't want to get ensnared here."

I bristled. "I'm not ensnared. He's a good and talented person and I happen to like him is all, and I think it's somethin' that he's going to get a novel published."

"Speculation, at best," Daddy said, gazing at me over his glasses. "Supposing they do publish anything by such an untested writer—unlikely, but not impossible, I'll give you that—then he'll be flush enough to buy himself a new topcoat or some such thing. Wonderful."

Katy entered the dining room and began clearing the salad plates while I was saying, "Don't you think we should credit him for having initiative?"

Daddy looked at me as if I was simple. "A man deserves credit when he accomplishes something of importance. Something that provides for the betterment of his life and his family's life and, whenever possible, mankind."

"But books *can* do that. I know you think so, or we wouldn't have so many of 'em in there." I pointed toward the library.

"Scott Fitzgerald is not Dickens, Baby. Nor is he James—who had family wealth, by the way, as do Edith Wharton and the rest of them. He's not a scholar, he's not a philosopher, he's not a man of property or business or even politics. He's—what? An Irish Yankee pup who enjoys liquor too much, didn't finish college, and is about to be shipped off to the war with no apparent prospects afterward—assuming he comes back in one piece." Daddy aimed his fork at me. "You had best set your feet on the ground and pull your head from the clouds, or one day you'll find yourself living in a shack like some nigger, washing your clothes in the river and eating peas for dinner every night."

"My goodness, Judge, what an image," Mama said. Then she patted my hand while saying, "Katy, we'll have the roast now."

"Yes'm."

I wanted to pursue the argument but was out of ammunition. As far as I knew or could otherwise prove, Daddy's opinion was indisputable.

"You do not," he continued, "want to ever have to work for your support."

And he was right, I didn't. No respectable married woman held a job if she had any choice about it, not in Alabama. We girls were trained up knowing there was only one goal to worry ourselves about, and that was marriage to the best sort of fella who would have us. As many rules as I was willing to break, I never gave that one a minute's thought. So the only thing for it was to make sure Scott would turn out to be right, and Daddy would turn out to be wrong.

4

"I can't stay to eat, but I needed to see you," Scott said.

It was an October evening, and I'd been waiting on the front porch for his arrival. Scott had been doing a lot of waiting of his own: to know the fate of his manuscript, which had been rejected once, revised, and submitted again; to ship out—which we knew would happen any day now; and for me to declare him first and best among my beaux, a possible husband, something I was still reluctant to do. He had no intention of returning to the South when the war was over, and, much as I cared for him, I was having trouble with the notion of leaving it. Who would I be, away from Montgomery?

Just the same, he kept riding the rickety bus from Camp Sheridan into town as often as he could get free. We'd go for long walks, we'd go to dances, he'd take me out for supper, and now and then we'd sit on the steps and porches of my friends' houses sipping gin from the men's flasks and telling stories, laughing the way only people who haven't ever suffered real loss or hardship can laugh. We spent a good lot of time perfecting our kissing skills, too, which I'd warned him was not binding—"Else I'd have been married well before now," I said.

Most of this I hid from Daddy, because as old Aunt Julia used to say, "Trouble, it don't need an engraved invitation." She'd been born one of

Granddaddy Machen's slaves and was Mama's childhood nurse before later coming to raise us Sayre kids; she said Emancipation just meant you had to get even better at looking out for yourself.

Now Scott's expression was grim, and his red-rimmed eyes suggested illness, or maybe a hangover. He'd told me how the strain of waiting to ship out was taking its toll; he and some of the other officers had been spending their nights drinking corn liquor and talking about all the ways they'd vanquish the enemy, if they ever got the chance. Maybe that's all this was. I hoped it wasn't the horrible Spanish influenza everyone was talking about.

"What is it? Are you ill?"

He reached into his pocket and withdrew a folded sheet of paper. "In a sense." He handed it over.

The letterhead read *Charles Scribner's Sons,* and I knew right away that his revision had not been sufficient. This letter was brief, apologetic, and seemed final.

"Aw, I'm sorry. You worked so hard."

He sat down on the top step—drooped onto it, as if the rejection had softened his bones. "You know, I was the worst student as a kid. No concentration. And since my father has a name but no real money . . ."

"Like us," I said, going down the steps to lean against the rail. "Neither Mama or Daddy inherited much—which he says is best anyway, a man ought to earn his way himself."

"He should. And my parents hoped I would, if I could just get serious about school. My aunt suggested Newman prep and paid for everything. Princeton, too. It was quite generous of her," he said flatly, picking at a hangnail. "But I hated that I was hardly better than a scholarship case. All my school friends with their millionaire fathers, their *houses,* their trips abroad, their society galas . . . why couldn't I have been born one of them?" He looked over at me, and I shrugged. "I wanted a place at their tables. My writing was supposed to get me there—not the millions, there's no hope of that, but the prestige. In America, you can invent your way to the top of any field. And when you do—well, you're in." He pointed at the letter still in my hand. "That, my dear girl, is the end of a dream."

I led him into the yard to get us out of earshot of whoever might be lurking near the porch's windows, then sat down on the grass. He plopped down next to me.

"Aren't there other publishers?" I asked.

"Scribner's was my best chance." He lay on his back, face up to the mauve sky, and sighed. "I might as well let the Huns use me for target practice."

"You're being ridiculous. You're as good a writer as there is. These Scribner people, they're just not smart enough to see it. Prob'ly a bunch of stuffy old men whose shirt collars are too tight."

He smiled dimly. "They *are* a conservative publisher. . . ." But then the smile drooped, too. "My ideas are too radical. And my style—it's not traditional enough."

I put the letter on his chest. "This Mr. Perkins doesn't think so, though."

Scott sighed again. "It doesn't matter what Perkins thinks if the answer's still no. God, I'm a failure. I should've taken orders—did I tell you? Monsignor Fay, my mentor, my friend, he's always felt I had a calling. I put him in the novel—which of course no one will ever read."

He sounded so desolate. I thought for a minute about how I might get him out of this gloom and back to his usual upbeat self. Maybe an appeal to his pride would work on him the way it had often worked on my brother. Tony was so moody, and tough talk did more to boost his moods than sympathy did.

I said, "Now really, is that what you want me to think? That you're a failure? Not only a failure, but a quitter? Francis Scott Key Fitzgerald, lately of Princeton University, is nothing but a weak-willed, washed-up has-been. Is that it?"

Scott sat up on his elbows and peered over at me, brow wrinkled, lips pursed. I raised my chin and gave him my most serious expression, the one I used when tutoring elementary-school children about poetry. You had to make the kids think you were fully sincere—especially, say, when it came to William Blake and his brightly burning tiger. They so often got off track about that tiger. Was it really on fire? Did it die? What made it burn? Was it lightning? Was it God? I had to make them believe that poetry was serious business; they'd come upon limericks soon enough.

Scott, here, needed to believe that his reputation with me was at risk. I gave him a disapproving glance, then looked away.

He said, "You do know I've taken a turn or two on the stage, don't you?"

"You did tell me that." He'd been active in Princeton's Triangle Club, writing scripts and lyrics and acting in several shows.

"Yes, so, right now, see, I'm playing the part of the Dejected Young Man. Honing my performance skills. A fellow has to keep in practice."

I forced myself not to smile as I turned toward him again. "You're *not* a failure, then?"

"No," he said heartily, sitting upright. "Of course not. I've had scores of things published in my schools' newspapers. Poems, lyrics, stories, reviews. A list as long as my arm. I wrote a musical! This is nothing. A minor setback. I can try again."

"That's pretty much what I was thinking. So you'll stay for supper?"

"I'd hate to disappoint your father."

On the day Scott's regiment shipped out, my sister Tilde, who'd now come to stay, too, while her husband was gone, found me sulking on the front-porch steps.

My closest sister by age, Tilde was twenty-seven years old, confident and capable, mother to a sweet baby boy named for his father. She was a real Gibson Girl type. Nothing ruffled her. With her dark-blond hair, her spectacles, her decisiveness, she looked and sounded a lot like Daddy.

She sat down next to me. "Scott's gone, then? Tootsie told me."

I picked apart a white cape jasmine bloom, dismembering the fragrant, silky flower and dropping its petals between my bare feet on the wooden plank. I looked over at Tilde. "Why do they do it?"

"What, volunteer?"

"Yes, that—and have wars to begin with. Why do they still think anything can be accomplished by having a bunch of young men meetin' up in fields and woods and towns, all shootin' at each other like it's goin' to prove that one side is righter than the other, all just for who gets to keep *that* field, or *this* river, or *those* buildings? Why does John care if the Germans get a chunk of France? Why does he care about that more than he cares about you?"

Tilde laced her fingers together over her knees. "Men don't think of it that way. They believe they're showing us their character. They're fighting for our benefit."

"How do *I* benefit from this war? How do *you*? Nobody's invadin' Montgomery, or any place in America."

"The war brought you Scott."

"And now it's taking him."

"Be patient, Baby. You're so young—you don't have to pin your hopes on any one man yet."

"Don't you like him?"

"From what little I've seen, I do. Though the way Mama tells it, he does seem to be like a little boy running around and yelling, 'Look at me! Look at me!'"

"What's wrong with that?"

"I worry, and so does Mama, that the two of you would wear each other out," Tilde said. "Anyway, the thing to do is wait and see what happens. I know you enjoy his company quite a lot, but even so, maybe he's not the one for you."

Thinking of how much better I'd feel if Tilde was right, how much simpler my life would become, I said, "I wish he wasn't, but I'm afraid he probably is."

5

—

1 November, 1918

Dearest Zelda,

    I write from Long Island, still stuck in port until my men are done with the 'flu and we can proceed at full capacity. The other officers and I pass the time with bad poetry and pretty good bourbon, wearing our overseas caps in the hope that we can will ourselves into health and action. Dear, dear girl, I miss your smile and the sound of your voice and the soft, rosewater scent of that delicate spot on your neck, just below your ear. Funny how eager I was to get to France before I knew that spot existed. . . . Now I'm just ready to be done with this damned war so that I can do what I'm truly meant for.

Desirously—
Scott

Not wanting to think about what awaited him in France, I kept my reply cheerful. I told him I'd begun an oil-painting class at the encouragement of Mrs. Davis, who'd been my art teacher at Sidney Lanier High and thought I'd shown real promise. I wrote, "We spent the entire first day learning to pronounce the technique terms *Grisaille* and *Chiaroscuro*, which don't exactly roll off the Southern tongue." I related a tale of how on the previous night I'd had two heavily spiked drinks before a dance at the Exchange Hotel and had subsequently climbed onto a tabletop to demonstrate steps to a sassy Negro dance called the Black Bottom before one of the chaperones pulled me down. I said,

> *The nice old woman informed me with great seriousness that it's a <u>scandalous</u> dance, and I told her with equal seriousness that she was preventing me from fulfilling my promise. Darling heart, do you think I could be good for anything besides entertainment? I hardly think I want to be—but of course it's you who I want to entertain most. And so I'm putting my sordid stories in my diary like always, so that you'll have some good reading when you do get back.*

He'd been gone all of three weeks when I came home one Monday to find Mama, all three of my sisters, and Marjorie's husband, Minor, surrounding Daddy, who was holding a newspaper before him like a trophy.

I shouldered in next to Tilde for a look. "What's going on?"

"It's over!" Tilde said, wrapping her arms around me. "The Huns surrendered!"

Daddy tapped the paper with the back of his hand, then turned it toward me. It was an *Extra* edition and proclaimed *PEACE. Fighting Ends! Armistice Signed.* "This morning, Paris time," he said. "We are victorious!"

Tilde said, "Tony and John and Newman are coming home!"

And Scott, I thought, awash with relief. He wouldn't have to sail the rough Atlantic to face the brutal enemy, would never be wrapped in those bandages I and so many others had rolled, would not be mired in muddy foxholes risking injury, infections, parasites, death, while I waited in my own kind of limbo for the war to end.

Home for him, though, would be New York, the city of his dreams. He'd told me how his Princeton friend Bunny Wilson had lived in Manhattan before the war, working as a reporter, sharing an apartment with a couple of men and a great many books, the clamor and attractions of the city all around them. Scott envisioned a life like Bunny's, not a life like he'd have here in sleepy Southern Montgomery, where the liveliest feature of a hot afternoon was a spinning ceiling fan.

"Aren't you thrilled?" Tootsie said, giving me a hug.

"Yes, course I am. Who wouldn't be?"

Scott returned to Montgomery briefly, to help close Camp Sheridan down. We pretended not to worry about where he'd live, spending most of our time together kissing passionately in out-of-the-way alcoves at the Club, or in the back row at the Empire Theater while some picture or other played. We joked about how our romance seemed always to have a musical accompaniment. "I bet that's how Lillian Gish feels, too," I said.

On a damp, cold early-February day, we went out for a walk in a stiff wind under scudding clouds just so we could be alone for a while. At the corner of Sayre and Mildred Streets he took my hands and said, "I'll send for you, would you like that? New York isn't much colder than it is here today."

I stared at him in surprise. His face was ruddy, his eyes bright and hopeful. "Is this an actual proposal?"

"I can repeat it in candlelight over dinner, if that makes it feel more official—but, yes, I want you to marry me." He dropped to one knee. "Marry me, Zelda. We'll make it all up as we go. What do you say?"

I looked around at my neighborhood, at the familiar homes, at the street sign that bore the Sayre name, at the sidewalks and post lamps and trees that had seen me through years of footraces, bicycling, roller skating, bubble-blowing, tag-playing—and, more recently, strolls with fellas who were as eager as this one to turn me into a bride. I loved Scott with all the enthusiasm of the most ardent eighteen-year-old girl, but did I love him enough to leave my home forever?

He saw the indecision on my face and, rising, said, "You don't have to answer now. Think it over. I'm yours, Zelda, if you'll have me."

When I closed my eyes that night, I saw myself as if I stood at an actual crossroads:

I'm out in the country. The air is still, and all is quiet around me as I wait for Fate's wind to blow, to push me in one direction or the other.

Standing there, looking down the long dirt road, I know that if I let Scott go, I'll most certainly end up married to some nice, proper fella from a good family whose people have deep roots in the South. I'll be the same girl I've always been, only the parties I go to will take place in drawing rooms instead of the Club or the Exchange Hotel. My husband will be, say, a cotton grower who golfs and hunts and drinks fine bourbon with his friends. My children will have colored nurses who mind them while I go to luncheons with my girlfriends and plan all the same kinds of social and cultural events the young me has taken part in over the years. I know this life, can see it clearly, love it the way I love my family, understand it, have no real desire to do anything differently.

Looking down the road in the other direction, I see the life Scott offers me, the life he outlined at the end of our walk. It's more unpredictable than Alabama's weather in springtime.

To start, he'll go to New York City, where he'll find some kind of writing job that will support us reasonably well, he's pretty sure, and then he'll send for me. He'll find us some place to live—an apartment, which will be old and small, he says, but cozy. Somehow, with my help, he says, he'll get his novel published and take his spot among the top writers of the day. We'll socialize with literary people and his friends from Princeton, who he's sure I'll find delightful. Sooner or later, we'll have kids. In the meantime, we'll be able to gorge ourselves on the kinds of entertainment we both love: music and dancing and plays and vaudeville. It will be an adventure—*adventure:* there's a word that worked on us both like a charm.

I could easily have chosen either life. But only one of them included the unique fella whose presence lit up a room—lit up *me,* and that was saying something. The question was, could he make it all work out? Which way was the wind going to blow?

I was eighteen years old; I was impatient; I decided, *Never mind waiting for the wind.* Around three A.M. I crept downstairs and placed a phone call to Scott's quarters. When he came to the phone, I said, "You'll make it worth my while, right?"

"And then some."

"Look at you," Sara Haardt said when I arrived at her parents' house for tea one gorgeous, fragrant afternoon in May. "Could you get any lovelier? You look like Botticelli's Venus."

Sara, born "blue" and always a slim girl, was thinner than the last time I'd seen her, and pale as ever. "And you're Mona Lisa," I said. "Think of the attention we'll get if we appear in public together."

"I can't imagine you're wanting for attention, all on your own."

I wasn't. Though Scott had sent his mother's diamond ring and I wore it with pride and pleasure, my social life was going on pretty much as it had before. The local fellas, all home now from France—except for the dozens who would never come home—seemed not to mind my long-term unavailability so long as in the short term I could still do a good two-step, and tell a good joke, and climb onto a chair or table now and then to demonstrate how well the little bit of fringe on my dress collar swayed when I shimmied. Also, Second Sara and I were volunteering as assistant wedding planners with Mrs. McKinney. Also, there was my painting class, where I was on my third pass at perfecting a dogwood bloom. Also, there was tennis. And now that the golf course had greened up, I was working hard on my drive, so as to maybe win the women's amateur trophy at the tournament next month.

I trailed Sara into the Haardts' parlor, where the maid was laying out the china tea service on a table near two floral-chintz chairs. Outside the picture window, three fledgling cardinals, their feathers sticking up in tufts, crowded together on a magnolia branch. I could hear their chatter through the glass.

Sara said, "What's the latest on Scott? No one can believe you've actually allowed a man to catch you—and take you off to New York City! What do your folks say?"

"Oh, they had a fit when I announced our plans, but I told them, 'I adore Scott. There's no one else like him. I've found my prince.' Daddy rolled his eyes, you can imagine. But Scott's wonderful is all," I said with a sigh. "Course, before he can carry me off, he has to do this quest, you know. Hardships must be overcome. Dragons must be slain. Then he can return for me, triumphant."

"You've been reading Tennyson, haven't you?"

"Isn't Lancelot marvelous?" I said. Then I leaned back and propped my feet on the table. "I used to think I'd never want to leave here, even for a fella as impressive as Scott, but now Eleanor's at her sister's in Canada, and you're in Baltimore most all the time, and my brother and sisters are away—well, except Marjorie—and, I don't know, plenty happens, but nothing *happens*."

Sara nodded. "I've been to some of the most interesting lectures recently. Have you heard about this new subject, sexology?"

"Don't let your mother hear you say that word."

"She went to one of the lectures! I was so proud of her." Sara poured our tea. "Sexology is concerned with women's power within the intimate relationship, and about understanding our unique physiological qualities so that we aren't shamed by our desires. We live in historic times, you know. Women are going to get the vote when Congress comes back into session and finishes ratification."

"Sounds like a witch's spell. *Ratification*—turns you into a rat."

Sara swatted me. "It's going to turn us into actual persons with rights," she said. "Women will be able to choose our next president."

"Right now, I've chosen me a husband, *if* he stops promising and actually comes through. He sold one story this spring, to some fancy magazine called *The Smart Set,* then spent the whole thirty dollars they paid him on a feathered fan for me and flannel pants for him. He can't find work he likes—he's writing advertising copy for ninety dollars a month and living in some terribly depressing apartment near . . . what did he say? Harlem? Some place kind of in the city but not really. He *hates* his job, but he keeps saying, *Soon,* and I have to tell you, the more he says it, the less I believe it.

How long is soon? It isn't days, or weeks, or a season. It's a placeholder is what it is, no measure at all." I leaned toward Sara. "Do you think I'm foolish to marry him? Tell me. I trust your opinion."

"Does he love you—and I mean genuinely, for the special person you are and not just some idealized feminine object?"

"He does, but—"

"But what?"

"If he doesn't succeed, he'll be miserable. I'd have a miserable husband and a miserable apartment. Romantic as I am, I'm pretty certain love does not conquer all. Plus I haven't had a letter from him in *two weeks*. He's got this whole other life. Other friends."

"So do you, from his perspective," Sara said. "Give him a little more time. If he regards you the way you say he does, he's a rare man, Zelda. Even in times as modern as ours is becoming, most men don't see any reason to get well acquainted with more of a woman than her vagina."

"Why, Sara Haardt," I said admiringly. "Goucher's given you quite the vocabulary."

"Are you *ever* serious?"

"You've known me my whole life."

"Right." She laughed. "Most women hear things like I just said—and I don't mean only that word—and want to put their fingers in their ears. 'What about romance?' they say. 'What about love?' We can have romance, love, sex, respect, self-respect, *and* fulfilling employment in whatever interests us, if we like. Motherhood doesn't need to be our whole lives—it can be one feature in a woman's broader life, the same as fatherhood is for men."

"You really think so?"

"If we had easy, legal ways to prevent pregnancy—other than the obvious one, I mean. Those are coming, too, thanks to women like Margaret Sanger."

And to women like Sara, who'd led the Montgomery campaign for women's rights. I said, "You are impressive, Sara Haardt. I really ought to at least try to be more like you."

"What fun would that be?"

"That's the problem in a nutshell, isn't it?"

In late May, I got bronchitis with a cough so severe that it kept me housebound. While I waited for the fever and cough to break and for Scott to report back on a lead he'd gotten for a newspaper job, I read. First was *Meditations* by Marcus Aurelius, which Daddy had given me. "Some food for thought," he said, "now that you have to sit still for a spell. See if it doesn't open your eyes about your future."

That wasn't the book for the job; that one amounted to a dry bunch of Stoic platitudes everyone had heard before but no lively person actually wanted to observe. "Do not act as if you were going to live ten thousand years. Death hangs over you. While you live, while it is in your power, be good." The man was a killjoy. Clearly, joy-killing was Daddy's intention, too.

The eye-opener was *Plashers Mead* by Compton Mackenzie, which Scott had sent. Its protagonist, Guy Hazlewood, resembled the romantic poet Scott said he saw in himself, and its heroine, Guy's fiancée, Pauline Grey, was a passionate woman Scott said reminded him of me. These characters were older than we were, and their circumstances were different from Scott's and mine, yet in reading the story I felt as if I was living a version of it. It was the strangest thing.

There was a line in the book, in the chapter titled "Another Summer," that jumped out at me, stuck itself into my brain and would not leave me alone. A friend of Guy's said this about him to Pauline:

He's such an extraordinarily brilliant person that it would be terrible if he let himself do nothing in the end.

That friend was speaking directly to me.

The newspaper job Scott was trying for: Did that add up to "nothing"? Scott didn't want to think so. For him, such a job appeared to be an answer to the problem of how he could support us properly in New York. But that was only one little part of things. He was giving too much credit to the idea that if he secured a new job, he'd be able to put the rest of his plan into action. New job, new wife, time for writing, cash for the theater and parties, great book, literary fame—he would make it all happen at once, by God, or die trying.

It was an impossible plan.

6

A few days later, Mama was on the phone with Tony when I came into the front hall. "I'll wire you the cash," she was saying, talking too loudly and leaning too close to the mouthpiece, as usual. She didn't trust telephones and treated them the way she'd treated Grandmother Musidora when Grandmother's hearing had nearly gone. "But this needs to be the end of it. You know how the Judge feels about a man living within his means—" She caught sight of me. "Your sister's here; do you want to say hello?"

She held up the receiver and I took it, while she moved out of the way.

"Hey, Tony," I said, my voice still raspy, "when are you comin' to see me?"

"Oh, soon," Tony said.

(*soon, soon . . .*)

"Can't get time away from this damned job right now. If I don't act like I'm supremely grateful to muck around in the swamp measurin' saw grass so's Montgomery can have a highway to Mobile, there's fifty unemployed former soldiers who will."

"Well, we sure do miss you. Maybe I'll come pay y'all a visit once I know I won't infect you. I have all kinds of time."

"Meanin' you still haven't set a wedding date."

"Scott's still tryin' to work out the details."

Tony laughed, but it wasn't a happy laugh. "I know fellas like that, senior engineers, here, fussin' over this and that while the rest of us go gray. Better marry a farmer—they *know* 'perfect' doesn't exist."

"Those senior engineers, though, they're just makin' sure it'll be a good road. Right?"

"It'll be *no* road unless someone gives them a swift kick."

"That's what I'm afraid of."

That night, when the house was quiet and there was only the sound of crickets at the windowsill and frogs in the trees, I sat at the desk in my bedroom and composed a letter. It took hours of careful thought—much longer than I'd expected—and, nauseated, I tore up my efforts twice, wanting to believe that what I was attempting to do wasn't necessary. Then I thought it through again and got back to work.

In the end, the letter was brief:

Dear Perry,

What a fine time we had last weekend in Atlanta!—but I'm afraid I went just a little too far by accepting your fraternity pin. Blame the gin. I regret having to wound such a tender heart, but your pin is enclosed. I can't accept it while I'm still promised to someone else. That may change, though, and if it does I'll certainly let you know.

Until then—
Zelda

I tucked the letter, along with a pin from an old beau, into an envelope, which I then addressed quite deliberately to Scott.

Sara Mayfield was with me when Scott's reply arrived the following week. Mama had sent her up to my room, aware that I'd been morose for days but unaware of the reason. When Sara arrived, I'd heard Mama say, "Go see if you can cheer her up. My moody children, goodness . . ." I couldn't tell Mama what I was up to; she'd have clucked about it endlessly and made everything worse.

Now Sara sat next to where I lay on the bed with damp eyes and the letter clutched in my hand. She patted my arm and asked, "What does he say?"

The lump in my throat made it hard for me to answer, so I handed her the letter, which was as brief as mine had been and amounted to *Never contact me again.*

Sara read it. "Wow, he sounds really hurt. But then, that's what you wanted."

"Mm."

"He'll be happy in the long run, I guess. If he gets his book published and all."

Wiping my eyes, I nodded my agreement.

"And if he loves you truly, he'll love you *then,* too. You had to do it, Zelda."

"For his own good."

"And yours." She took my hands and pulled me up from the bed. "Now come on, it's hot and I'm thirsty. Let's go down to the drugstore and have us some ice-cold dopes. There's more to life than fellas, right?"

"Not really," I said. My smile felt weak, but it was a start.

Ten days later, Scott stood in the hall of my house. "I had to *see* you," he said breathlessly, while Daddy scowled at us from the library's doorway. "This is all wrong."

He looked as desperate and miserable as I'd been when I'd gotten his letter. He wore a light brown suit that he'd obviously slept in—and run in, it seemed, likely all the way from the train station. Sweat was beaded on his forehead and made shiny trails along the sides of his face.

I took his hand; it was moist, too. With a glance at my father, I said, "Come outside."

As I led Scott to Mama's rose garden, he said, "It was all my fault for taking too long. Come back with me—we'll get the first train and get married right away."

My heart pounded in my chest. *Yes! Buy me a ticket, I'll pack my trunk!* I tried to say the words, they were right there in my throat, but—

He's such an extraordinarily brilliant person that it would be terrible if he let himself do nothing in the end.

Yes, I know, I thought—but I was stubborn, too, and he was right there with me looking so hopeful and impassioned, and I didn't want to let him down and I didn't want to give him up.

"Have you ever thought that writing should just be your hobby?" I asked hopefully, selfishly—stupidly too, 'cause I already knew better. "You could do something stable for a profession. Banking, maybe, like my brother-in-law Newman."

Scott shook his head. "I can't."

"Why can't you? Why does it *have* to be writing?"

"It's the only thing I know how to do. I don't have a single other talent or skill."

"You could learn one."

"I *can't.* You don't understand. I was terrible in the army. Worst aide-de-camp ever. I can't run an office. I can't lead men. I'm not a whiz with numbers. I've got no patience for administrative work—do you know what kinds of idiots head up these companies? But it doesn't matter. None of that matters. With you there to come home to . . . You'll *inspire* me. You *do* inspire me. I'll work so much better if I'm not worrying about you."

Such romantic words! If the scene were being played out in a dime novel or a picture show, the heroine, heart racing, would swoon and fall into the hero's arms. *We'll leave it to fate!* she'd say as she fainted. I guess I'm not the swooning type, though, because I knew Scott was giving himself a prescription:

I'll work so much better if I'm not worrying about you.

As I had already concluded, he was completely right, just not in the way he thought. He'd never give up on any of his goals—wasn't his appearance here clear proof of how ridiculously stubborn he was?—and if he didn't give up on any of them, he'd fail at them all.

So I swallowed hard and said, "You know, I think our love has run its course and we both need to just move on."

His mouth fell open. "What are you *talking* about? What—because I won't be something else, something your father would approve of, something soul-crushing and meaningless just to get a good paycheck?"

"If you want to see it that way." I shrugged.

Oh, the look on his face! It was awful. I thought flames might shoot from his eyes, that his hair might catch fire, that he might burst apart on the spot.

When he could speak again, he accused me of having led him on, of being self-centered and unwilling to sacrifice my comfortable life for the meager-but-honorable one he was offering. He pointed at me. "I never should have trusted a girl like you. You've obviously been lying to me all along."

I shrugged again and told him he should go.

"Zelda—" he tried once more, so angry, so confused.

I couldn't stay there and face that; I'd break down before long and then where would we be? I got up and walked away, head up, chin out, fists and teeth clenched, until I was safely inside the house, inside my bedroom.

There I stayed for hours, pacing, crying my eyes out, sure I'd done the wrong thing. I wanted him to come pounding at the door, insisting I elope with him—and at the same time I was terrified that he might.

He didn't return, though, and when my tears turned to hiccups and then to sighs, I took a bath and washed my face and got on with the business of being a heartsick, single, almost-nineteen-year-old Montgomery girl.

—Until October, when I came home one day to find a telegram waiting:

MISS ZELDA SAYRE
6 PLEASANT AVE MONTGOMERY ALA

MY DEAR SCRIBNERS TO PUBLISH MY NOVEL
MUST SEE YOU ARRIVING THURS. SCOTT.

When I saw him, he told me how, that summer, he had quit his job, gone home to St. Paul, and put all his effort into revising the novel once more. He said that he'd sent Scribner's the manuscript in September. The next spring, it would be published as *This Side of Paradise*—the book that started it all.

7

===

When Scott returned to visit in January, he took a room at an inn across town from my house. No need to explain the choice; I understood full well what he had in mind. Understood, and was as eager as he was.

In the twilight of that wintertime afternoon, I changed out of my wool dress into the green one I'd worn for my eighteenth birthday. Beneath my dress was only one undergarment: an ivory silk chemise I'd bought earlier that day.

Our engagement is rock solid, I told myself. Why not take this next step?

We had decided we'd wait 'til spring to marry, so that he'd have time to finish polishing up his manuscript and a bunch of short stories he hoped to sell. The advance he'd gotten for the book wasn't enough to live on, not by far. But he'd acquired a literary agent. Credibility. He'd written to my father to assure him that all the doors had now opened to him, that the two of us wouldn't be living on tins of fish and beans, that he'd keep a suitable roof over our heads.

It'll be fine. He loves me. There's no real risk.

Under cover of darkness and a heavy, figure-hiding old coat and head-scarf that had been Grandmother Musidora's, I went to see him at the inn.

He met me at the front door. "Aunt Myrna!" he said for the clerk's benefit. "So good of you to come. I brought some supper in; we can have it in my room. Come on, I'll bet you're hungry."

I hobbled along with him, head down, face hidden. "Good of you to anticipate your poor old Aunt Myrna's desires," I said, and Scott coughed.

"You'll see," he said as we reached the staircase. "I have such good things waiting for you."

The room could have been my grandmother's, too, that's what I thought when Scott ushered me inside. Flouncy draperies covered the windows. The chair and settee wore crocheted antimacassars. On the narrow bed was a beautiful but old-fashioned quilt. All of the furnishings were timeworn, as if they'd been bought from old estates and then given a new life here at the inn.

Scott pulled me to him. When he kissed me, I tasted bourbon.

"How 'bout a drink for your girl?" I said.

"Are you nervous?"

"No. Yes. No," I decided. "Not nervous. Just . . . It's all so momentous. I feel like you and me . . . we're this new creature just hatched into the world and there's nobody like us and we have to figure out every little thing fresh. But that's silly, isn't it? People've been fallin' in love and doin' the next natural thing for eons before us."

Scott pressed his forehead to mine. "It's not silly at all. We *are* making our own path. This *is* momentous." He kissed me again. "Let me pour you that drink."

The bourbon did what bourbon can do so well, and before long, Scott was admiring that new chemise with his eyes, then his hands, then he was moving it out of the way of places he wanted to admire with his mouth. I was admiring him as well.

We went about it slowly, a little awkward at first, me giggling, him shushing me and then laughing, too. Bare skin against bare skin, we entwined ourselves, eventually fitting together exactly as Nature intended. When Scott buried his face in my neck and moved against me, all thought fled my mind. There was nothing but sensation, this profoundly primal feeling I hadn't anticipated or even known could occur.

And while that first time lasted only a few intense minutes, it proved for certain that Scott and I had something exceptional, something irresistible to us both. For good or ill, that act, those feelings, defined everything my life was going to become.

Scott visited again in February. Again, I went to his room eagerly and in disguise. I don't recall us saying more than *Hello* before we were peeling off each other's clothes and falling into bed.

Afterward, I told him I thought I might be pregnant.

"You couldn't possibly know the minute it happens." He laughed.

"From before, I mean."

He stared at me for a moment, then said, "Well, I guess neither of us has any right to be surprised. Fatherhood, though." He shook his head. "I didn't imagine it would happen so easily—not that I don't want to have children."

"Me, too."

"It just feels awfully fast." He shifted so that he could sit up, then lit a cigarette.

I sat up, too, pulling the sheet up to cover us both. "I know, it does."

"Too fast. There are ways of . . . of managing the situation. Do you know about the, er, treatments? The pills and such?"

"Of course."

Tallu's sister, Eugenia—Gene—had informed us girls on this topic, along with all sorts of other salacious things that we were forever asking her to repeat. I did also learn some important things. To *prevent* pregnancy, there were devices and herbal teas and special rinses—none of which were considered fail-safe, and none of which I'd ever considered trying. Like Scott, I'd thought that getting pregnant would more likely take multiple exposures. It'd taken Marjorie years, after all, and Tootsie seemed to be on that same path.

And, Gene told us, to *undo* pregnancy there was another class of herbal teas and special rinses, along with a variety of pills that I'd seen advertised as providing "feminine relief." No girl I knew had used any of these things, but we all talked about them. There were, we all agreed, certain kinds of women and certain kinds of situations that would benefit from such things. For example, really poor women who had too many children already. And of course prostitutes.

Scott said, "So that's what you'll do, then."

"Hold on. First of all, I haven't even seen a doctor yet—"

"It'd be better to have a year or two to ourselves. I really need time to get established. A baby in the house . . . I can't imagine being able to concentrate on anything."

"Well, sure, but since we'd eventually have 'em anyway—"

"Eventually I hope to afford a nurse and a nanny and whatever other help you want. But that can't happen until I've got more things written, more things sold. You understand."

"There's still seven or eight months before the baby'd come," I said, "and then when they're first born, they pretty much sleep all the time. So that's at least a year."

Scott was shaking his head. "If I can't write, I don't make more money, and if I don't make more money, none of our plans will work out—and any money I've made already would go for the baby. I've paid in blood to get where I am, Zelda. You've got to take care of this. This isn't what we want right now."

"You have paid, I know. But a whole year should be—"

"Zelda." He shifted to face me. His eyes were stern, but fearful, too. "I'm so close. Everything I ever wanted, it's right *there*." He stretched out his arm as if literary success dangled like an apple on a tree.

"My father was a failure," he went on, getting out of bed to pull on his undershorts, then pour drinks for us both. "When he lost his job in Buffalo and we had to go back to St. Paul, only the charity of Mother's family kept us afloat. There we were, living in this grand house, acting as if we were as well-off as our rich neighbors, and it was all a farce."

He handed me my drink. "I can't be *almost* successful. I can't get this close to the life I've been witnessing, my face against the window like the Little Match Girl, and then see it dissolve like a mirage. When I get back to

New York, I'll see about some options, and we'll get the matter taken care of. You understand, don't you?"

"I guess I do."

The solution to my still-missing monthly arrived a week later wrapped in a paper packet tucked inside an envelope. The small, pale yellow pills looked innocent as aspirin. It would be easy enough to swallow them fast and then just not think about it anymore—until the effects came, at which time it'd be too late for anything but regret. I held them in my palm for a moment, then slid them back into the packet, tucked it underneath my mattress, and went downstairs.

At the piano, I paged through the pile of sheet music, rejecting the jazz piece I'd been working on, rejecting my father's favored tunes like "Dixie" and "On to the Battle," which I'd often played to get his attention and coax a smile. Then I saw "Dance of the Hours." I put it on the stand and began to play.

How simple everything had been that night I'd danced to this song. How easy. Nothing but laughter and the enchantment of a charming officer in his crisp dress uniform. Now everything was a tangle of hope and circumstance and connected fates.

Scott's happiness is my happiness, I thought. *'Til the end of time, amen.*

But . . . if I took the pills, if I ended a pregnancy just because it wasn't convenient, wasn't that the same as declaring that what we'd done was dirty and wrong? That I was no better than a whore?

On the other hand, if I had this possible baby and our life afterward proved to be nothing but misery, he'd be resentful forever, and what kind of life would that be?

But it wouldn't be misery, I was sure. He was overdramatizing—

"Zelda, for heaven's sake," Mama called from the library. "You needn't pound the keys!"

"Sorry, Mama!"

I'd never compromised on anything important, damn it. Leaving the piano for a minute, I ran upstairs for the pills, then returned to the parlor and put the packet into the fire.

As luck would have it, a few days later the matter resolved itself. I wrote to Scott, *Things have a way of working out for us, and this is just one more sign.*

I believed it, too. Who wouldn't have when, from about this time onward, nearly everything Scott had written in the previous year began to turn to gold?

"So his novel will be out soon," Daddy said. We were in the parlor, where Mama and I had been discussing my trousseau. "Good for him, but it's not a *job*. How long will it be before he can sell another, and what will you two live on in the meantime?"

I explained that Scott had begun selling his short stories. "*The Saturday Evening Post* bought one called 'Head and Shoulders' for four hundred dollars—and they liked it so well that they paid *nine hundred* for two more." When Daddy still didn't look impressed, I said, "Add that to how much he got for his novel and it's already as much as he'd have earned in *two years* at his old job. And he's got a pile of stories already done."

"I don't like it," Daddy said. "It's not a plan, it's luck. And when his luck runs out—"

A knock on the door interrupted him, and a moment later Katy came into the parlor to hand me a telegram.

I opened it quickly and read the short message, and then I whooped! "How about this, Daddy: the Metro Company is paying *two thousand five hundred dollars* for movie rights to 'Head and Shoulders'!"

For a girl who needed irrefutable proof that her father was plain wrong in his thinking, nothing could have been better. I danced around the parlor waving the telegram before me, and didn't care a bit that Daddy left the room in disgust.

Later that week, I was in my bedroom working on a story of my own when Mama came in with a small package. I was glad for the distraction; the story, which Scott had encouraged me to write, was going nowhere. I could give the most detailed examinations of my characters, but then couldn't seem to make them do anything interesting.

"This just came for you," Mama said.

Inside the plain brown paper was a short, square box, and inside that box was a hinged, velvet-covered one. I opened the lid and gasped.

Mama said, "Lord!"

It was a watch unlike anything I'd ever seen before. Its narrow rectangular face was set inside a perimeter of sparkling square-cut diamonds, with a band made up of diamonds laid out in an intricate, almost floral design.

I took it out. Beneath the watch, Scott had tucked a card that read, *To wear at our wedding—just a little "something new."*

"It's heavy!"

"I'll guess it's platinum," Mama said.

Engraved on the back was *From Scott to Zelda*. I turned it over again and again, marveling at the design, the shimmer, the very fact of it.

"Baby, do you have any idea what an extravagance this is? It had to have cost hundreds of dollars. He really ought not to spend this way; it's irresponsible. This is a time to *save*."

I fastened the watch onto my wrist. "I know how it seems. But he's earning a lot now, and his book's not even out yet. He's making his place in the world, Mama. It'll only get better from here." Everything he'd promised was coming true.

My mother sighed. She looked suddenly ancient, as if she'd aged ten years in one. Her hair had gone steely gray. Her skin had grown crêpey and was so pale—paler, even, than wintertime could explain. She didn't seem ill, just tired and worn. I felt I could disregard anything she said because what could such an old woman know about modern love and life?

I said, "It's different for us, Mama. We're not going to do things the same old ways."

She sighed again. "Honestly, I don't know whether to envy your optimism or pity it."

I took off the watch and turned it again to see the inscription, then flipped it back to admire the diamonds. As I did, I caught sight of Daddy standing in the doorway.

"When the novelty wears off," he said—and I got the feeling he was referring to more than just the watch—"you can trade that for a down payment on a house."

8

———

"Just think," Eleanor said, the night before I was to leave home, "New York City! Did you ever imagine?"

It was April 1, 1920; my wedding was set for April 3, one day before Easter and one week after the publication of *This Side of Paradise*. Eleanor and I were sitting cross-legged on my bedroom rug while I practiced how to look more sophisticated when I smoked. Along the wall were three new trunks filled with what little I'd take with me into married life: clothes and linens and shoes and books, a handful of photographs and a box of mementos, my diaries and my old doll, Alice. "Tilt your chin up a little more," Eleanor directed.

I did, saying, "New York's goin' to be grand. Scott made us a reservation at the Biltmore Hotel for our honeymoon." I handed Eleanor the advertisement Scott had torn out of a magazine and sent to me.

She read, " 'The Biltmore is the center of international social life in New York.' Just the place for you, then."

"He said there's nothing like it in Montgomery, not even close. Millionaires stay there."

"You can get room service."

"And swim in the indoor pool!" I said. "And he says there's a big ballroom on the twenty-second floor—twenty-two, and that's not nearly the tallest!—with a roof that opens up when it's warm out and you can eat under the stars."

Eleanor was speechless.

"And, I'm going to see the *Follies*." I took a sophisticated drag on my cigarette.

"And the Statue of Liberty."

"And skyscrapers!"

"And you'll be the wife of a famous man."

"Not *so* famous, not yet anyway; his book has only been out for a few days."

"Well, handsome then, and famous as soon as enough time has passed for people to know his name. Next thing you know, I'll be adding *rich* to my list of adjectives and everyone will say, 'Finally he's good enough for our Zelda.' Now show me that watch again."

My folks said their good-byes in our front hall. Not one of us mentioned that they weren't making the trip, too, or why that was. Mama and Daddy said little, in fact, beyond "Travel safely" and "Write soon" because my father had already said, "We think this is a poor choice and we won't condone it. Marry him, if that's what you think you want to do—we can't stop you. But we won't stand there and see it done." Mama had only sat nearby trying to be stoical, tears pooling in her eyes.

All the preparations had been made at Scott's end, with aid from Tootsie and Newman, who were now living nearby. There was no role for our parents and, really, little role for our siblings—and so Scott had told his folks and his sister to just stay home. My sisters were mainly participating because it was convenient for Marjorie to accompany me on the train, and convenient for Tootsie and Tilde, who'd also moved to New York State, to come into Manhattan. The three of them could enjoy a rare visit, and Marjorie could see the city; nothing more was necessary, or desired. Certainly

I didn't yearn for any further oversight. Excited as I was to be going, I'd hardly given the separation from home a thought. I could easily have hurried out the door without even a formal good-bye.

My friends had all gathered at the station for a surprise send-off. Here, the scene was emotional as they saw me onto the train with kisses and tears and flowers. I hugged everyone, dispensed jokes and advice while continually wiping my eyes, and promised I wasn't leaving forever—if only so that Eleanor and the Saras would let me go.

Once aboard the train and settled in our Pullman, I began to relax a little. As the engine chugged away from the station and Montgomery unspooled behind us, I drew a deep breath, exhaled, and tipped my head back against the seat. The car was new, sleek and modern-looking compared to the plush, older ones we'd taken before the government had commissioned all the trains for the war. There were window screens now, and dust deflectors. The carpet was unpatterned, and plain, smooth seats had replaced the old tufted ones. *Out with the old,* I thought, *and away goes the new.*

"I guess this will be a kind of adventure for you, too," I told Marjorie, who still looked startled by all the commotion in the station. Marjorie often looked startled, as if she was far more comfortable staying shut away in her simple little house, sewing and reading and cooking and tending Noonie, her daughter.

"Yes, I'm looking forward to seeing New York City. Tootsie thinks it's grand."

"I'm sure you all are going to excuse Scott and me from your tourin' schedule."

Marjorie smiled. "Honeymooners are excused." Then she added, "Now, Baby, I know you've had a lot more experience with boys than I ever did at your age—"

"At any age," I quipped. "Daddy said, 'Marry that fine fella Minor Brinson,' and you said, 'Yessir.'"

"That's a bit simplistic. But anyway, there are things you may not know that you *should* know before your wedding night."

"Did Mama put you up to this?"

"I volunteered, but she thought it was a wise plan."

"Sure, bein' that she's probably forgotten how such things as might happen on a girl's wedding night actually work."

"You do have hot pepper running through your veins, don't you? Where do you get that, do you suppose?"

"From the Machen side, I'm sure. The Sayres are such a dour bunch. Mama was pretty lively before her daddy put a leash on her."

"Fathers have to look out for their daughters. It's their duty."

I considered this. Our father was nothing if not dutiful, and so were my friends' fathers. Some had softer edges than others, but all of them were without question the heads of their households. I could think of only one exception: Eleanor Browder's household, where, from everything I'd seen, both parents were equally in charge. Mrs. Browder did not indulge in any of the routine, small deceptions that the other girls' mothers did—Mama included. She didn't need to.

In fact, at times Mrs. Browder's behavior bordered on obnoxious. Once, when I was at Eleanor's house, Mrs. Browder told us she wished Eleanor and I could trade places with her—that if she weren't so weighted down with her present duties and age, she would be out encouraging women to vote, and distributing Margaret Sanger's booklets to middle- and upper-class households, where, she said, the real facts of life needed to be known. "These women somehow believe that only the poor are subject to venereal diseases. Why, I could name a half-dozen of our neighbors who've been treated for 'female disturbances' that are in fact gonorrhea they've caught from their unfaithful husbands, who got it from the whorehouse!"

"Mama, heavens!"

We girls weren't against this kind of progress, necessarily. Rather, we didn't feel it concerned us. We weren't political; we were young and pretty and popular. Neither of us had any desire to be the kind of feminist Mrs. Browder wished to be, a fact the poor woman said she found wasteful and offensive.

Now I asked my sister, "The Judge never gave *you* any trouble, did he? Tilde says you were a model child."

"My veins run with cool water. Too cool sometimes." The thought brought a frown. Marjorie had "moods," Mama had said, and those moods could keep her in bed for days. Whereas I had "fits of temper" lasting minutes, usually, sometimes hours. Tootsie was "hard-nosed, but eventually she sees sense." Tony was "sensitive." Only Tilde's label was complimentary—she was "the cooperative child."

"Anyway, you were sayin'? About the wedding night?"

"You may be aware, there's a thing called 'the marital act' that happens first on the wedding night, and then, depending on the man, more or less frequently throughout a marriage. Its purpose is reproduction, but a lot of couples believe it's a . . . pleasurable thing to do." Her face reddened. "Men in particular find it pleasurable because their bodies are built . . . well, more efficiently in that regard."

I pretended wide-eyed fascination as Marjorie continued the lesson, quietly describing male genitalia and its arousal response, and then outlining what a man did with that aroused genitalia and how a wife was supposed to respond. Finally she paused and looked over at me.

"That is downright fascinating," I said heartily, then clamped my lips in an attempt to suppress my smile.

Understanding spread across Marjorie's face. "You devil. You knew all of that already, didn't you?"

"I'd never heard it explained quite that way, though."

"Hot pepper," Marjorie said, shaking her head.

PART II

Everybody's youth is a dream, a form of chemical madness.

—F. Scott Fitzgerald

9

Nothing can prepare the uninitiated for the truth of New York City. For all that Scott had talked dreamily about Manhattan, had told me about Broadway and the Hippodrome and the Gothic grandeur of the Woolworth Building— the tallest building in the world!—for all that he'd described the city as having a soul, of being a law unto itself, I was not prepared for what I would encounter after I got off the train at Pennsylvania Station.

Marjorie and I had traveled the final leg of the journey overnight. Our compartment was spacious with comfortable berths, but even so, my sleep had been filled with strange dreams. In the most vivid of them, I'd been able to fly. I glided over huge fields of pale violet Indian tobacco chanting, *"Lobelia inflata,"* repeatedly, worried that I was going to miss my botany exam. I soared along the tops of incredibly tall pines that grazed my naked stomach and breasts with a whisper-soft touch. All I needed to do to lift off each time was to stand on my toes with my arms outstretched, then bend my knees and spring upward. That little bounce, and then I was free. The air flowed around me as warm and soothing as a bath.

In the morning, I woke disoriented. The feeling would persist indefinitely.

Due to a three-hour delay somewhere in New Jersey, once the train rumbled through a tunnel beneath the Hudson River and came to a stop at Penn Station, we had only an hour to spare before the wedding itself and were already late for our rendezvous with Scott and the priest.

We disembarked onto a huge, glass-enclosed platform awash in brilliant sunshine, then stood awestruck, wordless and still. Passengers streamed around and past us. I was transfixed by the steel trusses that went up and up and up to wide glass panels and the blue, blue sky beyond. That glass-paned ceiling had to be more than a hundred feet high and was neatly segmented into the most pleasing steel arches and rectangular panes. Montgomery had some impressive buildings, but nothing that compared to this.

Still staring upward, I tugged at Marjorie's sleeve. "At breakfast, did you see any bottle labeled 'Drink Me'?"

"I didn't notice any bottles— Oh, like in *Alice's Adventures in Wonderland,* you mean."

"Mm," I said, gazing around us. "Bet there's a white rabbit here someplace."

"It's like an enormous greenhouse."

I sighed. "It's like heaven's depot. A place like this could only be built by angels, don't you think?"

We followed the last of our fellow passengers up a staircase to the concourse, where the space opened—*exploded,* I thought—into the biggest atrium I had ever seen and could not have ever imagined. Everywhere, steel and glass and arches . . . The seemingly endless ceiling was broad enough to cover a small town. It was magnificent, and dizzying.

"All the clockworks in my head are just spinning and springing apart," I said.

Marjorie only nodded. After a moment, she gathered herself and took my hand. "We should have let Tootsie and Newman meet us."

I was anxious, too, but I knew the surest way to make things worse was to indulge Marjorie's anxiety. "Scott says it's easy enough to get a taxicab— there's so many tourists coming that the drivers line up along the street out front all day long."

"It can only be easy if you don't feel as though you're in Wonderland. This place is a city all by itself."

Marjorie found a smartly dressed woman and asked for the quickest route to where the taxis would be waiting.

"Through there to the main waiting room," the woman said while checking the time on the huge clock behind Marjorie. "You'll see the exits—there are signs, too—and then outside any of them, there'll be a queue for cabs. You're first-timers here, I suppose?"

"Yes. My sister's getting married at St. Patrick's Cathedral at noon."

The woman's eyebrows rose almost to her hairline and I wondered if she could somehow tell I wasn't a Catholic. I said, "My soon-to-be-husband cleared it with the priest."

She gave me a quizzical look, then told Marjorie, "Yes, well, go right or left as soon as you're in the main room—don't spend all day meandering through here to Seventh. And you'll want to take this advice to heart: give the cabbie the address as though you're bored and have done it fifty times. If he thinks you're green, he'll run you all over the city before he lets you off."

We left the atrium through a passageway to the main waiting room, as the woman directed. Even the passageway's scale—thirty feet across and fifty high, all stone, arched, and with other passageways leading off it—was difficult to comprehend. It was like we'd disembarked into a dream even stranger than the ones I'd had overnight. I was Alice, or I was Jack, who, having tired of using the beanstalk to climb to the giant's lair, had elected to travel there by train. The feeling was amplified when we came to the stairs leading down into the main waiting room.

The wide, sunlit chamber was domed—how high the ceiling was, I couldn't guess—and built out of huge blocks of the same rose-colored stone that made up the atrium's lower walls. It was easily the size of a football field. Lampposts were stationed throughout, their scale ridiculously small in this vast space. The far end of the hall had tremendous arched windows divided by small frames into towers of squares. Stairways led off all four sides.

"In my wildest imaginings . . ." I began.

"It's after eleven," Marjorie said. "We have to move along. Left or right, do you think?"

"How can you be so practical?"

"You're on a *schedule*."

"Scott will understand if this makes us later—this stuff is part of the package he sold me to get me out of Montgomery, after all."

We walked into the hall and were crossing to the staircase that would take us to the exit when I stopped again.

I tilted my head back to see the ceiling from this aspect. Who carved all those hexagons—actually, a hexagon inside a hexagon inside a hexagon—that decorated the entire ceiling? Whose talent with a chisel rendered these tremendous columns? How had it been done? Where did the artists have a large enough work space to chisel the Corinthian curves and leaves that topped the columns?

If Marjorie hadn't taken me by the arm and said, "You have a wedding in an *hour*, remember?" I might have lain down right there on the floor in order to marvel properly.

Oh, and then outside! The buildings, the people, the noise of engines and whistles and voices, the commotion of cars clattering past! I glanced at my sister; she looked frightened. I laughed and said, "I might never leave."

I gawked at every single tall building and appealing storefront on our trip across town, then when we came around the block occupied by St. Patrick's, I gaped at its arched, stained-glass windows. Each was a work of art.

But when the entry and front spires of St. Patrick's came into view, my eyes filled with tears. I'd never seen a structure that was at once so ornate and so serene. The sight—the complexity of architecture, the graceful, intricately carved spires towering over the street, inlaid with smaller intricately carved spires, all of them topped by crosses—literally stole my breath. No wonder the woman at the station had looked impressed.

The thought of being married in this church felt overwhelming, but fitting, too; I was convinced that ours was no ordinary union. Scott was no ordinary fiancé. How, though, had he engineered *this*?

The sidewalk was crowded with tourists milling around the church. Marjorie said, "I wonder if it's always like this, or if tomorrow being Easter explains it."

I spotted Scott at the top of the wide steps, where he waited with

Tootsie and Newman and two unfamiliar men, and got out of the car before Marjorie had even opened her purse to extract the cab fare. Scott jogged down to the curb and swept me into an embrace.

"My dearest girl, my bride! We've done it, we've made it. Can you believe this? What do you think?"

"It's wonderful." I pulled back and smiled at him. His eyes were as green as they get, bright with pleasure and pride. "Look at you. My author husband."

He glowed. "Nearly *ten thousand* sold already, I'm told. And the reviews so far are pretty damn good. Some critics are even saying it's genius. They're putting me up there with Byron and Kipling!" His voice caught as he said, "*This,* now, here with you, is the top of the world."

"I'm so, so happy for you, darling."

"It's all because of you." He kissed my hands. "Because I had to have you."

Marjorie joined us as the others came down to the sidewalk. Scott turned to the priest. "Father, I'd like to introduce Miss Zelda Sayre and her sister Mrs. Marjorie Brinson. Ladies, this is Father Martin. He'll be doing us the honor."

"Delighted, ladies."

"Pleased to meet you," I said as I squinted up at the arched entryway, which sat beneath a stone peak that resided under an even grander one. Everywhere, peaks and spires reached heavenward—which, I supposed, was the idea.

"This is the most remarkable church I've ever seen," I said, still looking upward. "How many crosses are on this thing, do you suppose?" I looked back at the priest and smiled. "It's amazing. I have the sudden desire to become a Catholic."

"I believe that can be arranged."

Newman said, "We're told that the tallest of the spires reaches three hundred thirty feet."

"Practically to heaven's door," Tootsie quipped as she gave me a hug. "You look radiant, little sister."

I wore a suit the color of the evening sky, onto which I'd pinned the white orchid Scott had ordered for me from a Montgomery florist. He'd said it would keep overnight, and it had. My hat was the same fabric as my suit, trimmed out with gray leather ribbon and a silver buckle. I wore shoes to match and felt, as I'd told Eleanor when I tried on the suit for her, "like a proper lady—which might be the best costume I've worn so far in my life."

Scott then turned to the man beside him and said, "This chap is Ludlow Fowler."

Ludlow nodded to Marjorie and took my hand. "Fitz can't stop talking about you, you know. Thank God you're here—maybe now he'll stop bothering *us* and instead fill your ears with stories about us Princeton boys."

"As if the lot of you are worth my breath," Scott said.

Tootsie announced, "We're just waiting on Tilde and John. With all the last-minute arranging, we can only hope she remembered that you all settled on today instead of Monday."

Scott checked his watch. "What I should have arranged for was a car to pick them up." He turned to me. He looked like a horse at the starting gate waiting for the bell. "Scribner's store is just two blocks down. I can't wait to show you the book—we can go right afterward, if you like."

"Yes. Yes, of course, I can't wait to see."

"You two," Tootsie said. "It's your *wedding* day!"

"It's our everything day," I told her.

It was ten minutes before noon. Scott said, "We should go in and get things situated."

"I'll stay on post and keep an eye out for them," Newman offered.

Tootsie said, "Then if *they're* late, *you'll* miss it. That's silly. Come on."

Father Martin led us inside through the towering wood doors. The church's interior was enormous, and so stunningly beautiful in its architecture and finishings that I didn't know where to look first.

A long, straight ribbon of vanilla marble flowed far ahead of us to a magnificent altar. The ceiling towered overhead, formed by pale, graceful arching stone beams that seemed to bloom from tremendous stone columns that rose a hundred or more feet to the ceiling. Among the columns at floor level marched unending rows of polished wooden pews, nearly all of which were full.

I whispered, "These people, they're not all here for *us*?"

"No," Scott said. "We're going to the vestry; that was the compromise, since you didn't convert. Noon mass is about to begin."

The ceiling's arcs merged at regular points along the way to the front of the church, creating what looked to me like a row of poinsettia flowers. Interspersed high up the walls between the arcing beams were stained-glass windows depicting biblical scenes. Below, both sides of the room—if *room* was even the right word for this space—were lined by even larger window scenes, all glowing brightly in the midday sunshine. Statues, presumably of Roman figures, gazed down at visitors from pillars and nooks in poses of classic boredom, as if to say they were beyond such things as whatever impressed mortals, that heaven was *really* the thing to see.

Every surface, be it stone wall or ceiling, wooden balcony or bench, was sculpted or carved into one kind of artful form or another. Was all this about religion—an expression, say, of God's supposed glory? Was this, somehow, about being Catholic in New York City? Maybe all the world's great cities had cathedrals like this. . . .

For the first time, I had a glimmer of the immensity of the planet, of lives being lived as routinely or as vividly as my own had been at any given moment. The world contained who knew how many Pennsylvania Stations and St. Patrick's Cathedrals. If New York offered these two treasures within an hour of my arrival, what else would I discover here? What music? What dancing? What books? What plays? Beauty and art such as I'd never really considered were everywhere in this city, and probably all around the globe—and here I was, in this magnificent example, about to marry a man who had just added his own work of art to the collection.

When we were about halfway to the front of the church, I stopped and turned in a slow circle to take it all in. Marjorie did the same, saying, "Oh, I do wish Mama had come."

"Our parents say they're too old to travel so far," Tootsie explained to Father Martin. "And I'm sure Scott's parents wanted to be here as well."

"Certainly," the priest said.

I said, "You could park an airship in here!"

"Indeed," Father Martin replied. "We've considered the option—renting space to the government, should there be a need of maintenance funds."

"Sellout crowd today, though," Scott said.

Tootsie nodded. "I guess they heard that Mr. F. Scott Fitzgerald was about to be married here." She winked at me. I pinched her arm.

The vestry, though relatively intimate in size, was outfitted with rich wood millwork and leaded-glass windows. I breathed more easily in here. In this space, I could focus again on why we'd all come to be here in the first place. I could focus on Scott. How handsome and distinguished he looked in his dark gray suit, a finer cut than I'd seen him in before. He looked like the man he'd said he was going to be, and I thought, *I will never doubt him again*.

"It's nearly time," the priest said, inviting us to stand before him.

I looked at Tootsie and asked, "Any sign of Tilde?" Tootsie shook her head.

Scott said, "Father Martin has a full schedule today. Let's get started."

"But she'll hate to miss it," Marjorie said.

"We could end up waiting all afternoon." Scott looked at me; I nodded and he said, "Go ahead, Father. We're ready."

With Tootsie at my elbow and Ludlow Fowler at Scott's, the priest said all the things that needed saying in order for the Church and the state to consider us lawfully wed. While he spoke, I let his words flow over me. I stared into Scott's eyes, seeing there all the happiness, the pride, the love, the promise that we'd been striving for, together, since that July night almost two years earlier.

"Now." Tootsie nudged me.

"Oh—yes, yes, I do."

We exchanged simple wedding bands, then kissed sweetly, to the applause of our small audience. The door opened then, and a young man admitted Tilde and John into the room.

"You've just missed it," I said, going to my sister, whose unstructured dress and loose coat did a good job of disguising her advanced pregnancy—though of course the very fact of her wearing that style of clothing indicated her condition.

I put my hand on her belly and asked the baby, "Was it you who made them late?"

"The train." Tilde put her hand over mine. "But the good news is that the motion lulls him to sleep. This child is going to be an acrobat."

John squeezed my shoulder. "So he's made an honest woman of you?"

"Can you believe it?" I said, as Scott joined us. "They claimed it'd never happen, but here I am, a happily wed woman."

"One who's got a date at Scribner's." In my ear Scott added, "And then the Biltmore."

"Naughty," I whispered.

Tilde took in the vestry's scene. "Was the ceremony lovely?"

"It was quick. Here." I lowered my voice to imitate the priest's. "'We've come together before God on this fine day in order to ensure that these two crazy kids don't go to the devil.'" Then I kissed Scott the way I'd just done at the ceremony's conclusion and said, "'What God has joined together let no bunch of sisters interfere with.' And," I said in my own voice, "now we've got to get going."

Marjorie said, "What, Baby, just like that?"

"*I'd* like to see the book," Newman said. "Buy a copy, even."

Tootsie told him, "Later. Let this be their adventure. Besides, we've got to feed poor Tilde, who I'm sure is famished."

I hugged Tootsie. "Thank you."

Tilde looked crestfallen. "It would be so much nicer if you joined us. Tootsie, why didn't you help them set up something?"

"They didn't want any fuss."

"We'll visit you after the honeymoon," Scott said.

I nodded. "We're off, then. You all have a nice time catching up. Marjorie, get a copy of the book for the Judge and take it home, would you? I'll write to all of you; so long!"

Scott and I strolled the two blocks to Scribner's store hand in hand. I was so busy looking at everything around us that I didn't realize we were at the store until Scott pulled me over to a shop window.

"Here she is."

The window display featured a number of books individually. Copies of

Scott's, though, had been built into a pyramid that dominated the display. In front of the pyramid was a sign:

```
At only twenty-three years of age,
  Mr. F. Scott Fitzgerald is the youngest
  writer for whom Scribner's have ever
           published a novel.
```

I said, "Is that true?"

Scott nodded.

"This is my husband's book!" I shouted, pointing to the display. Passersby smiled. I turned to Scott and said, just to him, "And this is my husband."

10

═══

At the Biltmore Hotel, I couldn't resist petting every polished brass railing, every gilded table, every brocaded chairback along the way to our suite. I twirled beneath the crystal chandeliers, posed in front of the clock. I admired the brass buttons on the elevator operator's uniform. I admired the elevator. After a light meal in the hotel's lush dining room, I admired the three bottles of bootleg champagne awaiting us in our suite—sent over by Scott's Princeton friends, who I'd be meeting Tuesday night.

Soon after admiring the champagne (and its bubbles, and its flavor), I praised the wide bed and the way it accommodated the two of us no matter which way we lay or shifted while we made love. All this was so much grander than the life Scott had led me to imagine, and while I'd foreseen good things, this was simply *beyond*.

"Are we rich?" I asked.

"We are unstoppable."

We slept late on Sunday, lazed in bed with a room-service breakfast of fruit and cream and muffins, bathed together in the marble tub in the afternoon, then spent the evening in the Broadway district. Supper first, at a little diner on Forty-third Street, and then, as promised, a performance of Ziegfeld's *Follies* at the New Amsterdam Theatre. By the time we took our seats and the curtain went up and the stage revealed its remarkable sets and even more remarkable performers and, most remarkable of all, the Follies Girls' resplendent beaded, sequined, feathered, shimmering, sparkling costumes, I could only stare and grin and wonder at the crazy luck that had put Scott and me together and brought us to this place.

On Monday, we took a picnic lunch of cold fried chicken over to Central Park in the early afternoon. I hadn't expected statues or artful bridges or colorfully tiled tunnels. "They even make their *parks* like this?" I said, repeatedly, turning it into a joking refrain as we walked along the paths and over the bridges and beside the lakes. We ate in a sunny spot on the steps of the Bethesda Terrace near the Angel of the Waters, a benevolent statue that rose from the center of a wide, shallow fountain-pool. At the angel's feet were four cherubs that Scott said were meant to represent Health, Peace, Temperance, and Purity. I laughed at that. "The first two hardly matter if you have to mind the last two."

"That's my girl," Scott said.

Tuesday, I got my first real taste of what it was going to be like to be married to *F. Scott Fitzgerald*.

We had only just finished getting dressed when a knock sounded on our hotel-room door. A one o'clock appointment time for Scott's first magazine interview had sounded reasonable when Scott mentioned it on Saturday afternoon. That was before either of us realized we'd be staying up until near dawn every night. New York City's diversions were irresistible; if we could have survived without sleeping at all, we'd have done it.

Scott said, "Am I presentable?" as the rap on the door sounded again. "Coming!" he yelled.

I straightened his tie and kissed him. "Don't be nervous."

"Not a bit. He's a Princeton man."

Scott opened the door to Jim Ellis, a balding man of about thirty who had a soft, round face and eyes like a spaniel's. His brown suit jacket looked tight through the shoulders and at the waist, and its sleeves rode up over his fraying cuffs. The overall effect was that the suit had shrunk, or its owner had expanded, or possibly he'd borrowed it last minute from a room-mate or coworker. Ellis was a features writer for a magazine I'd never heard of. Some little start-up tabloid, Scott said.

Ellis shook Scott's hand. "Thank you for agreeing to talk with me. Our readers are eager to get to know the man behind the novel."

"Glad to do it."

Scott led him into the sitting room and indicated a chair to my left, where the man dutifully sat down. I smiled at him as though he was as important to Scott's career as Mr. Charles Scribner himself.

"Jim Ellis, meet my lovely bride of three days, Zelda Fitzgerald."

Zelda Fitzgerald. What a foreign sound to my ears!

I crossed my legs, letting my knee show, and leaned forward to offer my hand. "It's a pleasure."

Ellis's face reddened and he took my hand in a quick, shy clasp before turning back toward Scott. "Congratulations on your marriage."

I recognized Ellis's type. In my experience, there were two kinds of men. One type—no matter how plain or how poor he might be—is always will-ing to at least try his luck with an attractive girl. The other type looks upon all of those first types with envy. Ellis was among the second group. He probably wasn't married, or if he was, I ungenerously figured he'd found a girl even less confident than himself, a pairing that was sure to perpetuate a race of timid, boring people you'd never invite to a party unless for some reason you'd taken a shine to them and wanted to lift them out of their misery.

While Scott sat, Ellis took out a notebook and turned to a page where he'd already written some notes. He pointed at the copy of *This Side of Paradise* that sat on the table between his chair and Scott's. "I have to say, I read the novel and I fully agree with the *Times:* 'As a picture of the daily existence of what we call loosely *college men,* this book is as nearly perfect as such a work could be.' My sentiments exactly."

Scott nodded his thanks. "I'm always especially interested in how it plays with fellow alums."

"I wish my time there had been more like I hear yours was. I was a bit of a hermit."

I said, "Oh, I can't believe that. I'll bet you were just a sensible fella."

He glanced at me. Now his ears had gone red. He said to Scott, "What a thrill it must be to get a gold seal from the *Times*—and you being just twenty-three, first book . . ." Ellis shook his head with obvious envy.

I said, "He *is* impressive, isn't he?"

"Why, thank you, darling."

Ellis asked him, then, about how closely the experiences of Scott's main character, Amory Blaine, reflected Scott's own life.

Scott said, "Loosely. I've put a character into a version of my personal history, is what I've done."

"So Blaine's an alter ego."

"A somewhat naïve one, yes."

"Well, sure, of course, that makes sense; you couldn't write him so wisely if you *were* him."

Scott beamed.

"Now," Ellis continued, "about the women in this book—"

"It's a novel about flappers—you know the term? These independent, morally modern girls?—a flappers' story, for philosophers."

Ellis nodded and made a note. "And the selfish girl who breaks his heart—Rosalind. Is she . . ." He glanced at me again.

I said, "She bears me some resemblance, it's true—but you see, I *married my* Amory."

Scott added, "But only after her Amory proved he had a far better outlook and future than our poor hero here." He thumped the book. "Zelda was used to the finer things in life, things I couldn't provide until now. She wouldn't have me until I'd proven myself capable and had a few dollars in my account."

I said, "Actually, it wasn't quite as—"

"Darling," Scott said, opening his cigarette case, then snapping it shut, "I can't believe it, but I'm out. Would you ring for some while I finish up with Mr. Ellis?"

"Sorry?" I said, surprised that he'd interrupted me.

"Cigarettes. And something for you, Ellis?"

"If they've got a ham sandwich. I missed lunch—"

"Sure," I said, "but I just want to explain that I didn't—"

"No one thinks the worse of you for making me wait, darling. Women have to be practical."

I stood up and, in a tone suited to my supposed character, said coolly, "How about I just go find the concierge personally?"

Neither man replied, but I felt their eyes on me as I crossed the room. As I opened the door, I heard Scott saying, "These flapper girls, they're like racehorses." I slammed the door closed behind me. *To hell with them,* I thought. Let them find someone else to play fetch.

When I returned ninety minutes later, Ellis was gone and Scott was seated on the floor with half a dozen newspaper clippings laid in front of him. His nearly full cigarette case sat opened on the end table nearby.

"You said you were out!"

He stood up and came to me. "That was just a ruse, so that you'd stop trying to straighten the story. I didn't want you to dampen Ellis's interest. Did you see how he looked at you? To him, you *were* Rosalind. In the future, if anyone should bring up the subject of Rosalind being like you, don't split hairs; play it up. *Be* Rosalind. That's what they're hoping for."

I took a cigarette and lit it from his, dragged on it, then exhaled slowly. "But I'm *not* her. To start with, she's not Southern, not even a little bit. She's *New York* society, and I sure am not that."

He waved away the protest. "Artistic license."

"And she's a prissy snob, wouldn't you say?"

"What, for following her family's wishes and choosing a wealthy man over Amory? She's practical. *Chill-minded,* we might call her. These aren't bad traits necessarily. It's all about the context, all about how the traits are put to use."

"You want people to see me like that? Selfish? 'Chill-minded'?"

"Anyone who knows the real you knows you're warm and generous and smart. 'Most Popular' girl at Sidney Lanier High School—that's indisputable. For the papers and magazines, what difference does it make who you really are—or who *I* really am, for that matter? It's like in advertising: give the public what it thinks it wants, and they'll lay down their cash."

"Thinking they're getting some sob-sister confessional about us, sure. I'd think you'd want the book judged on merit."

"It's *been* judged—by most everyone who counts; look at these." He indicated the newspaper clippings. "The latest reviews from the weekend. My agent sent them, and they're *good*." His voice broke; he cleared his throat and added, "Max Perkins was a visionary, this proves him out."

"It proves *you* out," I said, softening. "You knew what you were talking about all along. It's a smart, funny, wise book, Scott, and you deserve all this."

"*We* deserve it. A lot of the dialogue in there came straight out of your diary."

"The way you gave my words to somebody I would *never* be is pretty keen. Sort of a magic trick, isn't it? It sure did work, though."

"It worked, and here we are."

I went to the window. "I never woulda thought it. Not like this." I turned back toward him. "You're sorta impressive."

He shrugged away the compliment, but his smile said he was pleased. "The thing now is *sales*. Popularity means we get to keep doing things like drinking champagne," he said, popping the cork from a bottle, "and wearing diamond wristwatches, *and*"—he tapped an envelope that lay on the table—"going to parties like the one next Friday night at George Jean Nathan's place."

"Another young Princetonian heir?"

"God no. He's one of this city's finest fixtures—editor of *The Smart Set*, plus he's a writer and a true theater critic of the first order. He knows everyone. Ev-ree-one. And he wants us."

I remembered *The Smart Set*, first of the prominent magazines to publish Scott's short stories. I hadn't realized at the time of the sale what a big deal it was; selling that story hadn't seemed to boost him much—he'd been focused on selling his novel, and on finding a better job. But that first gust had turned into a strong breeze bringing him all the things he had now: reviews from papers around the country. Books selling out of stores. New stories sold in new places. Steady money coming in. A wedding at St. Patrick's. A luxurious Biltmore suite. Reporters wanting to interview him—

"It's *you* this Nathan fella wants," I said.

"The invitation is for *Mr. and Mrs. Scott Fitzgerald*. And I think the occasion's going to call for a new dress."

"A dress for your Rosalind, you mean," I said, stepping up onto the sofa and walking across it, then stepping onto the back of it. I raised my arms overhead as I balanced, walking carefully along the narrow upholstered frame. "It was easier in Montgomery. I just had to keep on being me."

"Being you also meant being whatever character you portrayed onstage, didn't it?"

I jumped down onto the cushion. "I s'pose that's right."

"So . . ."

"So if I go along with this scheme, we'll be playing parts, that's what you're saying. Same as if we were doing this year's Folly Ball back home."

Scott handed me a glass of champagne. "Only this time, we're writing the parts ourselves."

11

We dined at the Cascades that night, on the Biltmore's top floor. While it was too cool outside for the roof to be open, we agreed that the fact that it *could* be opened was a thrill. The building was a wonder. Everything in New York City was a wonder, including Scott, who was treating me like the princess I'd once imagined I was. Fruit and cream from room service in the morning. Shopping and hair salon during the day. Dinner—that was the word refined Northerners used for the evening meal, Scott told me—at the top of a grand hotel. Dancing later, to the music of a first-rate orchestra. And champagne. We were drinking rivers of it. I'd told Scott the night before, "I bet you we'll be peeing bubbles before long!"

And we made love every chance we had. Quickly and vigorously in between activities; languorously when we had hours on our hands. We shared the bathroom sink when we brushed our teeth at night. We talked to each other from the toilet. Marriage suited us, there was no doubt about it.

As the waiter cleared our plates, Scott told me that the interview with Ellis had given him an idea, and he wanted to see what his publisher thought of it.

"I want to write a fictional interview that could then be placed with the *Times* or the *Tribune*. That way, we don't have to wait for the papers to decide they want someone to do it."

"A fictional interview? So, another bit of alter-egoism."

"Sort of. I haven't worked it out yet . . . but I have some ideas."

I could almost see those ideas swimming around in his head and watched, amused, as he took out his notebook and jotted things down.

"I have some ideas, too," I said suggestively, just before the waiter reappeared with our crème brûlée.

Scott glanced up at me, then caught my meaning and grinned. He asked the waiter, "Don't we make a fine pair?"

"Absolutely, sir. In fact, a couple at a nearby table was just inquiring whether you weren't famous, from the pictures or Broadway."

"Is that so?" Scott said. "Which couple?"

"There, with the spectacles." The waiter indicated a middle-aged man and woman several tables away.

Scott stood up then, and both the waiter and I watched him go straight over to the couple. He leaned down and spoke animatedly. They laughed, he laughed, then he took a pen from his breast pocket. He uncapped it and, as he did, must have said something that caused the couple to look over at me with appreciative smiles.

I waved graciously, as though this happened all the time.

Scott took the woman's napkin right out of her lap and spread it on the table, then wrote something on it. When he was finished, he bowed to the man, kissed the woman's hand, and returned to our table.

He said, "They'd hoped we were actors, but didn't mind settling for the autograph of the dashing young author of that *scandalous* new novel everyone's talking about."

The waiter took a quick look around. "Would you mind . . . ?" He laid Scott's napkin on the tabletop. "And remind me, what's the name of your book?"

The next morning, Scott arranged for a meeting at Scribner's, where he'd see Maxwell Perkins, his editor, along with the fellow who was in charge of publicity there. Left with time to myself, I decided to catch up on my correspondence. I owed letters to the Saras and to Livye and to my parents, and I needed to see whether Tallu was back in New York or still working in London, where she'd been finding an easier path to fame.

Everybody in New York is famous, she'd written me a few weeks earlier. *Everybody is beautiful. But England's dying for attractive girls. Hope I'll see you soon, but meanwhile, look up Gene. She's easy enough to find—just follow the trail of men.*

Scott returned with a spring in his step and a bag of sandwiches in his hands.

"It went well?"

"Oh, they think I have a screw loose, but they'll indulge me, all right. What do you think of this?" He took a folded page from his pocket, then opened it. "My interviewer's a guy I've named Carleton R. Davis. I've got him arriving as I'm here at loose ends. Things are in disarray—just like they are." He looked around at the mess. Living out of trunks did not encourage tidiness. "And I'm looking for my hat, and this tie," he said, patting the one he was wearing, blue with tiny white dots, "and my cigarettes, et cetera, but I encourage him to go ahead with his questions. We cover the usual 'How long did it take to write the book?' stuff, and I expound somewhat—"

"You, expound?"

He grinned. "Think you know me that well, do you?" He kissed me, then continued, reading from his notes, "He asks me what my plans are next."

"What *are* your plans next?"

He gazed at me over the top of the page. "I guess you mean my literary plans."

"No, Carleton R. Davis wants to know *those.*"

"Yes, yes, that's right." He looked at the page again. "And I shrug. 'I'll be darned if I know. The scope and depth and breadth of my writings lie in the laps of the gods.'"

"Who no doubt are reading *This Side of Paradise* as we speak—so's to give you appropriate guidance for the future."

"No doubt at all. And then I expound further, until I've impressed our

Mr. Davis sufficiently for him to ask whether I intend to be a part of the great literary tradition."

"Which you do."

"No! No, that's just it, that's just what people would guess a fellow in my shoes would say! But I don't. 'There is no such thing,' I say. 'The only real tradition is the death of preceding ones.'"

A thought grabbed him and he paused and began to search his pockets, coming up with a pencil. "Hold on." He laid the paper on the table and jotted something on it. Then he read, "'The smart literary son kills his own father.' What do you think?"

"Kinda Greek, isn't it?"

"The cradle of literature, dearest girl. All writers draw from that well—and how's that for mixing my metaphors?" He sat down next to me and said, "Give me a hero, and I will tell you a tragedy."

I started to reply when Scott added, "Wait— Give me a hero . . . Give me a hero and I'll tell you . . . no . . . I'll *show* you . . ."

He reached for the pencil and wrote in the paper's margin while I waited. It was so funny to see him transferring thoughts to words on paper as if he was taking dictation from those gods he mentioned.

"Here, I think I've got it: 'Show me a hero, and I'll write you a tragedy.' That's good. Don't know where I'll use it, but it's good."

"Isn't that Shakespeare?"

Scott thought for a moment, then shrugged. "Who can say?"

12

===

We'd invited Scott's friends to meet his bride in the Biltmore's Palm Court. Dressing for this date was no different from dressing for any party or dance back home, yet I was anxious. Without Montgomery's humidity, my hair didn't quite know how it should behave. Without Montgomery's context, I didn't know quite how *I* should behave.

Except for Ludlow Fowler, these men knew me only from whatever Scott had told or written them. I was accustomed to being assessed only for my *actual* actions—I had control over what I did and with whom, and once I'd made up my mind to act, I was happy to let the dust settle however it would. But God knew what things Scott had said after our breakup; to any or maybe all of them, I might be a fickle speed of a girl who'd led Scott on and then dashed his hopes and then roped him in again and finally caught him. Everybody knew of couples like that, where the poor man was obviously in over his head and miserable for it. If that was the Princeton pack's impression of me, I couldn't allow it to stand. Nor would I stand for them seeing me as Rosalind. That was fine for strangers, but these men were like brothers to Scott.

I'd be my most charming with them, and plainly affectionate with Scott, and I'd let him shine in his well-deserved limelight. They'd see, then, that what Scott and I had—regardless of anything he might have said before—was genuine love and mutual respect. I'd make Sara Haardt proud.

My dress was a navy-blue chiffon number that Scott had spotted in a shop window. He said everything I'd brought from home looked provincial when contrasted with what New York women were wearing—even I could see that. So, odd as it was to take fashion advice from a man, I'd had to admit that if I was going to be a famous author's wife—his apparently notorious wife—I needed to look the part. Gone were the simple cotton blouses and casual skirts that had been my everyday wear. Now I had finer cotton, and silk! My skirts and dresses showed my lower calves. I had smart hats and soft leather gloves and shoes in four different colors.

In truth, it had been awfully nice to walk into a shop and buy the thing I'd decided I wanted. No debating with my mother over color or style or length, no wheedling required, no discussion of sticking to Daddy's budget. Scott had peeled off ten-dollar bills and given them over to the shopgirl while encouraging me to buy more, if I liked.

Now Scott stood behind me at the mirror while I applied my lipstick and put on my hat. "Aren't you a wonder?" he said.

I smiled at his reflection. He wore a new striped tie that made his eyes silvery sage. His cheeks still had a rosy glow from our Central Park outing. He'd parted his hair in the center and combed it smoothly back, which made him look polished and confident. I said, "You aren't too bad yourself."

"In all the nonsense that will come from this lot tonight—and it's likely to be an arcane mix of football and poetry and literary journals and publishing and bourbon and war and girls—I want you to know that you, my dearest, darling wife, are the center of my universe."

"In that case," I said, turning to face him in person, "I might let you stay."

There were too many of them to keep straight at first. That first night, I hardly tried. It was enough to greet each of them in my new role, then sit among them as though I were an anthropologist who'd been drafted into a strange tribe.

Ludlow Fowler was easy to remember, having been at the wedding.

93

"Mrs. Fitzgerald," he said, taking both my hands and kissing my cheek. In his tailored suit and with freshly cut fine blond hair, he smelled like old money and somehow also of gardenias, as if his mother might still be sending him milled French soaps and he was still inclined to use them. Straightforward and confident in the way that born-rich men so often are, Ludlow reminded me of some of the well-off fellas back home.

The other five—who I'd later know as Bunny, Biggs, Townsend, Alec, and Bishop—I would have to study a bit, except for Edmund Wilson, the misnamed *Bunny,* who I'd heard so much about. He looked something like the reporter, Ellis, but Bunny's clothes fit better, and it was clear right off that Bunny fit better in the world. He likely belonged to the first type of men, the ones who believed they were entitled to a chance at any girl who enticed them—though I was certain that Bunny's tastes were very particular.

After the initial polite questions directed at me, who they surely saw as an odd new appendage that Scott had somehow acquired along with his new celebrity status, the men moved quickly into a hearty discussion of *This Side of Paradise.* Most of them had read it and had already offered Scott their critiques and their praise. What they wanted to know now was what it was like to be scrutinized so publicly, to be the latest literary sensation.

"You don't *look* famous," one said.

"Except that you seem to be wearing Fowler's suit," said another, a tall, blue-eyed, blond man who had a friendly smile.

Scott said, "That's what selling a story's film interest will do for a man; it's got nothing to do with the book."

"It's the book that made them look at the story."

"It's George Nathan that made them look at the story."

I followed the banter, amused.

"No," Scott said, "that story, 'Head and Shoulders,' went to *The Saturday Evening Post,* not *The Smart Set.* My agent, Harold Ober, got it to the movie people."

"*My agent.* Gad. He says it as if to the manor born."

"I still say it was Nathan. He's got a crush on you, Fitz." This was from the dark-haired, young-looking one.

Ludlow Fowler nodded toward me. "But we needn't worry about our boy's manhood now."

"Do we know any other fairies?"

The dark-haired one again: "I was in Greenwich not long ago and met a pair—that is, they weren't a *couple,* that is, they were two. Edna Millay and Djuna Barnes."

"Lesbians aren't fairies," Bunny Wilson said. "Christ, call yourself a wordsmith?"

Scott said, "Nathan's no fairy."

"Edna Millay is a lesbian?"

"I've seen her with men."

"I saw her with a woman."

Ludlow said, "Never mind that. How many stories have Nathan and Mencken taken from you now, Fitz?"

"Six. And *The Saturday Evening Post*'s taken four."

"Paying . . . ?" asked the dark-haired one.

"*The Post?*" Scott said. "Four hundred for one, four-fifty for the next two, and my agent's got them to five hundred for the new ones."

This stopped the conversation for a moment as all except Bunny and Ludlow stared at him, agog.

"And *The Smart Set* pays . . . ?"

"Thirty," Bunny answered, his voice as crisp and authoritative as three new ten-dollar bills. "Which won't cover much more than his room here tonight, but the literary cachet is invaluable, isn't that right, Fitz?"

Scott rubbed one hand over his hair and smiled.

The discussion went on for a time. Several of the men had brought flasks, which now began to appear more frequently; this then prompted a debate about the effectiveness of last October's Volstead Act, and alcohol's correct place within intelligent society. Did a thinking man need it? Did it hinder or enhance a writer's productivity?

Bunny turned to me. "Zelda, what do you think?"

"I believe it makes most men better dancers," I said, and held out my hand for his flask.

He complied, laughing. "I'm afraid that even liquor can't help me much there."

Scott caught my eye. His smile was one of gratitude. I had done something—perhaps everything—right.

This group, and this bookish world in which they lived and were simultaneously creating, was a collegiate literary circle puffed into wide proportions by the New York magazines and papers; that's how I saw it before long.

Before their reign, before a smart, young writer named Dorothy Parker said too much too well and was fired for it, before Scott's success, before people everywhere had been ravaged by war and flu, there'd been little glamour in the literary world. To be a writer then was to be a drab little mole who thought big thoughts and methodically committed them to paper, hoping for publication but not courting it, and then burrowing back into the hole to think again for a while.

With this group, though, and their counterparts from Yale, and the postwar push for life, for fun, for all the things Scott and I were seeking and embodying, the literary world put its foot into the circle of the entertainment world's spotlight. Not far; far enough, though, for the public to see the polished, well-cut shoe and wonder to whom it might belong.

It belonged to the Princeton boys who'd made a happy circus of what had once been considered the ultraserious Princeton journal *Nassau Lit*. It belonged to Scott.

Some of their influence would occur due simply to luck. For example, Bunny was at *Vanity Fair* primarily due to Dorothy Parker's lack of diplomacy (that's what got her fired), and their friend John Peale Bishop was there because of Bunny. The literary hub that was *Vanity Fair* and its likekind associations would soon grow new spokes and turn like a Ferris wheel set in the middle of Manhattan—a good ride, if you could get a ticket.

And these Princeton fellas all had one. The wheel might put you off in a prominent book review or an important essay assignment; it might drop you at a party with Florenz Ziegfeld or George Cohan; it might toss you in with the new Hollywood types, and before long you'd be writing for the pictures and making hundreds of dollars a week, or more.

Some of their influence would grow from design—as when Scott had explained to me the publicity game that he saw forming in our future, a game he'd conjured, almost, and wanted the two of us to play. Some grew from our giddy laughter in the Biltmore lobby at two and three A.M., from the singing that emanated from parties in our suite, from the dancing in the hallway, from the polite but firm request from management that sent us to finish our honeymoon in a new suite at the nearby Commodore Hotel. The future would be grander, stranger, and more precarious than any of us knew.

Just then, though, that influential little group was still a bunch of young, ambitious, intelligent men, along with me, a very young woman who hadn't known there would be this kind of carnival and wasn't sure she even wanted to ride the Ferris wheel—but was game enough to give it a try.

13

I was just done with my bath when I heard Scott answer the door, and then his friend Alec's voice:

"Did you see what they wrote about you two?"

"Of course we saw it—Zelda clipped it for her scrapbook."

"It" was a gossip-column mention of what had gone on the night before during a performance of *George White's Scandals.* The musical revue was similar to what we'd seen at the *Follies,* except that *Scandals* had Ann Pennington, and Ann Pennington knew how to shimmy. I could shimmy, too, and had, on occasion, during certain Montgomery parties after only a little encouragement and a little booze. The diminutive, dark-haired, wide-eyed Miss Pennington, however, did it while wearing strategically placed silver fringe, onstage, and with a spotlight trained on her. This had a dramatic effect on the audience, which responded with hoots and cheers and whistles and applause.

Amid this, Scott and I, having begun our evening with orange-blossom cocktails and at this point nicely tight, had been sitting close to the stage in the sixth row, talking quietly in each other's ear about each act and the range of talent and whether either of us might be able to do a better job of it. When it came to Ann Pennington and the shimmy, I'd shaken my head and said, "Lord, I'm pretty good, but I can't beat that."

"I'll bet I could," Scott said.

"Nah. You? You've got moves, sure, but not like those."

"You don't think so?"

As the number ended, he stood up and slowly peeled off his jacket. The people nearby us began to cheer. He unbuttoned his vest next and slid it off the way a stripper would. Catcalls and whistles followed, while onstage all action stopped. He loosened his tie, then began to unbutton his shirt. The cheering increased, and then suddenly a spotlight swung onto us. Scott got up on his seat so that more of the audience could see him while he slipped his tie over his head and dropped it into my lap. Then he stripped off his shirt, and the crowd went wild. Scott took his bows as three ushers moved in, and then the two of us—along with Scott's clothing—were escorted to the lobby and subsequently into a waiting cab.

The article Alec was referring to said, *Celebrated New Novelist Fitzgerald Scandalizes the Scandals.* It quoted theatergoers who'd been present with saying things like they hoped Scott would get a recurring role or at least some compensation, and how surprising it was that an *author* looked so pleasing without a shirt. Others said that New York standards represented a new low for the country; it was one thing to have that kind of activity done onstage in a revue, but when the public began acting out, clearly Prohibition had not gone far enough to curtail the wildness of today's youth. We'd read the article over coffee and toast, and then Scott had tossed the paper aside and rolled on top of me, with an offer to scandalize me once more before lunch.

"Why, sir," I'd said, "you may look fine without your shirt, but a lady's got her standards to consider."

Scott pressed himself into me. "I'll give you a standard to consider."

Afterward, still a little breathless, I told him, "You're gettin' awfully good at this."

"I'd hoped that was the case, and that you weren't calling out to the Lord for rescue."

"You were very godlike, I will say. Everybody calls you Fitz, but I think your nickname should be Deo, from the Latin. I'm goin' to call you that from now on."

Scott laughed. "And I'm going to let you."

And now Alec was saying, "You're not upset?"

"It's a game," Scott told him. "The press needs stories, and the more sensational, the better."

Alec still sounded troubled. "It's your reputation, though."

"We're just having a little fun," Scott said as I joined them. "They want to depict us a certain way because readers respond to that, so why not give them some material to work with?"

"What do *you* say, Zelda?"

"Do my buttons," I said, presenting my back to Alec.

Scott nodded at Alec and winked at me. "The book is selling like crazy— they can hardly print them fast enough. Everybody wants to know what it's like to be one of us." Scott gestured to include Alec in *us*. "The book and the news stories offer a vicarious thrill for anyone who can't or won't get on the progress train."

Alec was having trouble with my buttons. I could feel his hands shaking; it was sweet, and a little sad. Alec worked in advertising, the way Scott had done last year, and was living with his reportedly conservative mother. He didn't think of himself as part of *us,* I was sure, and likely wished he could trade places with Scott.

Alec said, "It sounds to me like you believe your own press."

"I'm a novelist," Scott replied, putting on his topcoat. "By definition, I live in a world of make-believe."

"And what about you, Zelda?"

I leaned over to strap on a shoe. "Darling, call me Rosalind."

Our destination was a Greenwich Village speakeasy, for a party being given by someone none of us had met.

A train rumbled over the Third Avenue elevated track as our taxi moved into the busy Forty-second Street traffic. That trains could and did traverse the city—not only here next to the wonderful Grand Central Terminal, but also all along Second and Sixth and Ninth Avenues—still seemed strange to me. Stranger still was the subway system, with lines called IRT and BMT and stations tucked like hornet hives beneath the streets all around the city. It was, however, a wonderfully efficient way for Manhattan's two million inhabitants to get around the island quickly.

Just for fun, Scott and I boarded once at South Ferry and rode all the way to the Bronx, where he then took me past the building he'd lived in on Claremont, "back when you broke my heart," he said. The building itself was a heartbreak, I thought—so plain and grim that it was no wonder he'd gotten depressed. What a tremendous difference ten months had made in both our lives.

Lower Manhattan was still new to me then. Here, the buildings were older and narrower than in midtown, and shorter, too; here was a New York City that hadn't known, yet, what it would grow up to become. The streets here were romantic in the twilight, and quieter than the bustling blocks around the hotels where we'd been staying.

Inside the little basement bar, cigarette smoke gave the space a blue haze that matched the low, mellow music being played by a quartet tucked into a corner of a tiny stage at the back of the narrow room. This music was jazz, but not like I'd heard before. Where the upbeat tunes of the *Follies* and *Scandals* made people want to tap their feet, to shimmy, this languid music, with lyrics sung by a colored woman who stood close to the band and swayed as she sang, made people want to drape themselves over one another as they sat, and smoked, and sipped from short glasses that in many cases were filled with what looked like green liquid. This music created half-lidded eyes and parted lips, and made the space between a dancing couple disappear.

"Whew!" I said, elbowing Alec. "Bet your mother wouldn't let you out of the house if she knew you were coming to a place like this."

Scott said, "And if she finds out, she's likely to have you arrested."

"Therefore," I said, "we will protect your identity while encouraging you to get acquainted with . . ." I scanned the room, then said, "That girl, there, in the dark blue dress."

Alec looked in the direction I was pointing. "They're all in dark blue dresses."

"Except the ones who are in black," Scott said. "We should try to find our host. Hostess, actually."

I smelled something that seemed green and earthy and mellow-sweet. "What's that scent, do you suppose?"

"Perfume," Scott said as a woman squeezed between them, her smile like the Cheshire cat's.

"I don't mean her. That smoky, earthy smell."

Scott sniffed. "Reefer, I'll bet."

"Reefer?"

"It's a plant you smoke, like tobacco, but with enhancements."

"I kinda like it."

"*Whose* party is this?" Alec asked Scott.

"A poet friend of Dorothy Parker's."

"Have you met Parker?"

"Not yet."

"Then . . . ?"

"Some chap phoned us," Scott told him. "Said he'd heard of us from Fowler, I think. Or maybe Bishop. Anyway, he said, 'Dorothy's friend'—well, he said her name, but I've forgotten it—'the friend has a new book of poems and would love for you to come hear her read.'"

"Oh, shit," Alec said. "A *poetry reading*?"

Scott shook his head sadly. "You have no soul."

"I need a drink."

"*I* need a drink," I said, taking Scott's hand. "Not 'cause of the poetry—we don't know how bad it is yet, so we gotta save our desperate drinking for after we make that judgment, don't you think?"

Scott clapped Alec's shoulder. "It might be fantastic."

"In which case," I said, "the liquor can only make it better."

We threaded through the crowd toward the bar, which seemed a make-shift affair. A wide, broad wooden plank rested on what looked like a series of stacked wooden boxes, though it was difficult to see it well. All of it had been painted black. I thought maybe it was supposed to be art.

I was studying what appeared to be a green drink when a voice said, "Zelda Sayre! Oh my God!" and two hands gripped my shoulders. I looked up to see Gene Bankhead's happy face.

"Gene!" I said, not simply glad to see an old friend, but glad to see someone familiar, someone from home—except the thought of home, of my mama and all my friends, suddenly made me wish I hadn't seen Gene after all.

"Tallu *said* you were coming up for a little hedonism—though why you bothered to get *hitched* first is beyond me. Is this gorgeous man the victim?" Gene asked, looking past me at Scott.

Scott held out his hand. "Scott Fitzgerald, at your service."

"Oh, at *my* service, too?" Gene arched an artfully drawn eyebrow and took his hand. Her voice was as sultry as the face and body to which it belonged.

"Meet Gene Bankhead," I told Scott, shaking my head. Just looking at Gene might be enough to set a man's hair on fire. "Whatever character faults I may have are her responsibility."

"Yes, yes," Gene said, waving her cigarette as she spoke, "I corrupted those poor girls as best I could." She leaned closer to Scott. "What do you say? Did I do a good job?"

"What do they have to drink around here?" Scott said, moving closer to the bar.

Gene reached out to pet Alec's cheek. "Babies, I am going to fix you *up*." Then she turned to the woman behind her. "Edie, you know that book everybody's talking about? The one with the petting parties that's got all the old folks frothing at the mouth? The handsome blond fella behind me's the author."

Edie went over to Scott, and then more Edie-like women did the same, and soon a crowd of marcel-haired Genes and Edies were asking him to *tell them everything*—as if anything he'd written could compare to the experiences they'd surely had. Alec and I could only stand back and watch as Scott became, that quickly, this strange little planet of a speakeasy's sun.

And then, oh my, Union Square.

Someone had said, *Hey, you ought to see Union Square,* and then, somehow, there I was. There *we* were, Scott and I and five or six people whose faces were unfamiliar and whose names I couldn't guess—except for the tall woman who looked like someone I'd seen in *Picture-Play,* maybe, or maybe I'd seen her onstage recently. Gene had suggested the green drink; I remembered that. It had tasted awful until I had more sugar put in, but regardless, it was so powerfully *green* that I hadn't been able to resist. There was not much green in New York in April. A few green cars. A green dress or two. So little green, amid all the tan and gray surroundings. The green drink helped mitigate the gray.

"The green drink!" I said.

Gene asked, "What's that you say, darling?"

Then, suddenly, there was a fountain.

"There's a fountain!" I said. I pulled off my shoes, unclipped my garters, peeled off my stockings, and ran to it. Then everyone else ran, too.

With my skirt hiked, I stepped up onto the broad, circular pool's lip. The stone was cold under my bare feet. My toes looked like stone toes in the dim light.

"Zelda here is a fantastic swimmer," Scott told the others. "She won every medal they give out in Montgomery, Alabama."

"Is that in Europe?" someone said, and then there was an "Ow!"

It was a cool night, but not cold. Certainly not anywhere near as cold as some of the spring days when I'd swum in the creek.

Or maybe it was colder. Really, it was hard to tell, and even harder to care.

The water looked black and deep, except at the center, where the fountain pulled the water up and then rained it down into a sparkling circle. It sounded like rain. When had it rained last? I looked up at the sky. A bright moon lighted thin clouds. So there *was* a sky over New York. This felt like a surprise.

Everyone was talking and laughing. Gene had stepped up onto the pool's edge, too, and was walking along it holding on to Scott's hand. *A tethered pony,* I thought, watching my onetime friend, whose long, dark hair streamed down her back like a mane. Scott was smiling up at Gene in a way that was supposed to be reserved for *me.*

I watched them a moment longer—too long, long enough to see Gene lean over and kiss Scott. *Kiss* him! Full on. Mouths, tongues. Scott's hand on Gene's thigh . . .

So I crouched down and put my hands on the stone, beside my feet. A moment later I was slicing through the cold water, my knees grazing the bottom of the pool. *Not so deep, then,* I thought, and was glad for the sensible part of my brain that had dictated a shallow dive.

I stood and shook the water from my hair. The group was cheering, and Scott was peeling off his jacket and laughing and motioning me to come to him.

Yes, I thought, looking for Gene. *Yes,* me.

I woke to sunshine stabbing my eyes, and checked the time: almost one o'clock. Scott, waking, reached for me.

My head was pounding, pressing images of the previous night into new recollection. I slid out of his grasp and got up, saying, "Wait, I'll ring up Gene for you."

"What are you talking about?" With his tousled hair and sleepy eyes, he looked like a little boy.

"You don't remember?"

He sat up against the pillows and reached for his cigarettes. Pensive, he lit one. "I remember some bad poetry, but I'm pretty sure that wasn't Gene."

"No, Gene was the one you were with at the fountain."

Now he looked thoroughly confused. "What fountain?"

Now *I* was confused. Had there ever actually been a fountain?

I went into the bathroom; there was my dress, piled near the tub in a wet heap. "Did it rain?" I said hopefully, while I shook some aspirin from a bottle. "Do you remember that?"

"Come back to bed, Zelda."

I went to the doorway. "Do you think Gene's beautiful?"

"Of course."

"Do you want her more than me?"

Scott kicked the sheet to the end of the bed, exposing his nakedness and his desire. "You tell me: Does this look like a man who's pining for another woman?"

"You have a good imagination. Maybe you're using it."

"It sounds like you're using *yours*. Come on." He patted the bed next to him.

"My head is killing me." I stepped back into the bathroom, where I filled a glass with water and swallowed the aspirin. "What was that green liquor?"

"Absinthe. Too much of a good thing?"

Leaving the bathroom, I said, "Everyone wants you. It's . . . it's one big candy shop for you every time we go out. They find out you're *you,* and I might as well be back in Alabama."

"Do you want to be back in Alabama, or do you want to be here with your clearly desirous and loving husband, who, yes, happens to be getting a little bit of extra attention right now?"

I went to him and sat on the bed's edge. "No, I don't want to go back. Just don't forget your lines."

"Which lines?"

"That you did it all in order to win *me.*"

14

As it is in the South, in New York City the buildings have names. And as it is in Society, some names carry more import than others. Our destination for George Jean Nathan's cocktail party was a high-society building named the Royalton, which was a hotel and residence, both.

The Royalton's marble columns were imposing, to say the least, but the massive, studded red-ocher doors offset the somberness like a ruby brooch on a widow's collar. We stopped on the sidewalk and considered those doors, which had no windows. They made the hotel seem an exotic fortress of some kind; the building might otherwise have been mistaken for a bank, or . . .

"It's like a Greek prison or something," I said. "He *lives* here? You wouldn't think a person would choose a place like this voluntarily."

Scott said, "New Yorkers are a different breed from anyone you'd have come across in the South—and I'm told Nathan's a species unto himself."

And so he was, as I saw after the doorman allowed us entry and directed us upstairs. George Jean Nathan had dark, expressive eyebrows and a knowing look about him. At almost forty, he was a tall, slender panther of a man in his fine black suit and glossy black shoes. His hair was almost as dark and as slick as his shoes. Seeing him there in the open doorway, I had a better idea of why this man lived in this building.

"Welcome!" he said, and waved us inside.

Scott shook his hand. "Scott Fitzgerald. It's such a pleasure to finally meet the man who now gets to say he discovered me. Meet my wife, Zelda."

"You were so thoughtful to include me tonight," I said.

"My God, Fitzgerald," he said, taking my hand but looking at Scott, "you're good, but I had no idea you were *this* good." He kissed my hand and asked, "How long have you and the new wonder boy been wed?"

"Three weeks tomorrow."

"Three weeks! What's he doing dragging you out to this miserable place during your honeymoon?" He took me by the arm. "I'm so sorry, my dear. Let me get you a cocktail to help you manage your obvious disappointment."

As George led me away, I glanced over my shoulder at Scott. He looked surprised, but also pleased. I lifted one shoulder, *Who would've thought?* and then waggled my fingers, *See you later.*

George said, "Zelda, Zelda. An exotic name for a girl who looks like sweet cream at sunrise. You're not from here."

"Nope," I said, assessing the other guests while he mixed a gin rickey. Scott and I were possibly the youngest people at the party, and just about the only ones who weren't dressed in black. My ivory georgette dress was about as opposite as you could get, in fact, which made me happy. "I'm Alabama-born, so a transplant here—but I think I could enjoy growing some roots."

"Then you like what you've seen of Manhattan?"

"It's a grown-ups' playground, isn't it?"

"These days. Before the war—before this Eighteenth Amendment Prohibition business, really—most of that playground was confined to Broadway. What you found if you went out uptown were blue bloods with yappy dogs and trailing furs, men and women with their noses upturned at the very idea of adults committing . . . shall we say *revelries.*"

"I haven't been uptown much. But I have been to Greenwich and Broadway—a few times, now—"

"So I've read. Your husband can't keep his clothes on, while you enjoy swimming in yours at Union Square—"

"These gossip writers, they don't miss anything, do they?" I laughed. "They got the bit about Scott paddling in the Plaza's fountain the other night, too."

"You two are so obviously noteworthy that I believe they've assigned a scout to trail you. Why, I imagine someone here tonight will be tattling on you in print tomorrow."

"I guess I ought to consider giving people something worth reading about, then."

George held out one hand to me and gestured to the center of the room with the other. "Shall we get started?"

The evening passed in a blur of new faces, laughter, flirtation, dancing, and liquor. The only time I wasn't holding a glass was when I was in some man's arms, moving to the new jazz music of Ben Selvin or Art Hickman's Orchestra being played on the grandest phonograph I'd ever seen or heard. It had no visible horn and was contained in a finely carved, hand-painted cabinet. George Jean Nathan took all of his interests seriously, that was plain enough.

I hardly saw Scott, until toward the end of the party when he found me in the midst of a conversation with two stage actresses whose primary concerns were cold cream and lice. He took me by the hand and led me over to meet a man he said was "the finest literary mind in the country."

"Finer than either of those two's?" I asked as we crossed the room. "I'm not sure that's possible."

"The one who was on your left gets three hundred a week."

"*Dollars?*"

"Yes—and probably love notes, too."

"Wait," I said, pretending I was about to turn around. "I need to get me the name of her cold cream."

The finest literary mind belonged to a man with a sober, somber round face that was framed by neatly combed dark hair parted severely in the center. His scalp was *actually white,* I thought, assessing him through a happy gin haze.

He appeared to be close in age to George, but worlds away in *joie de vivre.* He sat sedately in an armchair in the corner farthest from the phonograph, and at this point in the evening, when most of the men had mussed hair and had shed their jackets and loosened their ties, this man was as tidy as he must have been in front of his mirror earlier. He had a serious mouth and serious eyes. I wondered if he had a woman in his life. I wondered if he'd ever had one.

"Zelda, this is Mr. Henry Mencken. He's co-editor, with Mr. Nathan, of *The Smart Set.*"

I sat down on his chair's arm. "I sure do appreciate you taking such a shine to Scott's stories. He's awfully good, isn't he? It's so nice that people are finally taking notice and paying him so well for all his hard work. It's important that artists get recognition *and* money, don't you think? Otherwise, how else can someone like Scott afford to buy his wife a dress like the one I'm wearing?"

"I don't disagree," Mencken said, looking amused. "The trouble for the artist lies in the temptation to mistake the public's tastes—and thus their money—as a measure of actual value."

"So then, whose tastes matter?" I asked. Scott put his hand on my shoulder.

"The intellectual's. Someone who understands art—the history of it, its meaning to mankind."

"By 'mankind' you mean intellectuals," I said. Scott's grip tightened.

Mencken nodded. "I sound like a snob, I realize. Bad habit. I don't even have the formal education of this fellow, here." He indicated Scott.

"Princeton didn't give me much—"

"Except fodder for your novel, not to mention your newfound fame," Mencken quipped.

I said, "A thing can be popular *and* good. Scott's book proves it."

"How old are you?" Mencken asked.

"Almost twenty."

"Let's have this debate when you're thirty," Mencken said.

Scott took my arm and practically pushed me up onto my feet. "Mr. Nathan supplied some really fine gin tonight, didn't he? Come, darling, dance with your husband."

"What'd you think of Mencken?" Scott asked me in the morning. Or possibly it was afternoon; I wasn't sure.

I got up and shuffled to the bathroom. My mouth was dry. My eyeballs were dry. Dull, thick pain crept through my head.

"He seems kinda scary if you ask me," I said from the toilet. "I like George a lot better."

"And George likes you. Everyone likes you," Scott called. "Bring me some aspirin, would you?"

"Long as *you* like me, I don't care about everyone."

When I returned, Scott was sitting up in bed. He had a cigarette in one hand and a pencil in the other. A notebook was open on his lap. "There's not a finer man alive than Mencken, I mean that. He's got the keenest eye in literature—he's a natural. Taught himself everything he knows."

I gave Scott the aspirin bottle. "That's all well and good but he's so damn *serious*. Didn't it seem like he'd rather be most anywhere else than at a party?"

"Nathan says Mencken's anti–New York, only comes up when he begs him to. Says he tells Mencken there's no way he can get the pulse from his place in Baltimore. I told Mencken I'd send him a book, and he said he's *got* a copy, isn't that something?"

"And?"

"He hasn't read it yet. He thinks, though, that he'll have a look at it soon, and he wants me to send *The Flight of the Rocket* when it's out for review next winter."

"Doesn't that scare you?"

"*Scare* me? A review from Mencken . . . it's what writers *live* for. The honor of getting even an evisceration—"

"He wouldn't do that to you. He admires your work, if not your wife."

"Oh, I think he admires you—your fearlessness, at least. He's right about art, though. The most important work is too erudite for the masses."

"And for me, too, apparently, since I don't know what *erudite* is."

"Which is quite all right." Scott caught my hand and tugged me onto the bed. "You have other charms."

15

___

Dearest Second Sara,

I was delighted to get your high school graduation announcement.
Soon you'll be free as a lark! And it's no surprise to me at all that John
Sellers has taken a shine to you—he sees what we've all seen in you all
along: you're sweet and clever and have as much innocent sex appeal as
three Lillian Gishes. Mind you, there's no need to rush into anything.
Do like I did and wait until you know you've found your one true love.

New York is the most astonishing place, I must say, and Scott's popularity increases daily—it's truly impressive to behold. I'm just amazed,
and so proud of him. He gets at least a dozen fan letters every week, from
readers all 'round the country. And reporters are now starting to want to
talk to me, can you imagine? What will Montgomery say about Tallu
and me both being famous? You'll have to let me know, 'cause I'm sure
Mama will refrain from telling me anything that might swell my head.

Do come see us this summer. I think we're going to take a place in the
country so that Scott can get his next book done. Much love in the meantime,

Z-

Scott spotted her first: "Oh, darling, there she is: she is *the one*."

If we were going to live in the country, we would need a car. The beauty that caught his eye, here at the downtown sales lot, was a 1917 Marmon, a sleek, convertible red sports coupe. Scott waved to a salesman, then climbed inside.

While he talked to the salesman from the driver's seat, I examined the car's spoked wheels and wide running boards and the keen, leaf-patterned hood ornament. Then I got inside the red-leather-dressed interior next to Scott. He was holding on to the wooden steering wheel with one hand and stroking the wooden dashboard with the other. Nickel-plated gauges and levers and buttons filled the dashboard.

The salesman said, "Her first master was a Manhattan playboy. I'll let her go for the same price as a new, sedate 1920 sedan—how about that?"

"Let me just talk it over with the missus."

The salesman nodded and left us alone.

"It all comes down to materials," Scott told me. "The rich know this. Sure, we can get a newer car for the same price, but it won't look or drive like this one."

"We can afford it, right?"

"Our great friend Myra Harper's going to pay for it," he said, referring to the money he'd just gotten for selling movie rights to another of his short stories, "Myra Meets His Family."

I ran my hand across the sun-warmed seat tops. "Wow, our very first car. It's almost like we're grown-ups."

After a week of motoring about the countryside looking at houses for rent in a half dozen towns between Rye and Bridgeport, we fell in love with a gray-shingled house in Westport, Connecticut, about forty miles from Manhattan.

The house had a wide, deep front porch that reminded me of home, and sat on a road a few hundred feet away from the ocean—a happy fact that fascinated me to no end. I'd never seen the ocean before then, never seen any body of water larger than a big lake. Not much farther away was the Beach and Yacht Club, where we would get a summer membership. We thought it was the perfect setup for both of us: Scott would have the space and peace he needed for work, and I would have the beach, the club, and the ocean, and miles of old country roads to explore on foot or by bicycle. We told the real estate agent we'd take it through September, then we returned to Manhattan to pack our trunks.

On our first night in the house, we pulled two weathered rockers close together and sat outside on the porch, wrapped in blankets and drinking champagne by candlelight. The air smelled of salt, and cool, damp earth. We could hear the rhythmic boom of the surf.

"I always imagined the war would sound like this," Scott said. "Like heavy guns firing in the distance. Back then, even as I was sure I was going to war, I never saw myself in the action—and then I never *was* in the action."

"And a good thing, too."

"Maybe—but Bunny made it back. And Bishop, and Biggs."

"Well sure, but with no *B* in your name, you'd'a been in trouble."

"There you go, reminding me yet again why I love you," Scott said.

"The sound makes *me* think of Mama's story about when her house in Kentucky got shelled by Union troops. She was five years old, and the war was almost over but not quite. They had to hightail it to someplace in the country, and then they went to Canada, where her daddy was living so's not to get arrested for his Confederate activities."

"He left his family there in Kentucky?"

"They had a great big tobacco plantation, and a bunch of iron furnaces, and he needed my grandmama to keep an eye on all the business goings-on."

"Did he own slaves?"

"He did, sure. The plantation had six slave houses, Mama said—she and the other kids weren't allowed inside 'em, though. It's funny, 'cause I was *always* in old Aunt Julia's house, and the only difference was that we paid her for workin' for us."

"Which reminds me: Fowler said he'll phone you with the name of some agency out here where you can find a housekeeper."

"Thank goodness for that!"

"He'll know who's best—the Fowlers have only a little less money than God."

"What is it his family does?"

"Investments." Scott explained to me about bonds and stock and trading and interest, all of which I followed earnestly and then forgot immediately, retaining only the thought that none of that would ever intrigue me in the least.

"Anyway," he said, picking up the thread of our prior topic, "all respect due your grandfather, I can't imagine ever leaving my family the way he did."

"It turned out fine. After President Grant pardoned him—"

"The *president* pardoned him?"

"Well . . . yes. Who else would'a done it? And when they came back, he was almost nominated for president, and then he got on the Senate, and that's where he and my great-uncle met, and the two of them got Mama and Daddy together. So, see, if it weren't for my grandmama keepin' the business going in his absence, I wouldn't be here."

"Is that how you see it?" Scott laughed. "I'm not sure there's an actual connection."

"Course there is. Everything's connected."

"All those things could have happened even if he'd taken his family to Canada with him."

"Not if the Union had gotten control of his land and all. He'd'a been poor then, and you need money for politics. That's why my daddy's just a judge."

"*Just,*" Scott said. "He's one step from the highest seat in the state."

"And that's plenty good if you ask me. If he got any higher-and-mightier, he'd probably grow a beard and try'n elbow Zeus aside."

"What story will our kids be telling about *us* someday, do you suppose?"

"It'll be a lot more romantic than two senators matchmaking," I said. "They'll say that we were meant to be together no matter what. For us, stars aligned, the gods smiled—prob'ly there was a tidal wave someplace, too, and we just haven't heard about it yet."

"A Homeric epic, it sounds like. Have another glass of champagne and tell me more."

Ludlow did phone that week with the agency name, but despite my appreciation and despite our need, I was in no hurry to hire anyone, not until we'd run out of clean clothes and used up all the dishes and needed to have the pantry stocked again. We were still honeymooning then, and as glad as we were to be there on Compo Road, neither of us wanted to pop that perfect bubble of happiness we'd been floating in for nearly two months.

When the inevitable did arrive, I hired us a Japanese houseboy named Tana, all the regular—that is, female—domestics having already been installed in the homes of women who'd made their summer plans in the wintertime. I never have been able to be organized that way. Tana was a quiet and efficient fella who I liked very much, but who Scott and George deviled by pretending that *Tana* was short for *Tannenbaum,* and declaring that they believed him to be a German spy in disguise.

My time was occupied as anticipated: I swam at the club and at the beach; I explored the countryside; I wrote letters to all my friends, to Mama and Daddy, to my siblings, to Scott's friends who were now my friends, too. I read anything anyone recommended, and I gave a lot of thought to creating new cocktails for Scott and me and for the ever-increasing number of fellas Scott invited over. Ludlow and Alec were practically residents by summer's end, and we saw an awful lot of George, too.

Scott had page proofs to correct or revise for his upcoming story collection, *Flappers and Philosophers;* he drafted chapter after chapter of what he'd titled *Flight of the Rocket* but would become *The Beautiful and Damned;* he went into New York for lunch dates with Scribner's sales representatives and people associated with moviemaking. Already, he'd sold rights to three of his stories to the pictures—that was where the real money lay—and was looking for even more profitable ways to get involved.

How good life was! There was always an excuse to host a party or attend one. Every month, we got word that *Paradise* was going back to press for another five thousand copies. Scott wrote and sold three new stories. He befriended every actor, artist, writer, dancer, and bootlegger we came in contact with, and subsequently our house on weekends grew full of strange and lively and, yes, intoxicated people, but we almost always had a lovely time. Now and then he and I would get a drink or two past our limits, and a debate about, say, paganism versus Christianity would jump the fence of discourse and land in the slop trough of ugly argument, but there was nothing to such arguments; next day they'd be gone, along with all the food and the liquor, and we'd start fresh all 'round.

The single dark blot on that bright picture was my folks' visit in August. We did scale back our usual gaieties, knowing how they'd react; however, two of Scott's lesser Princeton classmates showed up drunk and uninvited at dinnertime one night. They barged in singing some bawdy fraternity song, and then before we were even out of our chairs, one of them puked in the kitchen sink. Daddy in particular was appalled; Scott got defensive; I tried to get rid of the friends, which only made Scott angry. He drank too much after dinner, and when my parents had gone to bed, we ended up in a truly ugly fight—and I ended up with a black eye. I was of the mind that I deserved what I got; it had seemed to me a fair fight, no different than I'd have had with my brother or any of the kids I'd grown up with. When my folks saw me in the morning, though, they were horrified.

It wasn't only my black eye; nothing about my life made sense to them. I defended my life with Scott as *our business*. I was so sure of our love then, so determined to prove to Mama and Daddy that we weren't doing things wrong, just differently. There was no way to know that certainty would one day become a luxury, too.

16

For that fall, 1920, imagine a scenario very much the same as the summer (minus the ugly fight), only see us in our little apartment on Fifty-ninth Street in Manhattan, right at the foot of Central Park. See us spitting distance from the Plaza, where, having put on our finery, we often drink cocktails in the lovely Japanese Garden. We no longer have Tana or any hired help; instead, we bring in our meals—from the Plaza's kitchen, mostly—and send out our wash.

Scott is still working on *The Beautiful and Damned. Flappers and Philosophers* is out and is selling nicely enough for a story collection, though nothing like *Paradise*. He's mostly happy about its reception—but Mencken's review, while lauding a couple of the stories, calls the others "atrociously bad stuff" and asks rhetorically whether Scott's going to be serious or be popular. Mencken doesn't know that the question is far from rhetorical for Scott.

Scott often had dark circles under his eyes at the time, and a restlessness I didn't quite understand. One minute he'd be agreeing with Mencken and Bunny and the other critics that the *Post* stories in the collection—the ones that paid for our life—were fluff at best and trash at worst, and then the next minute he'd be complaining that critics were rigid and hidebound, never willing to give due credit for anything that didn't fit in with their predetermined parameters of what fiction ought to be. He'd say, couldn't he be serious sometimes and popular other times? Wasn't it better—wasn't it *more* remarkable, he'd say—to have the ability to do both with real excellence? At those times, he was so sure he was right and everyone else was wrong.

On a Friday morning in late October, he handed me a roll of cash and said, "We're going to the Palais Royale tonight—to commemorate 'Head and Shoulders.' Dress, shoes, hair—whatever you want, do it up right."

The Palais Royale had made an appearance in that story, "Head and Shoulders," but I hadn't been there yet. That was the thing about New York: you could visit for months, you could *live* there, and still find a new place to go every time you went out.

As much as I liked the idea, I looked askance at the money. "Don't you think we've commemorated it a few times already?"

When it came to Scott's income, he gave me the highlights but I was not privy to the finer details. Even so, it was apparent that his earnings were unpredictable, and equally apparent that we were living awfully well. To spend even more, just on a whim like this, went beyond indulgence into luxury, which surely we couldn't afford. Yet here he was with money in his hand, so maybe I had it wrong. Maybe he'd invested well—maybe Ludlow had passed on some of the knowledge that had made the Fowlers so wealthy. What did I know about how finance worked? I trusted that Scott knew what he was doing.

He said, "One can never commemorate too often—haven't you ever heard that aphorism? I think Ben Franklin said it—or was it Mary Pickford?" He winked. "Get something really fabulous, something that'll turn every head in the place."

"I've got some nice things I haven't even worn—"

"Surely you're not going to turn down a chance to shop? Go on." He patted me on the behind. "I need to rework a couple of chapters—I've promised them to Max, and then I've got luncheon with some of the boys. I'll be tied up all day."

He liked to show me off, and I liked being shown off, so, "Have it your way," I said.

My first stop was a little boutique on Fifth Avenue that Scott's friend Marie Hersey had mentioned when she'd stopped in to see us the week before. *Parisian fashions for rich Americans* was how Marie had described the shop's goods, then she'd winked at Scott, who she'd known since they were children in St. Paul, and said, "Your bride deserves only the best, you told me so yourself."

Inside the boutique, the racks held luxurious, indulgent garments of every type. Delicate lingerie trimmed with exquisite lace or fur; lush velvet opera capes; heavy silk suits with embroidery and bows and buckles; furs that ranged from narrow wraps to full-length coats in ermine, in mink, in rabbit, squirrel, fox—I'd never had a fur, or even wanted one, until I stepped into that shop.

I stroked an ermine jacket while I surveyed the goods. Nothing in Montgomery came close to this. I thought, *What my girlfriends wouldn't give to be here with me right now.*

I missed the Eden-like environment of home, but the trade-offs I'd been enjoying for six months more than made up for it. And there, on a rack along the wall, was possibly the finest trade-off of all: a dress like I'd never seen before. It was black and sleeveless and simply cut—straight, almost, with just the slightest suggestion of a waistline. What was remarkable, though, was the decorative finish. One narrow line of silver sequins ran along the neckline, and then a river of tiny, ethereal silver beads flowed over the dress from the right shoulder all the way down to the hem, branching into an array of intricate flowers and vines.

A tall, slender, carefully made-up salesclerk came over to me. "Gorgeous, isn't it? All silk, the best there is. But wait," she said. "You are going to faint when you see this."

She retrieved the dress and turned it so that I could see its back. A smoke-colored mesh insert so fine that it was almost invisible was all there was to it, a deep U-shaped panel bordered by sequins and dropping almost to the point where a woman's tailbone might show. There, it joined the black silk that flowed around from the sides and into the back of the skirt, which had its own beaded riot of flowers and vines.

"My father would have me whipped," I said.

"You have the perfect figure for it—you've *got* to try it on. It's the very latest thing from Paris, a Patou design, *so* sexy, the way Parisian women are. Truly one of a kind."

I took the hanger. "You don't need to ask me twice."

Ten minutes later, the dress was being boxed and sent to the apartment, and I was on my way to the hair salon.

"What service may we provide for you today, Mrs. Fitzgerald?" asked the clerk when I arrived.

From my purse, I took a piece of folded paper and laid it out on the counter. "Life should imitate art, don't you think?"

The clerk read the headline, which was the title of Scott's May *Post* story, "Bernice Bobs Her Hair." She said, "I do, absolutely. Carmen will be delighted to assist with your mission."

"Quick, then, before I lose my nerve. How long does a person have to live here before they stop feelin' like everything they're doin' is criminal?"

I was back home before Scott returned. From the bathroom, I heard him come in. He was humming something that I wouldn't say was upbeat, exactly, but that he was humming at all was a good sign.

"What took you?" I called from the tub.

"Oh, you know. Business."

"Don't come in. I want to surprise you. Oh, I had the Plaza send up a light supper—*dinner*, I mean. Somethin' with potatoes and beets. I was hungry. We can still get a bite later, too, if you want."

"Are you in the tub?" he said from just behind the door.

"Do *not* come in here. I mean it!"

"All right then, I won't tell you *my* surprise either."

"What surprise?" I said, but he only laughed in reply.

I climbed from the tub, dried off, then took my time rubbing in the lilac-scented body cream I'd bought at the salon—where in addition to getting my hair bobbed, I'd had my first professional manicure. The deep red nail polish they'd talked me into still startled me—though not nearly so much as my hairstyle—but was going to look perfectly dramatic when paired with lipstick of the same shade.

I did my makeup, taking extra care with the eyeliner the way the salon girl had advised. A tiny hint of rouge, light powder, mascara, lipstick. *Goodness,* I thought, surveying the effect.

"What surprise?" I tried again.

"I'm afraid I can't hear you, darling. These ice cubes"—Scott rattled some in a glass—"are just *so* loud."

I said, "You're an evil man, Scott Fitzgerald, I just want you to know that," and resigned myself to waiting.

Sheer black, lace-topped silk stockings came next, with new garters. That was it for undergarments: the dress wouldn't allow anything more. I was genuinely grateful to have small breasts that required no support. The prospect of going out in public without even a chemise beneath my dress, however, was awfully strange. Scary and thrilling at once. I thought, *Those Parisian girls are brave.* Well, I was brave, too, New York brave, *Paris* brave, even, and all this would prove it.

I slipped the dress on, regarded myself in the mirror once more, stepped into my new black high heels, and then swung open the door.

Scott was seated at the desk. When he looked up, I turned in a slow circle. He stared at this new bob-haired, bead-draped, Parisian version of his wife, then gave a low whistle.

"Oh, perfect," he said.

George was waiting outside in a cab with the window rolled down. He saw me and whistled just as Scott had done. "Oh, doll, what *has* New York done to you?"

"Mind you, she's still married," Scott said, handing me into the cab and then climbing in after me.

George said, "If you have a point, I wish you'd get to it."

"And you didn't even see the back," I told him, then leaned forward and let my velvet wrap slip down off my shoulders.

"Fitz," George said, "where can we drop you?"

I asked George, "What do you think of this haircut? I'm hopin' I wear it better than Scott's Bernice."

"Darling," Scott began, "George might not have seen—"

"*The Post?*" George said. "The one with 'Bernice Bobs Her Hair' inside and *your name* on the cover?"

"*And* a handsome couple using a Ouija board," I said. "I liked that illustration."

Scott sounded almost apologetic as he told George, "That'd be the one. I would have offered you the piece, but I didn't think it was a *Smart Set* sort of tale."

"Wasn't that a sharp cover illustration?" I said. "Y'all should get that artist for *your* magazine. I talked to a spiritualist once about Scott and me; Ouija couldn't seem to get to the bottom of things."

George laughed. "I'll bet its turn as cover model got a lot of readers to part with their nickels, though."

"Let's hope so," Scott said. "It takes a lot of nickels to justify the five hundred bills they're paying me."

I said, " 'Bernice' is so much *fun*—people'd pay five cents for just that one story, if they had to. F. Scott Fitzgerald stories are *always* a good investment."

"There's a solid economic theory for current times," George said, nodding. "Not to mention a very charming, if woefully naïve, homage to a husband. He pay you to say this kind of thing in front of me? I can raise you to fifty dollars a story, Fitz—that's all we've got in the budget."

"But never mind all that," I said, swatting George's arm. "Wouldn't Daddy frown at me, goin' on about money? And this haircut! He'd say my morals have escaped me like a hound loosed for a hunt."

George said, "Fitz, I do hope you write this stuff down."

I ignored him. "Scott seems to like it, but I don't know, it sorta makes me feel like a boy."

"A boy!" George snorted. "Not any boy I've ever seen, and thank God. Doll, I think it's going to go over like a house on fire."

The Palais Royale at Forty-seventh and Broadway was lighted so brightly, it was as if the show was happening on the crowded sidewalk and street outside. Its marquee was strung across the second story, which housed the club and took up half the block, every shining letter in the name set inside a circle of lights. Above the marquee, perched on the roof's edge like hawks overlooking Broadway, were two rows of giant rectangular billboards more brightly lighted than the club.

There were ads for Pepsodent and Camel, Listerine and Lucky Strike, Gillette, Bayer, Cremo, Coca-Cola, Wrigley's, and Whiteway's—which was offering a "woodbine blend dry cider" for rheumatism and gout.

"Lonicera sempervirens," I said. The men looked at me blankly and I explained, pointing at the ad, "Honeysuckle—woodbine—in Latin."

They leaned over to see the billboard, then George said, "Amazing how many more people have gout, now that booze is illegal."

"Isn't it?" Scott said while rubbing his elbow theatrically. "Think I'm going to need some medicine myself before the night's out."

I thought we'd go inside right away, but as George wanted to wait for some friends, we stayed on the sidewalk near the corner entrance and watched the tourists stream by. Music wafted out into the evening whenever the door opened. I tapped my foot in time to the jazzy song and only half-listened to the men, who were going on about Haiti and someone named Eugene O'Neill—a playwright, I gathered, before I tuned them out entirely.

There was so much diversion here in New York, and especially in Times Square. Automobiles and streetcars and people who, like our little trio, had dressed to the nines for their Friday-night dates. Men in derbies like Nathan's, and in fedoras like Scott's, in top hats—real dandies, here—and a few fellows who were reliving summer, it seemed, with straw boaters and linen Ivy caps. Their companions wore every version of evening dress, from the old-fashioned gored-skirt style that made me think of Mama, to silk suits similar to the ones I'd seen in the boutiques, to stylish shirtwaists and skirts trimmed in tulle or satin or lace. No one had a dress like the one I was wearing; the salesgirl was right about my leading the trend.

I was about to ask Scott to tell me his surprise when a woman yelled, "George!"

Her voice made us all turn to look. The owner of the voice, a tall, curvy *girl,* really, was the blondest person I had ever seen. *Bottle blonde,* I thought, not ungenerously. Next to her was another girl almost as blond and almost as attractive. Both of them wore low-necked velvet dresses, one garnet-red, the other emerald-green, and coordinated feathered hats. They were sisters for sure, probably twins, and had figures that were ripe for a chorus line someplace. I suspected they had personalities to match.

"Good evening, ladies," George said. "You look remarkably pretty to-night."

The girl in garnet said, "Well, I told Mary, here, that this was no time to slouch, you know? It's *George Nathan*, I told her. Maybe he'll bring a friend, I said."

"She did say," said Mary.

"And you did bring a friend," said the first, indicating Scott. Then, eyeing me, she added, "But it looks like he brought a girl."

"*Some girl*, too," said Mary. Her gaze was direct and admiring—even envious, I thought.

"Indeed. Scott and Zelda Fitzgerald, meet Suzanne and Mary Walsh."

Suzanne's face lit up. "Oh, the girl is your *sister*."

"No, my dear," George said, putting his arm across her shoulders and steering her toward the door. "I should have said *Mr. and Mrs.* Scott Fitzgerald."

"But they look so much alike!" Suzanne protested.

"Why don't we start our evening at the pharmacy downstairs."

"There's a pharmacy?" said Mary. "I always thought it was a nightclub."

"I'll explain inside."

George let the girls precede him and glanced over his shoulder with a smile that I found both wicked and endearing.

The "pharmacy" was a basement cabaret called Moulin Rouge. The dark, loud, smoke-filled lounge had a small stage embraced by red velvet draperies. The stage had a backdrop meant to resemble Paris—I recognized La Tour Eiffel, and the famed bridges—and was being overrun by six flouncy-skirted dancing girls who circled a top-hatted, red-cheeked, mustachioed man. The music, a raucous accordion piece, was like nothing I'd heard before.

"Is this French music, then?" I asked Scott, almost yelling in order to be heard.

He nodded. "From the fin de siècle—so not modern, but when the girls move like that"—he pointed with his chin—"who cares!"

126

We found a tiny cocktail table and fitted ourselves around it. George sat between the sisters, with Scott and me to their right.

I leaned closer to Scott and said, "Now will you tell me the surprise?"

"Soon."

"I know 'soon' with you, mister."

"And it turned out to be worth the wait, didn't it?"

We'd all had a couple of cocktails by the time the revue finished. I was feeling pleasantly light-headed and altogether happy with the night so far, so much so that I'd nearly forgotten that there was supposed to be anything more to it.

Scott looked at his watch. "It's almost nine; let's go on upstairs."

"They're meeting us?" George said.

Scott nodded. "I reserved a booth."

"Who's meeting us?" I asked.

"A couple of Nathan's friends."

I grinned at George. "*Four* girls?"

"Your high esteem honors me, doll."

Scott told me, "But I ought to set this up for you first."

"You ought," George agreed. "Drawing it out is far better than unloading all at once." This made the sisters giggle.

"So then," Scott said, turning to me, "I've been in touch with some people who work in the pictures—"

"Who?" Mary said. "Can you introduce me?"

"And me!" Suzanne said.

Scott rolled his eyes. "Upstairs," he said close to my ear, nudging me to stand.

George grinned and put an arm around both Suzanne and Mary. "We'll find you later," he said. Somehow, I doubted that would happen.

Onstage upstairs in the Palais Royale, a young woman in a shimmering aqua gown crooned some sentimental tune. The whole room seemed wrapped in soft orchestral swells. Here was a nightclub like the ones I'd seen in illustrations; right away, I understood why Scott had chosen to put this one in the story. The wide, long room had deep brown walls, a broad stage with footlights, a pit for the orchestra, and a dance floor large enough to fit fifty people or more. The entire rest of the room was tiered, with eight or ten rows of plush and intimately lighted booths. I guessed that anyone who sat in them would appear lovelier or more handsome than they actually were, as a simple matter of reflected glory. I'd liked the vigor of the Moulin Rouge; here, though, I felt instantly more sophisticated, more desirable, fully worthy of the stares I was receiving from women and men both.

The maître d' led us to a big U-shaped booth at the edge of the dance floor. A man and woman who had been seated there stood up when we approached. Scott introduced them as John Emerson and his wife, Anita Loos. The names were new to me, and I glanced at Scott, expecting more information. He said nothing more, just stood there rocking back on his heels with his hands shoved into his pants pockets.

John Emerson, middle-aged, thinning hair, rectangular in face and body, stared at me and shook his head. "Unbelievable."

"Sorry?" I said.

"He *told* me you were screen-ready—and your photograph wasn't bad. But now I see you have real dimension, and there's something nice, something vulnerable yet mysterious, about your eyes." He turned to his wife. "What's your read?"

Anita was a little younger than John—thirty or so, I guessed, and pretty, but in a dark, studious way. "I can't disagree." She sounded almost sorry, or sad.

"Thanks, I guess."

"Let's sit, shall we?" Scott said.

When we were settled, John Emerson said helplessly, "And will you just look at the two of them together. You were right, Scott. I think we can pursue this further."

Scott said, "Fantastic!"

"Y'all will forgive my manners," I said, "but just what the devil is going on?"

John Emerson laughed. "Mrs. Fitzgerald—"

"Zelda."

"*Zelda,* tell me, how would you like to be a moving-picture star?"

"What, me? Gosh," I said. "There's something I never considered. Where

I come from, actresses are pretty common—that is, they don't have good families or good breeding—with Tallulah Bankhead being the exception. Course, Tallu having grown up with her father always gone, and her mother dead since just after her birth, and only her aunt to raise her and Gene, well, all that just made her *seem* common—"

A man appeared at our table then, and we all looked up. He was an oval-faced fella, fine enough in form but with features that, together, added up to *ugly*. You imagined him as having been one of those poor, homely children that even other children avoid, the sort who then gets too much attention from his mother and none from his father, whose burning desire as he grows up is to make everyone respect him one day.

This man was well dressed, and his manner was silky as he said, "So delightful to see you here, John, Anita. Can you forgive the interruption? Mr. Fitzgerald left word with my secretary that you'd all be here tonight."

Scott jumped up and proffered his hand. "You're Griffith!"

"Indeed. I had the advantage in recognizing you from the magazine portraits. They hardly did you justice, even that new one in *Vanity Fair*—why, you should be starring in pictures, not writing for them."

"Why not both?" I said, warming right up to the situation that seemed to be unfolding for us. I held out my hand and said, "Mr. Griffith, I'm Zelda, Scott's wife."

"Of course you are!"

I'd soon learn that this Mr. Griffith was *D. W.* Griffith, who along with Charlie Chaplin and Douglas Fairbanks and Mary Pickford had recently formed a company called United Artists. He sat down next to Scott, and before long the five of us were immersed in conversation that had nothing at all to do with literature, which I'll admit made a nice change of pace.

There were more cocktails, more music, and then the dancing began. Anita claimed to be tired and urged John to dance with me. He obliged, and then when we got back to the table, Scott and Mr. Griffith were gone.

An hour passed before Scott returned, alone. He had fire in his eyes. "We need to go," he said, reaching for my hand. "Good night, Anita, John—thanks for keeping Zelda out of trouble."

John said, "We'll talk next week." Scott only nodded and led me out.

"What is it?" I said, having to almost run to keep up with him.

"Taxi," he told the doorman, then said, "What is it? It's Dorothy Gish. She needs a new movie."

"And Mr. Griffith—"

"Will pay me *ten thousand dollars* if I can write up a suitable scenario."

While Scott stayed up all night sketching out ideas, I fell asleep to the happy thought that everything was possible, anything might happen, and circumstances could change with speed and drama no one in Montgomery would ever have believed. The Montgomery girl I still was on the inside kept wanting to stop and gape, to take in the wonder of the scene or event. The New York woman I was becoming, however, didn't have time for that girl. That girl was provincial and immature and frivolous; I was all too willing to leave her behind.

Scott wrote the scenario with his usual gusto, and two weeks after he'd gotten the assignment, he'd finished it.

"Let's get lunch out," he said, moving the curtain aside to look out the window. Central Park was now a half-naked forest of faded golds and deepening browns. The sky above was steely gray. "I'll see who's free to join us. Grab your coat and we'll go to that Irish place on Broadway for shepherd's pie."

He wanted to walk, saying that after being cooped up all that time, he needed fresh air and exercise. "I'm susceptible to lung ailments, you know."

I didn't know. What I *did* know was that outside, the biting wind stole my breath and gusted into my skirt and through the weave of my wool coat, and made my nose drip and my eyes water. With gloved hands, I dabbed my eyes frequently as we walked, hoping to keep my mascara from striping my cheeks.

At the restaurant, we entered the vestibule and I said, "Thank God! Another minute out there and my eyeballs would've frozen over."

Ludlow was waiting inside the door, at the end of the bar. His cheeks were ruddy and he still had his scarf wrapped around his neck. I said, "Hello there, Ludlow! You look like Hans Brinker."

"And you look distraught, though still beautiful—Fitz is beating you, isn't he?'

"Torturing me, in fact. He insisted we walk here!"

"You brute!" Ludlow said.

Scott gestured for me to follow the maître d', saying, "Obviously the South breeds sissies. Up North you build up a resistance."

"I don't need a resistance, I need a Caribbean villa. Right, Lud? I should have a villa."

"And a new husband."

"What you need," Scott said as we were seated, "is a fur coat. Ankle length and, what, ermine? Otter?"

"Oooh, yes, that's exactly what I need!"

Ludlow said, "What has he sold this time?"

"Nothing yet," I said sorrowfully.

Scott frowned. "This woman has no faith in me."

Ludlow declared, "This woman has too much faith in you."

"This woman needs a fur coat," I said.

After we'd placed our orders, I said, "How nice it must be to be covered in fur all the time. Animals have it good that way, don't you think? A day like this is nothing to them; nature insulated them exactly right for their surroundings. Why do you suppose humans persist in living where it's so cold that we'd want to cover ourselves up with another animal's skin and hair? It's sort of queer, isn't it?"

Ludlow nodded. "Not to mention expensive."

Scott had brought a bottle of brandy, which the three of us shared. As I polished off one glass and was into a second, the notion of actually owning a fur took hold of me as if of its own accord; I just couldn't stop talking about the subject: all the kinds, who wore them, what I liked, whether men should wear them, and Scott and Ludlow encouraged me.

Our food arrived, and Ludlow asked Scott, "Say, have you had a chance to read the smash-hit novel *Main Street*? They say Sinclair Lewis started out like you, Fitz, writing popular stuff for the magazines—he really built himself a following that way."

Scott's mouth tightened. "Nope, haven't gotten to it yet."

"He's been too busy," I said cheerfully, "working so that he can buy me a fur coat."

By meal's end, I was nicely warmed in every way and ready to face the elements. Ludlow left for an appointment with some investment adviser, and we headed back to Fifty-ninth. I wasn't paying any attention to the route we took home. We pushed against the wind, me chattering on about which movies I liked or didn't and how I might like being an actress and what Tallu had done and what she'd written me and how everyone back home secretly found her exotic and wonderful while saying that she'd— *Oh, isn't it so, so sad*—gone astray.

"What do you s'pose Montgomery will say about *me*? You can bet there'll be gossips claiming I only married you so's to get to New York, where I could get discovered."

"I rather like that scenario; it recasts me as sympathetic."

"Aw, the folks there all like you just fine—'specially now. It's change they don't like. And actresses."

"Here we are." Scott grabbed my arm and stopped some fifty feet from the corner, which confused me for a second. Then he tugged me toward a doorway and I saw that we were at a furrier.

"What are we—"

"You need a fur coat."

"Deo, wow, that's a wonderfully nice thought, and I know I went on and on about it, but *really* I just needed some brandy."

He said, "All right, then, *I* need you to have a fur coat," and led me inside.

Oh, didn't I have the grandest time wrapping myself in every kind and color of fur! Some were little more than elegant shrugs; some fell to the waist; some were swingy numbers that hit midthigh. The one that went home with us, though, was substantial in every way. It was made up of gray-squirrel pelts, with a full collar and wide cuffs, big, round buttons at the waist, and went down to my knees. The moment I slipped into it, I knew we were meant to be together. Scott wrote a check for seven hundred dollars as if he bought fur coats every day of the week, and then when we left, we walked six blocks out of our way so that I could "try it out," not to mention show it off.

Back in our apartment, we spread it on the floor in front of the fireplace and made love right there, right then in the middle of the afternoon.

I was blissfully certain that I had everything I could ever want.

17

=

Nov. 6, 1920

My Dear Sara,

    Your account of that Woman Movement meeting almost shames me, as all I've been doing lately is crowing about how my husband's novel was <u>the number one book for the whole entire United States in October</u>! If I were to die today, my headstone would read, "Proud Wife," and my death would probably be at the hands of angry feminists.

    I do realize I ought to consider doing something more with my time, but I can't help it, I really am proud of him and I can spend entire days just on grooming and dressing and then meeting friends, whereby I tell them Scott's fabulous news.

    Besides which, it's such great fun to have great fun—the few feminists I've met here wear long faces and dingy clothes and need hair dye desperately. Maybe I'll buy a case and distribute bottles to these poor needy women. I want to do my part to support the effort.

    You are the best of them, an exception in every way, and I'm proud of you. In fact, I'll toast you at tonight's dinner party—the hostess is some cosmetics heiress who's sure to miss the irony of my doing so there.

Please stay out of trouble, for once. All my love,

Z~

Tilde and John invited us to their house in Tarrytown for the day. The last time we'd seen them was in summer, not long after the baby was born. Tilde had been tired and irritable at the time, and a bit skeptical, still, about Scott and me. We could see it in the way she studied us with that intense, piercing gaze of hers, like she was analyzing our every word and move. We hadn't stayed long. Long enough, though, that now Scott felt the need to fortify himself before going over there again.

That fortification started with wine at lunchtime and continued with a steady stream of gin consumed throughout the drive, during which he sang Christmas-carol tunes but made up new lyrics to go with them.

"You should've been writing those down for me," he said as we parked in Tilde's driveway. "What was that line, from 'O Little Town of Bethlehem'?" He paused to recall it, then sang, " 'How gayfully and playfully the Christmas gifts are given / We do our parts to spare the hearts of all those but the heathens.' What do you think? A holiday music revue? That'd be right up George Cohan's alley." He grabbed his notebook and began writing down the lines.

Tilde saw us from the front window and waved. I said, "Can't we do this later?"

Scott ignored me and kept writing, so I climbed out of the car and went inside without him.

Tilde and John's baby, now six months old, was the sweetest thing imaginable. "Give him over," I said the second I stepped into their little brick house. It was a chilly day, crisp and cloudless; inside, the scent of apples and cinnamon simmering on the stovetop made the house seem even snugger and more inviting than it was. The baby had his own snuggly smell, like warm milk and rose-scented soap. I was wearing the squirrel coat and opened it so that I could tuck him right up against me. His skin was pure silk velvet. I put my nose up to his soft neck and inhaled deeply.

Tilde's older boy, little John, hovered close to her, one hand clutching her skirt—a skirt that was as long as ever, and more matronly than I'd seen her wear before. She was not even thirty yet, and already she looked middle-aged.

She said, "You remember Auntie Zelda." He shook his head and pulled her skirt in front of him like a curtain. "Our nurse has the day off," Tilde said apologetically.

"We don't mind a bit, do we?" I said to the baby, who gurgled happily in reply.

Scott came in then, still humming the song's tune. "Greetings, Palmers," he said, shaking John's hand heartily.

"How about it, you two?" my brother-in-law asked. "When can we expect a Fitzgerald cousin for our fellas?"

I held the baby overhead and kissed his tummy, which made him giggle. "No time soon," I said. "I've got to hang on to this figure a little longer. John Emerson—he's a director and producer—is thinking of me for one of his pictures."

"What?" Tilde said. "You, in the movies?"

"Why not? Everyone at home was always saying I had every bit as much talent and looks as any star. And Scott's just turned in a scenario for Dorothy Gish—she's Lillian's sister, you know—and we're chumming with lots of movie folks nowadays."

John offered to take our coats and then, as we gave them over, said, "What about books? I thought *that* was your thing, Scott."

"If I was among the independently wealthy, maybe. But I've got bills, and books won't pay them."

"Not unless it's Sinclair Lewis's book," I said—a glib mistake that I realized too late.

Scott glowered at me. By now we'd heard from almost every one of Scott's literary friends how that new book, *Main Street,* was selling so fast that the printers literally couldn't keep up, exceeding *Paradise* by far. Worse, Lewis was, like Scott, a Minnesotan. This novel that Scott had declared dreary and bleak when he'd read it, finally, a few days earlier, was usurping his book's place—*his* place, actually. He wanted to always be the favorite son.

He told John, "I'm awaiting word from a very powerful producer—head of *United Artists*," he said, as if Tilde and John would be impressed. "Then we'll have ten thousand to pay off our debts and start setting a little something aside."

"Start?" Tilde said, directing little John to a set of building blocks. "What happened to all the money you've gotten from selling all those stories and things? Mama wrote that Zelda said you can't stop making money. I'll suppose a lot of it went for that coat—"

"Now, Tilde, dear," John said, "that's not our business—"

"That's all right," Scott said too heartily. "We're *family*. It's true, I've made a tremendous amount of money, with which we've had a tremendously good time."

"The money's just irregular," I said, and Tilde gave me a look like *I'll say it's irregular!*

"You should buy bonds," she said. She took the baby from me before either he or I wanted her to, as if remembering that I was irresponsible. "Children need a secure, stable home—and heaven knows they're not inexpensive. A good nurse or nanny is worth her weight in gold."

"I told you, we aren't having any yet."

"You will, though—"

"Your sister makes a tremendously valid point," Scott said, and clapped me on the shoulder. "It's time we started acting like adults. No more of this lavish spending. No more John Emerson seduction scenes. It's tremendously improper—we know that," Scott told them with his sincerest frown.

Tilde looked alarmed. "Seduction scenes?"

"Not literally," I said. I glared at Scott; he was performing, putting on an act not for Tilde and John but for me, to punish me for having dared to utter Sinclair's name.

"I can't imagine telling friends in St. Paul that my wife's an *actress*," he continued. "Though I'm sure your good friend Nathan wouldn't mind it at all." When I started to speak, he held up his hand. "No, no, I'm going to have to put my foot down this time. I'm calling Emerson the minute we get back.

"Imagine!" he added, then leaned close to John as if to confess. "It's awfully embarrassing to think I was almost as swept away by the idea as Zelda was."

"*Almost?* You're the one who arranged for it!"

"Dearest," he said as he took his flask from his pocket, gave it a testing shake, uncapped it, and downed what little gin was left while my sister and John watched, eyes wide, mouths open. "Say, John," Scott interrupted himself, "what do you have on hand? I'll want a refill for the return trip."

Tilde answered in a huff, "We're not lawbreakers!"—but John's expression wasn't quite so definite.

Still, he kept silent and Scott went on, "Dearest darling wife, look at that magnificent little creature in your sister's arms. Don't you want one of those? I can't wait to be a father."

We fought the whole way home, and then he got right on the phone with John Emerson, saying I'd had second thoughts and was pining for motherhood—so no movie career for me. This wasn't a problem in itself, because in most ways what he'd said was actually true. I didn't actually want an acting career, and I did actually want to have a baby. I just resented Scott manipulating my life.

A silent night was followed by a silent morning, whereby our already-small apartment seemed to have shrunk to the size of an elevator car. I staked out a corner of the sofa to read the crime-fiction magazine George and Mencken had just launched, *Black Mask,* which was a terrific escape. Scott pretended to work for a while, then made a show of putting on his coat, hat, and gloves, surely expecting me to ask him where he was off to. When I didn't, he left the apartment in a huff.

Later, the phone rang and the operator put through Griffith's secretary, who said, "Would you please relay to Mr. Fitzgerald that Mr. Griffith and Miss Gish feel the scenario isn't quite what they were looking for? His efforts are much appreciated. Mr. Griffith will be in touch."

"I will tell him, you bet, and thanks very much."

Scott walked in just as I was hanging up the phone.

I said, "Griffith had his secretary phone to say you just don't have what it takes for the job. Looks like you're out of luck."

He stripped off his gloves nonchalantly, then his coat, then let all of it drop to the floor behind him. His hat remained on his head. "You should choose your pronouns more carefully," he said. His voice was loose. "*We* are out of luck. We're ruined, in fact."

"What are you saying? You're drunk."

"*I'm* drunk, and *we're* broke. Aren't pronouns fun?" Then he pulled his pockets inside out for effect. "I can't even buy us lunch."

"Go to the bank, then."

"No, I mean we have *no money at all*. Not in my pockets, not in my wallet, not in the bank. In fact, I had to borrow to pay for your coat."

"Borrow from who?"

"The Bank of Scribner, in this case, although sometimes I use the Bank of Ober."

I was confused. "Max and Harold *lend* you money?"

"Against royalties, or future earnings—it's all money I'm going to get eventually; just, *eventually* doesn't always arrive as quickly as I need it to."

I went to the closet, pulled the coat from its hanger, and shoved it at him. "Send it back!"

"Don't be ridiculous." He plopped down on the sofa. "You look fantastic in this coat. In fact, I think you should take off everything you're wearing and then put the coat on." His eyelids were drooping as he said this, and then they closed.

I watched him for a moment, thinking he'd fallen asleep. Then, without opening his eyes he said, "Don't hate me. I'm sorry. It's all for you."

Scott went on the wagon and finished his novel, *The Beautiful and Damned,* a story of a young society couple so indolent and overindulged that they ruin themselves. His self-discipline impressed me, so much so that I was pregnant by February.

18

Knowing—sort of—what parenthood would do to our lives, when Scott made a seven-thousand-dollar deal with *Metropolitan Magazine* for the serialization rights to *The Beautiful and Damned,* we decided we'd better go abroad and see some of the places so many of our friends had seen and told us about. Touring Europe was the thing to do, I guess, now that America had invested so much in its salvation. We booked first-class passage on the *Aquitania* and departed May 3.

Having never been on board any water vessel larger than a rowboat, I was as enraptured by the ship as I'd been by so many things in Manhattan. *Nine* decks, including a grand ballroom decorated with all the polished wood, wrought iron, stained glass, marble, and gilt-covered splendor any overspending couple could possibly wish for.

"I bet the *Titanic* looked like this," I said as we walked to our cabin.

A woman grabbed my arm and told me, "Hush! You're going to jinx everything."

"*Titanic, Titanic, Titanic,*" I said, pulling my arm away. "Better reserve your spot on a lifeboat."

We spent a whole lot of time in the Palladium Lounge, where velvet-upholstered chairs and a wide, ornate fireplace deferred the Atlantic's chill.

For a week, we danced to the ship's orchestra, dined on every variety of fish and prawn and pheasant dish imaginable, drank fine champagnes, and acquainted ourselves with a variety of people as dissipated as we would one day become. Scott was accosted by a fella who brought an opened copy of *Shadowland* magazine to our table. He dropped it in front of Scott and pointed at a paragraph, saying, "It says here that *you* are 'the recognized spokesman of the younger generation—the dancing, flirting, frivoling, lightly philosophizing America.'" Then he pumped Scott's hand like he thought Scott's mouth might open and gold coins would spill out. When the seas got rough, we all told shipwreck stories the way people tell ghost stories while in a cemetery—you want to be prepared, I guess.

In London, we met up with Scott's friend Shane Leslie—whose aunt was Lady Randolph Churchill, whose son Winston took luncheon with his mother and us and then went back to his duties at whichever important post he was assigned to at the time. Young as I was, I failed to be suitably impressed by both London and its celebrities, who seemed as stuffy and formal to me as I must have been unsophisticated and silly to them.

We saw Paris, we saw Venice, we saw Florence and Rome. It was strange to see liquor served right out in the open, though of course this made perfect sense, there being no Prohibition in Europe. After the first hundred impressive statues and cathedrals and fountains and alleyways and villas, our eyes and our brains took on a glaze. We were the most ignorant of tourists, and got little out of the experience because of that.

Our ignorance remained firmly in place upon our return to the States in July, when we went to Montgomery thinking we would live there, be near my family so that we'd have the support and help I'd be so appreciative of when the baby came. I wonder, were Scott and I just so distracted by the elements of our moment-to-moment life that neither of us recognized it was going to be as impossible for him to live there as it had been the first time around?

After a few days of visiting my family and seeing some friends, even I felt like a misfit, saturated as I was with my experiences since leaving New York. The South seemed so backward, so *slow*—not to mention unbearably hot for me in my ever-expanding state. My father's perpetual disapproval made it easy for us to alter our course: by the end of July we were house hunting in St. Paul.

There's a word for people who move from place to place, never seeming to be able to settle down for long: *peripatetic*. And there's a word for people who can't seem to stay out of trouble—well, there are a lot of words for such types: *unstable, irresponsible,* and *misguided* are some of them.

Trouble has lots of forms. There's financial trouble and marital trouble, there's trouble with friends and trouble with landlords and trouble with liquor and trouble with the law. Every sort of trouble I can think of, we've tried it out—become expert at some of it, even, so much so that I've come to wonder whether artists in particular seek out hard times the way flowers turn their faces toward the sun.

One element of my life that has never given me serious trouble, though, is my perfect baby girl, my sweet Scottie. She was born on October 26 that year, 1921, following a pregnancy that was unexceptional in every way.

My labor was long and awful—so, as unexceptional as my pregnancy had been. When I'd coughed and blinked my way out from underneath the anesthesia's effects, there Scott was at my bedside as the nurse brought the baby in. He held a notebook and wore a *Look what I've done!* smile, as if he was the first father on the planet and had birthed that child himself.

The white receiving blanket gave nothing away. "Is it a boy or girl?"

"You don't remember? You've been in and out," he said. "We've got a daughter! You said you hope she'll be 'a beautiful little fool,' but we won't hold you to that."

The nurse put the little swaddled bundle of baby girl into my arms, and my eyes pooled with tears. "Hello there, baby Patricia," I said, rubbing her soft chin with my knuckle.

Scott leaned over us and petted her downy head. "Actually, I was thinking that she doesn't really look like a Patricia. What would you say, darling, to naming her Frances—my name, but with an *e* instead of an *i*? Frances Scott Fitzgerald."

"But . . . she's Patricia. All this time, that's what I've been calling her."

"Frances Scott—it seems fitting, don't you think? Her having been born in my hometown, you know. We have to think of her future. There's nothing unique about being *Patricia Fitzgerald;* really, darling, it's too common. The Irish are forever naming their sons and daughters some version of Pat."

The nurse returned then, and Scott asked her, "What do you think of this: Frances—with an *e*—Scott Fitzgerald, and we'll call her Scottie."

"That's so clever! Named after her famous father—she'll like that, what a privilege!"

"Except that she's Patricia," I said, feeling foggy, still. This conversation was moving too quickly. "We agreed on Patricia."

"Oh, well, that's a perfectly nice name. Nothing special, but nice. You have to consider that she's not just any child, though, don't you?"

"Her legacy," Scott said.

"Exactly." The nurse took the baby from my arms. "Now, Mother needs her rest, so off with you"—she indicated Scott—"and *you,* little Frances."

"Scottie." He touched the baby's tiny nose.

"Patricia," I said.

I knew, though, that Scott would replay this scene with everyone he encountered, and that they'd all see it his way. No one would disagree with the charismatic hometown hero. Even so, I would stubbornly continue to assert my preference for weeks, the way you do when you allow hope to prevail over knowledge, and in the end, I would grow tired of the battle, and Scott would win.

19

We spent the exceptionally, ridiculously, unendingly frigid winter of 1921–22 in the company of an assortment of Scott's old friends. My drawl, never a problem in New York, was a hindrance here. "Would you repeat that, dear?" was a regular refrain. And if I said something like "If I never see another snowflake, it'll be too soon, I swear!" someone was sure to ask, "Is *ahswayah* a Southern term? I don't think we have that one here."

The women allowed me into their bridge groups, though, and invited me to join their committees—Lord, you never did see so few women create so many committees! They extended every courtesy whether they wanted to or not, unwilling to lose their connection to *F. Scott Fitzgerald* even if his wife was, unfortunately, a foreigner.

Scott's mother, however, always treated me like I was an orchid she'd discovered blooming in her parlor. Sadly, Scott was far less fond of her than she was of me. He thought her old-fashioned and eccentric and absentminded—the very qualities that made her so dear. His father was old-fashioned, too, but Scott thought him benign, like an old pocket watch that keeps time and has style but isn't worth much.

Whenever Scott and I weren't, say, out riding in horse-drawn sleighs and then rewarding ourselves afterward with hot toddies, we worked together on a musical revue, *Midnight Flappers*, for the Junior League's April fund-raiser. Scott wrote the script and was also the director; I was choreographer and, of course, would be one of the flappers—*if* I could get rid of all my leftover roundness, which, although I was nursing Scottie, stubbornly stuck with me as if I needed the fat to keep me warm. Scott and I collaborated so well and had so much fun that my irritation with him about the baby's name faded and then disappeared. She was Scottie; this seemed self-evident before long, and I was glad we hadn't named her Patricia.

She was a happy, indulged, adored infant. Nursing her was demanding but rewarding, too, most of the time. Scott had a bad habit of inviting friends up to our place without first seeing whether I'd welcome company. The commotion—and my goodness, between Scott and his former nemesis Sinclair Lewis and their third musketeer, Sherwood Anderson, there was always commotion—would wake the baby. She would want me, not the nanny Scott had hired, and so I'd have to go off and nurse her back to sleep. I'd hear the others talking and laughing, carrying on without a thought for me, for my having to go from gay socialite to milk producer in the space of a baby's cry. Fierce as my love was for my baby girl, it was no antidote for resentment.

Scottie was not even four months old when my monthly, which had returned, sort of, in January, went missing again. I couldn't be pregnant; my sisters had told me I'd be safe as long as I was nursing! But the doctor, after confirming what I hoped was not true, shrugged and told me, "The only sure method of prevention is abstention, and of course no husband can be expected to agree to that for long. Congratulations, Mrs. Fitzgerald, and give my best to Scott."

For the next couple of weeks, while we planned a trip to New York to see friends and celebrate the March 4 launch of *The Beautiful and Damned*, I kept the news to myself and chased my thoughts around and around inside my head, unable to be happy about my condition and miserable about that unhappiness. I just could not imagine celebrating Scottie's first birthday, still eight months away, by giving her a baby brother or sister. I couldn't stand the thought of gaining so much weight again. I couldn't see my way through the tall grass of sleep deprivation and milk-engorged breasts, couldn't face the prospect of managing the needs of *two* wonderful but helpless, demanding little beings, even with the nanny's help. I longed for my prepregnancy body and had just begun to wean Scottie in preparation for my being gone two weeks in New York.

Judge me harshly if you will—God knows I've spent the ensuing years judging myself that way—but I decided to assert my right to control my own fertility, as Margaret Sanger liked to say, and told Scott how it had to be.

"I can't do it, Deo, the timing is all wrong, I'll be awful to everyone if I do it, I just know I will. It would spoil our lives, we're hardly getting started, I don't want to be a baby-making factory, I just can't."

He didn't want that life either; he said, "Yes, all right, I understand," and the look of terror he'd worn the day I'd said, "I'm pregnant," changed to relief.

While we were in New York, Scott gave an interview to a reporter from the *New York World,* who, having read Scott's flapper stories and now the novel, wanted his opinion about women in Prohibition society.

"I think that just being in love and doing it well is work enough for any woman," Scott said. "If she keeps her house nicely, and makes herself look pretty when her husband comes home from work, and loves the fellow and helps him and encourages him, well, I think that's the sort of work that will save her."

I slipped out, then, for my appointment with a doctor who I'd heard was discreet and reliable for all types of "women's troubles." He supplied me with those little yellow pills I'd once been so opposed to.

"I've got it!"

Scott rousted me from sleep a week later with a shake. "You won't believe this, Zelda. It just came to me in a dream." He switched on the lamp and grabbed his notebook and pencil from the bedside table. "It's brilliant. A clerk who wanted to be a postman has delusions of becoming the president . . ."

Seemed to me that Scott was the one with delusions.

"Three acts," he said, scribbling some notes. "Broadway will *love* this."

I was still rubbing the sleep from my eyes when he said, "This is going to make our fortune—I'll never have to write for the slicks again." He tossed the notebook back onto the table. "Good-bye, *Saturday Evening Post*! Good-bye, *Hearst's*! A successful Broadway show will pay residuals for *years*—it'll make me a millionaire before I'm thirty, Zelda."

He jumped out of bed and grabbed the notebook. "We're going to have to move back to New York, of course. . . . Go back to sleep, darling, see you in the morning."

In late March I came home from a Women's Committee for the Betterment of St. Paul meeting to find the nanny—who'd insisted we call her Nanny—waiting for me near the door with Scottie in her arms. I reached for the baby, but Nanny held on to her and said in her stiff, Norwegian-accented English, "You have a message from Mr. Harold Ober."

"*I* do? You must mean *Mr.* Fitzgerald."

"No," she huffed. "I make no such mistake. The number is on the note-pad." She pointed toward the parlor as if sending me to my room, despite her being less than a year older than I was.

Scott had insisted we hire this sort of girl. "Ludlow once told me his nanny could cut his meat just by scowling at it. All the Fowler kids were terrified of her, which really kept them in line."

"She'll give the baby nightmares."

"She'll give the baby rules and structure—all the things you and I do so poorly."

Now I told Nanny, "All right, thanks. I'll just take the baby and—"

"Her diaper is soiled," Nanny said, already moving down the hallway. "We can't possibly let you hold her in this state."

No, I thought, watching Scottie recede, her wide eyes staring over Nanny's shoulder, *we can't possibly. We can't possibly put up with Battleship Nanny very much longer.*

In the study, I phoned Harold, wondering what he could possibly want with me. It had to be something to do with Scott—but what? Scott was in touch with Harold often and had most recently been discussing the play, which he was calling *The Vegetable*.

Harold got on the phone. "Thank you for returning my call so promptly. Burton Rascoe, an editor from the *New York Tribune,* phoned me this morning to see whether you might be interested in writing a review of *The Beautiful and Damned* for them."

"Sorry, am I hearing you right, Mr. Ober? They want Scott's *wife* to review his book?" I'd never heard of such a thing.

"That's it, yes. He thinks readers would love to have something from you personally, having heard so much *about* you."

"I'll guess you told him that I'm not a writer."

"I don't think he's too concerned. If it's rough, they'll clean it up. They'll pay you fifteen dollars for your trouble—and I'll forgo my ten percent. You could get a new pair of shoes, or a bag or such. My wife always loves an excuse to buy a new hat. What do you think?"

"I'll do it!"

"Oh—all right. Good."

"You thought I wouldn't?"

"I assumed you'd want to ask your husband first."

"He'll adore the idea, don't you worry. Tell me what this Rascoe fella wants and when he wants it, and I'll get right to work."

As was often true while we were in St. Paul, Scott was spending his day with Tom Boyd at Kilmarnock, Tom's renowned bookstore. Tom and his wife, Peggy, had become pretty good friends of ours—there was Tom, a fella who was all about books, and then Peggy, pregnant with her first at the same time I was pregnant with Scottie, so we were pretty well matched. Both Boyds were aspiring writers when we met them, and Scott gave Peggy a whole lot of good advice that she put to work in a novel, *The Love Legend,* which Scott recommended to Max Perkins and which Max had just agreed to publish.

Tom was doing a wonderful job with publicity for Scott's book: newspaper ads, posters, and even a short reel that was running at the movie houses. Scott, ever determined to influence the *what* and the *how* and the *when,* wrote to Max to say that Scribner's ought to do something more with advertising than they'd done in the past. Scott was worried that even though reviews had been good—even Mencken had admired it—sales of *The Beautiful and Damned* might fall short of the sixty thousand copies Scott had projected.

And so here it was, I thought, a ready-made invitation to put my informal writing education to work, and in such a way that would benefit Scott and me both. I was thrilled to be able to help.

With paper in hand, I found Nanny and told her, "I'll be in the den. I'm not to be disturbed."

"No, certainly," she said. "We would not think of such a thing."

I kissed Scottie's blond fuzzy-duckling head, then went to work.

Though my writing experience was limited to diaries and letters, I was sure this assignment had been ordained and I was more than up to the task. After paging through the novel to remind myself of its particulars, I framed an idea in my mind and started writing it down.

The words seemed to flow directly from my brain through my neck and arm and fingers, right through the pencil and onto the page. This was so much fun! So easy! Who wouldn't want to be a writer? I had the whole thing drafted by the time Scott came home.

"Deo, look at this," I called when I heard him come in. "I'm reviewing your book for the *Tribune*—the New York one. Harold Ober called. They'll *pay* me. Read it and tell me what you think."

"I think I'd like to take off my coat and boots."

"Fine, all right," I pouted, then went out to the foyer. After he'd put his things away, I thrust the pages into his hands. "It's funny, and I did what you and everyone always do when you're reviewing each other's books—it's not afraid to be kinda critical, 'cause nobody would take it seriously if it's all glowing praise. Right? You always say it's the balance of praise and thoughtful criticism that makes folks curious to decide for themselves."

He'd taken the pages but his eyes were still on me, and he had a bemused smile.

"What? Why are you looking at me like that?"

"Just listen to you. Next thing I know, you'll want to be Dorothy Parker."

"Nah, she doesn't have enough fun. Read it! I'm sure it's awful, but I think it's kinda brilliant, too."

Scott sat down at his desk and I paced the room while he read. His face revealed nothing. When he was done, he laid the notebook flat. "All right: it's got some pacing hiccups, and we'll need to address punctuation a little bit, but it's quite remarkable—your writing voice is almost precisely your spoken voice, even in essay form. *How* long did you work on this?"

"Just today. This afternoon. Since about three o'clock."

Scott sat back in the chair, a mixture of emotions playing across his face. "Huh. Well, I guess you've found yourself a new hobby. I'll call Harold tomorrow and see what else we might cook up for you."

The review ran two weeks later—and, soon after, spurred a request from *Metropolitan Magazine* for a flapper essay by me, then another request, from *McCall's*. I confess to feeling an outsize thrill when I saw the headline, *"Friend Husband's Latest" by Zelda Fitzgerald, wife of F. Scott Fitzgerald,* followed by the two thousand words *I'd* written, observations *I'd* made, quips *I'd* thought of, criticisms *I'd* noted and had refined with Scott's help. Scott was proud of me, too; we bought two dozen copies of the paper and sent clippings to all our friends.

Sara Haardt, now living in Baltimore, wrote in reply,

Zelda, my dear,

I can't tell you how much this pleases me! You, my lovely friend, are finally utilizing another of your many talents and being rightly recognized for it. Plus, I'm so glad to see you and Scott in such harmony. You give me hope for something similar in my own life one day. Meantime, I have just placed a story in a Richmond journal, The Reviewer, which I will send to you with much joy upon its publication. I always said we could make our own ways in this men's world. . . . My love to you, Scott, and the baby-

Sara

When my fifteen-dollar check arrived, I took it to the bank personally and asked the teller to please pay it out in one-dollar bills—not to make it seem like more money, but to make the counting out of it last just a little bit longer. Like having fifteen little bites of chocolate cream pie even though you could've finished off that slice in five.

"What will you buy?" Scott asked, when we were outside on the slushy sidewalk. "My first sale was thirty dollars, remember? I sent you a sweater."

"No, a feather fan. And you got yourself some white flannel pants."

"Are you sure?"

We'd come to the street corner. "Yep," I said, surveying the nearby shops.

"What'll it be for you, then? Matching white flannel pants?"

I turned to him and smiled. "Only if I want to get us thrown out of the country club."

"We should do it." He took my gloved hands in his, and I felt like we had stepped back in time, to those Montgomery days right after the war had ended. Scott's face was ruddy from the cold, and his eyes were as bright as I'd seen them lately. "Come on, I bet you'll look good in pants—and we're moving back to New York anyway, right? Let's show St. Paul what we're really made of."

20

Great Neck, New York, was, in the fall of 1922, a growing community of newly rich people who didn't have enough sense to move farther away from the temptations of Manhattan. The town sits about fifteen miles to the east of Manhattan, on the North Shore of Long Island, where the tremendously rich had already built mansions to rival the *Aquitania,* or Buckingham Palace.

We had a nice house, a spacious, lovely, but comparatively ordinary house, and it wasn't even ours; we paid three hundred a month to rent it. The truly wealthy folks had *estates,* with no mortgages, and spent three hundred a month on cigars.

They had tennis courts, and indoor swimming pools, and outdoor swimming pools. They had terraced gardens, where plants that had been imported and were cared for by teams of Japanese gardeners enjoyed invigorating views of the Long Island Sound—from which the owners gave their docked yachts views of the gardens. These wealthy folks had butlers, they had cooks, they had chambermaids and lady's maids, they had stables occupied by horses—and by horsemen, who would teach you to ride while also letting you know they were capable of other services, too, if your husband was one of those who had, essentially, built such a place and then spent his life living in hotels in London and Cairo and San Francisco.

Nineteen twenty-two had been good to us so far. Scott had written a strange and whimsical story, "The Curious Case of Benjamin Button," for which he'd earned a thousand dollars; I'd written three new essays, earning more than eight hundred dollars altogether, enough to pay for a *radio,* which became Scottie's and my most favorite thing—me, because now I had all kinds of music to dance to, and Scottie because I would hold her and spin us around the parlor, both of us giggling all the while.

We'd now seen four of Scott's works—three stories plus *The Beautiful and Damned*—made into movies. Scott's second story collection, *Tales of the Jazz Age,* had a good September launch, and overall his royalties income would end up, he said, in the fifteen-thousand-dollar range for the year. *The Vegetable* was in preproduction. There were opportunities that hadn't panned out—another movie scenario Scott wrote for David O. Selznick being the big one. In light of all the good, though, we were untroubled by the bad.

While I had only a vague sense of our expenses and our existing debts, Scott was brimming with ideas and was busy every day placing phone calls and arranging meetings, which said a lot. At night he was romantic, passionate, and assured, which said the rest.

Though Scott and I were, by comparison to some of our neighbors, lacking in every material way, we felt fortunate—because what we *did* have while we were anticipating Scott's big Broadway success was the camaraderie of our wonderful next-door neighbors, Ring and Ellis Lardner.

Scott and Ring were fast friends right from the start, a made-in-heaven pair like cherries and chocolate. One October weekend morning I was awakened by raised voices coming from somewhere in the house. I said, "Scott. Scott, wake up. I think I hear Nanny arguing with someone."

This was a new nanny, of course; she was less severe than the one in St. Paul, yet more possessive, hardly willing to let Scottie out of her sight. We had to force her to take days off just so we could spend time alone with our baby girl. I wondered whether we'd all been better off before.

Scott said, "Probably Albert. Is there aspirin on your nightstand?"

"It's not Albert; it's Sunday." We gave Albert and Angela, the live-in couple who served us as butler-cook-housekeeper-chambermaid for one-sixty a month, Sundays off.

"Sunday? What? That can't be right. It was just Thursday. You've had a nightmare. Go back to sleep."

It *was* just Thursday for Scott, who'd begun drinking while at tennis and had, along with Ring and writers John Dos Passos and Carl Van Vechten, kept the party going until the liquor ran out. Ellis and I had given up on our men by Friday evening and spent Saturday at the beach with the children—she had four boys. Scottie, almost a year old, toddled around on the sand like a drunkard herself, pointing to each new discovery as if it was her first ever, and yelling "Ma!" every time. Nanny, of course, hovered nearby, pesky as a horsefly.

That Sunday morning, what we heard next was a rich tenor from just beyond the bedroom door:

"Fitzgerald, *hoo*! I herald *yo-o-u*! The sun is creeping higher. You promised *mee* a symphon-*ee* of putters, woods, and drivers!"

"What did I tell you?" I said, throwing back the covers and reaching for my robe. With Ring, you could never be sure he wouldn't come right into the bedroom and take a seat at the foot of the bed to tell you all about the six fish he'd caught while out with one or other of the neighbors, or the six fish he planned to catch, or the six fish he was going to miss catching thanks to Scott's promise to play nine holes with him—and that was all right with him, he'd say magnanimously; such things couldn't be helped.

"My God, how does he do it?" Scott asked.

Differently than Scott had managed, that's all I knew.

We'd been in Great Neck for a little over a year when, in the weak afternoon sunlight of New Year's Day 1924, I sat at our kitchen table with a brand-new ledger book in front of me. It was green leather and had been a Christmas gift from Scott. "If you don't start keeping better track of things, it will all be lost to you later," he'd said. "I'd be an absolute disaster without mine."

Scottie was taking her after-lunch nap. Scott was still sleeping off the previous night's effects; we'd gone to a tremendous masquerade party at

Ziegfeld's four-story mansion, where I'd been dressed, quite extravagantly, as Madame du Barry. Most of our help had the afternoon off, so the house was quiet and still, perfect for me to try bringing into focus the blur our time at 6 Gateway Drive had been so far.

I wrote the date and our address, then began making a list of my impressions and recollections:

HERE IN GREAT NECK . . .
- *Salt in the air always.*
- *Insanely high prices for everything. Scott saying, more than once, that we'd run out of money.*
- *The train into Manhattan, drinks and parties at the Plaza and the Ritz-Carlton.*
- *Racing up and down Long Island in fast, fancy cars, laughing like crazy, picking bugs from our hair afterward.*
- *My Union Square fountain dive immortalized as a silhouette sewn onto the Greenwich Village Follies curtain—no sign of Gene Bankhead, though, anywhere.*
- *Scottie's first words: Mama, mine, no.*
- *The sale of This Side of Paradise to the movies.*

"We're getting our ten thousand dollars after all!" Scott had said when that deal came through, waltzing me around the living room while Albert and Angela looked on, probably anticipating a raise. Or anticipating new and better ways to pad the quantities of food and goods they were already filching, which Scott and I knew was going on but ignored because we feared losing them.

I was as relieved about that sale as I was delighted about it, because while I remained uninvolved in our finances, I always knew by Scott's moods when we were flush and when we weren't, and was getting a sense, too, of when he'd allowed us to creep into the red.

- *Astonishing parties at astonishing mansions: we met every movie star, every producer—Cohan, Ziegfeld—every suspected bootlegger millionaire—and got close to Gene and Helen Buck, Gene being Ziegfeld's main collaborator, a hugely talented songwriter and not coincidentally also a millionaire.*

- *Scott getting too close to Helen Buck; both of them denying there was anything to it.*
- *That first year's New Year's party, when I took everyone's hats and made a game of tossing them into the biggest bowl-shaped light fixture I'd ever seen. Not everyone was amused, but it seemed terribly gay to me at the time.*
- *Scott writing title cards and scenarios for the movies—his "Grit" scenario sells for $2000.*
- *Scott's play, <u>The Vegetable</u>, and its crushing failure.*

That was in November of '22, when it opened in Atlantic City and was so awfully bad that some of the audience walked out during the second act. I'd believed in *The Vegetable* as fully as Scott had and could never understand how what had seemed to work in rehearsal came off so badly at the tryout opening. I'd helped Scott write the play. Bunny had read and loved it. Max loved it—even published a revised version as a novel the next year. Sure, it had taken a long time to get a producer on board, but then it *did* get produced. So where had we gone wrong?

- *Scott, missing for two days soon after the play closed; he came home hungover and unsure of where he'd been, or with whom. Smell of perfume on his shirt.*
- *Scott on the wagon all of January, February, and March, so that he could write enough stories for the slicks—ten in all—to see us through last year (1923), during which he intended to write the novel that he'd put off writing in anticipation of the play's success. Novel still not done.*
- *My first real spells of uncertainty, of doubt.*
- *$2000-a-game croquet tournaments on Herbert Swope's manicured lawn, played after dark with car headlights to illuminate the course.*
- *Dancing with Scott, me in a gown, he in a tuxedo, on a wide canvas*

dance floor with torches lighting the night. Champagne, orchestras, canapés, kisses.

- Guests in our house always: Tootsie, Eleanor, Scott's Aunt Annabel, Max Perkins. John Dos Passos and Archie MacLeish (writers), Don Stewart (humorist), Gilbert Seldes (critic)—he loves Scott. Alec and his crush Esther Murphy.

- Unmarked, empty liquor bottles like lines of tired soldiers on our kitchen counters.

- The Hearst magazines option: gives them first-look at Scott's stories and a guarantee of $1500 for the ones they take; photograph of Scott and me together on the cover of Hearst International. We are stars!

- "Our Own Movie Queen," my first short story; Scott and Harold said it's better to send it out under Scott's name because I'd get more money for it. Harold sold it for $1000 to the Chicago Sunday Tribune.

- Scottie, with her little chubby legs, standing on Scott's shoulders, her hands in his, the two of them giggling wildly as he galloped her across the lawn.

- Interviews—of Scott, of me, of me and Scott together. "The Fitzgeralds are as popular as movie stars," we're told, and everyone wants to know how we see the world. They want to see us: so we, and Scottie, are photographed for numerous features and now we really feel like stars.

- Scott's "The Popular Girl" brings $1500 from the Post, his highest price so far.

- Helen Buck and me playing golf while tight; they say I went wandering down the fairways, but I don't recall that part.

- Eleanor's visit, when we met Scott at the Plaza. He had Anita Loos in tow, champagne in hand. He'd been drinking cause he hates the dentist, then celebrating his survival afterward. That night at home: some woman at the door in search of Scott. My accusations make Scott pull the tablecloth right off the table, dishes flying everywhere. El, Anita, and me so tight we could only laugh at him.

- Scott's "How to Live on $36,000 a Year" for the Post makes a funny story of our inability to make do with so much money.

That essay was all fiction—the "we" in the story is a couple who manage their money (or fail to) jointly, unlike the "we" in our real life. Daddy saw it and wrote me, "This is what Mama and I were afraid of. Our friends are aghast. However, the youngsters here think you two are gods, and if that doesn't trouble you, I fear you are lost for good."

- *A feeling, always, of standing on a precipice with a stiff wind at our backs. Nothing to hold on to.*

The ledger did help me, though, to hang on to the details of that time. What I realized in doing it, however, was that maybe we didn't know quite as much—about anything—as we'd thought we did.

And I was scared.

21

===

Early May 1924: What little snow we'd seen over the winter was long gone, and spring had exploded all over Long Island. Tiny leaves clung to every tree's limbs in uncertain but determined assurance to remain in place no matter what; cherry trees blossomed; tulips crowded around front stoops or carpeted entire lawns, their yellow and red and pink and white heads swaying languidly in the southerly breeze.

We were packing up, this time for a move to France in the hopes that our money would stretch further there and Scott would finally write his next book. Everyone said that Americans were living like kings there, so of course we wanted to go. On our last morning in Great Neck, Ring and Ellis came over to say a final good-bye. We stood outside on the lawn while a small team of workmen loaded our belongings onto a truck. What furniture we'd accumulated would go into storage; the rest of what we owned was now crammed into seventeen trunks of various sizes, half of which contained books.

In addition to this mountain of leather and canvas was one hundred feet of baled copper mesh. A man lifted the roll to load it, and Ring, pointing, said, "What in the world—"

"French mosquitoes have a taste for American blood," Scott told him. "Ungrateful bastards."

"And you intend, what, to wrap yourselves in that stuff like chain mail?"

"To screen our windows."

"They won't have screens already?"

"Can't take chances," Scott said.

"Um, you'll be living in *France*," Ring replied.

"Yes, where *all three of us* will be able to eat three meals apiece for a total of two dollars a day. I have got to get this damn book written, and I won't do it if I'm forever beholden to the slicks."

A brilliant yellow car pulled into the driveway behind the truck, and Esther Murphy, an artist, heiress, and wild woman we'd met through Alec, got out. I was startled to see her wearing snug-fitting trousers, which she'd tucked into a pair of boots.

"What's this?" she said, waving to us. "Scared you off, did we?"

"No, it's been grand here, but some of us still work for our living," Scott said as she approached. "Or are supposed to. We're getting a place in France for a while."

"Fewer distractions," I said. "He's going to finally get his book done."

"You *must* look up my brother. You'll adore him," Esther told us. "He's like me, only far, far sweeter, smarter, richer, and more talented. And I promise you, his wife, Sara, is a dream."

"*Another* Sara?" I asked. "It's like there's some kind of cosmological attraction—I have two of them already."

"She'll be worth any confusion you might suffer, you'll see."

With everything packed for transit, we took ourselves to the Plaza for a final night before sailing. I'd hoped for a quiet evening with just the baby and Scott; instead, Biggs and Alec stopped by for drinks, then Bunny and his new wife—Mary Blair, an actress, of all things—brought dinner, then Townsend arrived, then Ludlow, who had the waiters bring fruit crêpes and coffee. Scottie spent her last night in America stuffing herself with thick, sweet cream—which, inevitably, didn't agree with her, so *my* last night was a mostly sleepless one as I washed the vomit out of her clothes and hair, and mine.

Once we'd gotten on board the ship and were under way, though, all the world as we'd known it ceased to exist. *So long, New York. So long, America.* I stood at the rail with my squirrel coat wrapped tight around me and Scottie in my arms, and Manhattan receded as if waved away by her miniature hand and my larger one. Now, finally, at long last, the Ferris wheel had stopped turning. I'd ridden by choice—I'm not saying otherwise—but that doesn't mean I didn't need to, and want to, get off after a while.

During that week of crossing the Atlantic, I encouraged Scott to spend his time doing whatever he liked. "Go socialize," I told him over a lunch of poached salmon and boiled potatoes. The water goblets were crystal, the tablecloths white linen as clean and bright as fresh Minnesota snow. I urged him to write, to read—he'd brought the entire *Encyclopaedia Britannica* and claimed he was going to read the whole thing during transit—and I would indulge myself and my sweet girl, now two and a half years old, with uninterrupted togetherness.

"Go, Daddy," Scottie said, having piled her potatoes into a pyramid.

"There *is* a fellow on board I'm hoping to meet, an editor with some French magazine; Fowler told me to look him up."

Scottie and I saw Scott for meals, but otherwise our days were wondrous explorations of all kinds of things, like the elaborate designs woven into the carpeting, the colorful leaded-glass windowpanes, the filigreed wrought-iron railings, the labyrinthine paneled hallways, the fields of tables and chairs in the dining rooms and solariums and decks. A ship, for Scottie, was a planet.

I drew her pictures of zebras and elephants and giraffes and lions and made up little stories to go along with them. She slept beside me at night, knees and forehead pressed against me, little thumb resting against her little bow lips.

22

From our Paris hotel, I rang the Murphys' house and spoke to Sara III, whose cultured voice matched Esther's promise. "Come tomorrow for cocktails and dinner," she said. "We've assembled some truly lovely people who'll want to meet you both, I'm certain."

"We've got our two-year-old daughter with us," I told her. "No nanny as of yet."

"Oh, bring her! We have three wee ones of our own, and a wonderfully competent nanny. I'll give you the name of the agency we used, if you like. You'll need someone who's got good English, to start, and good references."

"Thank you! I'm already so glad that Esther put us in touch."

Still, when we arrived at the arched, gated entry to 3 rue Gounod in Saint-Cloud, an arrondissement that was just outside of Paris proper, my first sight of the house worried me. We'd known that Esther and Gerald Murphy owed their fortunes to their father's luxury leather-goods company, called Mark Cross. And thanks to shipboard gossip, we now also knew that Gerald's wife Sara's family had an ink-manufacturing company in Ohio, which gave Sara a small fortune of her own. Though this house wasn't a mansion, not in terms of what we'd seen on Long Island, it was three majestic stories of stone and wrought iron, set inside a little walled park. Our new life in France was going to be Great Neck all over again, I thought. There would be too much everything and not enough anything, and then where would that leave us?

There was no time to worry further, as the butler was showing us into the main salon and a handsome woman was saying, "I'm Sara, and *you* must be the famed miscreants of Manhattan and Long Island. Not you, of course," she said to Scottie, bending down and shaking Scottie's hand.

I looked over at Scott and mouthed, *Famed miscreants*. He winked.

Scottie, ever accustomed to meeting her mama and papa's friends, wrapped her arms around Sara's neck. "Mama told me to say *bone swohr*."

"And you did it so well," Sara said.

The house was spacious and luxe, done up in fine furniture and draperies and heavy-framed paintings of great variety, from classical nudes and still lifes to unidentifiable modernist compositions of colorful lines and shapes and spots. Several fashionably dressed people were already mingling, drinks in hand—though no one here wore anything like my Parisian dress from New York. This was not, I quickly knew, *that* kind of occasion, and I was glad I'd chosen a black and sage-metallic print dress that went on like a robe, with chiffon sleeves and a clasp and tie at the left hip. It covered everything but my calves. A slender man in a slim-cut tuxedo sat at the piano and played cheerful tunes for two dark-haired women who I guessed were in their thirties. The room smelled of money, refined.

My first impression of Sara: capable, classy, beautiful in an understated way. She had a great shock of chestnut-brown hair above a delicate, round face that was porcelain-pale and powder-smooth. She wore a white-trimmed, gray silk-and-chiffon dress, gray high-heeled shoes, and two long strands of white pearls. I guessed she was around my sister Marjorie's age, not quite forty. She smoothed a curl from Scottie's cheek, then stood and turned toward the drawing room and announced, "Everyone, meet Scott and Zelda."

Among *everyone* that evening were Gerald Murphy (naturally); singer-composer Cole Porter and his divorcée, high-society wife, Linda; painter Pablo Picasso and his wife, ballerina Olga Khokhlova; artist, poet, and novelist Jean Cocteau; and aspiring musician Dick Myers and his wife, Alice Lee; along with a few women who seemed to have been added for color. None of the names meant a thing to us before that night, mostly because either we hadn't had enough exposure to their work, or because their best work was still ahead of them.

Gerald, square-faced, square-shouldered, tall, with kind eyes, strode over to shake Scott's hand. "Esther telegraphed, calling you 'the Golden Boy,' and said you used to write lyrics at Princeton. Cole here got his start doing the same thing at Yale."

"It's true," Cole said. He'd swung around so that he sat with his back to the keyboard. " 'Bulldog! Bulldog!' The fight song, don't you know," he said in a voice that was as slight as he was. "There's ten minutes' work that will bring a lifetime of infamy."

Scott nodded and said, " 'Fie! Fie! Fi-Fi!'—just the lyrics, though. I'll venture that you write the tunes, too."

What followed was the most charming night of lighthearted conversation and music and laughter, uncorrupted by the heavy drinking we had been so accustomed to. It was as if the Murphys not only didn't behave like crass drunks but weren't even aware that one could.

Russian-born Olga, who'd danced for Sergei Diaghilev's incomparable Ballets Russes, intrigued me. She and Pablo met when he'd designed the costumes and set for the ballet *Parade,* which Jean had helped to write. "Gerald, here, 'as done the art for Sergei as well," Jean said in melodic French-accented English.

Olga said, "It is, what you say, a club with them." She sounded unhappy about this.

"Do you still dance for Diaghilev?"

"No, I do five years but give it up when I meet Pablo. I am not so good to be missed."

"It must have been something, though, dancing with that company," I said, careful to pronounce my *g*'s for this group. "I was always hearing about the Ballets Russes in New York. They don't have ballet, you know, so everyone has to come to Europe to see really great dance or to be a real dancer, isn't that silly? I love ballet."

Scott and I both were awed by how *cultured* all these folks appeared to be, how *intact* they all were. For a change, Scott listened more than he talked. They spoke of painting and music and dance—their own work as well as other artists'—with knowledge and candor and passion. If they felt rivalries, they expressed the situations as challenges, not jealousies. It wasn't a fraternity party, or a night at a cabaret, or a gauche demonstration of wealth; my worries eased a little. The Murphys' three children and the Myerses' daughter took to Scottie like she was a favorite cousin, while Gerald and Sara felt to me like older siblings I'd somehow forgotten I had.

We lunched with the Murphys the next day, on a sunny stone patio surrounded by ivy-covered walls, and Gerald told us, "Cole's persuaded us to try the Riviera for the summer—we're thinking Antibes; you'll have to come see us there."

Scott and I glanced at each other, and I could see that he felt the same way I did: we'd passed an important first exam. Could it be that we were saved after all?

After interviewing nannies at the agency Sara suggested, we again hired the one Scott thought best matched his ideal of what a nanny should be. With this new one, Lillian, in place, we went on to Hyères to find someone who could find us a house.

Lillian, a homely young British woman who'd been raised by nuns, stepped right into her role, showing all the authority and discipline we were paying her for—which made me a little sad. But life was in motion again, and if I wanted anything to turn out to my liking, I had to get involved, scout for houses, set things up—which I couldn't easily do if I was also trying to give Scottie the attention she deserved.

As with our search four years earlier, Scott and I had to survey all the prospective towns and rentals before making up our minds. We visited Nice, Monte Carlo, Cap d'Antibes, Cannes, and Saint-Raphael; Saint-Raphael turned out to be "it," for the moment anyway. No longer did I imagine that any place we lived would become permanent. The only question was how long we'd stay.

Saint-Raphael is a quaint and picturesque spot on the Mediterranean coast of France, not far from Cannes. We knew no one there—had chosen it for exactly that reason, so that Scott could settle down and work. It was not a fashionable place in 1924, not in the least. It was serene, though, with a rocky, verdant, slowly crumbling beauty that made me itch to try painting again. Having spoken with Pablo at the dinner party about his art—using Gerald, humorously, as translator—and having seen what Gerald was doing with his painting, too, I was suddenly aware of how much I hadn't learned yet and how much I *wanted* to learn, and how nice it would be to dabble some more myself and see what came of it.

A property agent helped us locate Villa Marie, an old but remarkable little compound high up on a hillside above the sea, with garden walls and a big stone house all draped in luscious pink bougainvillea—all this for only seventy-nine dollars a month!

Following Scott's *Post* essay about money, I'd managed to get him to tell me what sort of budget we were working from: we had seven thousand dollars, and no debts. We would have the villa, a nanny, a cook, and a housekeeper, all for one-fifty a month. We would buy a car. Scott would stay entirely sober, saving us a considerable amount of money on booze. The seven grand would be more than enough to see us through until the novel changed from an extensively outlined idea to a bound-and-wrapped fact. This was our plan.

We hired the servants, and I turned the villa into a version of home. One of our first orders of business was to explore the social scene, the cafés, the restaurants. As ever, Scott quizzed everyone he met, made copious notes about things, tried all the foods, taste-tested cocktails and offered bartenders his critiques. We liked to go to a little beach casino, where the festive crowd included a bunch of French aviators who were serving at an air station in nearby Fréjus. At that time, my French was more or less limited to understanding the phrase "Je souhaite à danser avec vous, si votre mari ne sera pas l'esprit," *I'd like to dance with you if your husband won't mind*—and replying, "Mais oui, dansons!"

Scott grew a mustache and read Byron and Shelley and Keats, all in preparation, he said, for the task ahead of him. How the mustache would help him write I couldn't say, and I don't think he could, either. And although his start was slow—it was early June by now, and he wasn't writing much and he hadn't given up alcohol yet—well, maybe that was how things needed to be. Becoming expatriates required a big adjustment.

Scott joined me on our terrace one evening where, after tucking Scottie in, I liked to sit and watch the sky darken and the stars appear, and to study the moon if it was around. The timelessness of nightfall comforted me. I was not quite twenty-four years old, and for all that I'd seen and done, when things quieted down I was still the old me, the Alabama girl who was as likely to swim in a moonlit creek as to dance a night away.

"Hi," I said as Scott sat down. "I had a letter from Sara Mayfield today—she's going to marry John Sellers. You remember John, he's one of the fellas I went with before I knew you. Never seriously, of course; he had a kind of an edge I just never quite warmed to—but I bet that's long gone now, if Sara'll have him."

"I'm ready," Scott said. "I'm restarting the book tomorrow. I've had a look at the draft, I know what needs to change—I can see it all like a vision before me." He set a pair of goblets and a wine carafe on the iron table between our chairs. "I can't even describe how marvelous it's going to be."

"You're going to write tomorrow after drinking tonight? Do you think that's a good idea?"

"Wine's not booze, dearest. Restaurants serve it with every meal."

"It is too booze. It's got alcohol in it, that's a fact, and you can't disbelieve a fact."

"Children drink wine here," he said.

"Maybe. But it doesn't prove your case."

"Are you planning to take over your father's seat on the court?" he said as he filled both glasses and handed me one.

"See, this is how you get when you know I'm right."

"This is how *you* act when you're determined to sabotage my work."

The remark surprised me. "That's right," I said, "I *want* you to fail at everything. That's why I followed you to New York, and Westport, and St. Paul, and Great Neck, and now France—all in, what, four years? Yes, I gave up my family in Montgomery, gave up my house and my friends and everything that was so good about our Great Neck life, in order to follow you halfway across the earth and then *sabotage you*."

He squinted at me, scratched his head, bit his thumbnail. "Poor word choice. Sorry. I've sampled the wine, maybe a bit too liberally?"

"I'll say."

"It's going to be a damned masterpiece, you know."

"The wine?"

"The book."

"That's quite a prediction."

"Everything I've sketched out so far needs to be rewritten, but, Zelda, I'm finally going to live up to my potential with this one. I'm going to *surpass* my potential. This book's going to prove that I'm the greatest writer of my age."

"Is that so?" I said, still annoyed.

"It *is* so. Greatest of my generation, and the top second-rater of all time."

Top second-rater. I had to laugh, and just like that my annoyance was gone. I said, "It's good that you've got it all in proper perspective."

I tried the wine; it had a dark, velvety flavor, like blackberries and vanilla and ancient hillside moss. Bats swooped past above the olive trees, keeping those bloodthirsty mosquitoes at bay. A church bell tolled in the distance. Nearer to us, a dog barked halfheartedly. The scent of lavender floated up the hillside from where it grew among the rocks at the sea's edge.

Scott said, "This is the place where we make it all happen. I can feel it."

"Well, I do have to say it's nice to hear you sound so certain again."

"It's nice to feel certain. It's been a tough couple of years."

"We did pretty well, though," I said. "There were some good times."

"Too many. I'm a wreck. Spongy"—he pinched his stomach, which did have some rolls now—"lazy, and my production is way, way off. Do you realize that for two years—more than two years, in fact—I hardly produced anything? One *failed* play, half a dozen stories, a few reviews, and a few articles. That was it, before I locked myself up and did those stories over the winter. This novel should've been *finished* a year ago. I'm twenty-seven years old. Time is running out."

"Running out how?" Stars had appeared now, and the moon was sneaking out from behind the distant mountains.

"I told you, it has to happen before I'm thirty."

"What has to happen?" I knew he didn't mean the book getting done; *that* had to happen before the money ran out.

"Immortality. By thirty, a writer's vitality is gone, and his unique vision with it. Anything he's got to say about the world has to be seen through his youth, his unjaded—or less jaded—eyes. Remember that article I wrote, 'What I Think and Feel at Twenty-five?' To the me who wrote *Paradise,* I'm already an old man."

"You're forgetting people like George. He's got lots of sharp thoughts and observations, and he's forty-two now."

"He doesn't write fiction."

"If you're so worried, I don't know what you're doing out here with me wasting your time. Get to work."

He stood up, and I thought he was going to do just what I'd said. But he took my hands and pulled me up from my chair.

"What I'm doing out here"—he put his arms around my waist and held me against him—"is reminding myself why it is I asked such a beautiful and impressive woman to follow me to and from—what was that list you made?—all those places, and making sure to thank her sincerely for doing so."

23

The first time I lost track of myself, truly lost all trace of me, the girl I'd been, the woman I thought I was becoming, would happen there in Saint-Raphael, while I was wrapped in the benevolent warmth of a Mediterranean summer.

The romantic ending to our night on the terrace was a romantic *ending,* period. With Scott shut away all day working in what would ordinarily have been Villa Marie's servant's cottage, and Lillian in charge of Scottie, and no cooking or housework for me to do—which I did poorly anyway, it's true—there was a very big hole in my day, every day. A big hole in my life, really, seeing as how this would be our routine indefinitely, and I had no friends at hand. Days longer than whole months crawled by. Though I read some and painted a little, restlessness was like a mosquito always buzzing about my head.

Lillian had firm ideas of what should constitute a toddler's day. I wrote to Mama,

> *She makes Scottie eat all her fruits and vegetables and has begun teaching her the alphabet forwards and backwards both. They have morning exercise and afternoon exercise and bath and tea and what Lillian calls "the lesson period." If I interrupt, Lillian scowls at me. I*

want to let her go, but Scott says—wisely, I suppose—that with the way I eat and my devil-may-care approach to the day, I'm no kind of teacher for a young child. He says Scottie needs structure and discipline or she's bound to turn out like me, and we wouldn't want that, would we?

And Mama wrote back,

In matters regarding the nanny, I would have to agree with Scott. We never did give you enough discipline in your early years, which resulted in some very trying times in your adolescence. I believe the Judge is still tired from raising you. The English are supposed to be superior nannies—though our old Aunt Julia was wonderful in her way—so my advice is that you find productive uses for your time. Write to your sisters; they worry about you, as do Daddy and I. But then, that habit will never leave a parent no matter how the child's life proceeds.

To pass my time, I reverted to my Westport habits of wandering the surrounding countryside during the cool mornings, and swimming at the beach in the afternoons. Oh, it was heaven to dive into the warm, so-blue waters at our little stretch of beach and swim until I was exhausted. The last of my stubborn post-baby fat disappeared, melting away into the sea, and my skin absorbed the sunshine and begged for more. Now and then I'd persuade Lillian to include beach time in Scottie's exercise periods, and now and then Scott would break from his work and join us, and we'd get a visitor for an afternoon or an overnight once in a while. Mostly, though, I was on my own.

I'd taken to bringing sketchbook and pencil and books to the beach with me. On a wide reed mat, I would lie in the sunshine like a sleek otter after a swim, and then I'd pass the day drawing anemones, reading James or Kipling or Ford Madox Ford and Colette's provocative French romance *Chéri,* which I'd selected to help improve my understanding of the language, but which may have seeded my brain for trouble. I might jot down story ideas or write to my sisters or my friends. Entire days could disappear this way, and did.

The aviators we knew from the casino also began to come to the beach, three in particular, Édouard, René, and Bobbé. Their schedules had them training at night. They would arrive in their white, white beach clothes and put their mats down near mine, and we'd talk, them with their iffy English, me with my slowly improving French. They thought Scott and I were so cosmopolitan, so glamorous; they wanted to know everything about New York and literary fame.

The men were, all of them, lean and handsome and inquisitive and good-natured. Édouard Jozan, though, had the keenest mind, the softest manner. On the occasions when we'd seen him in the casino, he and Scott and I had debated things like nationalism and heroism and the question of art versus action.

"To write the book—eh, *novel*—it is all very good, yes. *Mais* the young man must *demonstrate* the thought, not represent it in words. If he does not, there will be no change, no resistance. Anarchy will rule."

"What gives the acting man the instruction for what to do and how to do it, though?" Scott replied. "Books do! And novels do this best of all. They present the situation and model the hero so that you and your friends can emulate him—or not emulate him, as the case may be, dependent of course upon the story."

"*This* result we can achieve by discussion, though."

"The spoken word is fleeting. That's why novelists are so essential: we record everything we see, we dissect and analyze and reproduce the essence of what matters, for posterity."

"Too much time!" Édouard said, shaking his head. "This writing and the reading, it is wasted time, when things could instead get done. Zelda, don't fear your misguided husband, tell me, what is it you believe?"

"Surely there are times when there's too much thought and not enough action, and times when there's too much action without enough thought. What I *really* think, though," I continued, "is that somebody here had better take some action and dance with me before I run off and find somebody who will!"

I saw so little of Scott during my endless weeks, and even less of him solo. If he wasn't writing the book, he was thinking about it, or talking about it, or we were with Scottie or a friend, or we were out. In bed at night, he put off my affections: "I'm already exhausted. Making love will ruin me, Zelda. The energy I'd spend, well, I have to keep it stored and waiting for the book."

Édouard was a year older than me, and something in the way he listened so carefully made me think he valued me as more than just an amusing American. As June rolled into July, he began to show up to the beach without René and Bobbé. He'd put his mat right beside mine and then ask me to tell him about the South, and my childhood. "Tell everything, s'il vous plaît; your voice, it is my delight."

I had already sensed the attraction between us—it was apparent from the first time we met—but that sort of attraction was so usual that it didn't rate serious attention, let alone concern. When the attraction turned into something that smelled and tasted like substance, though, that was when things got complicated.

A married woman will first deny to herself that anything improper is going on. She'll make excuses for her eagerness to see the man in question. She likes his sharp mind, for example, or his fresh views or the stories he tells about his experiences, which are so different from her own. She'll dismiss as mere amusement her mind's tendency to wonder where he is and what he's doing and whether he's thinking of her. She might even avoid the fella for a day or two, to test herself: if she doesn't see him and she feels fine about that, she'll know there's no cause for concern. The test is false though, too, because she's lying to herself to make sure she passes the test, which will then justify her choice to see him again, often.

Imagine languorous days with no responsibilities. Loneliness and Dismay are your regular companions, but they're muted by soft sand, a sunfilled sky, and warm blue water, the sight and feel of which makes you drunk. Imagine your body is youthful, firm, a pleasure to live inside of—and you're wise enough already to know that this is fleeting, this body and its condition. It won't last. None of it will last. And because it won't, you allow the beautiful person who seeks you out to become as much a part of your day, a part of this place, as the poppies that grow beside the rocky paths you follow to get here. You allow affections to develop and grow as if they, too, are poppies. You let it happen because all of it is illusory anyway, that's how it feels, and that's what you believe.

This lovely illusion, though, this romantic fantasy, will begin to seem real if given a chance, every bit as surely as delusions are real to a person suffering a breakdown.

A week into July, I was sure I'd fallen in love.

At the open-air, beachfront café, Scott sat at the table across from me. Gerald was to my left, Sara to his left. The children ran about the beach, with Lillian and the Murphy children's nanny keeping watch. Lillian had dressed Scottie in a celery-colored jumper and a little straw hat; the hat hung down her back by its ribbons; the ribbon's ends blew about in the breeze. She and little Patrick, who was her same age almost to the day, held hands, even while running. *She has her little beach-love, too,* I thought.

"How do you feel about Venice, Zelda?"

"Sorry, what?"

"She's been terribly distracted lately," Scott said.

If that's not the pot calling the kettle black . . .

Gerald repeated, "We're contemplating a trip to Venice. Cole's doing a tremendous gala of some sort in this extravagant villa he and Linda found. Extravagant *palace,* rather. Forgive me for being gauche enough to say this, but they're paying *four thousand* a month in American dollars for the place. I find it hard to support that behavior."

"You know Linda's well-off," Sara told Scott and me. "Her first husband had to compensate her substantially when they divorced. But Cole came into a great deal of money of his own last year, and he seems determined to use it like water."

Gerald said, "His grandfather was J. O. Cole, of Indiana—whose money was in mining and timber. Well, it was in speculation, Cole says. Calls him 'the richest man in Indiana!' in that way he has, you know."

Scott said, "How rich is rich?"

"He didn't name a figure, and I didn't ask, of course, but how's this: he's hired Sergei Diaghilev and the entire Ballets Russes for entertainment."

The word *ballet* finally centered me on the discussion. "What's this about Diaghilev?"

Sara said, "We've all been close to Sergei for years; he's tireless, and so talented. Last year he put on Gerald and Cole's production, *Within the Quota*. Gerald did all the costume and set designs. It was a remarkable experience."

"I wish we'd seen it. I used to dance," I said.

"The man hired an entire ballet company to perform at a *party*?" Scott said. "The whole company?"

I thought we'd seen enough displays of wealth on Long Island that Scott would take another one in stride. Apparently not. This was, for me, yet another sign of why Édouard would be so much better for me than Scott had become. Édouard wouldn't sit there gaping at the idea of what Cole was doing. Édouard wouldn't care, except to express pleasure at the idea of this unusual presentation of fine performance art. "For the expression of life's truest agonies and beauty," he'd said to me, "nothing can exceed the dance."

Everything Scott said rankled; everything Édouard said reigned. I was a woman possessed.

Gerald was frowning at Scott. "The whole company, yes."

"His place there is *that* big, really?"

"He says it's quite large."

"Four thousand, you say?"

"Scott," I said, "quit bothering Gerald with all that."

"I'm just curious. In the book, see, I'm trying to work out the details about this wealthy character—"

"Let's stay on Gerald's subject, all right?"

Scott reached for one of Sara's hands and one of Gerald's. "Forgive me. My enthusiasm and curiosity sometimes overcome my good sense."

"Not a bit," Gerald said. "At any rate, we're not sure whether we should go. We've got so much to do, what with the renovations to the new villa starting; I don't feel we can get away."

I said, "For a ballet performance like this? Of course you can!"

"You say you danced?" Gerald asked.

"She was first-rate," Scott said. "In fact, the first time I laid eyes on her, she was performing a ballet solo."

His reminder of that long-ago night, the romance of it, the treasure it had once been in my memory, was a thin, sharp knife's thrust to the gut—but it was over so quickly that I could almost decide it hadn't happened at all. Scott hadn't seen it; Sara and Gerald couldn't tell.

"You could take Zelda," Gerald told his wife.

"Now there's a thought!" Sara replied brightly. "Should we plan on it?"

"Why not?" I said.

The next morning, Scott sulked about not being invited. "I want to see Venice again. I didn't fully appreciate it the first time. All that history!—you don't even care about that; you're only going for the party."

"I do care, and I'm going for the performance, and you have a book to finish."

"I think I'll find Dos Passos and see if he's interested in going to Monte Carlo."

"Book," I said.

"Or Dick Myers."

"Book."

"A few days won't ruin me."

"A few days of drinking and gambling—not the best idea."

"I deserve some time off. You're not the only one who deserves to have fun. In fact, *you* don't actually deserve it at all; what have you been doing all summer except flirting with those flyboys and lying in the sun?"

I said nothing.

"You should try living my life. Locked away all day, sweating blood over how to make this damned plot work. You should try being the one who's supporting a wife and child and household—that damn cook is cheating us blind, you know. Did you see the grocery bill?"

I left the table.

"Where are you going?"

"For a swim. I wouldn't want to disappoint you."

The morning was cloudy, the water cool. I wanted it colder, wanted it to shock my senses, help me understand what was happening, help me know what to do.

I hadn't confessed my feelings to Édouard—though I was certain he knew them. Knew them and returned them; why else was he seeing me alone, edging his mat closer to mine, lying there beside me talking of passion and life and love? What I was less sure of was what might happen next. How far was I willing to go?

Lying alongside Édouard on the beach that afternoon, I could smell his warm, musky skin, so exotic to me after five years of having only Scott so naked and near. With our eyes closed to the sun, were he and I both imagining the same things? I hoped so. Did he think of kissing my mouth, of stroking my belly, of rolling onto me, insistent with desire? I couldn't seem to clear these questions from my mind.

For long, agonizing minutes, I lay rigid with indecision, my breath shallow, my heart racing. When I glanced at Édouard, he seemed a bronzed god to me, and the image overwhelmed my senses. "I'm going over to la voiture de bain," I said. "Do you want to join me?"

The little wheeled, wooden building—a "bathing machine," in English—had been parked permanently and was now used sometimes by tourists who needed to change into and out of their bathing suits. But few tourists came to the Antibes beaches in summer back then, and none were there that day. We would be uninterrupted and unobserved.

Édouard opened his eyes, then sat up and cocked his head slightly. His irises were so dark they looked almost black. "Yes."

"I wouldn't have asked," Édouard began, when we were inside the dim, cool shelter. It smelled of salt and cedar and talc.

"No. I know that. You're an honorable man."

"Not so honorable; I think of you . . . I think of *this*." He kissed me gently, a testing kiss.

"And more?" I whispered.

He pressed me against the wall, the whole length of his body against mine. "So much more."

We didn't stay in there long, for the simple reason that the temptation to do so was so strong. While we were there, though, I reveled in every sensation his lips and hands and thighs provoked. He *wanted* me. I wanted him, or at least I wanted *that,* and for me at the time it was all one and the same.

"I could leave him, you know."

"For life as an aviator's wife? It would not be what you've had."

"Yes, exactly."

We reenacted the scene a few more times over the next week or so—not only in the *voiture* but also outside the casino after dark once, while Scott was inside and oblivious. Those moments with Édouard felt perfectly endless, their own vivid, multicolored dream of a world in which I was no longer *Mrs. F. Scott Fitzgerald,* and I wasn't Mrs. Édouard Jozan, either; I was becoming Zelda Sayre again. But not the popular Montgomery belle, swept away by a dashing young man who flew his plane in curling loops above my house—no. I was a strange new Zelda Sayre released from all constrictions, drunk with the timeless rhythms of sea and sun and passion, more daring and oblivious to danger than I'd ever been before.

An illusion, as I said.

Inside that illusion was a bachelor's small apartment, its shades closed to the midday heat. Inside that apartment was a man, naked atop cool sheets on a low bed, his hand extended in welcome.

24

I couldn't wait any longer for resolution.

Scottie was fast asleep. Lillian was in her room—probably doing another set of knee-bends while reading George du Maurier's titillating *Trilby*. The cook and maid had gone for the day.

"Join me on the terrace?" I asked Scott, who sat at a little table in the room we called the library, his hair sticking out in all directions, books and papers spread out in front of him. A single gaslight lit the table; the rest of the room was dark. A glass filled with ice and some clear liquid sat sweating near Scott's left elbow.

He finished whatever he was writing, than glanced up at me. "I'm working. It's too warm in the cottage tonight."

"How long will you be?"

"I've just had an idea about getting Tom and Myrtle to the Plaza—and a dog, I think. I'm arranging my thoughts, so I'll be a while yet. I won't wake you." He began to write again.

"Now would be better."

"What would be better now?" he asked without looking up.

"Scott. I need to talk to you."

He set down his pencil and looked up at me. "If this is about Venice, never mind. Just go on, have fun, see if you can charm Diaghilev a little;

I have some thoughts about a future production that could involve the ballet.

"Picture this," he went on, leaning back in his chair. "Our heroine is a showgirl, a shimmy dancer from a rotten upbringing who always yearned to be a ballerina, and—"

"I don't want to do this anymore," I said, shaking my head. "No more plays or books or schemes. I want to get divorced."

Scott stared at me while my words displaced the story he'd been framing. "What did you say? I couldn't have heard you right."

"No, you did."

Panic flickered in his eyes. "What have you been drinking?"

"Ginger ale. Come out to the terrace."

"Zelda—"

I walked away, giving him no choice except to follow me outside.

"What is this?" he asked when we were outside with the doors closed behind us. We usually weren't shy about airing our disputes in front of the servants. This time, however, I didn't want Lillian to hear.

I went and stood at the rail, facing the sea below. Not until I opened my mouth to speak did I know what I intended to say.

"It was all a mistake. We shouldn't have gotten married in the first place. I should have waited to see how things might go. It just . . . it just seemed like we were embarking on a great adventure, but that adventure turned into a party we couldn't resist, a five-year-long party, everybody in sparkling gowns and tuxedos with satin lapels, bottomless glasses of champagne . . . But that's not a marriage, that's not a way to live. Real life has to happen sometime."

"Since when did you want a so-called 'real life'? You've been living the life of a princess and loving every minute. Shoes, gowns, furs, *this*"—he swept his arm to indicate the house, the hills, the view—"who has a better life than you?"

"I want a husband who cares about me more than anything else, except his children maybe. With you, it's always the next story, play, novel, movie, the unending pursuit of some *stupid* critic's approval, an obsession over some magical number of copies sold, a terrible need for assurance that you're the finest living writer on the planet and every thinking man will worship your books forever!"

Scott stared at me, mouth open. Then, "The pursuit of *meaning*!" he yelled. "The pursuit of *excellence*! *That's* what I'm about. These things aren't about me at all. You—do you hear yourself? Do you hear how selfish you are? *You're* the one who wants to be worshipped."

I shook my head. "Not worshipped, just loved. I'm alone *all* the time. With you, I have nothing in my life." In the back of my throat trailed the words *I* am *nothing in my life*. . . . These I swallowed, and immediately I felt nauseated.

"Oh, and some other husband, some *worthy* man, he'd spend his entire day with only you, showering you with attention, is that it? I guess he'd have to be a wealthy man—a captain of industry, maybe—no, the captain's playboy son. A prince! That'd be perfect for you, princess, *that's* the man you need."

"Not at all," I said in a calm, low voice, hoping to keep the nausea at bay. "Édouard is only an army officer, but what counts is he prizes me above everything. And he's not *striving* all the time. He's *living* a good, regular life."

"Jozan?" Scott was incredulous. "You're in love with Édouard Jozan? *That's* what this is about?"

"Yes."

"Yes? You don't even deny it?"

"No, of course not. Why would I? I've fallen in love."

This silenced him for a moment, because for all that he might argue that I was selfish, he believed, as I did, that we are helpless to resist or influence what our hearts are bound to do.

"You can't do this to me now, Zelda. You can't *leave*. For Christ's sake, have you no mercy at all? I'm trying to write a book—the most important book of my life!" He began to pace the terrace. "How can you . . . how can you be so disloyal? This is not possible. I love you, for God's sake, of course I do. I love you so much that I can't even see straight sometimes, can't *breathe*. I'm so afraid that something might happen to you, or to Scottie. Why do you think I work so hard?"

"I hear what you say, but I also see what you do—and don't do."

"*Don't do?* What else can I possibly do? I started with nothing, Zelda, and look at what I've given you!"

"And look at how you've told your flapper stories for so long now that you've got me confused with all those selfish girls you invented! I agreed to marry you before you had one material thing to offer me."

His mouth opened, then closed, and he blinked a few times, fast. "I—that's true. So why did you marry me, then? Was it for the novelty? Was it . . . was it rebellion against your father? Did you ever really love me, or was it a lie all along?"

"No! God, of course I did. I *do*. It's different now, though. We never . . . Manhattan was supposed to be a honeymoon, and then sure, things happened that we didn't expect, and we had all these doors opening to us. . . . Even with the baby, we just couldn't resist. Parties and work, those seem like your priorities." I drew a deep breath, then let it out. "We're bad for each other, Scott. Mama and Tilde were right in saying we'd wear each other out."

His hands gripped the rail, knuckles pale and knobby in the gray moonlight. I thought of the calluses on his right hand, formed from years of holding a pencil, and hated them.

"I try so hard," Scott said in a low, strangled voice. "I want to give you and Scottie the best of everything. I want to succeed in whatever I do, so that I make you proud. I want people to see us and say, 'Those Fitzgeralds have it all figured out. Who wouldn't want to be them?' It's a juggler's act, I know—but I've been a pretty good juggler up to now. I thought I'd been."

He had been a pretty good juggler. Even there in the midst of my belief that there was nothing worth salvaging, I could feel the truth of his words. Our circus act, begun in the Biltmore Hotel four years earlier, had mostly been a success.

To admit as much, though, would be to undermine my argument. He would take the admission and twist it around in some way that would make him the victim and me the villain. I couldn't say what I knew: that I was the villain, too.

After a quiet minute, he went on, "Some days, though . . . I don't know if you understand how it's all I can do to face myself in the mirror, let alone sit at my desk and spin words into gold. There are days when I'm certain that everyone loathes me, that I'll never write another word worth a damn, let alone a dollar. There are times when I see you, you with your confidence and your fearlessness and your discipline and your beauty, and I'm terrified that it might all end up—well, like this."

I had no words.

"Please, Zelda, give me another chance."

I thought of Édouard, of *my* chance.

"You always said our love was everything to you, that you couldn't imagine life without me, wouldn't want it, would rather die. If you love me even a little—"

"Let me think about it," I said, knowing that if I let him continue, I might be lost forever.

INTERLUDE

When I met Scott, the first thing I knew about him, beyond his physical appearance, was that he was an army officer. Then I learned that he was a Yankee, and a writer. Initially, the first two matters seemed capable of sinking us. The third one, his being a writer, was the one I put all my faith in, as he'd done, too—and yet that third matter was the solid center of our crumbling world, not its beating heart but a cannonball.

Scott was the first serious writer I'd ever met. By 1924, though, I knew a bunch of them. Bunny and the Princeton boys—all of them serious if not all successful; Edna Millay, George Nathan, Shane Leslie, Dorothy Parker, Sinclair Lewis, Don Stewart, Sherwood Anderson, Tom Boyd, Peggy Boyd, Anita Loos, Carl Van Vechten, Ring Lardner, John Dos Passos, Archie MacLeish, Jean Cocteau, and of course my own beloved Sara Haardt. I'd become a writer myself, somewhat.

There are so many ways to be a writer, but I felt I understood writers in general, inasmuch as I think writers can be understood. We all have something to say, and we require the written word—as opposed to musical instruments, or paint and canvas, or clay, or marble, or what have you—to say it. Not all writers want to be profound (though an awful lot of them do); some want to entertain, some want to inform; some are trying to provoke the most basic, universal feelings using a minimum of words—I think of Emily Dickinson—to demonstrate how it is to be human in our crazy world today.

Yet, of all the writers I've heard of or met or come to know (the list has grown even longer since '24), I've never met another who's anything like Scott.

At the age when I was perfecting my cartwheels and learning to skate backward and stealing my brother's cigarettes to see what smoking was all about, Scott was writing one-act plays. He was writing poems and lyrics. Not long after that, his plays were full three-act structures with stage direction included. He wrote detective stories and adventure stories and dramatic stories. His plays began to be produced. He wrote more of everything, and then he wrote his novel, and then he wrote it again, and then again, and now he's written a play for *Broadway*, and a musical revue, and all kinds of movie scenarios and scripts, and so many stories I've lost track of them all. When he's not writing fiction, he's writing essays and articles and book reviews and letters. He's making notes and keeping ledgers where he tracks all of his stuff and my work, too.

Oh—I'd forgotten this, until just now:

We were newly married—still staying at the Commodore, I think—and had been out so late that we decided to go over to the East River to watch the sun rise. We were dressed up, still, from having been to a party at the apartment of a friend of one of George's friends—no one we knew, but we wouldn't think of refusing an invitation, and everyone there seemed to know us.

We walked from the host's East Side apartment, somewhere around Seventieth, I guess it was, over to the riverfront in the gray-washed predawn, still feeling tight and gay, me teetering now and then in heels higher than I was accustomed to. I wore Scott's jacket, and he wore my beaded hat.

The smell of the East River at dawn is dank and oily—though nothing so bad as Venice in August—and you get the sense that fish are decomposing all around you, just out of sight. Still, we found an empty stoop and sat there holding hands, oblivious. We sighed happily about the wonderfulness of being young and in love, of being in such demand simply because Scott had gotten some thoughts in his head and had written them down.

"You'd think anyone could do it," he said. "Writing sounds so easy. Even *I* think it sounds easy, and I've got a hundred and twenty-two rejections that clearly prove it's otherwise."

"How do you know if you're a writer, though? I mean, I've had thoughts and written them down— "

"Your diary, you mean— "

"My diary, yes. And I write my weight in letters every month, it seems. And I've tried a few story ideas like I told you, but I'm bad at it— "

"You'll get better."

"Maybe. What I'm sayin', though, is I never thought, 'I'm a writer.' But you did. *Why* did you? How did you know?"

"It was easy enough to tell: if I wasn't writing, I didn't exist."

So that night at Villa Marie, after I told Scott that I needed some time to think, I went inside for a pillow and some blankets and then made myself a bed on a chaise in the garden. There, on that July night beneath the lemon trees, I had a sort of conversation with myself about right and real, and wishes and truth.

Édouard was a good, dear man. We had chemistry, yes, and we had those outside-of-time Mediterranean days, and we had the excitement of doing something unusual and fraught, which itself appealed to people like us—risk-takers, you know. What else did we have, though? My French was still rudimentary and his English only a little better; when I thought it through, I recognized that our communications were quite basic. And while plenty of people had gotten married with even less in common, I'd already determined that such a marriage wasn't for me.

Here's what I figured: Édouard was less a man than a symbol for me, a symbol of my yearning for something I couldn't yet name. If I'd heard of Amelia Earhart at the time, I might have been as willing to follow her lead as I was Édouard's.

I wasn't in love with him, not really. Édouard was a symbol. Édouard was a symptom. Scott, for all his shortcomings, owned my heart.

By the time I went inside, the dew had settled; I tracked into the bedroom with wet feet. Scott was sitting up in bed. The end of his cigarette glowed.

I stripped off my damp clothes, then took the cigarette and put it aside.

"You'll stay?"

"Yes."

"No more beach, no lunches, you won't go anyplace without me while he's here."

"All right."

Neither of us said another word for the rest of that night—a remarkable thing by itself. That night, we kept quiet so that our truth could be heard, and seen, and felt, in the ways we touched each other's skin, the ways we sighed or gasped, our tentative glances, the press of my forehead to his.

When I didn't return to the beach for a week, nor send a note to Édouard, nor place a call, he stopped looking for me there. At the casino, he asked after "the Fitzgeralds" and got nothing more than a shrug. All this Scott learned from René, who'd said he was loath to reveal anything at all to Scott, but out of respect for the friendship they'd developed during those months, he thought it only right that Scott know what had almost happened.

Scott told me, "René says Jozan is heartbroken and confused and may never get over you."

"He will."

"Perhaps. Though if he doesn't, I won't be surprised. I said to René, 'Tell your friend that he's now a member of a very prestigious club.'"

25

===

October: Scott found me in the Villa Marie garden taking in the inspiring Mediterranean view for what would be one of the last times that year. "Here." He handed me a piece of paper that read,

Trimalchio
High Bouncing Lover
Among Ash Heaps and Millionaires
Trimalchio of West Egg
Gold Hatted Gatsby
On the Road to West Egg
Under the Red White and Blue
The Great Gatsby

Our lease would end when the month did, and then we'd migrate else-where the way the birds and our friends were all doing—most to Paris, some to Venice, or London, or Berlin. I'd persuaded Scott to tour Rome and Capri so that I could see a lot of the art and some of the artists that I'd been hearing about from the Murphys during our visits with them. After the tour, we'd get a place in Paris and—we reassured each other—be even more responsible about the partying and drinking and our marriage than we'd been here.

In Paris, we'd await and then celebrate his third novel's publication; he was more certain than ever that he'd accomplished everything he'd set out to do with this book, and at the same time he was terrified that he hadn't.

"What do you think?" he asked now. "I'm torn. I've been leaning toward one of the *Trimalchio* titles, but Max thinks the association's too obscure. I could make more of it in the book, I suppose—but I hate the thought of spoon-feeding my readers. God, I do too much of that for the slicks as it is. Still, *Trimalchio of West Egg* is a great title; it might be worth Nick making a little narrative sidestep in order to share the background."

This being my third go-round with Scott and his novels in prepublication madness, I knew there was no shortcut out of the anxiety; we both had to endure it the way you endure the headache, nausea, and malaise of a hangover.

As was now our tradition, I'd read his draft—had just finished the new one, in fact—and had been gathering my thoughts while I sat there. "Before we get into titles," I told him, "I have to say that there's something still kinda blurry about Gatsby. I can see Tom and Daisy, and Myrtle's poor husband! And even Nick is clear enough. . . . Maybe it's that Gatsby's *history* is murky. Wouldn't people know *something* about him? Or think they did?"

Scott crossed his arms. "These people don't care about how he made his money, they only care that he's rich and throws insanely great parties."

"You wanted my opinion."

"I did, I know." He uncrossed his arms. "Thank you."

"For titles, I like *The Great Gatsby*."

"You do?" He looked disappointed. "Really?"

"Really."

"That's the one Max wants, too."

"Remember when you revised the end of *Beautiful and Damned*?"

Scott sighed. "I'm too close to the work, that's what you're saying."

"That's what I'm saying. So listen, the Murphys are just about to pack up and head back to Saint-Cloud. While you're stewing over edits and titles and such, let's take Scottie over to see Patrick—she's been asking forever—and we can celebrate her birthday a little early. I was thinking I'd make a circus set for her—like paper dolls but the dolls will be animals. Camels, horses, tigers, elephants, lions, and a mistress of ceremonies who looks just like her. Maybe I'll add a unicorn, too."

"That all sounds marvelous, and I'm sure you'll do a bang-up job of it. *I* was thinking it might also be nice to give her a brother."

"Were you, now? All on your own?"

"With some help from the stork, of course."

"The stork's going to need more than seven weeks, you know."

He said, "Hm. I suppose that's right."

"But I guess we can *confer* with the stork. Place the order, you might say."

"Are you ready for that?" he asked.

"I believe I am."

I rested my head against his shoulder and we watched the sun set, just like you might see in the movies. We'd worked hard to create this lovely, new domestic bliss, and before *Gatsby*'s publication, right up until the book was printed and put into the hands of both the reading and the reviewing public, it looked as if we might actually succeed.

Wait: if I leave it at that, it'll sound like the novel's disappointing performance is to blame for the disaster we made of our lives, and that's not really so. Ernest Hemingway is to blame.

26

Sara Murphy looked sad as we all filed into the dining room for the season's final Dinner-Flowers-Gala, as she called these more formal events. The men were in tails, the women in slim, ankle-length summer gowns in all the colors of a Mediterranean summer. Sara stood next to her chair and sighed. "One final gathering—"

"Before the next one." Gerald kissed her forehead and took his seat at the opposite end of the table.

Present in this, their rented Antibes home, were Scott and me; Dick and Alice Lee; Pablo without Olga—they were on the outs; Pauline Pfeiffer, a friend of Sara's who worked as a writer for *Vogue* magazine; Dottie Parker; and Linda without Cole, who, she said, was "traveling." She said it like that, with quotation marks in her voice; no one asked her what she meant.

The weather had been perfect for us all week: clear skies, hot afternoons, the sea still warm enough for the children to spend all day splashing and playing. We'd toured the grounds and house that were slowly becoming the grand estate that the Murphys would name Villa America. In the evenings, the adults gathered for charades and bridge and a game Scott invented, whereby I sat at the piano while he named a theme, and then each of us had to ad-lib a story and sing it to one of the half dozen tunes I could play by heart. Every time I opened the keyboard, I apologized in advance: "Y'all will forgive me for not being Cole."

"And forgive me as well," Scott would say, but I knew he preferred it this way. Without Cole, the spotlight was all his.

Gerald's invented cocktails were a real help with our game, which Linda named "The Terribly Witty Ditties." Gerald poured the drinks while Scott exhorted everyone to come up with ever-more-creative rhymes. Then, when our imaginations could no longer meet the challenge, Scott would single out one or another of the group for Twenty Questions, which, depending on how much he'd had to drink, might go on well past twenty and into the night. His subjects always cooperated; who doesn't love being found unendingly interesting?

Now Sara sat down at the table across from Gerald, saying, "It might be *months* before we see these friends again."

At her right, Dick Myers reached over to Scott next to him and thumped him on the back. "One can hope."

"Have I exhausted your talents?" Scott asked.

"Prob'ly their patience," I said fondly.

"When he has exhausted yours," Pablo told me in heavily accented English, "you must come to mi estudio en Paris, sí? I will exhaust you all about art."

Sara put her hand on mine. "You must. And visit Gerald's studio, too. But see Rome's art first, then bring them every question that comes to mind. You won't find better mentors than this pair."

It was while standing in front of the Temple of Vesta that I first had the pain, a funny twinge low in my pelvis, near my right hip. Women get pains of this sort often enough that I paid it little mind, and it dutifully disappeared—for a while. Later that night it was back, and worse. Then it faded and was gone for a few days, only to return again.

The discomfort went on this way for five weeks. Sometimes I was cranky but functional, and we'd go out. We met up with some of the cast and crew of *Ben-Hur* during this time—who knows how Scott met them, to start? We were always being introduced to someone who knew someone whose husband was or brother was or great old friend was connected to someone or something we simply *had* to see. This happened so often that I'd stopped paying attention to the connections and concerned myself only with the results.

Too often, I spent half the day in bed clutching a water bottle to my hips like a lover. If you're thinking pregnancy was the culprit, well, you can join me in being wrong about that. One night in December, just as Scott led Scottie in to read a book with me in bed, he found me doubled over and in so much pain that I was wishing I could trade that pain for labor, for amputation, for anything that would be better than the aching, burning ball in my gut. Everything around me—my whole field of vision—seemed edged in white. "Take her and call a doctor," I gasped.

When Scott scooped her up by her middle, Scottie didn't protest being whisked away. She thought he'd begun a game. "Bye, Mama!" she called. I could hear her laughing as Scott carried her off. "Make me fly, Papa, I want to fly!"

The Italian doctor who arrived an hour later spoke no English and had French about on par with mine. He looked in my mouth and nose and eyes, he put his stethoscope on my belly, he pressed and prodded, asking, "Ici? Ici?" while I gritted my teeth and either flinched or didn't flinch in response. When he was done, his expression was grave, his words sober as he pronounced his conclusion, in French.

Scott, on the other side of the bed, looked panicked. "What's he saying?"

I told the doctor, "Yes. *Oui*. Fine, I don't care what you need to do, just make it stop."

"L'hopital Murphy," he told Scott, as he took a needle and syringe from his bag. "Maintenant. Comprenez-vous?"

"Zelda, for God's sake, what's he saying? *What* about the Murphys?"

I winced when the needle pierced my hip, a small but welcome pain that, within moments, delivered some miraculous something that allowed me to unclench my teeth enough to translate. "He thinks there's probably a water ball on my tube, which will require a knife to resolve. They have good knives at Murphy Hospital; we should go there now."

"A *what*?" Scott's eyes were wild as a scared horse's.

"A cyst," I said, translating further as the drug continued to dull the pain. The white edges began to recede from my vision. "On my ovary, I think." The pain faded, and faded, and I could breathe again.

Optimistically I asked the doctor, "Mais c'est bon un peu; est que l'hopital necessaire vrai?" which was supposed to mean *I'm feeling better now; do I really need to go to the hospital?*

The doctor scowled and unleashed a string of Italian curses—or so it sounded to me. Then he said in French, "Allez ou mourir." *Go, or die.*

The idea of submitting to surgery was only slightly less terrifying and undesirable than death, so I went.

Afterward, the pain wasn't gone so much as it was altered and muted. Recovering, first in the hospital and then in our hotel, *I* felt altered and muted. To a person who has hardly been sick in her life, sudden illness feels like a betrayal.

The doctor hadn't been able to assure us—not in Italian or French or English—that I would still be able to get pregnant now that one ovary was gone. When I translated this for Scott, he looked at me accusingly and asked the doctor, "Could medications for 'feminine troubles' have caused the problem?"

"Eh? Médicaments?"

I knew what Scott was talking about, even if the doctor didn't.

"Yes . . . to regulate cycles, and so forth."

The doctor looked to me for translation. "C'est rien," I said. "Il ne c'est pas ce qu'il dit, il est inquiet." *Never mind. He doesn't know what he's saying, he's just worried.*

"Ce médicament permettra de remédier à la douleur," the doctor said, nodding, and he wrote down a prescription for pain relief.

I told Scott, "He says no, it wasn't the pills, and this medication is our best bet."

For the next few weeks, I was tired and uncomfortable and crabby, and antisocial because of it. What I wanted was *home*. What I got was an assurance that we'd leave Rome soon for sunny, mild Capri. And in the meantime, Scott had written three new stories, then reviewed the *Gatsby* proofs, made corrections, and shipped the proofs back to New York. With that done, he grew bored. He went out a lot, then would turn up late in the evening glassy-eyed and pink-cheeked, often cheerful but sometimes belligerent.

"Suppose you can't get pregnant," he said on one of those nights. "Suppose that your abortion"—he spat the word—"got rid of my son. When *Gatsby* makes me an American literary legend, who's going to carry on my legacy, my name?"

"What, now you've decided that a daughter's not good enough? If you did have a son, I guess you'd name him Francis Scott Fitzgerald the Second—and what would you call *him*? Junior? Or would you take Scottie's name away from her and call her Fran or something?"

"You don't want another child," he accused.

"*You* didn't want what we thought would be the first one."

He slumped into the chair in the corner of the bedroom. "Women never understand this," he said, ignoring my point. "To you, every baby is just another child, no matter the sex. Men need *sons,* it's built into us, an imperative."

I knew he was anxious about *Gatsby,* not to mention inebriated, and enervated by everything we'd been through. But I was *tired.* I said, "What men need is to grow up."

27

Capri is an island, a big, gorgeous, rocky chunk of dirt and limestone that appears to have broken off Italy's southeast coast and lodged in the Tyrrhenian Sea. Sun-drenched and ancient, the island is an enclave for the young, the strange, the beautiful, the rich—heirs and heiresses to fortunes built wholly by their ambitious forebears and managed by teams of accountants and advisers. The beneficiaries dressed themselves in linen and silk and sat beneath striped awnings talking about polo, and travel, and how hard it was to find good help these days. But in that winter of 1924–25, it was an artists' haven, too—and I was intent on becoming an artist.

My incision was well healed, and the discomfort I'd suffered those weeks following the surgery had diminished enough for us to carry on as usual. While Scott went out, paying calls to writers like his old hero (and mine) Compton Mackenzie, I took Esther Murphy's advice to look up a woman named Natalie Barney and, through her, get acquainted with the artists' community here. Esther hadn't written much about Natalie, only saying, *Just meet her. She knows everyone.*

We met up at an outdoor café near the marina. Crying gulls skimmed overhead as a dark-eyed young woman seated us. She kept glancing shyly at Natalie but said nothing at all.

"So, Zelda Fitzgerald," Natalie said when we sat down, "the prettiest half of literature's Golden Couple. I'm glad to finally meet you."

She was handsome, tall and thin and dressed in a smartly tailored white shirt above a long split skirt of blue linen. Her lack of makeup surprised me—not that she needed it. The soft lines near her eyes and the glow of her skin gave plenty of character to a face that looked proud of its forty-plus years.

I said, "The feeling's mutual, I promise, but the truth is, I don't really know anything about who you are or what you do. Esther insisted I find you here is all."

"Well, when I'm not here amusing myself and seeing friends, I write poetry and plays and host a salon in the Latin Quarter in Paris."

"A salon?"

"You don't know salons? A ritual gathering place, a standing date, an open house for any and all artists, writers, thinkers. Do you know T. S. Eliot? Mina Loy, Ezra Pound?"

"Some of the names ring a bell," I lied; only Eliot's did, and only because Scott had insisted I read Eliot's strange "Prufrock" when we were en route to Rome. "You have all these people coming and going in your house all the time?"

She laughed. "It sometimes feels that way, but no, officially it's only on Saturday evenings. You'll have to come if you ever get to Paris."

"We're going this spring, in fact."

"Lovely! So now, when you phoned, you said you paint a little; tell me about your art."

"Well, I do oils, mostly, but I tried watercolor once—it's too risky, if you ask me. One mistake and that's it, you have to start all over."

"Who are your influences?"

"I was afraid you were going to ask me that. I'll tell you what I told Gerald. Where I grew up, pretty much all the art depicts the Glorious Confederacy. I like nature, so I guess you could say that was my influence, so far."

"You had lessons?"

"Sorta. Years ago, in the States, I took a class from a crusty old man who thought Michelangelo was modern."

"Well then, you must study with someone here. And in the meantime, we will expand your knowledge of what the art world has to offer. Tell me where you've traveled so far, and I'll tell you what you've seen."

The next week, Natalie took me to meet a painter friend of hers named Romaine Brooks. Romaine's studio was a vivid white square of a building hanging on to a cliff, nothing but the sea outside its windows. The natural light inside was incredible. Even more incredible was what I saw in the corner of the studio, what Romaine, who was a whippet-like woman with a serious brow and short, dark hair, had created while existing in that light: a portrait of a woman of such austere beauty that you wanted to pull up a chair and start a conversation with her, find out what was behind those knowing eyes.

I said as much, and Romaine replied, "Ah, yes; well, perhaps if I'd known the answers myself, she would not have left me."

Natalie nodded toward the portrait. "This was one of her lovers. They've just split up."

The woman in the painting had been Romaine's *lover*? Had I actually heard this right? Trying to mask my surprise at hearing her speak so plainly about something Montgomery folks wouldn't dare even whisper about, I said, "Oh. Gosh. I'm real sorry."

I didn't mask it well; the women looked at each other, and then Romaine changed the subject with "Why don't you describe the painting you've done. What subject matter do you like?"

When I repeated the story to Scott in bed that night, he said, "Mackenzie's got the strangest group of friends, too, I have to say. Fellows dressing in white linen pants and pastel-colored sweaters and talking about . . . about *pillows*—about fabrics and silk braid and bric-a-brac. And they're so clean, you know? Not a shadow of whiskers . . . sideburns *so* precise, back of their necks freshly shaved . . ." He rubbed his own fuzzy one. "In a way, they made me think of Cole—the mannerisms, that is. Except that these couple of guys, well, they just about said outright that they're fairies."

"Mackenzie's married, though, right?"

"He is. In fact, his wife, Faith, was just telling me that she's related to the Fowlers through some common distant cousin or something. I'll bet half the people on this island know the Fowlers. Imagine being heir to millions of dollars—and they don't appreciate what they've got, most of them. Wealth is wasted on the rich boys—"

He reached for his notebook and pencil, then repeated the phrase while writing it down. After he put the notebook back on the bedside table, he said, "The rich live an entirely different life from the rest of us, you know. That entitlement—it colors everything. If I didn't like Ludlow so well, I'd hate the bastard."

Scott spent the next several days drafting a story he called "The Rich Boy," then set it aside and returned to his routine of having cocktails with those very same types.

Staying in Capri that winter offered more than mild weather and exposure to people whose money or sexuality puzzled and, to be honest, intrigued us; it brought me Nicola Matthews, a petite, graying, tremendously knowledgeable artist who had the time, interest, and patience to teach me all about form, composition, technique, style—and all about life as she understood it.

In her tiny studio in the hills above the harbor, as I practiced sketching, brushstrokes, paint-mixing, Nicola spoke of a kind of feminism that was about developing women's natural tendencies to exist in groups with other women and with children, rather than in traditional marriages. Men would be used primarily for procreative sex, but weren't otherwise needed. She talked about Sappho, and Lesbos, and sexual attraction being variable for some people while inflexible for others.

"Women are formed for love, yes, but also for purpose, and the highest state for a woman—for all humans, in fact—comes when one discovers and then achieves one's ultimate purpose."

"Interesting," I said, thinking what a nice intellectual exercise it all was. I was twenty-four years old, I was still just beginning to find my way; *ultimate* purpose wasn't something that concerned me in the least.

28

We got acquainted with Hemingway the writer before we met Hemingway the man. Bob McAlmon, a scrappy writer and publisher we'd first met when we were in London and saw again in Capri, had done a small printing of Hemingway's work the year before and mentioned him to Scott. McAlmon said Hemingway was a true talent, "though he's having a damnably hard time getting the attention of the *Post*."

"Is that so?" Scott said. "I'll have to read him, maybe put in a word. I've got a little pull there."

While we were in Rome again, on our way to Paris from Capri, Scott tracked down copies of two Hemingway collections, with a mind to bring another fledgling under his wing. On an afternoon when Lillian was visiting home and I was entertaining Scottie with an art lesson and then a manicure, he lounged on a settee in our hotel suite and read the first of the books, *Three Stories and Ten Poems*, a slim, paperbound volume that, honestly, looked like something that had been assembled by a junior high poetry club.

When he finished a short time later, he stood and stretched and then dropped the volume onto the table near me, saying only, "Tell me if you think he's an up-and-comer."

Scottie, her fingernails now a glorious bright pink, said, "What's a nuppincomer?"

"A nuppincomer is a person your papa thinks has talent, but will never be as talented as *he* is." I winked at Scott, and he grinned.

I read Hemingway's *in our time,* along with McAlmon's edition of *Three Stories and Ten Poems,* at Scottie's bedside a couple of nights later; my girl, being in between homes, wouldn't go to sleep unless I was in the room with her.

"'Mitragliatrice,'" I said, reading the first poem's title. "That's a word? Am I going to need a dictionary to get through this?" Scottie blinked at me sleepily, then nodded off while I read the short poem.

Its last line ended with another mouthful word, *mitrailleuse,* which I supposed was French. Not knowing its meaning, though, meant the poem's message was lost on me—and a lot of other people, too, I guessed. "Why would you do that?" I muttered, annoyed. "Show-off."

I went to find Scott, who was sitting on the bedroom floor with magazine pages spread neatly around him—copies of all the stories he'd published since *The Beautiful and Damned,* from which he was trying to choose ten for a new collection. He saw me and said, "If I can finish 'The Rich Boy' and place it quickly, I think it'll do a lot for the book's chances."

"Well, *I've* finished these Ernest Hemingway bits," I said, setting the books on the bed.

"And?"

"He sounds a lot like your pal Sherwood, except without the warmth. That prose, it's clean and precise, sure, but it distracts you just like a cobra does with its dance before it strikes its victim. It's a sham. There's no substance there, no heart."

Scott shook his head. "It's spare, true. But I think you're simply not seeing the substance, the character of it—maybe it takes a poet to spot it."

"Oh, please. The two of you are no more genuine poets than I am. You—and I'll venture every third writer in Europe nowadays—fancies himself a poet, when all you're doing is building little towers of words set prettily on a page. His poems aren't *awful,* they're just not profound or impressive. He's sure not Robert Frost, or Coleridge, or even Blake."

"Darling . . . don't take this the wrong way, but you're not really the best judge of what makes a skillful or profound poem. You may read a lot, and, yes, you've written a little, and you're a great help with my stories—but you aren't *serious* about literature."

"What, just because I don't spend my every free minute reading or talking about *that* book or *this* author or the context and import and relevance and representational pulchritude of *this* image in *that* poem or story?"

Scott burst into laughter. "Okay, fine, you win, if only because you're so gorgeous when you're impassioned." Scott filed the books in his satchel. "This Hemingway fellow's prose has force, though. You can't argue with that."

I said, "Hammers have force, too, but they're pretty limited in what they're good for."

April 10, *The Great Gatsby*'s publication day, arrived, and we celebrated by having lunch with friends at a café in Rome's Centro Storico. Scottie amused herself in the gravel beneath the table; she pretended to be a dog, and we all fed her tidbits. I tried not to think about what Mama would say if she saw such a thing.

Our being in transit, abroad, meant we were in the dark about the book's reception back home. It would be a good two weeks before the day's papers could catch up to us—and who knew which papers would review for certain, let alone when any one review might run? Maybe three days had passed when Scott said, "I can't stand it. I'm going to cable Max."

We were out with Scottie at the Trevi Fountain, letting her toss bits of apple into the water to "feed" the carved horses. "It's too early to know anything, Deo."

"No, it isn't, there's a pattern to these things."

My stomach had begun to cramp a bit; I shifted Scottie to my other hip in hopes that would help ease the pain. "Not when it's only been a few days. You'd get just as good information by having some mystic over by the Vatican read your tea leaves."

"You don't understand, Zelda, and you never will because *your* life is nothing but a series of low-risk amusements. Shopping and hair appointments and painting lessons and parties. I seek information about my *very existence,* my *fate,* not out of some idle curiosity but because our future depends on this book's performance. Do you think your surgery was free?"

Scottie threaded the fingers of one hand into my hair and put her head on my shoulder, her thumb in her mouth.

If Scott hadn't been in such a state, I might've debated his view of my life. And I sure would have defended myself against his suggestion that I'd developed a life-threatening condition by choice. He *was* in a state, though, and that meant nothing would get through to him. So I said, "I'm sorry, I know you're anxious. Fine, go cable him, we'll meet you back at the hotel."

Scott waited ten days for Max's reply, which would find us in Marseille. In the meantime he ate little and slept less. Every hour was a battle in the warring factions of confidence, hope, and fear. Was he right? Had he synthesized all the past criticism and learned from it and produced an undeniably excellent and satisfying novel? *Gatsby* was short—around fifty thousand words—but in that brevity was a lot of nuance. He expected the critics to be smart enough to recognize all the subtleties they'd claimed were missing in his previous books. And when they did, their glowing responses would ensure that the public—who could not be so trusted, he said, but who needn't bother with what was highbrow about it anyway—would flock to the stores with as much enthusiasm as they'd shown for *This Side of Paradise.*

Scott's hands were like a palsied old man's when he opened Max's telegram. Over his shoulder I read,

SALES SITUATION DOUBTFUL. EXCELLENT REVIEWS

Scott crumpled the telegram and dropped it onto the floor.

Max was truthful on the first count, but he'd overstated the second: when the first packet of reviews from the clippings bureau found us in Lyon, there was praise, but it was mild and, most often, in the nature of "Fitzgerald shows he's not quite as awful as we feared and may have even grown a bit."

Even Scott's hero Henry Mencken, who had privately written Scott a praise-filled letter, in public made the book out to be "a glorified anecdote." Scott read that review in full silence, and even before I knew the actual substance of it, I saw in Scott's open mouth, furrowed brow, and wounded eyes a kind of confusion mixed with horrified disbelief. It wasn't so much what Mencken said, but what he *didn't* say, which was anything that amounted to "You must read this book!"

I didn't speak. After a moment Scott appeared to recover somewhat. Handing me the review, he said, "Scribner's will be lucky to move even the twenty thousand they've printed."

His outlook would improve a little over the next week, when Max's and Harold's letters included two very positive reviews. As we moved on from Lyon to Paris, Scott would write lists and letters that analyzed and strategized and summarized his thoughts on what he'd done wrong and what might yet be done to help the situation.

This was Scott. This *is* Scott, always looking back to try to figure out how to go forward, where happiness and prosperity must surely await.

PART III

Always be drunk.
That's it! The great imperative!
In order not to feel Time's horrible burden
*   weighting your shoulders,*
grinding you into the earth,
Get drunk and stay that way.
On what?
On wine, poetry, virtue, as you please.
But get drunk.
And if you sometimes happen to awake on
*   the steps of a palace,*
in the green grass of a ditch,
in the dismal loneliness of your own room,
with your drunkenness gone or disappearing,
ask the wind, the wave, the star, the bird, the
*   clock,*
ask everything that flees, everything that groans,
*   or rolls, or sings, everything that speaks—*
ask what time it is;
and the wind, the wave, the star, the bird, the
*   clock will answer you:*
"Time to get drunk!
If you are not to be the martyred slaves of Time,
Get drunk! Stay drunk!
On wine, poetry, or virtue, as you please."
                              —Charles Baudelaire

29

Paris in 1925 was filling up with American writers and artists and dancers and singers and musicians of all stripes. And in the same way that high school students congregate in cliques and clubs and groups, so were the expatriates sorting themselves into like-minded collections, each with its favored gathering spot in town. Some chose restaurants and cafés on the Right Bank, where the establishments tended to be American in flavor, while others preferred the grittier and truer Paris of the Left Bank's cabarets and cafés and bars.

Though Scott would prove to be a Right Banker in his heart, we'd spend a great deal of time on the Left, too, depending on which circus train we'd either hitched our wagon to or started pulling ourselves. The streets, the bridges, the glowing pink streetlights, all of it blurred so easily during a night of trailing from one place to another, our excursions an ever-movable cocktail party in search of the best people or the best drink or the best singer or songs.

Our apartment was on the Right Bank in the stately, elegant limestone building 14 rue de Tilsitt, right off the Champs-Élysées. We were on the fifth floor, surrounded by an assortment of wallpaper and furnishings that were "circa Grandmama," as I told Scott when we saw the place.

If the décor was antiquated and as heavy to the senses as a plateful of friands foie gras, it was at least spacious, with rooms for Scottie and Lillian and a cook, plus a small suite for Scott and me. Most important, it had indoor plumbing, a feature for which I was willing to pay a great deal even under regular circumstances but which would prove a blessing when new health problems began to plague me in the months ahead. That we had a view of the Arc de Triomphe from the corner window impressed my sisters to no end.

Paris was the most remarkable place, even to a girl who'd spent a good deal of time enjoying everything fine and fun about New York City. Amid those cobblestone streets, the smells of roasting nuts and burning coal, the sculpted and carved stone façades that had witnessed Napoléon's march, the 1870 Siege, the Great War's miracle on the Marne, you felt that you were part of something, some*place* much greater than yourself. While I'd felt something similar in Rome, it seemed more personal in Paris. You didn't just *see* the antiquity, the history; you felt it was ongoing. You inhabited it and it inhabited you.

Shortly upon our return, we spent an evening at Gerald and Sara's Saint-Cloud house. Sara and I enlisted the children to help bake a belated "book-day cake" for Scott, which they smeared with blue icing in more or less the color of *Gatsby*'s wrapper. Scottie declared that she had to lay the buttercups around the base of the cake, saying, "It's *my* daddy's book-day," while the Murphy offspring, Honoria and Patrick and Baoth, watched her with the fascination of children who've never had the opportunity to be selfish.

We took our cake and tea in the parlor. Now when I gazed at the art hung on the walls here, I understood that Sara admired Renoir's work for its vivid and delicate humanity. Gerald's choices—Fernand Léger, Georges Braque, Juan Gris—expressed his modern taste and vision. I recognized the deliberation that had gone into each artist's choices for the work. What was the focus? Where was the light source? How much black in the mix for that little girl's hair? How much yellow in that sky?

In this setting, and maybe also owing to his depression, Scott was modest and subdued about the book. This was still early in our friendship with the Murphys, and Scott looked up to Gerald and Sara both; he wanted always to impress them and to win their high regard. The Murphys had this effect on everyone who knew them. We all endeavored to be our best selves because *they* were so excellent and genuine.

Our routine quickly became dominated by social gatherings with the people we knew already: we saw the Murphys and Porters and Myerses, we saw Dos Passos and Sherwood and met Ezra Pound. And just like in New York, then St. Paul, then Great Neck, our social circle expanded rapidly with every party; there were always new people to meet.

There would be no easing into the scene—when did Scott and I ever ease into anything? Even had I wanted to slow things down, Scott wanted to be everywhere with everyone, jovially encouraging his rise to the top of American letters. Every day had double the hours of days elsewhere in the world, yet at the same time I was half as aware of how I used all those hours—as if the Parisian air that heightened my other senses muddled my sense of time.

At first, my days were busy with lunch dates and shopping forays, and craft-making with Scottie, who'd become fascinated with beads. Nights were an endless succession of bars and cabarets, liquor and music and dancing. I came to adore a colored woman with vivid dyed-red hair whose name was Ada "Bricktop" Smith, after meeting her at one of Cole's parties, where she'd been hired to teach us all the Black Bottom—which was now being called the Charleston.

She'd lined us up and announced the dance. "I learned this one when I was a girl," I said, waving my arm in the air like the boisterous student I'd been.

Ada looked me over. "That was when, five minutes ago?"

"Feels more like five centuries, some days."

She tsked and said, "Well, let it loose, girl!" So I did.

Before going out to a bar called Le Select one night at the end of April, we had dinner at home with Scottie, a light meal of her then-favorite foods, the sorts of things a three-and-a-half-year-old will eat: chicken legs, along with carrot disks and squares of little French cheeses, which we'd all eaten using toothpicks.

Scott had directed Lillian to begin teaching Scottie French—a sign that told me he believed France would be home for us, that he believed he could be at the top of the order here in a much more genuine way than he'd been in New York. I practiced my French with Scottie while we ate, naming the foods and then putting their names into silly sentences.

"Les carottes ne veulent pas être mangées ce soir," I said. *The carrots do not want to be eaten tonight.* And Scottie said, "Les carottes mangent le soir."

I laughed. "*The carrots eat the night*—I like that better than what I said."

"Do another!"

"Les petits fromages sont prêts pour leur bain." *The little cheeses are ready for their bath.*

"Les petits fromages *mangent* leur bain," Scottie said, giggling.

"Oh, now we have cheeses eating the bath! Aren't you just the cleverest little lambkin?"

"You know it's useless for you to do this," Scott said. "There's too much Alabama in your voice, she'll never get the pronunciation right."

"You're probably right—but we don't care, do we, ma petite quinte-feuille?"

Scottie had become engrossed in stacking carrots on a toothpick and ignored us.

"*You* could take a turn," I said. "My French is mediocre, but yours is deplorable. You could use the practice even more than her."

He waved away the suggestion. "As long as I can read a menu and settle a bill, that's good enough for me."

At the Select, we joined a group that included our beloved Alec, who was passing through Paris. There were maybe eight of us all told, four other men and a woman, all of whom were Scott's newfound friends. The woman spoke no English. All of the men were writers, some still aspiring to any kind of publication, others having placed stories in small American-run

Parisian journals. Writerly barnacles, they were, who'd drifted to Paris after the war and had attached themselves to the literary community's pillars and anchors. Who knew whether they were decent writers?

Two hours in, Scott was on his fourth cocktail and was leaning forward, his hands pressing the tabletop, his face alight with impassioned enthusiasm for his subject.

"Tell me one name," he was saying, "one man who understands and can represent the beating heart of the American experience better than I've done with my *Gatsby*. Don't say Lewis, don't say Boyd—the prairies and small towns and factories might be in the heart*land* but they aren't America's *heart*! They're the somnolent feet, dragging along, depressing us with their bleak, bloodless prose."

Was I the only one who noticed that he was talking just slightly out of alignment? Everyone watched him with expressions of rapt adoration on their faces; did they admire him so much already, or was it the absinthe?

Scott continued, "And none of those depressing wartime dramas either, American soldiers and their sordid, bloody tales—that's the past. Zelda, darling, you've read *The Great Gatsby*—and she's tremendously well-read in general—you tell them: Have I written the preeminent American novel, literature's shining city on a hill?"

By this time I'd come to recognize the warning signs that said Scott would, if no one stopped him, tumble over the cliff. So, while I would have supported him anyway, I took the extra measure and said, "There's no doubt about it. It's *dazzling*, people. His best work yet, and better'n everybody's out there. Now is there any chance we'll have some music here tonight?" I looked around for signs of a jazz quartet, at least. "'Cause I'd really like to dance with a preeminent American novelist, if one happens to be around."

30

At a Left Bank bar called the Dingo a day or two later, we had just taken a table when Ezra Pound spotted us and came strolling over. With his crazy, thick hair and his Spaniard's mustache and the mad glint in his eyes, Pound was one of my favorites among the Paris crowd. Married to one woman and publicly involved with another, passionate about women and politics and art, he was lawless and profound and genuine in both his life and his poetry. Because of that, I—and everyone, really—accepted him fully.

He said, "Just my luck! I've got someone you need to meet."

"Who's that?" Scott asked.

Pound led us to the bar. A dark-haired, mustached man wearing what appeared to be two thick, gray sweaters was saying good-bye to a pair of women I'd later know as Duff and Kitty. He looked to be in his mid-twenties, same as me, strikingly attractive, his face suntanned—from ski-ing, we'd learn—his hair mussed and curling onto his forehead, his dark eyes keen and brooding.

Pound said, "Wem, meet Scott Fitzgerald. Scott, this pup's named Er-nest Hemingway. Can you imagine such a name? It's ludicrous. You can call him Wem or Hem or Wemedge or Ernie—or anything you think suits."

While Pound was speaking, the man's face had lit up with a smile that, if directed toward a girl, would no doubt make her swoon. He grabbed

Scott's shoulders. "Damn glad to meet you. Saw your story in *American Mercury*—good stuff, true and moving, really fine writing."

Scott bowed a little and then backed out of the embrace in order to turn toward me. "Meet my wife, Zelda."

"Don't mind if I do," Hemingway said, giving me the most charming, rakish look before gazing back at Scott. "To the victor go the spoils, eh?"

"So they say."

"Um, pardon me," I said in mock annoyance, hands on my hips. "I am not some prize."

"I beg to differ." Hemingway pulled out a chair. "Sit, please. Pound and I were just tiring of each other."

"*I* was tiring of *you*. How are you, Fitz?"

I said, "He's as fickle as the weather here, touchy as a feral cat—"

"I've been reading the latest opinions on my latest book," Scott explained. "They correspond to the sales figures."

"Neither are as bad as he'll make you think," I said. "It's a marvelous book, everybody ought to buy ten copies."

Scott smiled at this show of faith. "*I* would like to start with buying a drink."

"Critics are all a bunch of goddamned eunuchs. What's the book?" Hemingway asked.

"*The Great Gatsby*. It's a novel—my third."

"I've heard only good things," Pound said. "Everything excellent. First-rate."

"You, my friend, are a poor liar. No, look," Scott told Hemingway, "the reception has been mixed—but wait," he said, interrupting himself. "Hemingway! Bunny Wilson and Bob McAlmon talked you up so much that I went out and found your books. You're good!"

Hemingway gave a crooked smile and scratched his scalp. "Yeah? Thanks. I've left McAlmon for Boni and Liveright, who've promised to take my novel—assuming I'll have one to give them. I'm here in Paris to make a go of it."

"Ah, I'm sorry for you then—talented as you are. It's a hard-knock occupation."

"How can you say that? You're a celebrity by all accounts. I haven't read your novels yet, but I sure have heard of 'em."

"I get a lot of attention, no question. But if you stay in this godforsaken business, you'll see that you only ever really believe the bad things they say."

"Because they speak to your own fears." Hemingway jabbed Scott's chest. "Yet you've continued to write and to face down the devils, to surmount your fear. To my mind, that makes you strong and heroic and true."

"Waiter!" Scott called while pointing at Hemingway. "Put this fellow's drinks on my tab."

Scott asked Hemingway where he was from, and when Hemingway told him Chicago and Michigan, they went about extolling the virtues of a Midwestern upbringing. Scott's enthusiasms were all about growing up in a city like St. Paul, with its modest museums, libraries, concerts, plays; whereas Hemingway went into detail about the settings we'd seen in his stories—the rivers and forests where, he said, he'd spent as much time as he could steal from his overbearing family. "Nature tests you, and if it finds you worthy, it lets you live another day."

The discussion went on into details about game and gear and survival techniques. Hemingway was enthusiastic and knowledgeable about his subjects, there was no doubt about that. And he had personality aplenty. He wowed you such that you could easily miss what, to me at least, was apparent in his writing: he was trying awfully hard to be a man's man. Still, he seemed likable enough, and sufficiently interesting and different that Scott, with his boundless curiosity, was captivated.

I left them talking and went to find Pound, who'd gone over to the bar. "Dance with me, won't you?"

He laughed. "There's no band."

"I'll hum in your ear. Do you like a waltz—or maybe you're game for a tango?"

"You hum, I'll follow," he said jovially.

"I'll hum, but if you want to hang on to your masculine reputation in this town, you'd better lead."

Scott and I walked through Montparnasse later, on our way to Les Folies Bobino to hear Georges Guibourg sing. This district was the pulsating center of Parisian life, with all its messy, joyous, tragic, fearful, heartening, disheartening ways. We edged along sidewalk cafés still crowded with men arguing or laughing or singing songs from their homelands. We passed fragrant flower and tobacco carts being packed up for the night, beggars in rags—fragrant in a less pleasant way, so we gave them a wide berth despite our sympathy.

A pair of sooty little boys in short pants ran up to us with their palms out. These boys tugged at my heart; why weren't they home in bed? Did they have homes? Did they have childhoods? They deserved more—upbringings like I'd had or Scott had, or even Hemingway's, with all its apparent masculine overemphasis. Anything but a life on the streets.

I put some coins in their hands while telling Scott, "That Hemingway just oozes manliness, doesn't he? All that talk about fishing and hunting and skinning what you catch—"

"He's an outdoorsman; that's what outdoorsmen do."

"Merci, madame! Merci, merci beaucoup, belle dame!"

"De rien. Rentrer à la maison, aller au lit!" I told the boys. Scott and I walked on and I said, "I know . . . but I grew up with fellas who did all those things, and they didn't sit around and *talk* about it all day, give it all that romantic minutiae the way Wem or Hem or whatever he goes by was doing back there. I mean, really, he's a *writer* who lives in *Paris,* that's what he is, just like all the rest of them, just like you."

"I've never been fishing, did you know that? I didn't want to tell him—"

"You'd hate fishing. You have to sit cramped up in a little boat, or on some log or rock for *hours.* And fish smell bad—and then of course there's the bait. . . ."

"Sounds to me like *you* hate fishing. I think he's right—there's something honorable and true about pitting yourself against nature."

"Did he mention a wife while I was dancing with Pound?"

"Watch out for him," Scott said.

"Who, Hemingway?"

"Pound."

I let go of Scott's hand to turn a few pirouettes. "He's got his hands full as it is. Besides which, I'm not so good at sharing."

"Ernest's wife is called Hadley, she's from St. Louis. And they have a boy who's about eighteen months. Remember Scottie at that age? All that roundness? What did Ring and Ellis call her—I can't remember. Not Pumpkin . . ."

"Little Miss Dimple." I stopped turning and fell into step with him again.

"What? No. I don't recall that."

"I'm surprised you recall anything from Great Neck. I'm surprised *I* do. What I want to know is, what woman thought it'd be a good idea to throw her lot in with *Wem*."

"You know, don't you, that there are people who wonder the same thing about you after they've met or heard about me."

"Maybe," I said, linking my arm through his. "But the difference is that you don't have a false bone in your body."

"You think he does?"

"Anybody who uses the word *true* as much as he does can only be the opposite."

Scott shook his head. "You're wrong. He's too young, too sincere, for it to be an act. He's the real thing; just give him a chance, Zelda, and you'll see."

Scott was especially vigorous in bed that night, and then afterward he said, "If you don't get pregnant by summer, we should find a specialist to check you over. There might be some treatment or procedure—"

"We have to give it some time, Deo. It hasn't even been six months since my surgery."

"Those wop doctors, I doubt they had any real idea what they were talking about. You should see someone *here;* the French are far more advanced in medicine than the Italians."

He plumped his pillow and turned onto his side, throwing one arm over my hip while closing his eyes. "I'll see about getting you an appointment with someone who's tops in the field. I'd really like to have a son."

31

As we'd soon learn, Gertrude Stein, an American expat whose salon rivaled Natalie's, lived by her own rules. You never got the sense of her having been young; she seemed to have been planted at 27 rue de Fleurus as a middle-aged woman fully conceived in both physical form and reputation. Everyone knew Miss Stein, everyone admired her—and no one more than Ernest Hemingway, at least at the time.

"You just *want* to be around her," Hemingway told us during dinner at his apartment on a Saturday evening in late May.

This was the first time we'd met Hemingway's wife, Hadley. When she'd opened the apartment door, her appearance had shocked me nearly as much as the building's horrible, stinking stairway had. I'd imagined someone pert and sweet like Sara Mayfield back home, or else one of those simmering, sultry types, like Tallu. Hadley was neither of those, nor any other type you might think would win herself a handsome, energetic he-man.

She was, in fact, just about homely. Her hair was dark and of no particular style—though I suspected it had at some time in the past been bobbed like mine. She wore a gray shirtwaist with a long, darker gray wool skirt and an apron over the top, and shoes similar to those I'd seen on peasant women plodding along the cobblestone alleyways with big cloth bundles on their backs. Her features were round and boyish—but her smile was genuine, and her eyes were warm; I liked her right away.

Hadley was saying about Gertrude Stein, "We've named her as Bumby's godmother. She's been lovely to Tatie, here. Very encouraging with her critiques."

"You let her read your work?" Scott said with surprise. My surprise was in hearing Hadley call Hemingway *Tatie*. Sure, I had my nickname for Scott, which anyone hearing might find somewhat odd—and that's why I didn't use it around company. *Tatie,* I thought. *Weird.*

We passed around simple china bowls filled with potatoes, peas, slices of beef roast in gravy, and Hemingway said, "Sure I let her read it. There's no better eye than Gertrude's, no better mind."

Scott looked dubious. "She's, what, a fifty-year-old never-married woman, right, and a Jew to boot? Hardly seems like someone who'd be authoritative about modern writing. But I guess I'll take your word for it."

"It's true," Hadley said. "She's been hosting a salon for artists and intel-lectuals every Saturday since, well, forever. It's held in her home, which is a veritable art gallery. You should see it."

"I'm surprised you haven't already been," Hemingway said. "So, good—we'll bring you around tonight. I'm sure she'd want me to, and no time like the present, eh, Fitzgerald?"

"I'm game for anything."

"So I hear, so I hear. How about boxing?" he said, and I made a serious effort not to roll my eyes. "Ever take a turn in the ring?"

Gertrude Stein was what you might call amply proportioned. Her skin was smooth, her features unexceptional save for her eyes, which had the clarity, humor, and wisdom I'd seen in old Aunt Julia's ancient mother, Mama Clio, who I'd known when I was a little girl. Mama Clio was half-Haitian, half-African, and had the pruniest skin I've ever seen; she must have been near a hundred years old when she passed. She knew *everything* about life and the world; it was all there in her eyes, and she could tell you all about it. Gertrude Stein had those same eyes.

"I've been hearing a great deal about you," she told Scott after Hemingway presented us to her in her anteroom. "Our friend Sherwood Anderson found your book very satisfying and sent it to me to read, and I've found much about it worth reading."

Scott smiled—not the polite, secretly condescending smile I'd seen him give to other writers who saw themselves as superior to him, but a genuinely pleased grin. He said, "That's very good to hear."

We followed her into the whitewashed, high-ceilinged main room. Unframed paintings filled every wall; I recognized Pablo's serene, lovely *Head of a Sleeping Woman,* which Sara Murphy had praised, and his striking portrait of our hostess, which hung at the head of a long table in the corner to our right. Small statuary done in marble and plaster and carved wood sat on sideboards and side tables throughout the room.

"Sit there," she directed Scott, pointing to an armchair near the hearth. "Hemingway, pull up a chair for yourself as well, and ladies, Alice will get some tea."

This Alice, who I guessed we were supposed to either know about already or not pay attention to at all, was looming silently nearby.

She said, "Come."

I didn't imagine that we "ladies" wouldn't also gather at the hearth, but Alice led us past it into a distant corner of the room. Nice as the corner was—plush wool rug, upholstered settee and chairs, lovely spindle-legged side tables with hand-painted Chinese lamps—it wasn't central, and I was used to being in the middle of things.

Alice left us, saying, "Please, make yourselves comfortable. I'll just be a minute."

I must have let my irritation show, because Hadley whispered, "I should have warned you. The wives sit over here."

"And you don't mind that?"

She shrugged. "I'm not a writer, or an artist either. I wouldn't have much to contribute."

I was both—which neither Scott nor I seemed capable of pointing out, here in the revered Miss Stein's apartment. And so I said, "Is Alice her sister?"

"Her . . . companion," Hadley said in a low voice.

"Oh." I looked over at Miss Stein, trying to see her as the object of anyone's desire, let alone another woman's.

My stomach chose that moment to cramp, and I became far more concerned about those implications than about Miss Stein's romantic life or whether I was worthy of an audience with her. Rather than tell Hadley about my stomach trouble and have her think her cooking was to blame, I stood up and said, "Well then, I hope you'll excuse me. Not that it hasn't been grand to visit with you, but there are other things that need my attention."

I stopped beside Scott and said, "Miss Stein, it was purely a delight to meet you. I'm afraid I've promised myself elsewhere."

Scott looked up at me with surprise and concern while Hemingway joked, "She's got a date with Pound."

"Dancing on a Saturday night—why not?" Then I leaned down and said in Scott's ear, "It's my stomach. Stay as long as you like." I hurried off, calling, "Good night, all," and barely made it back home in time to save myself an awful embarrassment.

32

A typical day that Paris summer would go something like this: I'd paint in the morning while Scottie had her lessons and Scott was still asleep—at this time I was using watercolors and gouaches on paper, which was simplest given the limited space in our apartment. I might have lunch with Scottie or I might meet up at Deux Magots with one of the women I'd met at Natalie Barney's salon, which I preferred over an evening at Miss Stein's. I'd paid my first visit when Scott and Hemingway went off to Lyon to retrieve our car, damaged during transit from Marseille. "He'll be good company," Scott had said, packing a bag with more clothes and books than he could possibly need. "And I think he could use my counsel."

The luncheons sometimes turned into afternoon outings to a studio or gallery; *sponge-time,* I called those outings, wherein I soaked up everything I saw and was told about Impressionism, Realism, Rayonism, Post-Impressionism, Cubism, Modernism, Pointillism, Synthetism, Art Nouveau—and more. You couldn't take a step in that district, Saint-Germain-des-Prés, without bumping into *art.* In addition to the galleries, along the riverfront on Quai Malaquai and Quai de Conti were artists and easels and, truth be told, a whole lot of really bad paintings.

Scott usually got up around eleven and then, with or without me, went out to the cafés in search of other writers who, like him, were doing a fine job of conversing about other people's writing while producing very little work themselves. He'd finalized his choices for the new story collection, which would be published the following February as *All the Sad Young Men,* and talked a great deal about his unwritten next novel, as if by discussing it he would conjure a finished manuscript into being. There'd be wine at lunch—which lasted well into the afternoon—and then came late-afternoon cocktails before he'd return to the apartment to change clothes for the evening's events. Throughout it all he exuded the same sort of pleasant buzz he must have been feeling.

Scott's idea of an evening well spent began with a stroll among the horse-chestnut trees that line the Champs-Élysées, then cocktails at the Ritz, after which we'd often head into the Latin Quarter to meet up with the Hemingways at one or another of the *bal-musettes* for dinner, dancing, and drinks.

These had the potential of being good times, and to be fair, I enjoyed myself when the music began and I could set aside every thought and let the sounds infuse me from scalp to toes. A roomful of dancing, sweating, laughing people is a beautiful thing. Scott would dance with me some; more often he and Hemingway would drop out and I'd find them later at a table outside, debating not the finer points of sentence structure or the state of literary theory, but the merits or failings of various boxers whose matches they intended to see, or the intimate lives of their writer friends.

We would migrate from one place to another, getting progressively tighter and collecting friends as we went, and the party might go on until sunrise, at which time Scott would realize we'd lost the Hemingways hours earlier, Ernest having the self-discipline to leave early and get up, clear-headed, to write the next day. At home, Scott would want sex—except that sometimes his brain was more willing than his body, and nothing I tried made a difference. He'd push me away then, saying, "Never mind," and we'd both just sleep it off.

I learned that if I consented to his outings regularly enough, on other nights I could go do what I preferred. On "my" nights, I would join the Murphys, or sometimes just Sara, or sometimes no one, for a performance of the Ballets Russes or a production at La Cigale theater. Here, amid the swelling orchestral music, the grace and beauty of the dancers, was the life of my childhood imagination.

As much as I loved the spectacle of the dance and the drama, I also loved being able to see the sets afterward, to meet the artists Gerald spoke of with admiration and high regard. In particular, Gerald introduced me to Mikhail Larionov, whose designs for the Ballets Russes that season were astonishing. Larionov fractured color into kaleidoscopic scenes that had sophistication and whimsy, both. You didn't just view his wild sets and costumes; you *felt* them, responded to them. Or I did, anyway.

At the first of what would be many post-show coffee dates, the Murphys, Larionov, and I ran into Sara's friend Pauline Pfeiffer and two of Pauline's friends from *Vogue* at Deux Magots.

"So good to see you again, Zelda," Pauline said. As usual, she wore an up-to-the-minute dress, in this case a gorgeous peony-and-birds print with gold metallic lace sleeves. "Didn't we have great fun last summer in Antibes?" she went on. "Sara, do say we can all come to Villa America this year—I'm dying to see it done, and Zelda's so good at that game we played."

"We have grand plans to see everyone," Sara assured her. "Have you met Mikhail Larionov, artiste extraordinaire? He's promised to share all his brilliant secrets with us. Join us, why don't you?"

"You're sweet," Pauline said while holding her hand out to Larionov. "Pauline Pfeiffer, *not* an artist. And thank you, Sara, but no. We're on our way to the Dingo to meet some fellows." She made a show, then, of kissing Gerald, then Sara, then me in the way the French do, before wagging her fingers and following her friends out.

I took Larionov's arm and said, "Never mind those show-plates; let's get a table, and then you need to tell me *everything*."

His enthusiasm for his work was boundless. After two hours of conversation, he said, "I have much to add, but I must be on my way. Please seek me out anytime you come to a show."

And so I did.

"Tell me how an artist makes a name for himself," I urged him during our next meeting, just the two of us this time. "I want to know so I don't end up like the proverbial grasshopper."

He looked at me quizzically, and I explained, "Caught unprepared when winter comes."

"Of what winter is it you speak?"

"I don't know. I can't describe it. It's just a feeling I have—that anything can happen and I need to be prepared."

He smiled generously. "A woman of your beauty will never find herself alone. I think you will always be warm when winter comes."

"Thank you," I said. "Just the same: How did you come to work with the Ballets Russes? When Diaghilev says he's got a new ballet to stage, how do you begin forming your vision? Do you need to see the dancers in rehearsal, or just hear the music, or . . ."

We met weekly, then, and I wasn't exactly deceiving Scott when I neglected to mention these platonic post-performance dates. He was always out when I got home, and by the time he was awake and sober the next day, his mind was occupied with the future, so why volunteer the information and give him the opportunity to overreact? My silence was a protection from distraction, that's how I thought of it.

All was well until one night in June, when we attended a small party to celebrate Cole's thirty-fourth birthday. The party was being held in one of the Ritz's opulent private salons. Before we went in, though, Scott wanted to pay a visit to the Ritz bar, where he had quickly become a favored patron.

As always, we were greeted warmly by the maître d' and the staff of liveried waiters and the bartender, whose regard was maybe one grin shy of obsequious. Here at the Ritz, Scott was *le suprême Américain,* the role he'd been born to play.

"Champagne, my good fellow," he told our waiter. We were dressed in our finery, Scott in a tuxedo with a bow tie, me in sleeveless teal silk and fringe.

"Monsieur has an occasion?"

"That's what I want to know," I said. "It's *Cole's* birthday, darling. Are we going to practice our toasts?"

Scott said, "Au contraire; we're celebrating." He sent the waiter off, then placed a square velvet box in the center of the table. "I have *this,* to go with *this*," he said, then took a folded bit of newspaper from his jacket pocket and laid it out on the table beside the box.

The newspaper clipping's headline read, *"Our Own Movie Queen" by F. Scott Fitzgerald,* and was followed by the story, *my* story, the one I'd written back in Great Neck.

"What's the matter?" Scott said when I didn't speak or react. "I know it took forever, but I thought you'd be ecstatic."

"I . . . it's great," I said, my eyes scanning the words that I'd labored over. My Gracie Axelrod was now as alive as she'd ever become, here in the *Chicago Sunday Tribune.* Right below Scott's name.

"It's real exciting," I added, forcing cheer into my voice.

"It is!" He pushed the box over to me. "Open it."

I did; inside was a black-enameled, diamond-bejeweled film-reel brooch made of gold, about a half inch in size. "I had it custom-made," Scott said, beaming.

Had I accepted the gift with grace and gratitude, the night might have ended better. Neither of those feelings came to me, though. My mind was warring with my heart over the disappointment I felt as I looked, again, at Scott's name beside my story's title.

This was my own doing. I'd agreed to let Harold sell the story as Scott's, never guessing the result would depress me so. We'd gotten a thousand dollars, but where had that thousand dollars gone? What did I have to show for it—except this brooch that, pretty and thoughtful as it was, announced nothing of my talent, my imagination, my skill.

"I don't want it," I said. "It's lovely, but you haven't sold anything since winter. We can't afford this sort of thing right now."

Scott's eyes narrowed the littlest bit, a flinch, really, and he glanced around to see whether I'd been overheard.

"That's *my* concern, darling," he said heartily, and now his voice had the false cheer. His eyes were wary, as if he was dealing with an impostor; *his* wife *loved* gifts, and had always before been thrilled with publication.

Heeding the warning, I said, "Yes, of course it is. Thank you." I closed the box and tucked it into my handbag, then picked up my glass and downed the contents fast. I called out, "Garçon," and signaled the waiter with my glass. "Bring us a bottle."

Cole was at the piano when we joined the party. The room was afire with gilt and crystal, awash with gleaming silver and white tablecloths, abuzz with music, sequins, beads, feathers. Cole was in the middle of a jazzy tune we hadn't heard before:

> *No one knows what a glimpse of paradise*
> *Someone who's naughty showed to someone who's nice . . .*

Linda, elegant in a powder-blue sequined suit, greeted us near the piano and said, "He's test-driving this one—"

"If you hate it, don't tell me," Cole said as he continued to play. "At my advanced age, I can't handle disappointment."

He sang, " 'I'm in love again . . .' "

Scott said, "Does it make you think of Jozan, darling?" which alarmed me until he continued, "Linda, did Zelda ever tell you about the man who fell in love with her last year on the Riviera? Poor fellow took his own life when she rejected him for me."

"My God!" Linda said. "How awfully sad."

Jozan had not done any such thing, but I played along, affecting a bored look. "Yes, but what can you do? Men are so irrational about love."

It seemed that Scott had decided to overlook my out-of-character reaction from earlier, so I tried to let myself relax and enjoy the party. Drinking, mingling, dancing: it was a routine so familiar to me that I ought to be able to do it automatically. I found, though, that this time the best I could do was listen politely while carrying a drink with me as a prop; the champagne and events of earlier had soured my stomach and my mood.

That mood lifted some when Mikhail Larionov saw me and came to say hello. He hugged me with all the warmth of an old friend. "Your art, how does it progress?" he said.

"Like a snail over boulders," I told him, aware that Scott had come up beside me. Scott held a highball glass half-full of what looked like bourbon, and I just knew he was sniffing Larionov for trouble.

I went on, "Paris is too full of distractions for me to get much done. Mikhail Larionov, meet my husband, Scott Fitzgerald."

"What line are you in?" Scott said, keeping his free hand in his pocket— and another warning bell rang in my head. "Do you write? Paint? Fly for the navy?"

A string trio had taken over for Cole, and he and Linda were hamming things up on the dance floor with an exaggerated waltz. They were an ideal pair, always affectionate, supportive, funny, sweet. *Why*, I thought, *can't that be us?*

Larionov said, "I paint and sculpt, and do the stage sets and costumes for the Ballets Russes." He nodded toward Diaghilev, who was waltzing with Sara.

"How good of you, then, to take Zelda's little pastime seriously."

Larionov raised an eyebrow. "Her mind is the artist's," he said. "And while I've not yet seen her work, I have quite enjoyed our conversations after the shows."

"Oh, have you?" It was Scott's brow that rose now, along with his pitch and volume. "And where have we been going for these delightful tête-à-têtes?" I started to answer but Scott went on, "Paris is such a marvelous city, so romantic, don't you think? An ideal setting for intimate talks, walks along the Seine, conferences in quaint little hotel lobbies—or apartments— where doormen keep the riffraff out."

"Isn't that all true?" I said oh so brightly, and put my arms around Scott. His body was as rigid as his voice, but I persisted, "And so well put, darling. Of course Mikhail is a huge fan of yours, I've told him everything abou—"

Scott unwound my arms and set me apart from him, saying, "How do you suppose it looks, you out there alone, carrying on with men who aren't your husband?"

My face grew hot. "There's no carrying on, just a few of us having a coffee before going our separate ways."

The song had ended and Sara came over, saying, "What's this? You two aren't quarreling?"

Scott said, "Coffee, sure. I'll guess that's *his* story, too." He looked on the verge of tears. "And yours, Sara—you've all rehearsed this, haven't you?"

"What is he on about?" Sara asked me, while Larionov was telling Scott, "It is nothing, all innocent—"

Now Gerald had joined us; I could hear him murmuring apologies to Larionov while Scott said, "You've got no business out running around Paris at all hours. I won't have it, Zelda." The music had stopped and his voice was now the loudest sound in the room.

"You're hardly in a spot to complain," Gerald said impatiently. "When are you ever home?"

Scott looked shocked. Gerald had never spoken harshly to him before. "I am the husband!" Scott yelled, poking his own chest and stumbling backward a step.

Everyone in the room was watching him, watching *us*. My face and neck and ears were so hot I thought they'd catch flame.

Abruptly, Scott sat down on the gold-and-black-patterned carpet, just plopped down like a child worn out from a tantrum. In a voice that was almost a whimper, he said, "*I* am the husband," and started to cry.

The next day, he seemed to have blanked out everything except his suspicion. His first words when he joined Scottie and me at the table were "You can forget going out without me."

"Says you," I told him, not caring that both the cook and the nanny were in the room. I'd used up all my tolerance the night before, barely keeping my head high while Gerald and two other men practically carried Scott out to a cab. "I'm not giving up my interests just because you drink too much and have irrational jealous fits. Come along, if you don't like me going by myself."

"You know I can't stand the ballet."

"Well, I love it, so I'm going."

"Then you'll come straight home after," Scott said.

Scottie popped strawberries into her mouth and watched us volley as she chewed.

I said, "When did you decide to become my father?"

"If your father had kept a tighter rein on you, I wouldn't have to worry about your behavior."

"Who says you need to worry in the first place?"

"You seem to be forgetting our friend Édouard Jozan."

What defense did I have against that? Game, set, match.

But Scott went on, "They all want you, Zelda. Every man out there. What happens when you've had a few drinks and then some man tries to—"

"You think that doesn't happen when you're right there? It does. And I handle it, same as I've always done. You don't need to act like some crazy, overprotective ogre." I raised my arms and curled my hands in an ogre imitation, and Scottie giggled.

"I don't *want* to be an ogre," Scott said. "But what can I do? I love you beyond reason, I can't help myself."

Scottie tugged his sleeve. "Daddy, *you* do an ogre. Be a growly one," she added, climbing out of her chair. "And I'll be the princess in the forest and you *chase* me!"

"Really, can you blame me, Zelda?" Scott said, and then he went running after Scottie.

I let it go at that. It wasn't wise to let him excuse his bad behavior with apologies and declarations of best intentions and helpless love. I knew that every time he got away with it, there was an increasing chance he'd behave badly again. I knew it, and yet I went along, as helpless to resist a bad choice as he was.

33

The next time I went to the ballet, Scott and I didn't rehash the argument; we just made plans for me to meet *him* afterward. So when the performance was over, I left Sara and took a cab to the Dingo, where Scott was supposed to be playing cards.

The night was warm, the air scented with roasting chestnuts, and my head was aswim with the sights and sounds of *Flore et Zéphire*. The cab let me off at the corner of rue Delambre; I leaned into the window to pay, and then when I stepped away from the car, there was Hemingway walking in my direction, toward the boulevard du Montparnasse.

"The incomparable Zelda Fitzgerald," he said, embracing me and then kissing both my cheeks. He smelled of soap and sweat and whiskey. "Fine night, isn't it?"

"I'll guess it has been for you. You seem jolly."

"Yes, now that your husband has graciously lent me a hundred so that I can make a trip to Pamplona to see the bulls. We went a couple of rounds in there," he said, raising his fists while he inclined his head toward the bar. "I almost let him win."

"So he's here, then. Good." I wondered how badly bruised Scott was going to be. *What is it with men*, I thought, *that the ones who don't instigate these stupid contests can't seem to resist a challenge?*

"He's a real sport, your husband. Gifted. Lucky. Soused, I should add. He's right now holding court on the bar—note that I say *on* and not *at* or even *in*."

"My English teachers always did stress the importance of prepositions."

I imagined Scott seated *on* the bar, legs dangling, a coterie of the also-soused grouped around him on barstools. "Where's Hadley tonight? Be sure to tell her hello for me."

"Insecure, though, isn't he?" Hemingway went on, as if I hadn't spoken. He put his hand out against the wall and leaned on it, blocking my path forward. "Obsessive. Can't stop worrying about *Gatsby*'s sales and make progress on a new book. A writer's life is a difficult one. He should accept this and embrace it fully. No greatness is possible without failure and sacrifice."

"We've sacrificed plenty for the writer's life he's living—sleep, mostly," I joked.

Hemingway put his free hand on my shoulder, then slid it down my arm to my wrist, which he gripped tightly. "All the men want you, you know."

"And *speaking* of sleep," I said, trying not to let my annoyance show, "seems like you could use some."

"But you're discriminating. You think most men are fools, I've seen it in your eyes. I know you're devoted to Scott and I admire that and it raises you up above many women. No one would say he's manly, though, and I see your passionate nature and wonder if you've ever been truly satisfied."

He'd been drinking, which excused his behavior somewhat—and certainly I was accustomed to excusing the poor behavior of inebriated men. This man, though, had crossed a line no one had crossed with me before. There were no *best intentions* here.

How could he disregard his wife like this, not to mention his supposedly great new friend who also happened to be my husband? What made him think he could approach me this way? I'd certainly never encouraged him—but then, he didn't need encouragement. I stood there for a moment, looking into his eyes. A glint of humor told me this wasn't the first time he'd behaved this way with someone else's wife, which only made me angrier.

"Is this what you do? You can't box with women, so you try and seduce 'em?"

"I *am* a man." He maneuvered us so that my back was pressed against a door and he pressed against me. His interest in me, or at least in sex, was plain. He put his palms on the wall, bracketing me between his arms. "It's man's nature to prove himself, to take what he desires."

Bad enough that he'd spoiled what had been a gorgeous night of music, dance, and art; I was not about to become one of his conquests. Thinking my anger would only amuse him, I decided to turn the tables on him instead. I reached between us and put my hand on his erection through his pants. I rubbed the length of it, taking my time, letting him think he might yet take advantage of *both* Fitzgeralds tonight.

"Not bad," I said, my mouth real close to his ear, and he chuckled. "But," I added as I ducked beneath his arm and slid out, "here's yet another area where Scott's got you beat." Laughing, I hurried away toward the Dingo's door, sure that I'd gotten the better of him.

"Bitch," he said with such calm assurance that the hair on my neck stood up, and I knew right then I'd made a mistake. "Go on. Go make sure you tell your half-impotent hero what a cocktease he's married to. I can't wait to hear how he takes it."

I'd underestimated how astute Hemingway was, how much he already knew about us: He had seen into Scott's soft heart and knew what hapless prey he'd be if he should decide to attack. And he knew that I wouldn't tell Scott what had just gone on between us, that I would want to avoid provoking another bout of jealous misapprehension. Whether Scott had told him about Cole's party or not, he knew.

I continued on to the Dingo without looking back, without replying. My step never faltered but my stomach lurched, as if it understood better than I did just how awfully stupid I'd been, and what it was going to cost me.

34

====

"I'm eager to see Villa America done," Scott said as we cruised along the coast road en route to Antibes. "It's a damn shame my father didn't make something of himself the way Gerald's old man did, and Sara's; imagine having a place like they've built here—and two fantastic Paris apartments. All because old man Murphy knew that belts and shoes were at least as lucrative as saddles and such, and Sara's father—what's his name? Wiborg?— liked mixing chemicals. Do you know he was a millionaire before forty?"

This early-August trip was the first time in ages that Scott and I had been absolutely alone together. The daylong trek to southern France gave me a chance to really *look* at my husband, study him, assess him—and what I saw worried me. He'd grown soft in the face and neck and middle, blurring him, you could say. His hands were stained yellow-brown with nicotine, his hair was losing its luster; he looked ten years older than the almost twenty-nine he was.

I'd marked my twenty-fifth birthday a week before the trip. Twenty-five not being a milestone, I hadn't expected anything—though I couldn't help recollecting, as I did on every birthday, the party Scott had devised for my eighteenth. He sure had obsessed over me in those days; now he was obsessing over Ernest Hemingway.

—*"I'm meeting Ernest for lunch."*

—*"Ernest and I are going to the fights."*

—*"Go ahead and go to bed without me; I told Ernest I'd read some of his stories before I see him tomorrow."*

—*"Gertrude wants Ernest and me to come 'round tonight."*

—*"Ernest thinks . . ."*

—*"Ernest says . . ."*

—*"Ernest wants . . ."*

Every time we saw Hemingway, he'd smile at me like we shared an evil secret, something worse than if I'd succumbed to his manly charms. My mind would urge, *Tell Scott!* but my gut said, *Wait—suppose he takes Hemingway's side?* Better to let it be.

For the first time in my life, I chose to avoid confrontations. I'd hidden out for most of June and July, and I told myself that I was doing it more because of my stomach trouble than because Hemingway intimidated me.

As we drove, Scott went on talking about Mark Cross leather goods and about the Wiborg's Ohio ink empire and about how wise we'd been to send Scottie and the nanny to Antibes by train.

"Ernest said he wished he could make his trip to Spain this way: just a man, a car, and a road."

"At what speed do you s'pose it's safe to jump?"

"What? Oh! I'm sorry, darling, I'm lost in my own head is all. Are you looking forward to the beach? Hasn't it been *forever* since last summer and Jozan? Gad—there's something absolutely mystical about how time behaves in Paris. Oh, speaking of Jozan: I told Ernest our tale about Jozan being tragically in love with you. This time, I said he couldn't bear the thought of your rejection, and killed himself in his plane by crashing it into the sea."

"What did Hemingway say?"

"That he could understand a man wanting to kill himself over you. It makes a grand tale, don't you think? I can see it as a stage play, or even better, a movie . . ."

What was it about Paris, what had *happened* to us, that our crisis of the summer before could now so easily be reimagined for entertainment, our renewed connection not put aside, exactly, but not tended to, either?

Scott would later record in his ledger that the year had been "1000 parties and no work"; that summarized it for sure, but it didn't explain a thing.

On the Riviera, my stomachaches were no more frequent than they'd been—which is to say, one every week or two—but they'd begun to hurt more. There we'd all be, us and the Murphys and Dottie Parker and Esther and Archie MacLeish and his wife, say (there were so many people there that month), strolling through Villa America's seven lush acres of terraced groves and gardens, or down at *la plage de la Garoupe* on what everyone called Gerald's Beach, and the cramping would sneak up on me and strike without warning. Within minutes I'd be hobbled by the pain or need to quickly use the toilet, and have to abandon the group. The walk back to the guesthouse took all of time and beyond, that's how it seemed.

Once there, I'd swallow one of the pills from after my surgery and stay shut away inside the bedroom, curled into a ball on the bed while I waited for the medicine's too-slow relief. Every time it happened, I'd tell myself, *It'll pass, it'll pass* . . . and it would, and then I would sleep for an hour or two and awake as fine-feeling as if nothing had ever hurt to begin with. A couple of times the drug didn't work at all, though, and then Scott would get a doctor in, an angel, a savior bearing a hypodermic bearing morphine.

I found that if I ate carefully and avoided drinking, I could minimize the symptoms. I didn't want to be involved with all the group's activities, but neither did I want to be "Fitz's sick wife," so I made every effort to at least be present for luncheons on the terrace, afternoons on the beach, evening cocktail hour in whichever scenic spot Gerald was inclined to hold it.

After dinner there were games of cards and charades and, once Cole and Linda joined us, long evenings spent playing our favorite game of the previous summer—except with Cole at the piano instead of me. Scott said he could sometimes see a pinched look in my eyes and around my mouth, and Sara said she'd know I was uncomfortable because I'd get stiller, and quiet. I was glad to know that they were paying attention and that they cared.

Care, of course, can materialize—or not materialize—in so many different ways. Scott and I hadn't made love since arriving in Antibes. We hadn't
made love since well before that, in fact, though I couldn't place quite when
the last time had been. Given how often I felt poorly, I should have viewed
Scott's not approaching me as a blessing; if he didn't ask, I didn't have to beg
off. What I felt, though, was rejected and undesirable. There was none of the
sweet affection that signaled his interest, none of those cues that married
couples develop—the flirtations, the significant gazes—to help me know
that he still wanted me whenever I did feel well.

I guess *pitiful and insecure* is what I was feeling when we went to dinner
one night in Saint-Paul-de-Vence, at a restaurant set right into the rocky
hillside overlooking the sea. It being August, the sun still graced the sky
well into the evening. It washed the stone orange, then rosy, then lavender,
while we sat on the outdoor patio eating fish and olives and drinking a
local wine Gerald was excited about.

"It's extraordinary," he said as the waiter filled our glasses. "Not at all
the table wine you find everywhere—and not that peasant stuff they like to
serve on the Left Bank, so thick you just about have to chew it. This will
transport you." And because he was Gerald and, being Gerald, never exu-
berant without good reason, I had not one, not two, but three glasses of
that wine before the sun had finished its descent, even knowing that I
would pay later.

At about the time I was draining that third glass, someone—who can
remember just who it was?—noticed, aloud, that the glamorous and beloved dancer Isadora Duncan, one of my own idols, was having dinner at a
table across the patio.

"What? Really?" Scott said, and then he was out of his seat and in seconds had either fallen or collapsed or thrown himself onto the ground at
her feet; I wasn't equipped at this point to comprehend the finer details.

Miss Duncan reached for him, petting his face and smoothing his hair
while he beamed up at her. "How lovely and golden you are, my faithful
centurion!"

"My life is but to serve you," Scott said.

What the hell? I thought. She was mine. He was mine. I got up out of my chair and, seeing that the shortest path to the steps that led down the hill away from the patio was across our table, I got up onto my chair, walked across the table, stepped onto the stone wall, and jumped into the stairwell.

If only the steps had been a fountain, like the one in Union Square—but no. No, they were old, solid stone, and my high heels were not so good for making an upright landing. Next thing I knew, I was on my throbbing hands and knees and Sara was there with her arm around me, helping me to my feet. Blood trickled down my shins, and I remember being glad I hadn't worn stockings.

"I purely hate it when he does shit like that," I said.

I remember, too, that Scott was far less distressed by my actions than the Murphys and MacLeishes were. In fact I think he appreciated the display—which might well be why I made it.

We were near to the end of our stay when, late one night after everyone was asleep, sharp pain woke me from a dream in which I'd been arguing with Alice's Mad Hatter about whether cloche hats were still in style. (*Feathers!* he'd kept shouting. *Brims!*) I was disoriented for a moment, then got my bearings and tried to relieve my discomfort by rolling onto my side. When that didn't work, I got up and headed to the bathroom.

The guesthouse was a sort of loose U of a building curled around a courtyard. To get to the bathroom, you went outside along a breezeway, to a door beside the kitchen. I'd hardly gotten there when the pain sharpened, making my knees buckle. It was as if someone had cut into me with a wide butcher knife and was digging around my belly with it, just cutting and twisting. . . . I thought I was going to die, wished, almost, that I would. I couldn't move, couldn't speak, could hardly breathe without the knife twisting more.

When one pill didn't seem to be helping, I took a second and waited, doubled over, breathing, breathing, waiting, breathing . . . "Please, God" was my refrain this time, and when it seemed as if forever had passed and *still* no relief, I took more pills, desperate for the damned things to do their merciful job. Just a little letup, and then I'd go wake Scott and have him get a doctor.

Later, Scott told me he'd awakened and wondered where I'd gone. When I didn't come back, he went looking and discovered me on the bathroom floor, slumped against the wall. He ran for help. Gerald and Sara sent one of their groundskeepers for a doctor, then the three of them got me up and walked me around for hours, they said. Meanwhile the sun was rising and the birds were racing from branch to branch throughout the garden.

The doctor wouldn't show up until almost noon, having been dispatched to deliver a baby in nearby Le Ponteil, so around the gardens we went. Only when I could respond coherently to their questions did they allow me to lie down and sleep off the remaining effects. I remember nothing about any of that; only the all-encompassing blankness, an ethereal kind of joy that, *Thank you, God,* the pain had diminished, dissolved, and nothing would ever harm me again.

35

Feb. 5th, 1926

My dearest Second Sara,

    That you're in Paris to study at the Sorbonne cheers me immensely, though I am so sorry that John couldn't be a better husband to you. Divorce is awful hard, I'm sure.

    Your letter found me in the Pyrenees, where we've come to the town of Salies-de-Béarn so that I can take the cure for what my doctor says is colitis. Daily baths in the hot salt springs will remedy everything, I gather, except the fact that my being here means I can't see you until we return to Paris in March!

    We're at the Hotel Bellevue, with only five other guests in the entire place. Colitis must be woefully out of style—why didn't anyone tell me? The village is a lovely, quiet, restful place, which of course means Scott hates it. What he really hates is that he can't be right in the thick of things with that fella Hemingway I told you about. He's made bringing Hemingway to Max Perkins at Scribner his holy mission. I've washed my hands of it; Hemingway wrote a nasty little "satire" of our good friend Sherwood Anderson's book (his own first mentor, I should add!) and insists that whichever publisher wins him for the "highly serious novel" he's writing about bullshit—I mean bullfighting—must also agree to publish this other book, Torrents of Spring.

Even his wife thinks he's doing wrong. He's a perfect bully but Scott won't see it. Not only won't see it, but thinks I'm jealous of the attention he's giving his best good friend. Incidentally, Scott was against the book at first, but Hemingway pushed and Scott toppled. You'd never know Scott was the older of the two of them.

Do you think the salts will cure me of both colonic and pessimistic irritation?

Some good news: The Great Gatsby is now playing on Broadway. Reviews are solid and there's a movie deal in the works, so Scott is on top of the world again.

We've left Scottie with her nanny—do go see her, she's a four-year-old butterball and after almost a year here speaks French admirablement; we can take lessons from her.

What a gift it is to have you so nearby. —See? The salts are working already!

With all my heart—

Z-

While I rested and bathed and painted and read and corresponded there at the Bellevue, Scott was busy trading letters with all manner of people. He tracked Hemingway's trip to New York to visit publishers and cheered when he read Max's letter and then Hemingway's, announcing the new addition to Scott's Scribner's Writers' Club. None of them called it that, you understand, but I had come to think of it that way. Scott considered himself a hero for making the match—even knowing that both he and Hemingway had lost Sherwood's friendship and were on the outs with Gertrude Stein, who thought *Torrents* deplorable.

On our return to Paris, Scott told anyone who would listen, "His novel's the real deal. I've had a look at some of the early pages and it's great stuff. My publisher—Scribner's—gave him fifteen hundred dollars up front." And as if this weren't enough, he'd add, "I'm predicting *The Sun Also Rises* will go fifty thousand copies"—the same number of copies that each of Scott's first two novels had eventually sold. I watched Scott extol Hemingway and understood something that explained everything and terrified me: Hemingway had become Scott's alter ego.

At noon one day in March, Sara Mayfield and I met at Rotonde. "I understand what you mean about that character Hemingway," she said, her wide blue eyes full of intensity and purpose.

"Tell me."

"I was having lunch with a fellow student here a week ago, and there was a group behind us, a bunch of women all got up in belted dresses—like yours, but even fancier, in silk and such, you know? They all had the latest hats, the latest shoes, the careful, artful makeup. Anyway, I wasn't minding their business at all until I heard one of them say 'Zelda,' and then I listened close; how many Zeldas can there be around here, after all?"

"None that I know of."

"Right. So the woman says, 'Drum thinks *he's* decent—though he thought that one critic, Gilbert Seldes, was far too kind about his novel. But *she's* odd, I've seen it myself—Drum says she's *crazy,* maybe even dangerous, and he knows them well.' Then she says, and I quote, 'Drum believes she's a huge liability—he told Scott as much.' Of course the friends wanted to know what Scott said; she tells them, 'Oh, he agrees, but he's working to get her under control.'"

Drum. That could only be Hemingway. I asked Sara, "What did this supposed authority on my mental state and my marriage look like?" From her description of the group, I was sure I knew, but hoped I was wrong.

"You don't sound real surprised."

"Did you get a look at her?"

"No—I mean, I saw them all when they came in, but which one slandered you, I don't know."

"I think I do."

Later I repeated the story to Scott, who said, "I don't believe a word of it. Pauline might have said some version of that, but it didn't come from Ernest."

"So he never told you I'm a liability?"

Scott's gaze slid from mine. "He knows how much I love you, and how that distracts me sometimes."

"Because of how I'm always throwing myself at some fella or other, is that it?"

"No, of course not; but you are awfully sociable sometimes. You can't blame me for worrying, not after——"

"If you bring up Jozan again, I swear I'll pop you one."

Laughing, Scott wrapped me up in his arms, pinning my arms to my side. "Let me go."

"I can't, sorry. I'm working to get you under control."

Two days later, despite my insistence that I had no appetite and wanted to spend my day reading Theodore Dreiser's new *An American Tragedy*, Scott dragged me out to Deux Magots for lunch. I'd recently read Dreiser's first novel, *Sister Carrie*, having met him at some Hôtel du Cap soiree the summer before, and was interested in seeing what scandalous tale he'd written in the new book. There's nothing like losing yourself in someone else's troubles to make you forget your own.

Scott took the book from me, saying, "You read *Gatsby*, so you've already gotten the gist. Come on, I need to get out for a while."

Before we were seated, I saw Hemingway rising from his seat at a table on the far end of the room. On the other side of the table was Pauline Pfeiffer, wearing a red silk chiffon dress that, in my opinion, made her look like she was trying too hard to be what everyone had decided she was: chic and smart and independent.

Scott said, "Hey, there's Pauline and Ernest—he must be just back from New York." His surprise struck a false note, and I suddenly knew that our being here at the same time was no coincidence.

Hemingway began to turn from the table, and Pauline reached out and grabbed his hand. Reluctance was evident in every part of her body, if not in her attire. Hemingway chucked her under the chin and then left her there alone. I wanted to go slap her, wake her out of her selfishness and stupidity—and might have, if not for what Sara Mayfield had overheard.

"Scott, my friend, my champion," Hemingway boomed, crossing the room toward us. He was grinning. "I see you've got the little missus in tow. How are you, Zelda? Nerves under control now?"

"It was a stomach ailment."

"Anxiety will cause that. My father has nervous bouts, and good *God* you didn't want to use the bathroom—or be in the house!—when he was having one of his spells. Let's get a table, shall we?"

While I disassembled and then rearranged a veiny corned-beef sandwich, Scott encouraged Hemingway to recount his New York trip. Scott wanted every detail about which editors Hemingway had seen and how the staff had treated him and what Max had said and whether the Scribner's people had mentioned *him,* Scott, and how Hadley felt about the whole thing—he had to know it all. He said, "Hadley must be excited. It's a tremendous step forward for your career."

"She's pleased." Hemingway's voice was level. Then he smiled and said, "Pfife, though"—he inclined his head toward Pauline, who had remained at her table for a few minutes and was now making her way to the door—"she got *Torrents,* she saw the deal coming, she supported the whole thing. She's been just amazing." His eyes and voice lingered on her before he turned back to face us, saying, "And she's a great friend to Hadley, too."

"I'll guess you're thinking of Ford?" Scott asked. "Trying that out?"

He was referring to writer Ford Madox Ford, who we'd all heard was living like a polygamist with both his second wife, Stella, and a smart, thoughtful writer named Jean Rhys. *Variations on a theme,* that's all it was, that's what everyone was saying.

Monogamy was old-fashioned and unnecessary, and wasn't it better if these alternate relationships were conducted out in the open? Honesty and acceptance, that made all the difference; then there was no need for secrets, and everyone could get along happily. So the theory went—and it seemed that some people were succeeding at it, Ezra Pound included. The gossips said Pound's mistress, Olga, wanted no distractions during her time with him, and so after following him and his wife to Italy, she'd given over her newborn daughter to a woman in the village and Pound was paying the woman to raise the child. This wasn't "modern" to me, it was despicable; I'd liked Pound, and Olga, too, but now I wasn't sure which of them I hated more.

Maybe I was alone in finding all these things distasteful. Maybe Hadley would be as acquiescent as Stella was, and Dorothy Pound. Maybe she'd be fine with sharing her extra-manly man. I sure couldn't predict the outcome; any woman who was willing to take Hemingway in the first place was a mystery to me.

Hemingway said with a shrug, "All I know is it's going to be interesting in Antibes this year."

Scott leaned forward. "Did I tell you? We've got a place there, too, we're leaving next week. Great little villa in Juan-les-Pins, half a mile from Villa America."

I stared at Scott. As far as I knew, we were staying put in Paris just as we'd done the previous year and would visit the Murphys for a few weeks late in the summer. Hadn't Scott told me that he'd assured both Harold and Max that he was going to buckle down and finish his novel, now that we were back from Salies-de-Béarn? He'd even rented a garret for the summer, "Like Ernest's got," he'd said, and planned to go on the wagon until the book was done. Surely he wouldn't alter his plans—*our* plans—without consulting me, without *informing* me, even. He wasn't that kind of husband.

And yet.

"That's grand," Hemingway said, smiling at me. I, however, couldn't bring myself to speak.

Scott went on cheerfully, "So whenever you need another set of eyes on the manuscript, I'm your man. And of course you can count on our support with Pauline and all that."

"I hoped I could," Hemingway replied to Scott, but he was still watching me.

After Hemingway had gone, I said, "It was real thoughtful of you to check with your *wife* before you went and made plans."

"I intended it as a surprise. You've had such a difficult year; I thought a few months of sunshine and sea air would thrill you."

"Well, you sure surprised me all right. Funny the approach you used, though—seemed more like you were surprising your great good friend. And when did you get on the two-wives bandwagon, or is there somethin' else you've been meaning to tell me?"

My sarcasm was wearing on him. "Maybe you ought to make some friends of your own, then, if you're so jealous of mine."

I slapped the bread back onto my sandwich. "Cancel the villa; I want to stay here. I'm working on a painting, I've got Scottie signed up for ballet— you'll break her heart if you make her wait 'til fall."

"She can dance around Villa America with Honoria," he said. "What difference can it make to a five-year-old?"

"It makes a difference to me."

"It's always about you, isn't it? You don't like Ernest, you don't like Gertrude, you don't like Pound, you don't feel well—and I understand, I accommodate your feelings, I do everything I can to help. Now *I* need something, some time away from Paris. I've already paid for the place up front. We're going."

36

Shortly after our arrival on the Riviera, Scott and I got invited to a farewell party being given for Alexander Woollcott. To Scott, this was proof that the season was off to a good start. There was little joy for me, fixated as I was on Scott's ability to deceive me so smoothly and easily, and without the least bit of remorse. He looked relaxed, though, his skin now lightly tanned from spending a few afternoons at the beach. I had to admit that the time here was already doing him good.

The party took place in one of the Antibes casinos. Mr. Woollcott was a slight acquaintance of ours from when we'd lived in Manhattan and Great Neck. Like George Nathan, he was a theater critic. Unlike George, he was doughy and sexless, but pleasant and kind, with a rich sense of humor.

At such parties, the thing was to sit around at great big tables eating and drinking and taking turns making either sentimental or ribald speeches about the man of the hour. Since Mr. Woollcott was *not* George, the speeches at this party tended to be the sentimental sort. Only playwright Noël Coward had anything witty to say, and it was too brief and too early in the evening for his words to have much effect.

Scott had helped himself generously to the wine. I wasn't drinking at all and was growing restless and bored. On it went: *Alexander was charming, Alexander was wonderful, Alexander was witty and wise, Alexander would be missed*—nice speeches, really nice, but not captivating, and I needed to be captivated because my mind kept trying to drag me back to my outrage over having been made to come here when the life I was trying to lead was in Paris.

Working against that outrage, though, was my recollection of Mama's latest letter. She'd written,

> *Baby, I'm not sure what gives you the notion that your husband—or any woman's husband—is bound to consider his wife's wishes when making decisions such as this. It's so hard to understand the life you're leading so far away from home. . . . Have you become one of those awful feminists? By my measure, your life has become foreign in <u>every</u> way if you are somehow led to believe that women are due equal say. We are meant to keep a respectable home and care for our husbands and children, and in return for this effort, our husbands support us entirely. Is this not the case for women in France? Certainly women deserve time to pursue hobbies and such, and can find fulfillment in interests of their own, but we are not entitled to assert them over our husbands' priorities and wishes. Perhaps if you will accept this, your health will improve and subsequently so will your happiness.*

Part of me chafed against Mama's old-fashioned attitudes. These were modern times, and women were more than chattel. Part of me worried that she was right; maybe I *would* be happier if I accepted the traditional thinking, rejected this particular aspect of the modern woman's approach to marriage. It was so much easier to be led, to be pampered and powdered and petted for being an agreeable wife.

Easier, I thought, but boring. And not only boring, but plain wrong. Who really believed that men could be trusted to always get things right?

I stirred the ice in my water glass and watched the other women. They were bored, too, but doing their damnedest to hide it. All these men in their dapper suits, their slicked hair and waxed mustaches and tight collars—we women were all here trying to please these men, and for what? So that they could drag us to another boring, self-congratulatory event tomorrow, and the next day, and the next? We were with them for the support they provided.

Single women could work all they wanted; married women locked themselves into a gilded cage. All of that had seemed natural before. Now, it made me angry. Now, I saw how a woman might sometimes want to steer her own course rather than trail her husband like a favored dog.

With all the laudatory speeches done, all the Woollcott well-wishers began turning back to their companions and food and drink.

"Hold on," I said, seized by the need to take some kind of action, even if it was wrong. I stood up on my chair. "Hold on, everybody. Here you all are talking about Mr. Woollcott with praise that I'm sure he appreciates, but it seems kinda like you're shortchanging him, don't you think? Where I come from, which is a very highly traditional place in America called the state of Alabama, we never send our friends off without also giving them gifts. I'll start," I said. Then I reached up under my dress and shimmied out of my black silk-and-lace panties, which I tossed onto the table, knowing they'd land near Scott. "Bon voyage, Mr. Woollcott—this was the best I could do on short notice."

That sure raised eyebrows—but what didn't, that spring?

Take also poor Hadley, arriving at Villa America with only Bumby while everyone knew that Hemingway, in Madrid for the moment, was carrying on with Pauline—though we weren't certain yet whether Hadley knew.

Worse, Bumby brought an awful cough with him, and when it turned out to be whooping cough, Sara went white with fear that any of the other children should catch it. We were having coffee in the Murphys' olive garden when the doctor came from the guesthouse and said that, while the worst of Bumby's illness had already passed, he was directing two weeks' quarantine in order to prevent the rest of us from getting sick.

"We can't keep them here," Sara said, and then, as Hadley appeared behind the doctor, told her, "Hadley, I'm so sorry. I'll find you a hotel, and we'll send along whatever you'll need. I'm so very sorry," she repeated, already moving toward the house to make arrangements. "We can't take any chances."

"Sara—wait," I called. "We'll just trade with Hadley. There's six more weeks on our lease."

"We'll get another place," Scott amended. "Villa Paquita is a little damp for me, but should be just the thing for Bumby's cough—you don't want anything too dry, it irritates the lungs' lining, don't you know."

Why was he lying? The villa wasn't damp, it was wonderful, perfect, he'd said so himself.

"I couldn't—" Hadley looked lost, as if all this was beyond her capacity to take in.

"Of course not," Scott said, "but *we must*. You'll be doing us the grandest favor. I've had my eye on this other spot, Villa St. Louis, right on the water's edge, and needed an excuse to rent it."

I stared at him. This was the first I'd heard of Villa St. Louis. Why would we take on yet another expense when we could use the guesthouse for these two short weeks?—and then it hit me: *He's leaving the guesthouse to Hemingway and Pauline.*

He was saying, "The place has forty rooms, imagine! Why, we'd be doing *them* a favor by filling a half-dozen or so until the family's return at summer's end—so how lucky it is that poor Bumby is ill!"

"All right then," Hadley said, nodding. "We'll do that. It'll be so nice for Bumby."

"And even nicer for me," he said. "If I didn't put myself first, you'd all think *I* had taken ill."

"That was the perfect solution," Sara said later, thanking Scott. "I couldn't turn her out but couldn't keep her here, and with you in the guesthouse, where would we have put Ernest?"

With his wife and son, I thought, and why hadn't that solution been foremost in everyone's mind—including Hadley's? *Especially* Hadley's.

Hemingway arrived a few days later, temporarily alone. "I heard what you did," he told Scott at dinner that night. "There's no finer, truer friend. All of you," he said with a sweep of his arm, "you're incomparable. A man counts his fortune in the number of true and generous friends, and so while I've hardly got two francs to rub together, I am a rich man indeed."

To celebrate his new books (*Torrents* just published and *Sun* forthcoming), Sara and Gerald hosted a party at the casino. Every person we knew on the Riviera that spring turned out for the party; of course they did. Who would miss a Murphy event, regardless of the purpose? It was certain to feature wonderful food, great music, and even better company. Pablo and Olga were there, and Coco Chanel, who I'd been wanting to meet. The MacLeishes, the Myerses, Man Ray, Diaghilev, Dottie Parker, Dos Passos, and a new fellow, a Canadian writer and friend of Hemingway's named Morley Callaghan. It was, for me, another version of the scene from our earliest days in Manhattan, the Princeton boys now supplanted by this influential bunch.

That such a thing was happening on Hemingway's behalf hadn't sat well with Scott, who'd been grumbling, too, about the "war boys' club" of Hemingway, Dos Passos, and MacLeish, all of them writers who'd been in the thick of things during the Great War, whereas Scott's attempted sacrifice had been thwarted by the armistice.

We were dressing for the party, Scott standing at the mirror adjusting his tie, his mouth set in a hard line. He was wearing one of his better suits, nicely cut, brown summer-weight wool, and wore a striped tie that matched the color of his eyes. Except for his expression, he looked as good as I'd seen him lately.

He said, "Not to take anything away from Ernest, but I had a book out this spring, too—as if anyone gives a damn."

"A story collection's different." My intent was to sound fully supportive, but Scottie, who'd just helped herself to one of my lipsticks and was using it like eye shadow, distracted me. "Here, sugar, give that to Mama. I'll show you where it goes."

I looked over my shoulder at Scott. "It's just an assemblage of stuff you already published."

"Which took a damn lot more effort than *Torrents*!" He turned from the mirror. "Jesus, Zelda, does she really need to be wearing lipstick? Nanny!" he yelled, then said, "Nobody appreciates how difficult it is to get a story in the *Saturday Evening Post*. Christ, they're all agog at Ernest's fifteen-hundred-dollar advance when I'm getting *twice* that for a short story."

Lillian appeared, assessed the situation, and swept Scottie out of the room with a promise of fresh lemon parfait.

I said, "Maybe *they'd* appreciate it more if *you* did; you're always disparaging the slicks and saying how you hate writing for 'em—as if somebody's holding your feet to the fire 'til you spit out another flapper tale."

"My feet *are* to the fire. And if I don't complain, they'll all think I'm done with serious work, finished trying to be relevant. I need the money, and I need my novels to be taken seriously."

"Honestly, Scott, I don't see how you can have it both ways, or why you even persist in trying. What's wrong with being purely popular, as long as the quality is high? Look at Ziegfeld—do you suppose he worries about his critical reputation?"

"He doesn't need to worry, he's a millionaire."

"Yes—because of dancing girls and bawdy songs and sentimental tear-jerker, crowd-pleasing acts. And yet everybody thinks he's tops."

Scott checked his collar and adjusted his tie once more. "The standards are different in literature."

"But they don't *need* to be—they're arbitrary, and you all just perpetuate the problem by acting like they aren't. A coupla critics decide what's important, what *matters,* and then you all go along with it like it's been decreed by God himself!"

"You're oversimplifying. Literature is an art, it has an effect—it *matters*."

"I'm not saying otherwise. But good is good." I followed him down the hallway to the front room, my heels clacking on the marble tile. "And there's all different kinds of value, all of 'em legitimate. Fine artists understand this; why don't writers? And why is this serious literary acclaim so important to you anyway? You're popular, beloved—Deo, you still get fan mail from *Post* readers every week!"

Scott sighed. "Let's just go," he said.

252

At the casino, Hemingway looked different than he had when I'd seen him last. Smug in one way, edgy and watchful in another. Thanks in large part to Scott, he'd taken a great stride forward in his career and likely had a sense that things were going to improve even more in times to come—but he'd also begun shedding some of the very people whose friendship, guidance, and influence had led to his progress. Now his eyes seemed to be saying, *Which of you want to latch onto me? Which of you will be of use to me next? Which of you can be trusted to serve my purposes?* All around him he saw good prospects and faithful supporters—except when his eyes rested on me.

With a glass of champagne in one hand and caviar piled upon toast in his other, Hemingway raised his glass and said, "What a fine set of friends you are, and how fortunate I am to be here among you. To the Murphys I give my humblest thanks and highest regard, for there are no finer people on the planet."

Gerald bowed. "We couldn't be prouder of you. As many of you know, Ernest has been away watching the bullfights in Madrid. Tell us all about the *corrida*!"

He did, endlessly, and Hadley, the ever-dutiful wife, stood by getting slowly drunk.

I did my best to tune him out by talking with Coco Chanel. Sara had said Coco was involved with the Duke of Westminster, and Dottie Parker had said Coco saw Edward, Prince of Wales, too. I wanted to know which of the men was behind the astonishing diamond, pearl, and sapphire choker she wore to the party with her simple white sheath dress. And her eyebrows—they were so artful and expressive; I wanted to find out whether she did them herself.

While I sought distraction, Scott couldn't seem to separate himself from the attention his great good friend was commanding. Every time I glanced across the room, there he was at Hemingway's elbow.

If Hemingway was the king that night, then Scott was the court jester—or he tried to be, at least. Midway through the party, just when Coco, hand to throat, was saying, "This incredible decoration was a gift from—" Sara found me and pulled me aside.

"He's asking the oddest things of the other guests. I wonder if you ought to claim a stomachache or something and have him take you home."

"Only to turn back up like a bad penny later," I said. "You know how he's gotten. Leaving has to be his idea or it won't stick."

"Well, his idea right now seems to be finding out what color underwear the women have on, whether the men believe extramarital intercourse is a sin, and whether Dottie might be—and I quote—'a fine piece of tail despite her big mouth.'"

"Oh, Lord, I'm sorry. He's feeling a lot of pressure to turn in his novel, which of course isn't nearly done. All of this attention on Hemingway . . ." I shrugged. "You should get Gerald to talk to him—he's sure to have better luck than I would."

I went to the ladies' room, just to escape all the nonsense. It turned out to be no escape at all, though, because there was Hadley, sitting on a chair in the corner, crying.

"Oh, Zelda," she said when she saw me, "I'm the biggest fool. Ernest and Pauline have been carrying on for God knows how long, he doesn't even deny it. What am I supposed to do with this?"

I had no answers for her. Maybe I ought to have put her together with Coco, who might have enlightened us both about the impracticality and undesirability of giving one's whole self to any man—for all the good it would have done.

When I saw Scott next, he was attempting to juggle three glass ashtrays and was managing pretty well until some man I didn't recognize called out, "Say, Fitzgerald, when are *you* ever going to write another book?" Scott threw one of the ashtrays at the offender, grazing the man's head.

"Enough!" Gerald hissed. He took Scott's arm and led him toward the door. "You might have killed him. Christ almighty, Scott, go home and sleep it off."

Scott's eyes brimmed with tears. "I'm sorry." Gerald turned from him and Scott clutched his hand. "I'm *sorry*. Please, don't make me leave."

I had to intervene. "Scott, darling," I said soothingly, "your aim is a little off, yet. Let's go back to our place and practice a little by chucking some rocks into the water. We can come back later."

His bleary eyes lit up. "Yes! Grand. That's just what we'll do," he said, and I led him out of the casino wondering how I was ever going to survive the summer.

There were so many people at the Riviera that year, and Scott was making it his business to befriend every one of them. In addition to those of us attached to the Murphys, there were theater and film people like Rex Ingram, whose film studio in Nice was a sort of second Hollywood, and playwright Charlie MacArthur, and actresses like Grace Moore—we'd first seen Grace in a musical during our honeymoon in New York—plus a number of those playboy types who enjoyed being wherever the actresses were.

Scott was forever meeting people at casinos and cafés and bringing them home with him, staying up until all hours, and then the whole lot of them would pass out wherever they happened to be when drink got the better of them. Mornings, I'd sometimes lead Scottie past a snoring man draped over a chair; or we'd see some actress, her eyeliner now raccooned around her eyes and lipstick bleeding around her mouth like a clown's, sprawled in a garden chaise, undisturbed by the raucous *gatah-gatah!* calls of the pintail sandgrouse out for their morning drink.

To save my sanity, I tried to give most of my attention to painting. My head was still full of Larionov and his abstract work, his passion for rejecting conformity and realism in favor of works that *expressed*. My new oil would feature my impression of a young girl in a swaying orange dress, and a cheerful little dog as her companion—*if* I could get it right. With all my new education, my ideals had grown far loftier than my talent could accommodate.

The other problem was that Villa St. Louis, while ordinarily beautiful and serene, was the last place I wanted to be. Hemingway was there almost daily—and though I couldn't know for sure, I suspected he was feeding Scott a steady diet of advice on how to manage a "crazy" wife like me. One evening during cocktail hour, Hemingway had said in front of everyone, "A woman who knows how not to be a distraction to her husband's work and career is a good and fine and honorable woman." He apparently had two such women, and if Scott took his advice, Scott might yet have one, too.

Though my colitis had improved a great deal since I'd taken the cure in Salies-de-Béarn, new twinges of pain made me scared that a relapse was imminent. Fear dragged me down and stole my appetite. I woke almost every day in a fog of dread that took an hour or two to shake off. Everything was bad, I thought, and getting worse. When I learned that Sara Mayfield was coming to Antibes for her summer holiday, I actually cried with relief.

We met at a tiny café in the old-town section of the city, in view of the Marché Provençal, a covered outdoor market where vendors hawked fresh beans, parsley, carrots, berries, scores of spices, hundreds of cheeses, ropes of dried peppers and garlic. There were bunches of lavender, buckets of roses, baskets of turnips, potatoes, squash. Alongside all of this were silk scarves dyed in colors even rainbows hadn't thought of, tied like nautical flags along a length of clothesline and waving in the sea's breeze.

We'd hardly ordered our shrimp cocktails before I started in about Hemingway's latest insult. "They go out drinking all the time, and he knows Scott will be useless in every way afterward. He encourages Scott's bad habits and then blames the effects of them on me."

Sara said, "There's something not right about him." She was quiet for a few seconds. "I'll guess you don't know what Bob McAlmon has been saying. I wasn't goin' to tell you, but—"

"Saying about what?"

"About *who;* Scott and Hemingway, that's who. McAlmon says that something scandalous happened between himself and Hem a while back, and that now it's Scott who's caught Hemingway's eye, if you know what I mean."

Skeptical, I shook my head. "I never heard this."

"Who would tell you—besides me?"

"He thinks Hemingway's a *fairy?*"

256

"If you believe 'it takes one to know one,' then I'll guess he *knows* that's the case."

"*He's* a fairy?"

"They say he goes both ways. Could be our mighty Hem does, too."

"I don't know . . ." I said, thinking of that night outside the Dingo bar. "He propositioned me once—and now he's got two women tangled up with him. I wrote you about Hadley and Pauline, didn't I?"

She nodded. "He tried to rope *you* into his sordid circle? What did you say?"

"That he's got nothin' on Scott. You can bet he didn't like hearing that." The recollection chilled me. "Scott doesn't know. No one does, so don't say anything."

Sara reached for my hand. "He's a shit, Zelda. You should give Scott an ultimatum: his pal Ernest, or you. Pick."

"And if he doesn't choose me, then what do I do, run home to Montgomery like some whipped dog?" I couldn't imagine it. Montgomery, compared to Paris?

"Of course he'll choose you. He's crazy about you. You have a daughter together. You're his muse."

"Yes, well, he doesn't need a muse if he's going to spend all his time working on someone *else's* book."

Our food arrived. I picked at mine and said, "I just can't imagine what the appeal is; they're about as alike as parsnips and pachyderms."

"Maybe it's this," Sara said. "*Scott* thinks he's *being* the hero, while Hemingway thinks Scott's *worshipping* the hero."

I nodded and sighed. "Sounds about right. Do you really think McAlmon is telling the truth?"

Sara speared a shrimp. "Why would he say it otherwise?"

"Why do any of them do the strange things they do?"

"The real question is, what are *you* goin' to do?"

"Wait it out, I guess."

37

The first time I'd seen a doctor about my stomach troubles, I'd been reluctant to describe all the symptoms. It's so much more embarrassing to talk about such disorders with a man than with, say, a girlfriend—more embarrassing, even, than discussing fertility troubles, with those intimate *how-often, what-position, do-you/does-he* questions. I'd done it, though, and that doctor, who was old and pleasant and sympathetic, made it as easy on me as it could be made.

The prospect of going through it all again with a stranger made me reluctant to seek care when the pains came back and refused to leave. For days, I put off taking action, staying in bed while Scott took off for his adventures and Lillian took Scottie off for hers. The so-blue sky and sea outside my window taunted me, *Here we are, here we are,* so I closed my eyes and slept . . . until I was awakened one afternoon by a strange man standing at the foot of my bed beside Scott.

He had beady eyes and thin, firm lips and dealt with my assessment real matter-of-factly, which I appreciated. Even so, I was mortified the whole time.

"The pains are where? . . . You see blood every time or only sometimes? . . . Describe the stool's consistency . . ."

At least his English was good.

After the exam, he administered some morphine and pronounced, "Until we get in there and see it, we can't know for certain whether it's the ovary, the uterus, the colon, or the appendix. We'll schedule a surgery and see if we can excise the thing that's troubling you. It may not be possible, you understand."

I understood all too well.

Scott was worried that the Antibes hospital was too far behind the times and insisted I have the operation at the American Hospital in Paris. I let him worry to his heart's content, let him take over the planning, let him step back into his role as my protector, all the while secretly pleased to have wrested his attention from Hemingway. Fate was intervening to give me back my husband, at least for a little while. Before we left for Paris, I told Sara, "If things get out of hand again, I guess I can always have my tonsils out."

The Paris doctors removed some scar tissue and my appendix and pronounced me cured, which I was willing to believe without reservation. I hardly cared that my lower belly was now and would forever be a map of scars; I was luxuriating in Scott's attentive presence at my bedside throughout visiting hours every day. He read to me, we played cards, we wrote letters, we talked . . .

Apparently, though, it was the pain medication that made me so dreamy and content, because when my last day approached and I said I thought we should stay in Paris and send for Scottie, Scott said, "Stay? God, no. I've just finished writing a full evaluation of Ernest's manuscript. There are some things he really has to address before we let Max have a look at it."

Ernest. Again.

I said, "Can he not just leave you be? Have you heard what Bob McAlmon's been saying about you two?"

"McAlmon's still seething over having lost Ernest to Boni and Liveright—who are now very sorry to have lost him to Scribner's."

The doctor came in then, and Scott said, "I'd like to take her back to Antibes. Don't you agree that it would be better for her to avoid the city—the germs and filth and such—when she's in this condition?"

"Quite right," the doctor said. "I could do with a summer at the coast myself."

And so to the Riviera we went, where Scott could return to the thick of the drama, the place in which he felt most at home. Surely this, not Hemingway, was what was truly drawing him back.

Late one night in July, Scott woke me by switching on the bedside light and shaking my shoulder.

"What? What's the matter?" I said, immediately awake and certain that someone must have died—until I saw Scott's face.

He looked giddy. "What do you get when you mix three different alcoholics together?"

Hemingway and the others had gone off to Pamplona a week earlier. Citing my delicate post-surgery condition, I'd refused to go, which made it easy for Scott to pretend that he *would have* gone, if not for me. The fact was, he had no stomach for the bullfights or for anything gritty or brutal beyond its presence in photographs or inside the pages of a book. He'd taken up, then, with Charlie MacArthur and playboy Ben Finney.

Scott and his new friends played all sorts of pranks on hapless waiters and musicians. Once, they persuaded a pair of waiters to come out for a ride with them, then drove to a cliff and acted as if they intended to kill the young men. They claimed to have been so convincing that one of the fellows wet himself before they confessed the joke, and then they took the pair out for a steak dinner and fine bourbon to make up for the trouble they'd caused.

Now I wanted to punch Scott. "I was *sleeping*. That's what people do this time of night. Shut that light off."

"Don't be such a poor sport. Come on, tell me, what do you get when you mix three alcoholics?" He reeked of bourbon, and cigar smoke.

"Don't you mean *alcohols*?"

"No—*alcoholics*. I am a wordsmith, you know. I always, *always* choose le mot juste."

"If I answer, will you promise to bathe before you come to bed?"

"Sorry, madam, you've taken too long. You get *Love's Betrayal, or A Simple Story of Incest*." He leaped off the bed and began loosening his belt.

"I've just finished the screenplay, and we're shooting it over at Grace Moore's villa, starting tomorrow."

"Tell me I didn't hear you right. Y'all are making a movie about *incest*?"

"Don't scowl like that, it puts the most unattractive lines across your forehead." He dropped back onto the bed still half-dressed and leaned against his pillow. "Oh, God, is it going to be funny. Grace will play Princess Alluria, the most wicked woman in Europe—"

"I don't need to know any more. Turn the light off so I can get some sleep."

"And we're going to paint all the title cards right on the walls, to save the trouble of cutting them into the film."

He held his arms out the way a director might when framing a scene. "'Her tits were perfect halves of peaches, firm and ripe and golden from the sun.'"

"I said I don't want to hear this. Just keep it to yourself."

"'These she displayed at any urging. But her juices she saved for only those she favored most.'"

I got out of bed, grabbed my pillow, and left the room.

In mid-August, Scott returned from a luncheon at Villa America. "Hadley's given up." He said this as if it was Hadley we should blame; the old girl was obviously deficient in some way. "They say they're getting a divorce. Ernest's just a mess over it."

"Is he, now?" I was on the terrace at my easel, trying to perfect the shades of orange in my dancing girl's dress.

"You don't sound sympathetic in the least."

"I have great sympathy—for Hadley. If you see her before I do, tell her I said, 'Good riddance.'"

The marriage wasn't over yet, though. Hem being Hem, he would prolong the agony when they got back to Paris, acting the innocent while letting his marriage bleed for months, until he'd tortured Hadley sufficiently for her to finally put the sword between the bull's shoulder blades herself.

Scribner published *The Sun Also Rises* in October of that year, 1926. Its sales were respectable but not astonishing, and its reviews generally good but not an avalanche of praise. All of this sat well with Scott—far better than the performance of Hemingway's next book would. For now, in his mind he was still the more prominent, more experienced, more successful of the two.

Though the Riviera season had ended, we stayed on through the fall. Scott's new friends and admirers had such a hold on him that he attended every party, frequented every casino and bar. Too often, he would drink to excess, become argumentative or crass, embarrass me, and embarrass himself. There were fistfights. There was an arrest. There were mornings I woke to find him asleep at the kitchen table, the servants going about their business around him and averting their eyes from mine. I complained to him, he apologized to me, and we both acted as if *There, that ought to fix it.* Until the next time.

If I refused to accompany him in the evenings—and I did, often, claiming illness twice as many times as was true—he would stay out all night, and then, when he finally showed up at home, he'd refuse to say where he'd spent the night. He wanted to punish me for leaving him on his own. Other times he'd say things like "You deserve so much better than a louse like me, Zelda. I don't mean to mistreat you. . . . I want us to be like we were. Two of a kind. 'The Golden Couple.' Didn't everyone love us then?"

And because I missed those happier days, too, I forgave him.

There were limits, though. I was in the kitchen one November day, slicing mangoes for Scottie, who was playing hopscotch in the courtyard outside, when Scott appeared looking like death itself.

He was pale, unshaven. His hand shook as he reached for the cupboard door. "We've got to leave this country before it ruins me."

This time I tried, but failed, to summon sympathy for his misery, and tried, but failed, to be agreeable. "How 'bout we leave this *town* and go back to *Paris.*"

"Max has been asking when we're coming stateside, my parents want us home. . . . . I need to be someplace where I'm not going to be tempted by so many distractions."

"We're always leaving a place that we went to because the previous place had too many distractions. Do you even see that?"

"And no more of the hard stuff." He rubbed his forehead. "Water, from now on. I can do it if we're back in the States."

"How do you figure? Prohibition never slowed you down before."

"I feel bad enough as it is, Zelda; couldn't you show me a little faith, a little support? I'm trying to turn over a new leaf."

"There are plenty of leaves in Paris. Come on, Deo; it'd be so much easier to go there than to change continents—you can use that room you rented," I said, a setup that would benefit me as much as him. "And then while you're working, just act like you don't know anybody in town."

"Renting that room was a mistake. I can't work in a garret." Meaning he'd decided that he couldn't imitate his great good friend Ernest's habits and still retain his superiority.

"And I don't want you there hanging around with all those lesbians, that crowd with Esther and Natalie and those bull dykes. We need a fine, new, fresh place, a fresh start. Paris is unwholesome."

"That's pretty rich coming from you. And where'd you get that word, *bull dyke*? I don't like it, it's unkind."

"I don't know where I heard it. It's around. Those women who look like men, wearing suits with pants, for God's sake—"

"I bet it was Hemingway."

"Right, blame Ernest, everything is Ernest's fault." He looked genuinely perplexed when he said, "*What* do you have against him?"

"He's rotten inside. I can't believe you still don't see—"

"He's a fine person, he just needs a little guidance. You know, I genuinely hope you get over the colitis and whatever else has made you so bitchy this year. I haven't been an entirely model husband, but that never used to bother you. You used to have a fine sense of humor."

I pointed the knife at him. "If I hear you use the word *fine* one more time, I'll use this to take out your tongue."

We let Lillian and the rest of the staff go, then sailed on the *Conte Bianca-mano* in December. To leave Europe was both a relief and a disappoint-ment. The relief lay in knowing that Scott would be separated from his playmates. For me, though, I was once again being torn from the people and places that provided me with a sense of balance. An evening at Natalie Barney's salon, a day wandering the galleries of Saint-Germain, another day at the Louvre, an ad-libbed dance solo performed with a cooperative orchestra's accompaniment—all these had given me purpose or brought me pleasure. We weren't sure, yet, where we'd settle, but it would be some-place remote, and then what would I do with my time?

On our first evening aboard ship, I was at the rail watching the sun dis-solve into the sea and wondering why I couldn't have one of those marriages where my husband was content to lead his own life—if not in a respectable manner then at least a separate one—and let me lead mine. Where I'd once been so central to his life, now I felt like an afterthought. And that was all right; I didn't need to be central, not anymore. But if he couldn't make our family the center of his life, then what I needed was to be left in peace. Being left in *Paris* would be even better. For that, I needed money of my own, more money than anyone in my family could give me if I were willing to ask, which I wasn't.

"Zelda!"

I turned to see Ludlow Fowler coming toward me. He said, "What a delightful surprise!" I guess I was scowling because he added, "Or maybe I'm the only one who's delighted?"

I hugged him. "Do I look that bad off?"

"You are as lovely as ever, but plainly not thrilled—even by my pres-ence."

"No, it *is* a treat to see you here. Where's your new bride?"

"Elsie's in the cabin—hasn't got her sea legs yet, poor girl. But I'm hop-ing she'll be fit for the salon later." His eyes and his voice were aglow with affection and concern.

"I envy you two, being at the start of everything. . . . Can you believe it's only been six years since we were in St. Patrick's Cathedral together? Feels like it's been twice as many, and all of them spent swinging a pick into a rock pile."

Ludlow smiled sympathetically. "I'm sure it's just a rough stretch of sea—"

"—on a fruitless voyage. Listen, if you want your marriage to be any good, don't let drinking get you into the same position it's gotten Scott."

"Speaking of the devil, I ought to find him and—what?—punch him?"

"If I thought it'd do any good."

"He loves you, Zelda. I hope you aren't questioning that."

"What good is it, though, when all he really wants is to somehow have been you? He was born into the wrong life, and Scottie and me, we have to pay for that mistake."

"How is she, anyway? I loved the photo you sent, you three in the canoe."

"She's well." Scottie, at five years old and with no recollection of life before France, fully believed what her papa claimed: that we were embarking on our biggest, best, most incredible adventure yet. "Still young enough that she's mostly oblivious to her parents' foolishness," I added with a grateful sigh. "The question is whether we'll improve in time to save her."

PART IV

No evil dooms us hopelessly except the evil
we love, and desire to continue in, and
make no effort to escape from.
—George Eliot

38

———

"Listen to this!" Scott said. "Thirty-five hundred up front . . . *twelve thousand five hundred dollars* if the script's accepted; we're going to California!"

We'd disembarked the ship a day earlier and were at the Plaza in New York City. Scott had just retrieved the bundle of mail that had been routed to his bank there, a common practice for rootless people like us. Among the letters was the offer he'd just trumpeted, which had come from Douglas Fairbanks at United Artists. He was producing a new film and wanted Scott to write it.

I said, "What about your book? You told Max—"

"I've often thought my real genius was for stage and film," Scott said while putting his coat back on. "It was just a matter of the industry catching up to that eventuality."

"Where are you going?"

"To cable Fairbanks. And we'll need train tickets. Oh—would you phone my mother and tell them we've had a change of plans? She'll take it better if she hears it direct from you."

Scott's parents had moved to Washington, D.C., and assured us we would love the area. *Join us here,* his mother had written. *We could be such a help to you and Zelda, and Scottie deserves to know her grandparents, don't you think?* It was the best thing for Scott, so of course we'd agreed that, yes, we'd find a quiet place to rent nearby and settle in for a while, live like regular folks.

"So, we're not going to move to Maryland?"

Scott put his hat on. "Ask Mother to keep Scottie while we're away. I'm not sure how long it'll be—a month or two for sure."

I shook my head. "We'll just bring her."

"There's no time to find a nanny."

"Then I'll stay."

"I need you with me, Zelda, and I need you free. This could be my biggest break, and you know socializing is a huge part of that. Don't worry, she'll love being spoiled by her granny," he said, and then he was out the door.

What didn't I love about Hollywood, once we'd finally arrived? It was all so wonderful, at first.

There was the trellis thick with fragrant roses outside the window of our Ambassador Hotel bungalow; the aquamarine parrot calling us to join him beside the brilliant aquamarine swimming pool; the heat, the eucalyptus, the palms and poinsettia trees; the surprisingly low-key parties to which I wore a new, smart black suit or green dress or creamy silk blouse with a kaleidoscope skirt. I loved that we were celebrities again and looked forward to the luncheon Douglas Fairbanks was going to hold in our honor. I loved that Scott hadn't mentioned his great good friend since before we'd gotten off the train.

Scott loved going to his office at United Artists. He loved the idea of himself as a screenwriter, the prospect of the money he could make, the attention of the film-to-be's star, Constance Talmadge, the sight of the new celebrity estates dotting the hills above town. At the Fairbanks luncheon, I heard him telling a young lady—a guest's teenage daughter, I assumed—how he loved the way Hollywood was all about invention and reinvention, that a little talent combined with a lot of effort could lead just about anyone to home ownership in those hills.

That teenager turned out to be a starlet, a supposed nuppincomer named Lois Moran. She wasn't all that pretty. Her face was too round, her nose too sharp, her hair—like mine—too frizzy without serious attention by the likes of an Elizabeth Arden salon. She had something, though; that's what they say in Hollywood when you don't look like Mary Pickford or Greta Garbo. She was sweet and smart and had landed a prime role in *Stella Dallas,* a movie that came at the end of the silent-films era, too bad for her: she had a tiny voice, impossible for the talkies.

At first, it seemed that Scott was doing with Lois what he had so often done for an admiring and aspiring new friend: taking an interest, sharing his expertise, making connections or recommendations. We, or he, would see Lois and her mother at brunch, or for tea, or bump into them at a restaurant and end up spending the evening together. These events were mixed in with a lot of other similar brunches or lunches or teatimes or dinners with some other actor or writer. Lois's mother was ever present as her chaperone, so I had no qualms about Scott spending time with her. She was not quite eighteen years old.

I was at the pool one afternoon, writing to Scottie about my earlier trip to the zoo, when Scott appeared. The workday being done, I'd been expecting him and was expecting that we'd then get ready for dinner out with the Van Vechtens, who we'd known since Great Neck.

Scott sat down in the lounge chair next to mine. "Change of plans. We're not meeting Carl and Fania tonight, something came up. I have to run and change my shirt. Have dinner here, this place is beautiful." Then he was off, hurrying toward the bungalows. Over his shoulder he called, "I'll be back by eleven or so."

I watched him go, then continued my letter.

> *Daddy is so busy here, with more energy than a bouncy kangaroo. We ought to take a trip to Australia one day, would you like that? The koala bears and kangaroos would all love my little lamby-pie, I'm sure. I miss you dreadfully and wish you'd write to me soon.*

At eleven or so, Scott turned up as predicted—but with his tie loosened, his collar undone, his hair mussed, his lips redder than they could get on their own. Without his saying a word, I knew that somehow little Lois had given her mother the slip.

"How far did it go?" I asked tersely.

"What's that, darling?"

"You and the teenager—I do hope you didn't take advantage of her."

"You're crazy," he said as he headed to the bedroom. "I was with a couple of the fellows from the studio."

I followed him, then leaned against the bedroom door frame while he hung his jacket in the wardrobe. All the while, my heart was racing madly. "Then I'll suppose you dressed up in drag."

"*What* are you talking about? We had dinner at Musso and Frank."

"Is that right? So if I pop in there tomorrow and tell them how Mr. F. Scott Fitzgerald sure did enjoy his dinner with those fellas from UA, they'll know all about it?"

Scott closed the wardrobe door and turned to face me, his arms crossed the way a guilty man's would be. "You're a fine one to talk about trust."

"*I* never denied a thing."

"No, you just hid the truth until you were ready to throw me over."

"So your tactic is, what, obfuscation now, confession later?"

"All right, if you really want to know, Lois asked me to meet her for dinner; she wants me to write something for her. There's no money in it up front, of course—she's not earning all that much yet. But if we can sell it to Fairbanks, it'll be a perfect next step for her and me both."

I might have asked him to tell me why he'd lied to begin with, or whether her mother had been present—except I already knew the answers. I knew the answer to my next question, too, but—call me a masochist—I wanted to hear what he'd come up with.

"And your lips are so red why?"

He touched them with two fingers, then went over to the mirror. "Huh. Must be from the wine."

"*What* is so special about her? Why are you bothering?"

"She's talented and bright, and she's doing something about it. I admire that. I want to help her achieve her potential."

"You want to be everybody's hero." *Except mine.*

"I like to help people, what's wrong with that? She's so organized and focused. You could learn something from her," he said.

We would remain in Hollywood for two increasingly difficult months. Scott would struggle to finish the script he'd been hired to write, fight with me about Lois, fight with the star about the script, spend everything he'd been paid (and more), see Lois ever more frequently, and at the end of it all—well, the end looked like this:

Scott had been out who knows where and returned to the bungalow late, drunk, disheveled, distraught. He swayed as he stood inside the door. "That bitch hates me."

I'd been reading, but now I set the book aside. "Who hates you? Surely not your little Lois?"

"No, no—the precious *star*," he sneered. "She made Fairbanks reject the script."

"Serves you right for making her mad."

He didn't have enough energy left to fight with me. All he did was frown. "Pack up, we're leaving tomorrow."

"Good." I went into the bedroom and locked the door behind me.

In the morning, I woke to find that he'd piled all the living-room furniture into the center of the room. At the very top of the pile, tacked onto the leg of an upturned chair, was the Ambassador's bill for all the charges we'd accrued during our stay. In big red letters Scott had written, C/O UNITED ARTISTS.

He was still in the suit he'd been wearing the night before. When he saw me, he said calmly, "All right, then. Get dressed and let's go."

39

See us living in a columned behemoth of a house called Ellerslie, a plantation, almost, in the Delaware hamlet of Edgemoor. Three full floors of
great, square, high-ceilinged rooms defy me to furnish them sufficiently.
We pay only $150 a month to rent this twenty-seven-room Greek Revival
home on a hill overlooking the Delaware River, though we'll spend nearly
that much each month in winter to heat it.

Beyond our royal lawn, the river flows past, broad and brown and silent, unconcerned with the little party gathered at its bank on this afternoon, the twenty-first of May. It's 1927, but could be a hundred years
earlier or a thousand or three; the river doesn't know or care. It doesn't care,
either, about the dramas playing out among the people at this picnic, or
about the one taking place in the sky far to the northeast, where Charles
Lindbergh is attempting to cross the Atlantic Ocean to Paris with a single
engine in a single flight.

If the river has a soul, it's a peaceful one. If it has a lesson to impart, that
lesson is patience. There will be drought, it says; there will be floods; the ice
will form, the ice will melt; the water will flow and blend into the river's
brackish mouth, then join the ocean between Lewes and Cape May, endlessly, forever, amen.

Who's listening, though? See us on the river's bank, our picnic blankets outspread on the clover. Here are Scott's parents, Molly and Edward, looking amazed at what their boy has acquired; here are Carl and Fania Van Vechten; here is a fellow Southerner, critic and novelist James Boyd; here are Lois Moran and her mother—who are the fêted guests because we have been away from Hollywood for two entire months and Scott is badly in need of a fix-up, a dose of the girl whose "absolutely platonic affections" have for him become paramount. Does anyone besides the two of them and me know this is the case? The river says, *Who cares?* but I'm too distracted to pay it any mind.

The blanket is checkered in a picnic-proper red-and-white design. The ice bucket is kept filled by a pair of colored women, who Edward eyes with a mixture of curiosity and suspicion. His world has always been white. We are post-sandwiches and pre-dinner, so our time is occupied with gin martinis and croquet.

Lois wears gingham and acts the innocent, as if the floorboards outside her bedroom don't creak mere minutes after I wake in the night to an empty bed.

Scott is in a Brooks Brothers poplin suit that's far sharper than the man inside it, the man who, only a few days earlier, wrote his agent that his novel, still only two chapters long, will be finished in July. This is the same man who, when July arrives, will interrupt his wife at the ballet barre she installed against his wishes to say, in a trembly panic, that he is on the verge of something horrible—either nervous breakdown or death. This he'll do three times before August ends, and then to prevent further frights he'll switch to a lower-nicotine cigarette and forswear the gingham girl. He'll try to quit drinking and will succeed for two days, until he declares that the world is far too raw and bright for him to be able to settle down and work—he needs a little something to soften it and steady him. A new bad habit will be born, along with a series of stories for the slicks and lots of letters to his great good friend Ernest—but no novel. In winter, he'll attempt to give a speech at Princeton, but will appear at the podium drunk and mute; he'll arrive home—where his sister-in-law Tootsie is visiting—still crying tears of mortification, then fight with his wife about her breaking the liquor cabinet's lock, and bloody her nose in the process.

My dress for this picnic is as brown as the river. As much as I'm succeeding in imitating the river's appearance, I haven't been able to assimilate its wisdom—and won't, not until years later. Right now I'm the woman who, in an attempt to escape her husband's life, has begun taking ballet lessons three days a week. She's not needed at home; her husband directs the maids and the cook and the governess that both she and her daughter despise. And so the woman studies books about art and works on paintings in between dance lessons, then works on essays and stories when her painter's eye is spent, and if any hours remain between these activities and sleep, she passes those hours in as thorough an alcoholic haze as can be achieved without ending up horizontal. Guests will come and go and come and go. Her husband will do the same. She will dance and paint and write—and many remarkable things will come of her efforts: beautiful painted furniture and lampshades that delight her daughter; publication, interviews, opportunities, acclaim. These are the good things she'll hold on to later, when she's in the thick morass of the bad.

The sight of one of the maids standing on the porch and waving a dish towel gets our attention. "It was on the radio!" she calls. "Mr. Lindbergh just landed his plane in Paris!"

We foolishly look up at the sky past the treetops, as if we can see the plane, see it descending lower, lower, then disappearing from our sight. It is the end of an astonishing journey, I think. All done now, nothing more to see.

40

Carmel Myers was a lovely, dark, sultry woman, a real beauty with hooded eyes and lips that were shaped in such a way that her mouth was always slightly open. When we ran into her in the lobby of our Genoa hotel in late March 1928, she said, "You've *got* to come meet Fred and me tonight for dinner." Who could turn her down?

Fred was Fred Niblo, who'd directed Carmel in *Ben-Hur*. He was twice Carmel's age, and married, not that it mattered. For all we knew, the two of them being in Genoa together was as coincidental as our seeing them there while en route to Paris for a visit.

"Excellent to see you again!" Fred said as we joined them at the hotel's restaurant. He pointed to a name on the menu. "Have you ever tried this brandy? It's an experience, I'm telling you. Four glasses," he told the waiter in English, holding up four fingers and then indicating all of us. "Four glasses, two bottles," he tapped the brandy's name on the menu, then made a *V* with his fingers. "*Doo-ay*. To start."

Carmel said, "We'll toast to your return visit to Europe—how exciting to be spending the summer in Paris! How was the journey? Don't you love traveling by ship? It's so intimate, so romantic, don't you think?"

Scott and I glanced at each other. Our answers, unsaid, were both *Hell no*. The weather had been terrible—rough seas, cold rain—and all we'd done for the first two days was argue about my intention to continue dance lessons when we got to Paris. Tiring of that, we spent the next seven days ignoring each other entirely, reconciling somewhat only on the last day, when relief at the sight of land gave us something in common again.

A small orchestra performed dance tunes I recalled from my childhood. Dinner was some kind of fish, some kind of vegetable—nothing special, and I didn't eat much. The brandy, though, was memorable; I sipped it with pleasure, enjoying the little bit of escape a good drink can provide. Fred and Scott finished a whole bottle between them before dessert arrived.

Scott's was a tart that looked richer than my stomach would be able to handle gracefully, so when he said, "It's fantastic; here, try a bite," I demurred.

"You go ahead. I'm full."

He looked so disappointed. "But you can't miss out on this, it's delicious."

"*I'll* have a bite," Carmel said, and she held those lips of hers open a little wider than usual.

Scott stared at her mouth, just stared like he was hypnotized, paralyzed, like that crimson *O* was the answer to all of life's problems, or maybe just his prayers. I kicked his shin to break the spell, which worked; he blinked, then ate the bite himself as if he'd never even offered it to anyone at all. I looked frankly at Carmel; her expression was innocently amused.

There are women whose whole selves are engaged in being a public commodity, and Carmel was one of these. Every gesture she made, every syllable she uttered, the tinkle of her laughter, the way her dress's fabric draped over her breasts, all of it was self-conscious and deliberate, designed to elicit admiration in women, desire in men. This isn't to say I held any of that against her. Not a bit. I liked her, in fact. The way I saw it, she was a kind of living work of art, and funny and thoughtful besides. Was it her fault if she, as had happened to me, sometimes provoked the basest feelings in a man?

Scott and Fred made short work of that second bottle of brandy while Carmel's and my glasses still held our initial pour. I'd found that drinking very much of any kind of alcohol still did bad things to my stomach. Carmel might have found that it did bad things to her self-preservation; I know that if I looked like her, I'd never let down my guard.

Fred entertained us with an ongoing routine of self-deprecating jokes about why Jews (like himself, and Carmel) were so prevalent in the entertainment world. Carmel rolled her eyes a lot, that perfect-*O* mouth open to express mock disapproval. The more brandy Scott drank, the less he was able or willing to tear his eyes from that red *O*—until I finally slapped the table and said, "All right, that's it!"

Everyone jumped, and I went on, "*Why* are men so taken with women's mouths? Is it just . . . you know, what they wish that mouth would do to them?"

Scott said, "Zelda!"

"What? You're the one who's fixated."

Fred said, "No, no, it's so much more than what you think. Consider: The mouth is the only bit of erotic landscape visible when a woman is dressed. It is the symbol of every moist cavern a woman possesses, which all men are bound to seek out, we have no choice."

Scott looped his arm around Fred's shoulders and said, "You see? You *are* an artist!"

"Who doubted it?"

This set the three of them off into a discussion about whether filmmaking was a legitimate art form and who thought so and who thought not, and whether talkies like last fall's *The Jazz Singer* were going to alter Hollywood forever.

I'd resigned myself to waiting out the remainder of the night, my mind already wandering to subjects of more interest to me—Natalie's salon; ballet with a serious, European teacher; brioches from my favorite *boulangerie*—when I noticed that Scott was staring at me.

"What? Why are you looking at me like that?"

He stood up and offered his hand. "Dance with me. It's a waltz."

I listened to the band; sure enough, they were playing "Kiss Me Again," which I'd heard on the radio and loved.

"Go on," Carmel said, nudging me. "Dance with your husband. Or I will."

But Scott shook his head as I reached for his hand. "No one but Zelda for me."

41

June 27, 1928

My dearest Second Sara,

It's been three very full months in Paris. We're staying at 58 rue de Vaugirard—the Left Bank, this time. I meant to write sooner, but as usual I'm burning my candles from both ends.

Scott meant for us to be close to you-know-who, and was disappointed when we arrived to find out that the great man's new wife was with child and wanted to give birth on U.S. soil—any minute now, I'm told. So she shuttled them off to Key West, Florida, which I think is a perfect out-of-the-way spot for them to settle. His last letter to Scott was all about conquering man-sized fish.

I am conquering age and gravity with a new ballet teacher, Lubov Egorova, who came recommended by the Murphys—Honoria takes lessons at her studio, and now Scottie's going, too. Egorova is also <u>Princess Nikita Troubetska</u>, isn't that wonderful? And even better, she is a formidable teacher and the most lovely and lyrical of ballerinas. When I grow up, I want to be her.

Things are otherwise much the same, though Paris is not—there are hardly any French people left here. Every boulevard is packed with

Americans whose mispronunciations make me sound like I'm native. Scott and I had a row last weekend and haven't spoken since—but as we are going to Sylvia Beach's dinner for James Joyce tonight, I'll once again have to put on my <u>Mrs. F. Scott</u> costume and try to play nice with him and the other children. Whose life is this, anyway? Only when I'm sweating rivers perfecting my pliés in the studio do I feel like a whole and real person. Is this how you felt when you were reaching the end with John?

Enough of that. Pray tell, when do you return to Paris? We're here until September, then back to Ellerslie for the winter, during which Scott may or may not finish his novel.

Yours as ever—

Z~

Plus!

Etire!

Plus haute!

Plus grande!

A ballerina's training looks nothing like the result of her work, her performance. In training she is bludgeoned repeatedly by words that have every bit the impact of a cudgel, if not more. She's a prisoner, a slave by choice. She asks to be tortured; she tortures herself. More! Stretch! Higher! Taller! And at the end of every series of commands comes the most dreaded one: "Encore!"

Do it again!

In Madame Egorova's studio, I spent my hours lined up at the barre next to fourteen other women, all of them clustered at the cusp of twenty years of age. The day my twenty-eighth birthday came, I observed it silently except for the huffs and grunts and sighs that corresponded with my motions. The other girls all knew I was older than they were, that I had a husband and a child. But if my arabesques looked like theirs, if my jetés were executed as crisply, if I could turn, and turn, and turn, and turn, and turn, and turn, and turn, I wouldn't be bullied more than anyone else was, and I'd be allowed to stay.

The regimen was brutal—we were allowed no poisons in our bodies (meaning alcohol), no pollutants (meaning drugs), not if we wanted to be professionals. I loved it. I loved the strict rules, the strict diet, the aching muscles, the bleeding toenails, loved it all because Madame had answered my question "Puis-je devenir une professionnelle?" with "Mais oui." She said that if I *hadn't* shown the potential to dance professionally, she would never have allowed me into the advanced class.

And I loved the regimen because it had done what the appendectomy had not quite managed to do: it cured me. My colitis was now completely gone.

Scott, however, was convinced that I adhered to the rules as a selfish excuse not to go out socializing with him. For example:

On that birthday afternoon, I arrived at the apartment twenty minutes before he did and collapsed facedown on the bed, clothes still damp, hair escaping wildly from the tight bun I forced it into for lessons. He'd been asleep when I left that morning and, as far as I knew, had then spent his afternoon with his friends watching fights at the American Club. He was wild about boxer Gene Tunney that summer, who he'd latched onto through playwright Thornton Wilder, that's how these things went.

"Hello, birthday girl," he announced when he came in. "I got us a dinner reservation at La Tour d'Argent, how about that? We'll eat like royalty, watch the sunset color the Seine, see Notre Dame in twilight . . . The Murphys want us to come by afterward—Sara's got a cake for you, and then they're leaving again for Antibes tomorrow."

Too much effort for too little reward, I thought, silently apologizing to Sara. I rolled onto my back. "What I would really like for my birthday is a bath."

"A quick one, then." He stripped off his tie and went to the wardrobe. "Fowler is going to meet us at the Ritz at six o'clock."

I watched him take his shirt off. His undershirt was doing a poor job of hiding his fleshiness, which looked all the worse when compared with the lean body I saw in my reflection.

"Let's do this on the weekend," I said. "Class was really hard today. We did a lot of center work—you know, away from the barre, nothing to support you but you. Fouettés, mostly—a whipping sort of turn that begins with a plié, then a—"

"It's your birthday *now*. You need a night out; no excuses."

"Exhaustion's not an excuse, it's a reason."

"Whatever it is, it's interfering with our life. I'm glad you like dancing. It's nice that you're still good at it. It's taking over, though. Maybe you don't see that. Which is why," he said, tugging my arm, "you need to listen to your husband and get yourself ready for a *birthday celebration*."

I pulled my arm from his grip and sat up. "Since it's *my* birthday, I ought to have the say—and I say all I want is a bath and then dinner here with Scottie and you."

"You see!" I thought he might stamp his foot. "*This* is why—"

He stopped, so I said, "What? This is why *what*?"

"This kind of thing is why men like Pound and Ernest take up with other women."

"Their wives were the opposite of me! I'm *doing* something—"

"Yes, something all about *you*. Pauline, she understands where she should be placing her extra attention."

"Hadley was a slave to him! Don't you go tryin' to make it like his affair was her fault."

"Regardless. Never mind. The point is, men need compensation for the pressures they face every day. They need to know that all their effort *matters* to the woman in their life. We give up our freedom, devote our entire selves to *one* woman—"

"—at a time, maybe—"

"—so is it too much to want that woman to make us her favorite activity? To accept our attentions and offerings with pleasure?"

I said, "What about Lois?"

He looked confused.

"Don't you remember? 'She's so organized and focused,' you said. 'You could learn something from her, Zelda.'"

"Completely different situation. I wasn't suggesting you take up a *career*."

"What, then?"

"She was . . . There was something . . . fresh about her. I admired her spirit." His voice was wistful. "I *wanted* to admire yours, but you were always criticizing me, or the help. She looked up to me, just like you used to."

She never had to live with you.

Tired of the argument, I got up and, as I passed Scott on my way to run my bath, said, "Please give Ludlow and Elsie my love and regrets. As for Sara, I'll phone her and explain."

"No, I won't, and no, you won't. I'm tired of this, Zelda. You're not a ballerina, you know; you're my *wife*. You need to start devoting your time to your actual duties."

In the bathroom, I started the water and then returned to the doorway. In my most guileless voice I said, "*Actual duties,* right. We all should tend to our actual duties, that's a good philosophy. Tell me, darling, how much writing did you get done today?"

He looked hurt, then angry. "You know, I always defend you when Ernest says that your jealousy and disruptiveness is ruining me. But he's right. Jesus, he's been right all along."

Then he turned and left the room, slamming the door as he went.

Still in my clothes, I stepped into the tub, got down on my hands and knees, and put my head under the faucet, letting the noise and the rush of the water on my head cancel everything out.

42

Ellerslie again; early December 1928. I was in the chintz-bedecked southern parlor reading an article Sara Haardt had sent about Virginia Woolf's recent Cambridge lectures, after I'd told her I'd been writing some new things—

> *Are women not subjugated, prevented by fathers and husbands from having the wherewithal to produce the stories of their experiences? Mrs. Woolf says, too, that so long as men are the primary voices of women's experiences, Woman shall remain powerless in her own society. "False constrictions deny fulfillment of one's talents," Woolf claims, "and the world is poorer for it."*

Sara, ever urging me to become a feminist. But I was writing pretty much whatever I wanted to write; I had no dog in this hunt.

Scott was . . . well, he might actually have been upstairs writing something. One of his Basil Duke Lee stories, probably; the novel remained stalled where he'd left it before we'd sailed for the States—which is to say at chapter four or five.

Scottie was playing on the parlor floor with a set of Red Riding Hood paper dolls I'd made for her, but leapt up when a knock sounded on the door. She went running to answer it. Now seven years old, she had lost most of the little-girl chubbiness I'd loved so much and was becoming a leggy little colt who wanted to be involved in everything.

"Daddy!" she yelled from the foyer. "Telegram for you!"

Curious, I went to the foyer while Scott came down the stairs.

He opened the telegram and read it. "Oh, hell," he said, then handed it to me and went to get his coat.

```
        PHILADELPHIA PA 6 DEC 1928
MR. SCOTT FITZGERALD   ELLERSLIE, EDGEMOOR DE
    REGRET ASKING. FATHER DIED AM STUCK
IN PHILLY WITH BUMBY NEED CASH TO SEND HIM
ON TO FL. ME TO OAKPARK. WIRE ME C/O NORTH
      PHILLY STATION THANKS ERNEST
```

Scott put on his coat and hat, saying, "I'm going to drive up to Philadelphia—I'll probably stay overnight."

"What? It's at least two hours to Philly, why would you *go* there? Just wire it to him like he says."

"My God, Zelda, are you heartless? The man's father just died."

He went off toward the back of the house where the kitchen and servants' rooms were located, yelling for his so-called manservant, Philippe, a former boxer and taxidriver Scott had met in Paris and had imported here to work for us. "Get the car! Allons-y! We need to go help our friend Ernest!"

Scottie tugged my arm and whispered, "Mama, are they going to bring a dead man here?"

"No, lambkins. Daddy's just going to lend money to Mr. Hemingway," *who always knows just who to ask when he's short of funds.*

I hated Philippe almost as much as I hated Hemingway. He was surly, Scott's man only, as much a drinking buddy as a butler/chauffeur/handyman. When I practiced ballet at home, he sometimes lurked at the doorway, his expression unreadable. May and Ella, the maids, said he watched them, too; they'd begun keeping a pistol in their room, and I'd have done the same, except that if Philippe was home, Scott was, too, so there was no real danger for me. There wasn't for the maids, either, so much as we all knew, but who could blame them for assuming the worst?

Between Philippe and haughty Mademoiselle Delplangue, the new governess Scott had hired, I felt like an unwelcome guest in my own home. Even Scottie complained that she didn't like Miss Del, earning a stern lecture from Scott about having proper respect for adults.

When I later told Scott that I wanted him to send Philippe back and to replace Delplangue with someone who wasn't a tyrant, he said, "If you're forever too busy *dancing* to manage your own home, you'll just have to live with the selections I make."

I was starting to worry that I hated Scott, too.

43

January 30, 1929

Dear Zelda,

We've just finished reading the article by you and Scott in the latest _Harper's Bazaar_. "The Changing Beauty of Park Avenue" is a brilliant essay, just beautifully done! We always felt you possessed underutilized literary talents, and this proves it. We hope you'll keep writing. Congratulations to you both!

We Murphys have all been suffering greater or lesser versions of cough, fever, and malaise. Patrick's lingered, but he's well now. I'm to tell you that he misses Scottie—and will she be at Villa America this summer?

Will she? We heard from Scott that he's setting his novel in Paris and that you'll be returning this spring, in order to make sure he gets the details right. As it appears that Scott is mending his ways, we will be only too happy to see all of you wherever, whenever.

Much love to you and Scott and Scottie too—
Sara

Feb. 13, 1929

Dear Sara,

Your praise was very much welcomed—but despite the byline, the article is all mine, how about that? I have another coming in June in College Humor, *and have just sold them one more. Scott and his agent feel the joint byline is what enables me to place my work with these national magazines—which I agreed to, so as to use the money to pay for my ballet lessons. It's an uneasy compromise but a necessary one.*

Yes, we'll be in Paris in March or April, depending on our route. I've been maintaining my dance lessons here, and I'm writing Madame Egorova to ask for a place again in one of her classes. I can't afford to interrupt my training for yet another season of debauchery. Tell Patrick that Scottie can't wait to see him—as we are awfully eager to see his parents.

Best love to all—

Z-

I think it was the painter Henri Matisse who'd told us about the Beau Rivage hotel in Nice. Scott, though he had no interest in Matisse's work, hated to miss anything grand, so he booked us rooms for two weeks in March, as a landing point for our journey from the States. We'd go on to Paris from there.

Who Scott spent his time with during those two weeks I can't begin to say. I hardly saw him between sundown and sunup, except for the night the police detective phoned to say they'd arrested Monsieur for assault and public drunkenness, and did Madame wish to come post his bail? *Non*, Madame did *not* wish to—Madame *wished* she could leave him there until such time as he would somehow regain some self-control, not to mention self-respect; she had a seven-year-old daughter asleep in her suite. Madame put a nice young bellhop into a cab, francs in hand, on a reconnaissance mission to the jail.

"No more," I told Scott when I let him into the suite two hours later. His right eye was swollen half-shut and turning all sorts of shades of purple. Blood had caked along his hairline and was spattered on his shirt. Thank God Scottie wasn't seeing him like this.

"I'm so sorry," he said, and looked it. "But the son of a bitch said he wouldn't read my work no matter what, that he had no interest in anything written by a fairy. Goddamn McAlmon."

I felt for Scott, I truly did. "Aw, Deo, that's rotten." There was no lower blow for Scott than someone dismissing his work, especially for such a wrongheaded reason. "I don't blame you for giving him what for."

Scott's face bloomed with surprise. "Thank you." His grateful smile was an amusing contrast to his beat-up face.

"Of course. Now come on, let's get you cleaned up. Paris tomorrow, all right?"

He nodded, and when morning came he was in good spirits again. He told Scottie, "Look at this—I went out for cigarettes last night and had a run-in with an orangutan."

"Daddy," she scolded him. "Orangutans live in Asia."

"They do, but they have very long arms."

In Paris, we took an apartment on the rue Palatine, in the same neighborhood as our last place, which made it feel like home. The lovely stone-and-iron Gothic building, the kind Paris does so well, was right by the remarkable Église Saint-Sulpice—one of those churches I'd once imagined might exist after I'd first seen St. Patrick's.

Here, it was a five-minute walk to Natalie's on rue Jacob, another five to the Seine, and a short cab ride to Madame Egorova's beloved, timeworn studio. Perfect geography, if not perfect circumstances.

No surprise, the Hemingways were also back in Paris. What was surprising, to Scott anyway, was that he had written Ernest for his street address and gotten no reply. Then he'd written Max, who, gentleman that he is, delicately explained that Hemingway had asked him to keep his location private. Something about avoiding late-night serenades that could wake little Patrick or, worse, get Hemingway evicted.

Even knowing this, Scott wanted to pay Hemingway a visit first thing. So while I was once again immersed in unpacking and contacting agencies for household help that Scott would then approve or reject, Scott went out in search of Hemingway or a friend who'd lead him to Hem, whoever he found first. "It'll be fine," he said when I asked whether he ought to wait for the great man to find him. "He doesn't mean anything serious by it, he's just making a point.

"And anyway," he added just before he left, "I'm certain it was Pauline who made him hold back the information. He's still pretty torn up about his father's suicide, you know. He'll probably do anything she says."

44

I'm sure Hemingway was indeed distressed that his father had put a re-
volver to his head and taken his life. Anyone would be. Hadley sure had
been when her father had done the same—though she'd been young
when it happened, so when she told me how awful it had been, she'd described it all with a quiet detachment and gentle regret. *Gentle regret*
described her attitude about her divorce, as well, by all accounts. The
woman didn't have an excitable bone in her. Her ex-husband, on the
other hand, needed to express himself in a wide variety of ways—one of
which was a new book.

"Ernest channeled a lot of his grief into the story," Scott said one
evening in May, laying a copy of *Scribner's Magazine* on the sofa next
to me. "He's calling it *A Farewell to Arms,* but I'm not wild about that
title."

I had a notebook in hand and was writing what would be my third
short story for *College Humor* magazine, "Southern Girl." Following the
sale of my essays to them, we'd sold the first story of the series in March,
and I was looking forward to its July appearance.

I glanced at the magazine, then said, "You know, this joint-byline business is making me cranky. I'm going to tell Harold to make 'em change it
to just my name after the first two stories are out."

"But they're all joint efforts. You rely on my critiques and my connections to get them publishable and published."

"If that's so, why isn't Hemingway's first book also by you? Why isn't Peggy Boyd's?"

"You and I are a team." Scott looked surprised that I didn't know this answer. "You're using our joint experiences, and what are essentially my ideas—or my themes, at least."

Thinking of all the ways I'd assisted with his work, I said, "Then why isn't *my* name also on *your* stories and books?"

"That's not the same thing at all."

"No? You tell me what the difference is, 'cause I sure don't see it."

"It's the difference between the amateur and the professional. I'm a writer, it's my profession, how I earn my living. Whereas you dabble at it, the same way you dabble in painting and dance."

"So all those times when you wanted my help to work out a plot or—"

"I was trying out ideas on you. Thinking out loud, or surveying opinion. I didn't *need* your help."

He was so convinced of his view that there was nothing more I could say. And there was no one I could go to on my own; what agent would be willing to cross a woman's husband—especially when her husband was *F. Scott Fitzgerald*? Like it or not, if I wanted to see my stories in the world, I had to dress them in Scott's clothes.

I picked up the copy of *Scribner's*, which had Hemingway's name on the cover. They were serializing the book ahead of its publication. "Far as I've seen, Hemingway has put his energy into boxing, liquor, and hauling his most faithful drinking partner all around the Left Bank."

"It's his right to enjoy himself, now that—"

—*his novel's done.*

Scott couldn't say that, though, knowing that my retort would surely be *Then what's your rationale?* So he said, "The first installment's there in the magazine. Read it for yourself." He went to the window and looked out, up the street toward the church. "Granted, the serialization leaves plenty to be desired. I told him to give me the manuscript and I'll help him shape it up before the book goes to print."

Another way of avoiding work on his own novel while asserting his role as mentor—which I suspected Hemingway was beginning to resent. In this, Hemingway and I had something in common.

Even with my resentment, knowing that Scott was struggling with his novel troubled me. It was a dilemma: his drinking habits prevented him from working on anything that required more than a day or two's attention, while his inability to do more than produce more short stories demeaned him in his own eyes—which made him want to drink more. Getting tight soothed the insecurities that Hemingway had cued into so quickly and so well; but they came raging back if he indulged too much. I felt bad for Scott in one way, impatient with him in a whole bunch of others. Where was the man I'd married?

"Maybe I'll read it when I'm done with this," I said. *But don't hold your breath.*

Scott turned. "I'm going to have a bath. We're meeting the Callaghans tonight, don't forget."

"I did forget, and I intend to forget again. I'm tired, Deo, and I need to get this story done. Harold's expecting it next week, latest."

Scott held his hand out for mine. "All work and no play makes Zelda a dull wife."

A dull wife. Like Hadley. Who was now a divorced wife, a replaced wife, a possibly happier but possibly destitute former wife, who now had to share her little boy with the woman who'd replaced her.

"Dull, huh? I'm going to go, but only 'cause I don't appreciate that adjective." I took his hand and let him pull me to my feet.

At Deux Magots, we ate dinner with Morley and his pretty new wife, Loretto. They'd gotten married in the spring and were still shiny with newlywed gloss—lots of hand-holding and sweet smiles and meaningful looks. Though he was short and stocky and had small teeth and a receding hairline, Morley was no question Adonis to his more attractive bride. Watching them made me sad for what Scott and I had lost. *Not lost; misplaced,* I decided. *If it's real, it must exist* somewhere.

"Is your food all right?" Loretto asked.

"What? Oh, it's fine, I'm sure. You're real sweet to ask. Guess I'm just not hungry tonight."

After the dishes had been cleared, Scott took the copy of *Scribner's* from his pocket, saying, "Morley, you'll want to hear this—it's from Hemingway's latest," then read a short passage using full theatrical technique:

The town was very nice and our house was very fine. The river ran behind us and the town had been captured very handsomely but the mountain...

On Scott went, and then after he was done, he said to Morley, "Pretty damned impressive, isn't it? Bet you never thought the Ernest you knew back in his Toronto days could produce anything like *that*. I've been working with him since, gosh, '25—four years, now, and I think this shows how far he's come."

Morley shrugged. "Some might say so."

"It's in *Scribner's*," Scott said, with the air of superiority he often assumed when he was about one drink past jolly but still several away from fully obnoxious. "They only publish top work."

I rolled my eyes. Probably everybody in the place did the same.

Morley said, "Well, 'top' is a matter of opinion, you should know that."

Morley was seven years younger than Scott and had only one novel in print at that time, so Scott gave him a dismissive look. "You'll learn."

"I don't need to 'learn,' I already *know*. It's too deliberate, too forced. He's trying to be something he isn't."

I said, "See, that's just what I've been saying all along! What Hemingway really ought to be is an actor. Well, in my opinion he *is* an actor, and Bob McAlmon says—"

"That's enough, Zelda," Scott said, and told them, "She's not good at holding her liquor."

I said, "Don't be stupid. *I'm* not drunk—and even if I was, my opinion would be the same."

"You're hardly qualified to judge—"

"I've had nearly as many things published as he has, not to mention my nine years of marriage to someone who never stops talking about writing, so how am I not qualified?" To the Callaghans I said, "Right now I'm working on a story for *College Humor*—they're taking six of 'em, it's a series, they're about different girls who find themselves in all sorts of unusual situations and have to try to figure out what's right and best—and they don't always, but—"

Scott put his hand on mine. "You're being a bore, don't you think, all this talk about yourself?"

"What I *am* is bored with you trying to act like I'm boring," I said, pulling my hand from beneath his and turning to the Callaghans. "Whatever you two do, make sure you avoid using the Fitzgeralds as role models. We used to be sorta like you, and then, wow, we just lost control; it was like flying a kite in a windstorm. So let that be a lesson. Now, what do you say we all go roller-skating over at—"

"I think you ought to call it a night." Scott grabbed my wrist. "You're obviously tired."

"I'm not—" I began, and then, realizing he was handing me my escape, said, "Actually, yes, yes, I am, I'm purely exhausted—I just run on like this when I'm tired, and nice as it's been to see you—and meet you, Loretto—I believe my dearest darling husband is right."

"I'll get you a cab," Scott said, then signaled for the check. "Morley, Ernest's sparring with some fellows over at the American Club. Why don't you send your lovely wife home and we'll join him there?"

"Another time," Morley said.

We were all outside at the curb awaiting our cabs when a light rain began to fall. We opened our umbrellas while, fifty feet away, a boy no older than Scottie took a newspaper from the stack he was attempting to sell and held it above his head. The rain fell harder, fast becoming a deluge that turned the paper into a soggy hat.

Scott said, "Hang on," and he went running off with the umbrella, leaving me in the rain.

I ducked in with Loretto and Morley, and we watched while Scott handed the boy his umbrella, then took out his wallet, withdrew some bills, and gave the money to the boy. Then Scott picked up the whole stack of soggy papers and said, "There, you did a great job tonight, go on home." Whether or not the boy understood English, he understood that he'd been freed. Off he went into the wet Paris night.

As Scott started back toward us, Morley asked me, "Was that for the kid's benefit, or ours?"

"Honey," Loretto scolded, "now really, what a thing to say!"

Morley looked at me.

"I wish I knew," I said.

Some hours later, a crashing noise woke me and I bolted upright, ears straining in the darkness.

"Shit!" Scott muttered from somewhere in the living room. Then came Scottie's voice from down the hall, "Mama?" and the sound of Delplangue's door opening, and then another crash as I was hurrying into the hall.

I pushed the switch, lighting the hallway. To my right, Delplangue was at Scottie's door. I nodded to her, then went left, toward Scott, who had pitched face-first over a table and onto the Oriental rug. Beside him was a ceramic lamp, now in pieces.

"Are you all right? Get up."

He groaned and lifted his head slightly, then let it drop forehead first against the rug. "I 'it the lamb," he mumbled. "Goddamn lamb."

Lamb? Oh—*lamp*. "Yes, it's damned for sure. Now, *come on*."

"Ernest." He rolled onto his side and then blinked at the light from the hallway. He squinted at me. "Oh. 'M I home?"

"Lord knows how you made it here, but, yep, you're home, and you need to get to bed before your daughter sees you like this."

"Whyza lamb there?" he said sorrowfully.

"Never mind. Up."

An eternity seemed to pass while he gathered himself sufficiently to get onto his knees, then his feet. Once up, he swayed to one side, then the other, and then his knees began to buckle. I barely caught him by putting myself in the path of his fall. "Holy Christ, Scott, how much did you drink?"

298

He swung his arms wide-open, saying, "'Smuch," and knocking us both against the wall.

I pushed him upright, my teeth clenched with the effort. "*When* are you going to learn?"

"'E said 's okay."

"What?"

Scott peered hard at me and didn't answer.

I helped him to the bedroom, silently promising to pay Delplangue extra if she managed to invent a convincing story to explain the commotion to Scottie.

In bed again a while later, I couldn't sleep. Scott was as bad as I'd ever seen him, and I was worried about alcohol poisoning. We'd all heard the stories about bums found dead in the gutters, having literally drunk themselves to death. One young fella, an artist who'd come over from Wales, had done it, too. With him it had been a drinking contest against a Frenchman twice his size. I could all too easily imagine a similar contest between Hemingway and Scott.

Lying on his stomach, Scott snored then stopped, snored then stopped, mumbled, snored, mumbled, snored. After a good while of this I grew more annoyed than worried, and finally I gave him a shove.

"Come on, roll over."

"Mmmm," he moaned, stretching one arm up past his head. "No more, baby, I can't . . ." His tone was half-protest, half-pleasure. "'S so good but 's *wrong*," he mumbled. Then he chuckled this throaty, low chuckle and moaned again, more quietly . . . and then nothing, just sleep-heavy breathing.

My heart was thumping hard. No question about it: wherever he thought he was, sex was involved. I waited for him to say more. And waited. And waited. Then I got tired of waiting, and my thoughts started to drift like thoughts do when you're not quite asleep in your bed in the dark middle of the night.

Just as I was beginning to slide into another of my dreams about flying, Scott shifted and moaned a little, waking me. He muttered, "C'mon, Ern, no . . . ," and then gave a sigh of pleasure.

All my senses snapped to attention, heart galloping, eyes wide. C'mon, *Ern*?

So there was that. And then there was this, a few nights later:

After having dinner together at Prunier's pub, Scott and Hemingway went to the American Club, where Morley and Hemingway were going to square off. They gave Scott a stopwatch and told him to time the rounds: three minutes per round with a one-minute rest in between. The fighters stripped down, donned their gloves, climbed into the ring, and went at it.

The first round was mostly a warm-up, neither opponent prevailing, and Scott called time right at three minutes.

One minute rest.

Round two: now Hemingway was getting aggressive—more aggressive than he'd been when they'd sparred before, Morley later reported to Loretto; he wondered whether that wasn't because Scott was there.

Morley had some actual boxing training in his past. Hemingway's talents, such as they were, were proudly self-taught. Hemingway was swinging hard, but mostly missing. Morley blocked and jabbed and circled and dodged, and Hemingway cursed and spat. On it went, and then Morley drew his arm back and really let Hemingway have it. One swift, hard punch to Hem's head and down he went.

"Oh my God," Scott cried after looking at the stopwatch. "I let the round go four minutes!"

Hemingway said, "If you want to see the shit kicked out of me, Scott, just say so. But don't say you made a mistake." Then he picked himself up off the canvas and went storming off to the showers.

"Morley said it was like a lovers' spat," Loretto told me.

The apartment was empty, a rare event and one I intended to make the most of. I'd waited six days for this opportunity, the chance to pick the lock of Scott's private trunk and see if proof of Bob McAlmon's assertion was hiding inside.

With two hairpins and a recollection of instructions my brother had shared with me twenty years earlier, I worked on that tiny steel lock. Outside, taxidrivers blew their horns and vendors called out from their carts and the wind changed direction, blowing the bedroom's long, gauze curtains in, making them dance over me like ghosts—and still I crouched there, determined to get at the truth. Then the lock clicked open suddenly, and I tipped onto my backside.

Gathering myself, I opened the trunk's lid and saw, first, the ordinary things I'd anticipated, given that I'd seen Scott using this trunk for years: stacks of journals, cardboard boxes, folders, notebooks, files. His unused overseas cap was in here, along with photo albums and scrapbooks begun when he was a boy.

The most recent journal sat on top. Inside its cover, Scott had written

F. Scott Fitzgerald
14 November 1928—

We'd been at Ellerslie in November. I turned the page and began scanning the scrawled musings for Hemingway's name.

A lot of what was there concerned Scott's thoughts on his works-in-progress, along with reminders like *Tell John to try Scribner's mag* and *Harold: $400 but keep pressing*, and notes such as *'Flu two weeks*. Nothing real deep, and no mentions of his pal, beyond *E's father suicide $100; Re-reading in our time; E $50 for bet, lost Tunney*. There were several other notes about lending *E* money. There were even more about the money Scott had asked Max or Harold to deposit into one account or another. I blinked at these without taking time to calculate.

Tucked along one side of the trunk was a folder of letters from Hemingway. Here, then, would be the evidence. I sat down on the rug with my back to the bed and began to read. The letters—there were dozens—dated all the way back to July of 1925, when Hemingway had gone to Pamplona. It was no surprise that Scott had saved them; inside the trunk were other folders containing all the letters I'd written him, all the letters he'd gotten from his parents and his sister, his correspondence with Max, with Harold, with the Princeton boys, with just about every English-speaking writer on the planet. What surprised me was that Hemingway had written so many.

In that first one, he'd said,

> *I'll bet heaven for you would be an unending cocktail party with all the best and powerful members of the best powerful families there. A wealthy and faithful bunch they'd be. Your hell would be some seedy bar that had run out of booze where the unfaithful husbands sit waiting forever for a drink.*
>
> *Whereas for me heaven has the corrida and my own stream full of trout; nearby I'd have two houses, one with my family and my most loving wife and the other full of beautiful women all seeing to my needs and I'd have all the worthless lit magazines printed on soft tissue and stocked in the toilets.*

Most of the letters were like this. They were casual, humorous, and surprisingly personal. Truly, they were the letters of a good friend. Only the more recent ones seemed edgier, critical, moody. The most damning things I found were endearments that might, through a certain lens, seem a little too chummy—but those were plainly in jest, as were the occasional closings like *With salacious sincerity, Ernestine.* A few times Hemingway had said things like *I wish to hell I could see you*—but I'd written things like that to my friends and that didn't make me a lesbian. On the other hand, *I sure do miss you. I've been trying and trying to get down there to see you* concerned me. Did men who weren't fairies write to each other this way?

Occupied as I was, I hadn't noticed the shifting daylight, nor did I hear the apartment door open and close. Not until the sound of footsteps right there in the room caught my attention did I even glance up from the letters, which I'd spread on the floor all around me.

"Find what you're looking for?" Scott asked.

I was too saturated with Hemingway's words to be startled, I guess, because all I did was look up at Scott and say, "Are you two in love?"

He leaned down and took all the letters and tucked them back into the folder. His hands shook, and I smelled wine on his breath as he said, "He's my good friend, Zelda. Christ, now you're after us, too?"

"The other night—"

"What about it?" To my practiced ear, he sounded defensive.

"You were talking in your sleep. About him. And you sounded . . . amorous."

"That's crazy." He closed and locked the trunk, then turned to leave the room.

I followed him into the hallway. "You were drunk—do you even recall coming in and breaking that lamp? *Sloppy* drunk." Throat tight, the pressure of tears behind my eyes, I said, "Maybe even drunk to the point of unedited honesty."

Scott turned. "What did you say?"

I was crying now, couldn't seem to help it. "I *said,* maybe McAlmon isn't the 'goddamned liar' you two call him." Scott's eyes widened. "Maybe you're both . . . *fairies,* and, and"—I drew a breath as his eyes widened even farther—"and it could be you just hide the truth in plain sight the way so many of the other fairies try to do."

Scott shook his head as if to clear it. "You really are insane. You don't have one shred of evidence—"

"You said his name a couple of times, and you said, 'No more, baby,' and you were moaning, and you've been just, my God, *consumed* with him and his career—"

"Stop it." He grabbed my upper arm. "Do you hear me? I am *not* a fairy. *Ernest* is not a fairy. If I ever . . ." He paused, then swallowed and said, "If you ever so much as even accuse us in your *thoughts,* let alone suggest such a thing to anyone, I swear I will take my daughter and you'll never see her or me again."

"I'm *sorry,*" I cried. "It just seemed like . . . I mean, you don't want *me* anymore."

He released my arm. "What man would want a woman who thinks he's a secret homosexual? Not to mention all you talk about is ballet and artists and—Jesus, Zelda—"

"What?"

"Nothing," he said, his voice swollen with disgust. "I'm going out."

He left me standing there in the hallway, the whole encounter spinning in my head. I had to brace my hands against the walls, could barely walk a straight line to the sofa.

When my emotions finally settled, though, I thought I understood what was probably true: When it came to Scott's affections, I'd been displaced if not replaced and had only made the situation worse by confronting him. Probably, Scott loved Hemingway truly but platonically. Probably, he couldn't see that Hemingway's feelings weren't so clean. That was the thing with Scott: if he loved you truly, he had trouble seeing your flaws. *What a gift*, I thought. *What a curse*.

Probably, I had my answers. And yet I was no happier than I'd been before.

45

A Saturday in early July: I was with three of my ballet classmates at a café when Pauline rolled her pram up past our table and parked it beside a broad ivy arch. Even in her Patou suit, Pauline looked harried. Motherhood hadn't otherwise changed her, not visibly at least; possibly she'd made a connection between Hadley and motherhood and Hemingway's roving eye. Predictable though it seems now, she didn't know—none of us knew—that it wouldn't matter a bit what she did or tried to do to keep that eye focused on her. She was trying to be his best wife, the same aspiration all of us had been taught to aim for. Which didn't mean I liked her any better.

"Hi," she said. "I saw you here and thought I'd just stop over and see whether you and Scott will be at Sara's latest Dinner-Flowers-Gala next week, before everyone runs off for the summer."

"That's our plan."

"What are you going to wear? I just bought this sweet little shift, Drum said it's darling on me, but I don't know—it's rose-colored linen, with a nice contrasting—"

"Sounds perfect. I don't know what I'm wearing; I guess I'll decide that day."

Pauline said, "Sure, I know you're so busy these days with your dance lessons. You look fantastic; I just know that everything you could wear will look gorgeous on you. And of course Sara will wear something très élégant, and the apartment will be all decked out with flowers, and there'll be a fine band, and, well, you know Sara, nothing halfway."

I nodded. "Yep."

The baby started fussing. Pauline stood, saying, "Just like his father, he hates to sit still. I'm off to the market, then."

I ignored the invitation in her voice, the longing for me—or someone, anyone—to join her. If she was lonely, well, she'd made that bed for herself when she ended her single-girl-at-*Vogue* life while stealing another woman's husband.

I visited with Tom Eliot and Jean Cocteau at Natalie's salon that night, along with a group that included two women journalists who both were engaged and told me they intended to keep their jobs after marriage.

"It can be done," one said. She was tall and solid, with brown eyes that dared anyone to argue with her—about anything, I suspected. "You just have to set the ground rules up front."

"*Women* couples are doing it," said the other. She was petite, and as thin and pale as Sara Haardt. "They don't put restrictions on each other's work."

"And there are plenty of married women working in factories or as domestics," said the first. "Sure, it's because the family needs the cash, but so what? Their husbands accept this. Mine will, too."

I said, "I envy you two, getting married now. Ten years ago when I was engaged—well, I was in the American South, so there's that—but still, we were just getting around to having such high-minded ideals."

Leaving them, I went to find Natalie, thinking, *Women couples. They seem to have all the answers.*

How funny, I thought, that Natalie was a lesbian, and Romaine was, and Djuna Barnes, and Sylvia Beach, and this didn't bother me at all. Yet I'd twisted myself up into knots wondering about Scott and Hemingway, thinking that if they were lovers, it would be a disgusting, horrible thing.

How could I have one standard for the women and a different one for men? Or maybe it wasn't different for *all* men; I liked Bob McAlmon just fine, and I adored Cole—though we *had* been startled when Sara told us, somewhat reluctantly, that, yes, the rumors were true, he preferred fellas in bed. At the moment, he was doing a poor job of hiding a new affair with some young man, almost as if he didn't care whether everyone knew.

Homosexuality did seem unnatural, and puzzling, too, but to each his—or her—own, that's the way I'd thought of it. Maybe my standard was just different for the one man who was supposed to be mine.

Leaving all of that aside, I saw Natalie and followed her into the kitchen, where I told her about having seen Pauline earlier that day. I said, "She seems stuck, if you ask me. Stuck, and a little desperate."

Natalie refreshed her drink, saying, "It's a matter of making a full commitment to one's life—and if you can take an honest assessment without hating me for it, I'd like to observe that you, my dear, seem stuck, too."

"Me?"

"Are you a dancer? Are you a writer? Are you a painter, a mother, a wife?"

"*Yes.*"

She smiled. "And Pauline right now is several things, too. But look around us: when you see any of these people, don't you identify them by *one* label—the one they themselves have chosen? Me: poet. Djuna: journalist. Sylvia, there: book vendeuse. We are all other things as well, but these are us *foremost.*"

"I guess I see what you mean. But you all don't have to worry about husbands."

"Maybe you should stop worrying about yours. What are you doing to help refine yourself?"

"Well, my dance company had a recital last week, a small one, and Madame gave me a featured role. Representatives from all the top European ballets were there."

"So you hope to dance professionally despite your marriage, yes? This is good. Be a model for other wives. Lead."

"I'm too selfish to lead, don't you think? Scott won't have it anyway, and

I can't afford to leave him. I don't want to *have* to leave him. I *want* him to quit being so stubborn."

Natalie winked. "You may as well ask him to quit being a man."

That night I lay in bed alone, sleepless, restless. Scott was out who knew where doing who knew what with who knew whom. I shoved that thought away, and in its place came bits of my conversations from earlier:

You know Sara, nothing halfway.

Whereas I did *every*thing in my life halfway, or worse.

You, my dear, seem stuck, too.

And I was. What did I commit to absolutely? In my heart I was fully committed to Scottie, sure, but in my days I was, at best, ten percent. Everything else—Scott, painting, writing, dance, friendships, family—got less of my heart by far, even if I did give it more of my time. How did Sara manage *nothing halfway*? Was it built into her character? Or something she'd aspired to when she was younger, maybe? Something she'd worked at and then achieved? What chance did I have? Surely Sara had been born perfect.

For days, while at my morning and afternoon dance classes, while I ate, while I bathed, while I tried but failed to sleep, I considered how I might become more like the women I respected and admired. Surrounded as I was by such ambitious, accomplished women, I couldn't ignore the little voice in my head that said maybe I was supposed to shed *halfway* and do something significant. Contribute something. Accomplish something. Choose. Be.

I was a Sayre, after all; a woman, yes, but still a *Sayre;* my life was intended to mean something beyond daughter-wife-mother. Wasn't it?

Oh, just let it go, a different voice urged me. *What difference could your puny achievements possibly make?*

All the difference, the other voice answered.

Which of my many possible lives did I want to define me? Which one could I have?

And the question that troubled me most: Was it even really up to me?

46

September, Cannes—so that Scott could do research for the novel and try, again, to write it. He'd been shoring up his eroding confidence with stories that now brought an astonishing four thousand dollars apiece, but always there was the novel, the novel, he needed to write the novel. And it had to be phenomenally good, he said; critics would expect a masterpiece, given that more than four years had elapsed since *Gatsby*.

We had come to Cannes in July. To keep up my training, I took lessons with ballet master Andre Nevalskaya, who'd worked for the Nice Opera. I'd done three recitals in Cannes and Nice, earning no money but a lot of admiration and praise. At each performance's conclusion, I faced the applauding audience and thought, *I am a dancer*.

This day, I'd just finished class and returned to our lovely rental, Villa Fleur des Bois, to find an intriguing envelope awaiting me. Like the villas we'd rented on the Riviera before, Villa Fleur was a spacious collection of marble-floored rooms with pretty millwork and ironwork and wide French doors. There were twice as many rooms as we needed, most of which sat unused. We never economized; the very word *economy* was abhorrent to Scott's thinking. I'd once heard him tell Gerald, "Truly big men spend money freely. I hate avarice, but I hate caution even more."

The letter's postmark read *Naples, Italy*, but it was the sender's name, Julie Sedowa, that got my attention.

23 Sept. 1929

Mrs. Fitzgerald,

Having seen your July recital in Paris and last month's in Nice, it is my distinct pleasure to write you this morning with an invitation to join the San Carlo Opera Ballet Company as a premier dancer and soloist. We first wish to offer a very worthwhile solo number in <u>Aïda</u>, and think you would find our theater to be a magnificent venue in which to perform regularly.

Should you decide to join us for the duration of the season, we can offer you a monthly salary which we will discuss. It cannot be a tremendous amount unfortunately, as we do not have a budget such as the Ballets Russes, but the experience would be of great value itself, and also, Naples is inexpensive. One can find good lodging and board for only 35 lire a day.

Please advise soonest as to your disposition in this. We would be most pleased to have you.

Sincerely,
Julie Sedowa
Director, San Carlo Opera Ballet Company

I sank into a nearby chair for support and then read the lines again. Here it was, just handed right to me, my chance to be a professional dancer. This offer had to be fate.

How, though, to tell Scott? His routine since we'd come to Cannes was not so different from the way he'd been doing things for a long while, except that now he drank vodka before, during, and after his afternoon writing sessions, when he'd shut himself away in the villa's tiny maid's quarters and work until about eleven at night. He went out afterward and usually didn't return for a day or sometimes two. We hardly saw each other—even when we were in the same room.

Scottie and her governess came in and found me still sitting in the hallway. "Mama!" my girl said, and wrapped her arms around me. She wrinkled her nose and pressed it to mine. "You smell like salt and apples."

"You're making me hungry."

She sat down on my lap. "I told Mam'selle that I should have sailing lessons, and she says I need to ask my papa. Is he home?"

"I'm not sure, I just got in. *Sailing* lessons?"

"And un petit bateau."

"Mais oui."

"Will *you* ask him?" she said.

"Your chances are better if it comes from you."

I waited until after Scottie had sought him, found him, and softened him with her charms and her charming request before going to talk to him myself. Besides the obvious advantage of finding him in a better mood, I needed time to frame my more unusual request, see if I could put things in such a way as to make him think that my joining the San Carlo ballet would only benefit him, and in ways he might not have considered before. Something like *I can be your wife and a dancer, both. We'll be leaders, Deo, we'll be relevant, modern, we'll set the trends again.*

Scott was sitting on a sofa in the little conservatory, his feet up on the cushion, a neat pile of handwritten pages resting on his thighs. The doors stood open to the stone-paved courtyard, where red bougainvillea competed with honeysuckle and purple clematis for space and glory.

He had a glass of something clear in his hand and a tender smile on his lips. "I told her she can have the lessons," he said when he saw me, "but that the boat will have to wait until she's proven her mettle."

"That's both generous and fair." I lifted his feet and sat down in their spot, then let them rest on my lap. This was the most intimate we'd gotten in months. "Now I have something to ask. You know how you're always saying I just dabble at my interests? Well, I'm a dabbler no more: I've been invited to dance with a Naples company, and I want to take the job."

I handed Scott the letter. His lips tightened as he read. Then he sighed and handed the letter back. "It's flattering, I'm sure, but you can't run off to Italy to become a dancer."

"I thought *we* would go—you see where she says it's cheap to live there.

It'd just be for a year. Not even a whole year. Eight months, I think the season is."

He was shaking his head. "Our life is in France. And I hate the Italians—remember our first trip to Rome, when they tried to arrest me for stealing a bicycle?"

"You did take it without permission. Who cares about that anyway? That was Rome eight years ago, this is Naples now."

"I have a book to finish. I don't have time to find another apartment and another set of servants and another governess if Delplangue won't go, all while you're off playing ballerina for at most a couple thousand lire a month."

" 'Off playing ballerina'? It's a *professional position*—they're offering me a solo. I'm *good,* Scott, and I want to make something of my life while I've still got this"—I indicated my body—"to work with. And besides, if we do this, we'll be trendsetters again. We'll be—"

Scott pulled his feet off my lap and got up. "Oh, you want to 'make something' of your life, do you? Scottie and I, the Fitzgerald family, all that is nothing to you—I see. Just one more thing you dabbled in on your way to your serious, professional life in the ballet."

"What is *wrong* with you?" I said, my temper rising. "I have trailed you all over this continent and back and forth across an ocean and across another continent besides, all so that you can chase movie stars and drunken friends while you drown yourself in liquor, and fuss about your sad circumstances, and pretend you're going to write another book. And now I ask you for one thing that matters, *one thing* that's about *my* ambitions, something that could also put you at the forefront again, and this is what I get? You hate that I might succeed while you . . . you rot away from the inside out!"

Scott pointed at himself. "*I* am in charge of this family, Zelda. If not for *my* blood, *my* sweat, my—my—my *determination,* you'd be nobody special, just another aging debutante wasting away the years somewhere in Alabama, getting fat off of biscuits and preserves. It's *my* life that made yours worthwhile! And yet all I get is selfish ingratitude."

We glared at each other then, with the kind of hatred that comes from being deliberately wounded in one's softest, most vulnerable places by a person who used to love you passionately.

"So that's your position." I rose to my feet. He nodded, so I said, "All right. Don't come to Naples, but *I'm* going. I'm sure I can find a place that will suit Scottie and Del—"

"Scottie's not going. You're not going to abandon me and take my daughter with you."

"*Abandon* you? It's a few months apart, so that I can maybe become the kind of person every thinking woman these days would expect F. Scott Fitzgerald's 'First Flapper' to be."

"Then they're as misguided as you are. All of that flapper business was just to sell books. When are you going to understand that what I want is for you to get your priorities straight?"

Translation: *Worshipping me should be your only desire.*

I said, "When are you going to become someone who deserves to be my priority?"

After making some discreet inquiries, I learned that the law, being less progressive even than Scott, would favor him in all matters relating to Scottie's custody. If a woman left the marriage, the father kept the children—unless he chose otherwise, and Scott never would.

I wrote back to Julie Sedowa with my regrets.

47

My short story "The Girl with Talent" was written just before we left Cannes in October—right before we learned that, back home, the stock market had crashed. What's more, Bunny had checked himself into the Clifton Springs Sanitarium in upstate New York because of a nervous collapse.

Scott's face was bloodless as he laid down Bunny's letter. "He says it's 'alcohol and panic attacks and a complete inability to work.' God."

"Bunny, really?" I said. It seemed so out of character, and he'd seemed so . . . *Bunny-like* when we'd seen him the previous winter—but then what did we know about him and his life, really? We hardly understood our own.

As for the markets, well, if you'd never managed to invest, you had no money to lose.

Harold got me eight hundred dollars for my story, which, in Paris again, I used for the coming winter's lessons with my beloved Madame Egorova. Dance now became a different, more obsessive escape for me. My hopes of being a first-rate professional persisted—I might yet get on with a company here in Paris, which would make it harder for Scott to protest. But I also couldn't stand to be still.

My mornings began with one poached egg and one small cup of coffee. I dressed in my tights and leotard, my leggings, my sweaters, my skirt, my boots. I bound up my hair, then wrapped myself in my coat and scarf. Instead of taking a taxi, I walked through the Parisian winter mornings, sometimes stopping to buy a scarf or a book to give to Madame, who had become the shining light that powered my world. Madame understood me, she encouraged me, she made me believe I had every reason to continue striving for perfection.

For eight or nine hours each day, I trained with the other girls, forcing my body to defy time and gravity and metabolic needs. I shredded my muscles and taped them back into place and went on throwing myself across the worn wood, eyeing my reflection in the wall of mirrors with admiration and loathing. I needed to jump higher. I needed to be thinner. My body's lines were still a little off. *Failli, cabriole, cabriole, failli* . . . thirty times. Fifty. Afterward I went home, ate a brioche, had a bath, and went to bed. My sleep was deep and it was dark, bottomless, empty, cold. The next day I awoke and repeated the routine.

On the weekends, I practiced in the studio on my own, then went home in the afternoon to paint and to write.

A Millionaire's Girl

Twilights were wonderful just after the war. They hung above New York like indigo wash, forming themselves from asphalt dust and sooty shadows under the cornices . . .

Scott was writing, too, claiming progress on his novel. Life became calm if not happy. *Stagnant* is a better word; that's how I felt when, for example, I followed Scott to "an important gathering" at Gertrude Stein's on a Saturday in December and sat at the tea table with Alice and Pauline while the people who *mattered*—Scott, Hemingway, Ford Madox Ford—talked Art with Miss Stein. The woman I'd been at twenty would have tried to shake things up; the woman I was now, at twenty-nine, was, instead, inert.

"You look awfully wrung out," Pauline told me. "Don't you agree, Alice? Drum says you spend all your time at lessons and Scott's awfully cross about it—you should spend more time at home if you don't want to lose your husband." She leaned closer and added, "Zelda, I say this as your friend: you really do need to gain some weight. Your clothes, well, they're hanging on you. It's not flattering."

"What do you know about Scott or me or ambition or purpose?" I said. "You gave your life away just to be Hemingway's whore."

Pauline jerked back as if I'd slapped her. "Suit yourself."

In February, the nuisance cough I'd been trying to ignore turned into a hacking cough, with fever. I coughed my way through my morning routine and through my lessons and through the evening and through the night. Everyone around me urged me to go to the doctor, go to bed, do *something*— and a part of me understood that, yes, I should, yet I went on this way for two weeks, dazed, unable to exist in the world if I didn't persist.

Scott stopped me at the door one morning. "We're going to Africa. Just the two of us. You've got to take a break and get away from this climate before I get a call from Egorova saying you're dead."

"Africa?"

"Some new ground. It'll be good for us, don't you think?"

I just blinked at him. Apparently *no,* I didn't think, not very clearly or very well.

Algiers, Biskra, camels, beggars in white sheets; black ants, Arabs, desert, strange cries in the night. All of it as if experienced through a haze of black gauze. No conversation. No love. No sex, even. Why did we go? I had no idea.

See me post-Africa: dancing again, little food, sometimes vodka—to help me finish "A Millionaire's Girl." The vodka is a writing technique I've borrowed from Scott.

Harold somehow mistakes the story as Scott's and sends it to the *Post. They love it!* he reports by cable, and says they offer the now-usual four thousand dollars. "*If* it runs under Scott's name only," Harold tells us, after I make Scott phone him about the mistake. Scott says, "We need the money, Zelda, and what's the difference? You know the story's excellent or they'd never take it. That's what counts."

"Is that what counts?" I ask Gerald, who sits beside me in a movie house. Sara is on my other side. It's an April afternoon, a day in a week in a month in which I've felt agitated all the time, and two beats off the rhythm of everything around me. Scattered. Fearful. Restless.

I've ignored this, excused it, chalked it up to sleep deprivation, to irritation with Scott, to the pressure of new recitals that might yet land me a new offer, a new chance to get my way.

"I danced beautifully last night," I tell Gerald. "I could support myself that way, you know."

Gerald, trying to pay attention to the movie, whispers, "Sorry, what?"

"Money. I could make my own money."

"What are you talking about?" He's frowning at me, a strange, long, exaggerated frown.

"Sorry. I was thinking of something."

"Could you think quietly?" he says kindly.

I love you, Gerald, I think. Watching him, I feel strange, bleary. Is his mouth misshapen? Something is happening to his face—or is it just the theater's darkness, the strange light bouncing off the screen?

When I turn back toward the screen, it's difficult to focus. I blink at the shapes, which seem to be forming into something large, something solid, something with long legs—tentacles? *An octopus, it's an octopus, it's propelling itself off the screen!* I dive to the floor, sure that the beast will snatch me up and haul me off. "Help me," I whimper.

Sara's voice comes from far away: "Zelda, darling, Zelda, it's all right. Is she taking medication?"

"How should I know?"

More voices:

—*What's going on?*

—*Should we send for a doctor?*

—*Is that woman drunk?*

—We ought to get her home.

The floor is cold under my hands and knees. I'm shivering. I let Gerald help me upright while I cast about for signs that I'm safe. "The octopus—"

"What octopus?" he says.

I risk a glance at the screen. A man and woman are speaking. I recognize them from a movie poster for *Hold Everything.*

"Hold everything," I say, feeling muddled, dazed.

Sara takes my arm. "Yes, that's right—but we'll come back to see the rest, maybe tomorrow. You feel clammy, darling; we're going to get you home and make sure you're not coming down with something."

"Yes, good, thanks."

Outside, the muddled feeling eases a little amid the evening traffic, and by the time we get to my apartment, I'm more exhausted than terrified. Or rather the terror has seeped into my skin, making my entire body buzz with the knowledge that I am no longer in full control of what's going on inside my head.

"I'm fine, honest," I tell the Murphys. "Tired, but fine. I must'a been half-asleep, is all."

"A bad dream," Sara says, nodding. "Get some rest."

But I *am* coming down with something, something I'm too frightened to talk about, something I persuade myself will go away if I just work a little harder to get my leaps high enough, my turns sharper, my lines a little cleaner.

I dance mornings, I dance afternoons, I roam the streets in search of . . . nothing. Colors all look wrong to me, too bright. Music lives in my head like a ferret running on a wheel. My dreams are of ballet moves: soubresaut, sous-sous, rond de jambe, relevé; it doesn't matter that there's no sense to it, no logic or flow. I don't even notice now. It's all one with my waking dream, with the echoing voices rising from flower stands, the undulating pavement beneath and around me, the desperate desire for Madame's attentions, caresses, adoration—*Please, someone must love me*—and the horrible sensation, just before my collapse, that the world is running out of oxygen.

I can't breathe, can't breathe, can't—

PART V

"I don't know what you mean by 'glory,'"
Alice said.

Humpty Dumpty smiled contemptu-
ously. "Of course you don't—till I tell you. I
meant 'there's a nice knock-down argument
for you!'"

"But 'glory' doesn't mean 'a nice knock-
down argument,'" Alice objected.

"When I use a word," Humpty Dumpty
said, in rather a scornful tone, "it means just
what I choose it to mean—neither more nor
less."

"The question is," said Alice, "whether
you can make words mean so many differ-
ent things."

"The question is," said Humpty Dumpty,
"which is to be master—that's all."

Alice was too much puzzled to say any-
thing, so after a minute Humpty Dumpty
began again. "They've a temper, some of
them—particularly verbs, they're the
proudest—adjectives you can do anything
with, but not verbs—however, I can manage
the whole lot! Impenetrability! That's what
I say!"

—Lewis Carroll

48

"Schiz-o-phren-i-a," Scott said in a soft, careful voice, as though verbally tiptoeing around broken glass.

He was seated across from me at a little wooden table in the sunny salon of Les Rives de Prangins, a Swiss hospital on the shore of Lake Geneva. A chessboard sat between us, carved ivory pieces all in place and waiting for battle orders. He'd brought it from the apartment he'd taken in nearby Lausanne, where he intended to live for the duration of my stay here. Scottie was in the care of her governess in Paris.

I'd arrived in May after a short stint at the aptly named Malmaison clinic in Paris. The doctors there had directed me to rest and eat; I did, and then as soon as I'd regained my energy, I bolted. Back to the dance studio I went, desperate to make up for the time I'd lost. Unfortunately, I brought my terrors with me and was soon a true nervous wreck—a nervous *disaster,* practically the *Titanic*—all over again. Confused, angry, exhausted, skinny, sick, scared, and broken-down, I'd agreed to come here to Prangins. I would have agreed to anything that promised relief.

I said, "Yes, that's the diagnosis they've settled on. It means 'split mind.'"

Scott put his fingers atop a rook, tracing the toothlike surface. "Yes, I know, Dr. Forel told me." This was Dr. Oscar Forel, the renowned psychiatrist and Prangins founder the inmates—two dozen women, all well-off, all "nervous cases" like me—secretly called The Warden.

"And they won't let me dance, not at all, not even the exercises. Ballet is a trigger, they said." I swallowed my resentment, tried to ignore the pull of a desire still as strong as the most addictive drug. "How about you? How was Paris and your visit with Scottie?"

"Oh, she's well enough. Busy with her friends."

My heart clenched. "Does she miss me? Did you give her my drawing?"

"Yes, she loved the princess—wants you to do her as a paper doll if you can. And this was great: I met up with a writer Max has taken on—Thomas Wolfe, from North Carolina. He's got a novel called *Look Homeward, Angel*. I brought it." Scott leaned down to take the book from his satchel. "His writing is like Ernest's but with this soft vitality . . . he's hugely impressive, I think you'll love the book."

I looked at it without enthusiasm. "Maybe, if I ever get my concentration back."

"You will. You *will*." He reached for my hand. "Dr. Forel says it's your ambitions that drove you to the breaking point, but you're here now. There's every reason to believe you'll be fine."

"You might deliver that last line again, 'cause you don't sound a bit convincing."

"I *want* to be convinced, but, well, you have to quit doing things like trying to run away, or refusing your medications—you *have got to* be more cooperative. I'm paying a thousand dollars a month for you to be here, Zelda, so every delay—"

"I'm sure sorry to have done this to you." I pulled away from him. "How thoughtless of me—get it? Thought-less? Meaning mindless, empty-headed, vacant, and what's worse, *expensive*."

"Darling, come on, I didn't mean to—"

"It's *awful* here. Sure, it looks like this beautiful lakeside hotel, but the treatments—I feel like one of the undead," I said. "Half the time I'm sick to my stomach, just all muddled and bloated . . . and no one here speaks decent English, and you know my French is below par, and for God's sake, when I tried to leave, they sedated me and *tied me to my bed*—"

"Don't you want to get better, Zelda? *Cooperate*. Admit how damaging it is for you to compete with me. Agree to give up dancing. They've told you that all of this is necessary to your getting well."

They had. And I was learning to weave some fine baskets, too.

He said, "Scottie misses you dreadfully. We just want you home. There's no need for you to be a professional dancer, writer, anything. Be a *mother*. Be a *wife*. I've made a good life for you, Zelda; stop rejecting it."

"And then what?"

"And then your mind will mend itself. The split will heal. The doctors will put you back in balance here, if you'll let them."

The therapies I'd undergone in my three months here had diminished the terrors, the delusions—*psychosis,* they called it—and I was grateful for that. In their place, though, was this sticky, bleary bleakness. I'd tried to describe how I felt: "Pas de couleur," I told one of my doctors, *No color*. His solution: a watercolors paintbox, an easel, and paper, all of which I appreciated greatly without being able to tell for sure whether he'd understood my meaning.

"What I meant was, what will I *do*?"

Scott looked at me blankly.

"With all my time," I said.

He pushed his fingers through his hair. "You'll just *enjoy* yourself. Christ."

The first of the torturous patches began as a red spot on the right side of my neck. A mosquito bite, I thought. The spot, though, became an area. It grew scales. It itched. It wept. It throbbed. It crept along my skin until my neck was covered and my face became a dragon's, all scabby from my clawing, all oily from creams that had no effect. I breathed fire at my nurses and my doctors, demanding some kind of relief.

I felt like my head and neck had been dipped and floured and were continuously frying in hot oil. Dante would have adapted this torturous rash—*eczema* is its innocent name—to the *Inferno* with glee, and Dr. Forel would have devised a special circle of hell for women who, like me, resisted reeducation.

Wrapped in salve and gauze and waiting for my next dose of that old savior morphine, I wrote to Tootsie, *Emma Bovary wouldn't have hung around for this.*

49

One of the Swiss doctors had written in his notebook, in English, "A jazz-age train wreck in slow motion." I pointed and asked, "Est-ce le vôtre?" *Is that yours?*

He tilted the notebook so that I couldn't read from it. "Madame Fitzgerald, veuillez répondre à la question." *Please answer the question.*

"I'm tired this morning; can we do this in English? And call me Zelda, won't you? It's been nearly a year, after all. I think we're acquainted."

The doctor and I were seated in armchairs that had been upholstered with dense brown silk. Here were polished maple shelves filled with medical volumes; damask draperies framing the kind of bucolic view Wordsworth and Coleridge and Shelley wrote about so eloquently; a carved desk holding a tooled-leather blotter, silver inkwell, silver-framed photographs of three perfect blond children and a perfectly conservative-looking blond wife. Bland wife, in fact. No flapper, no party girl, no dancing *artiste* for this doctor, who looked only a little older than Scott's thirty-four years. This doctor was without question a sensible man.

"Madame Fitzgerald, the matter of evaluating your progress—"

"'Cause that sentence sounds like Scott," I said, reaching over to tap the notebook. "That's his term, you know. *Jazz age.* From *Tales of the Jazz Age,* his second story collection, in 1922. Have you read his books?"

The doctor's gaze was level, expressionless. If he was judging me, he didn't let on. But I had to wonder if Scott had persuaded them that I was the one who'd derailed our life, the same way his letters had tried to persuade *me*. We'd both written reams of recriminations over the past year, purging ourselves of all the feelings we'd held inside for so long.

"Let us continue," the doctor said. His name was Brandt, and I'd seen him three or four times before. He said, "Yes, you have been with us for eleven months, so we evaluate your progress once again." He glanced at his notebook. "How do you feel presently about Mr. Fitzgerald's success in relation to your own failed attempts?"

"Sorry?"

"Ah, you feel remorse." The doctor wrote something in the notebook. "You realize now that a wife must first tend to *domestic* matters. Good. This is paramount to every woman's happiness."

"No, I mean I don't understand the question. *Failed* attempts? How did I fail, except in having the stamina to continue?"

He looked at me blankly. "You are not sorry? Do I misunderstand? Préféreriez-vous de parler en français?"

"No, God—it's bad enough trying to do this in English. I *mean,* I don't think I've failed, not in the way you seem to be saying. And Scott, well, he hasn't been all that successful in the past few years. And he sure wasn't tending to domestic matters either, and I'd say *that's* paramount to a woman's happiness."

When the doctor said nothing, didn't even blink, I added, "Maybe my stories and essays aren't as fine as Scott's, but who says I have to be just like him? I'm not him. No writer should be the same as another, that's not art. My articles and stories have been published in lots of places. Ask him, he'll tell you I've succeeded on my own."

Dr. Brandt said, "We have asked him, yes." He scratched his chin, then said, "Dr. Forel feels that since hypnosis was so helpful with the eczema and you are feeling stronger, it is best for you to write down your recollections and opinions, which we can compare with your husband's. Monsieur Fitzgerald has been extremely forthcoming."

"I bet. So I write my thoughts, and then what? You'll hand down a final judgment like my father would?"

This thought about my father tugged at my heart, making it flutter. The tug was not about Daddy, exactly, but about *home*. Some home. *Any* home. I was well now and had been well for a good while. Several thousand dollars' worth of while, in fact; continuing to stay here just to perfect my carpentry and volleyball skills was absurd.

I'd said as much to Scott during a recent outing to Geneva, begged him, "Deo, just tell 'em you're satisfied with the job they did and now we're going back to Paris."

Being away from the clinic made me feel wholly human, reminded me that I'd once had a life as real as any of the people we passed on the quai.

Scott took my hand. "These doctors are the finest psychiatric minds in the world. We can't second-guess their knowledge."

"But the expense—"

"I'm handling it. Of more concern to me is that Dr. Forel says you're still resisting some of their suggestions. Even though you *feel* better, you aren't fully cured."

"Forel isn't God. And even if he was, I don't understand how we can afford—"

"The *Post* has been taking everything I write," Scott said, quite pleased with himself. "My productivity's the best it's been in ages."

Not only was he pleased, he was *happy*. I was suddenly suspicious. "Are you seeing someone?"

"What? No!"

"Then why don't you want me out of there?" Then I realized he'd given me the answer already. "Never mind," I said. "I understand."

Now Dr. Brandt was saying, "A judgment, yes."

"Okay then. Let's get this done. Only—you have to guarantee that Scott doesn't get to read what I write. No editorial oversight from my husband. No consulting. You can't even *tell* him. If he knows I'm doing it, he'll insist on having a look. There'd be no point, if that's how it goes."

"Yes, we agree." Dr. Brandt nodded. "We wish to make the objective evaluation."

Knowing that was impossible, I said, "I would like that very much."

He gave me some pages of blank paper and a pencil and left me to it. I started with this:

The Recollections of one Zelda Sayre Fitzgerald,
as begun on this day, 21 March 1931, at the suggestion of Dr. Forel

You said to begin anywhere, so here is a poem I especially like, by Emily Dickinson:

I know a place where summer strives
With such a practiced frost,
She each year leads her daisies back,
Recording briefly, "Lost."

But when the south wind stirs the pools
And struggles in the lanes,
Her heart misgives her for her vow,
And she pours soft refrains

Into the lap of adamant,
And spices, and the dew,
That stiffens quietly to quartz,
Upon her amber shoe.

Even from here, from Prangins today, when I haven't seen my daughter in three months and no one's willing to say whether I'm truly well or how much longer it might be before I get to leave, I sit bathed in sunshine that streams through the window and feel a sense of hopefulness, of possibility. Spring always did make me feel this way, before. So I think this is progress.

You asked me to say what happened, so I'll tell you. Scott might tell you a different story about the same things—but then, hasn't he always?

The world was strange and perilous when I met Scott in 1918, with the Great War in progress and influenza raging across every continent, taking more than fifty million lives by 1919. This horror, along with knowing that fifteen million soldiers and civilians were killed in the war, infected everyone's spirits if not our bodies. Life seemed more tenuous than ever. But Scott and I were lively and eager, unfettered by conventional ideals. We were sailing at the leading edge of a storm.

Maybe we asked too much of everyone and everything right from the start. Our parents were kids during the American Civil War, you know; their world was a divided one. Scott and I weren't supposed to even mingle much, let alone fall in love. And to make it worse, Scott wanted to be a professional novelist, which was not really a recognized occupation. We didn't care. For us, it was a time to make everything up, to create our lives from scratch using unfamiliar ingredients and untested methods—only to now arrive at this unforeseeable result.

Now that the stories about us, about "the Fitzgeralds," have grown like wild Chinese wisteria past the borders of cocktail party gossip and are starting to encroach on literary myth, I hear that some of my friends have started saying I made Scott the writer he is—and you can imagine how well that goes over with him. His friends—and especially one in particular—are saying I've held him back, interfered with his talent and his work ethic—which is of course what he has said, too.

Depending on who you ask, you'll hear Scott's either a misunderstood genius or a pathetic son-of-a-bitch who never met a liquor he didn't want to cozy up to. He drinks too much, it's true, and he has not always been good to me or to himself, but I think he's broken somewhere inside, and he drinks to try to fill the cracks.

———

I've had a letter from one of my dearest, oldest friends, Sara Haardt, saying that she's marrying another old friend of ours, Henry Mencken. She's been frail with tuberculosis for a long while, but that didn't sway him in the least.

She wrote, "I'm not sure I'll be any good at marriage, having gone without for so long. Your letters from over the years make a good primer, though; for all the troubles, I've never seen devotion such as you and Scott enjoy."

Sara must have had spies in Annecy, as Scott and my sweet baby girl and I have just returned from the most perfect two weeks there. We danced and dined and it was even better than old times for having Scottie always at my side, her soft hand in mine, and at night, Scott's reassuring form curled behind me. I wish, oh, you have no idea how much, that I could bottle up those days and then climb inside that bottle too.

———

Here's an anecdote, a memory that comes to mind as I'm writing: For our first trip to Europe, in 1921, we sailed on the Aquitania. There was a lot of drinking and, when the seas got rough, a lot of nervous humor over the prospect of going down with the ship. That would be the end for us all, everyone said.

"Not for me," I declared, and Scott said, "That's right. My wife is not only beautiful, she's an excellent swimmer. You'll save us both, darling, won't you?"

That's what I'm doing here, I'm swimming.

After reviewing the journal I'd been keeping for three months, Dr. Forel came in to see me. I was up and dressed and had eaten my usual fruit and yogurt, but was still shaking off the effects of my sleep medication.

"Bonjour," he said, all bright and cheerful. He wore a tweedy brown suit with vest and tie, and his beard—also tweedy—looked freshly trimmed.

"Not so *bon*. I would like to try eliminating the sleeping pills."

"Eh? This is unexpected. Your regimen has been most effective; it would be unwise to alter it now."

"I always feel like my head's been stuffed with cotton and I have to spend the morning plucking it out through my ears."

"It's so?" He frowned, then smiled and said, "Ah, with you this is not a literal statement. What did you tell me before—such a thing is spoken figuratively, yes? Except when one is experiencing delusions. But you are past that."

"Past the delusions, still stuck on the metaphors. So how about it?"

"I will consult with Dr. Brandt. Your quality of rest is of great import, as you are aware."

He gestured to the pair of ladder-back chairs that faced my window, and we sat down there. "We are finding much that is of interest," he said, handing the book over to me. "We notice a pleasing amount of melancholia in your recollections. Clearly you have an enduring affection for your husband—would you say this is the case?"

"Of course I do. We've been through everything together."

Outside, clouds—like the figurative cotton from my head—filled a lavender-blue sky. A tall, thin woman in a broad-brimmed hat shuffled along the garden path, her arm held securely by a young nurse.

"Yet this affection, it was greatly diminished before you came to us," Dr. Forel said. "Shrouded by your anger. It is like this?"

"It was a difficult time, that's what I would say. I was a real mess. Angry? Sure, before my collapse I'd been real angry with him. He was drunk all the time. He let me down."

"And also you let him down, this we have established, no? A wife owes fidelity of all kinds. Her husband, her family, these are the things that must be foremost in her mind, always. When this is not the case, there are breakdowns. Some severe—as with your situation, when indeed the woman has pulled far away from her domestic circle, that place where the only genuine happiness can be found."

In the garden, the tall woman stopped abruptly. I could see the nurse speaking to her, but she didn't respond, just stared off into the hedge. *Poor thing*, I thought, understanding too well her condition despite not knowing anything about it, or her.

I said, "I'm not saying I don't agree about what can happen—'cause I sure was awfully unhappy for a long time—but you know, sometimes being away from Scott, being in class with Madame and the others, *sometimes* that was the only place I *was* happy."

Dr. Forel nodded. "Yes, that is part of the delusion's complex. Schizophrenia divides the mind, deceives it. You are showing us, however, that your capacity to recognize the consequences of your choices is returning. I am persuaded that you now see the effects of your failure to create and maintain a secure hearth, which, had you done so, would have tethered your husband in ways that would have prevented his difficulties."

So there it was, in plain enough English: my main failure, the reason for all our troubles, was that I hadn't created a secure hearth, a tether for my husband. I wondered if it was *possible* to tether Scott, but kept that thought to myself.

"Yes," Dr. Forel said, rising, "we are pleased."

"Well, since I've also mastered shuffleboard and woven more baskets than there were locusts in Egypt, will you consent to my release?"

He smiled as if he found my question quaint. "Not yet. But you may cease the journal. And the baskets." He started to bow, then stopped himself. "I would, however, like to pose a question, which you may, if you wish, explore in the journal before we meet next: What is woman's duty to her husband, philosophically speaking? You are a person of true intelligence; I'm interested to know your thoughts."

A Woman's Duty in Marriage

The specific details of how a woman enacts her duty to her husband will depend upon many different circumstances. What is the couple's social standing? What is the husband's occupation? Do the couple have children? Do they have money? What is his personality—independent? Needy? Demanding? A woman has to assess her circumstances with thoughtfulness and thoroughness before she knows how she will be expected to comport herself in her role as wife. Once she understands what's needed, she must endeavor to anticipate her husband's desires in all matters. She must make the creation of a stable, comfortable household her primary occupation, however that translates to her particular situation.

Nature has created roles for male and female, which in the case of the higher species such as humans comes with a moral component as well. Because most women are supported by their husbands entirely, the women are bound to offer support of an equivalent nature in return. This is a cooperative arrangement, and a correct one.

When I finished the essay, I thought, *There, that oughta do the trick,* and presented it to Dr. Forel with contrived—but apparently convincing—sincerity. He and Scott agreed that after sixteen months they'd finally, successfully reeducated me, and it was time for me to go home. If the reeducation had actually succeeded, that might have been the end of it. As it was, the worst was yet to come.

50

Believing Europe had turned toxic, or at least toxic for us, we moved to a charming little house in Montgomery, where I would have my family to help me readjust.

Little had changed in the eleven years we'd been away, but for me, everything had changed. *I* had changed. Freedom from Prangins had been my greatest desire, yet like a slave after emancipation, I wasn't quite sure how to exist in this quiet, calm, open-ended world, how to be a mother to my cautious daughter, a wife to any man—let alone one as observant and particular as Scott. When he left Scottie and me for an unexpected six-week job in Hollywood for MGM, my moods and my confidence rolled like the ocean in a storm, leaving me seasick, sometimes, and scared. I'd been forbidden to resume ballet—and was so out of condition that I was hardly tempted anyway—so to steady myself I wrote, and I wrote, and I wrote: essays, stories, letters to friends, an article for *Esquire*, the start of a book.

My father had been ill when we arrived in September, having had an awful bout of the flu in the spring and then pneumonia in summer, which laid him lower still. Daddy was legendary in Alabama, still on the bench at seventy-three, still a vital legal and moral force for the state. His old body just could not keep up with his stubbornly healthy mind, though, and he passed in November, while Scott was still in Hollywood.

At the end, he was such a small version of himself—but still Daddy: "I don't know why you don't divorce that boy" were among his last words to me.

"What's that on your neck?" Scott asked. "Did you get bit? Do we need to go inside?"

It was February of '32, and we were on the veranda at the towering, pink Don CeSar resort in Tampa, Florida, during our "getaway on the Gulf," a little holiday for just the two of us. Scott hated the Montgomery quiet, the calm. Home two months from Hollywood, he'd gotten stir-crazy. My mother and Marjorie's constant hovering over the three of us hadn't helped a bit. We would move again soon.

There on the veranda, he'd been elaborating on a new plan for his novel. Where originally the story had been about matricide, now it would be the story of a psychiatrist who falls in love with one of his patients, a poor, sad woman in a mental hospital. He'd lay the story in Europe as planned, he'd use the places we'd been, the people we'd met, all the things he'd learned while helping Dr. Forel treat my illness, he said. "You don't mind, do you, darling?"

And then he noticed the spot.

I put my hand up to where he pointed and felt angry skin. My fingers knew too well what was happening. My hand trembled as I lowered it. "Eczema."

"From what? You're not having trouble, are you? You seem fine."

I shrugged, not trusting my voice. I'd been trying hard to remain steady, to avoid overexcitement, to eat properly. I, too, had thought I was more or less fine.

I am, I am, I am. Nothing to worry about. Do not worry! Do not scratch! Think about the palm trees, look at the water, isn't it lovely here? Nice place, nice trip, nice husband to bring me here . . .

A few days later, a second spot appeared, and the first had grown larger. Something was going very wrong. I wasn't as well as I thought. My confidence crumbled. "I need to go home, Deo. I need to see my doctor before this gets any worse." My voice was now as shaky as my hands.

The doctor recommended a rest cure at the Johns Hopkins Hospital's Phipps Clinic. Some time away from anything or anyone who might upset me—Scott interpreted this to mean Mama—would surely set me right again.

My official overseer was gruff, formal Dr. Adolf Meyer, the very prototype of a rigid German overlord. At my admission exam, he poked and frowned and squinted as he looked me over, saying, "Vut haf vee here?"

I frowned and squinted back at him and refused to answer.

His assistant, Dr. Mildred Squires, was a godsend. Unlike her male counterparts, she drifted through the institution's ugliness like a rare butterfly, somehow above the coarseness of it all. To me she was Sara Murphy in a white coat and spectacles, dispensing care and wisdom and encouraging you to rise above the indignities of your treatment—the intestinal cleanses, the stupor that followed sedation—and assert your humanity, if only to yourself. I loved her.

To right myself, I would *write* myself. Well, not me, exactly, but a version of me, and a version of Scott, and a dramatization of the not-me's life, including her struggles as the ballet-dancing wife of a popular artist, and the breakdown that came as a result. The more I wrote, the less I itched, to the point where I nearly forgot the eczema altogether and it began to fade.

Weeks passed in a blur of story, a complete escape into the depths of my imagination. I'd named my not-Scott after his first novel's protagonist, Amory Blaine. To me, this was a nod, a public sign that I had studied at École Fitzgerald and was a devotee. As Scott had done with *This Side of Paradise* and Hemingway had done with *The Sun Also Rises,* I'd fictionalized my characters while maintaining, I thought, the truth of our lives and our society. I tried to marry modernist art to modern fiction, using words to paint vivid, fractured images that would evoke my desired responses. When the handwritten draft was done, I had an aide find me someone to turn it into a typescript.

"Two copies," I told the young woman when I gave her my handwritten pages. "Thanks so much."

Dr. Squires stopped in at my room one day and, upon seeing typed, stacked pages done up with twine, said, "You're not finished with your book already?"

That stack was a beautiful thing to have sitting atop my desk, an affirmation that I wasn't only a useless burden in life. I grinned and told her, "I am. Beginning, middle, end. Hard to believe, I know."

"It's only been, what, a little over a month since you started writing?"

"I sketched some of it when Scott was away in Hollywood."

"Even so! May I read it?"

"I hoped you would."

Dr. Squires's admiration puffed me up—and I got puffier still after she read and praised my efforts.

"What a story," she said when she brought the pages back. "So creative, so compelling. What do you plan to do with it?"

"Well, first I'll have to see what Scott thinks." I'd told him only that I was going to try my hand at a novel, not what the story would be or how I'd approach it. "Then I'm hoping Scribner's will want to publish the book."

"Very good, Zelda. This story is saying some important things, and with such unique style."

I mailed one copy to Max straightaway.

Was sending it to Max first a kind of subterfuge? Yes. Was it necessary? Without question. Scott had been laboring for six years on a book that was still a long way from done. *Six years,* versus one month; that matchup promised disaster and I knew it. But I could no more stop myself than I could fly to the moon on gossamer wings. The novel had to be written and evaluated independently of Scott, that's just the way it was.

When he came to see me next, I had the other typescript waiting for him. I handed him the bundled pages.

"What this?"

"It's my novel."

"What, finished?"

I nodded. "I already sent it to Max—I didn't want to trouble you with it when I knew you were concentrating on your book. But now that you're on a break, I'd love to get your thoughts. I'm sure it's awful and will benefit greatly from a master's eye."

"Finished?" His face reddened and his voice rose. "You did all this behind my back, on my dollar, while I was slaving away to keep your life, our family, my career, all of it, from disintegration? Unbelievable!" He threw the bundle onto the floor.

"No, Deo, you knew I was working on it, and what does it matter?" I said, retrieving it. "Aren't you proud of me that I finished something? That I made good use of my time here? Scott, *I wrote a novel,* and I tried to put to use all the things you've taught me. Won't you please at least have a look?"

He snatched the pages from me and tucked them under his arm, then stormed out the door.

Days went by with no sign of him, no telephone call, nothing. Had he returned to Montgomery? Would he read it at all? Maybe he'd burn it; good thing I'd already sent a typescript to Max.

I chewed at the skin on the inside of my lower lip, and watched the ducks paddle along the lakeshore, and walked, and ate, and slept, and waited.

The response came by mail:

> *Good God, Zelda, if your intent is to ruin me, you've made good headway here. Your Amory is an alcoholic caricature of me, Zelda, wearing only the thinnest of veils, and everyone will know it! You may as well flay me and leave me in the sun for the flies and vultures to feast on, Jesus!*
>
> *If I allow Max to pursue this, you will submit to my editorial direction, is that clear?*

At about the same time, Max cabled to say he was quite impressed, that there was much to appreciate, some truly beautiful descriptions and turns of phrase, and that, yes, he would like to publish it.

"So there," I whispered.

Oh, I knew I wouldn't get my way, not entirely. In the months to come, Scott would take over the project as if he were Cecil B. DeMille himself. He'd scold the Phipps staff for allowing me such free rein. He'd make me cut or revise anything that rang too true for his comfort. He'd direct Scribner's to apply any money the book made to his preexisting debt with them. He'd tell them to minimize efforts at publicity—supposedly to protect me from "overweening expectations." It didn't matter. None of that mattered. As far as I was concerned, I'd won.

Or had I?

I cut as directed and patched somewhat, and then the book was rushed to publication in October without any oversight save Scott's, and no advertising support at all. Scott told me, "The doctors don't want you getting egotistical about having a book out, it would only cause you more emotional trouble. A small start is best."

"Sure, okay," I said, caught up in the thrill of having a whole book of my own, a book printed with my title, *Save Me the Waltz,* and my name all by itself below.

Then came the reviews. *The Saturday Review of Literature* used words like *implausible, unconvincing, strained,* and full of *obfuscations.* Oh, and also *disharmonious. The New York Times* was slightly kinder; the reviewer there seemed more puzzled than antagonistic; he found the story a *curious muddle* and was unable to get past the author's *atrocious* writing style.

As bad as that? I thought, when I set the clippings aside. I felt weak, nauseated, ashamed. Where was the thrill? The pride of accomplishment? Could it all be undone by two strangers who hardly seemed to have given it a chance?

Scott had been watching my face as I read the reviews; when I looked up, he said, "Now you know how I feel. Now you know what it's like."

I had believed I was writing my way to salvation, but just like that night outside the Dingo with Hemingway, I'd miscalculated, overestimated what I could do.

In the end, the novel sold only a thousand copies or so. The cover should have read,

Another Failed Endeavor
by Zelda Fitzgerald

51

The sound of the back door closing told me Scott was home, "home" this time being a porches-balconies-turrets Victorian on twenty snow-covered acres in Towson, Maryland, another pastoral rental taken in hopes of us reordering our life so that Scott could finish his book. *Gatsby* was now more than seven years in our past.

Scott had rented the house, La Paix—which means *peace,* a moniker that would grow ever more ironic—not long after I completed my novel. Coming off his most lucrative writing year ever, thanks to the *Post* buying nine stories written while I was locked away in Prangins, he'd splurged. Again. I had been released from Phipps in late summer and come home to find we had fifteen rooms, four live-in servants, tennis courts, and a lake. We also had dowdy, kind Isabel Owens, a secretary who managed Scott's affairs and the household, too, when I wasn't around.

What we didn't have much of was furniture, but not much company to use it, either. We did see a lot of Scott's mother, Mollie, who was sweet, if forever puzzled by her son's irregular life and his irregular wife. Next door were the Turnbulls, an old-money pair who made good landlords and whose three children made good playmates for Scottie but, being a "dry" couple, not such good playmates for Scott.

Upon my release, Dr. Meyer had directed me not to drink alcohol and had gone 'round with Scott about how much more successful my treatment would be if Scott licked liquor, too. Scott's reply: "I've done the reading about schizophrenia and, with due respect, see nothing that even suggests the illness can be triggered by *a spouse's* alcohol use."

"It presents unnecessary stress," Dr. Meyer said.

"It relieves unnecessary stress," Scott replied.

Now I heard Scott tossing his keys into the dish near the door, and then the creak of the stair treads. I expect he assumed, as I did, that everyone was asleep. Probably he hoped he could haul himself upstairs and fall into bed as usual, and probably he would have done so if I hadn't still been up and painting in my little studio, which was the first room at the top of the back stairs.

When Scott saw me, he stopped and, holding on to the doorjamb, leaned in. He'd taken off his coat and shoes, but was still wearing his hat. His mouth was slack, his skin pasty, his eyes dulled by whatever he'd been drinking on the train from New York, and from whatever he'd been drinking with Ernest Hemingway before getting on the train.

Hemingway had recently published *Death in the Afternoon,* a book of his thoughts on bullfighting, and was in the city to give a speech of some kind—something Scott was both eager and loath to witness. Afterward they would meet up with Bunny Wilson, whose second wife, Margaret, had died a few months before after falling on some stairs. Hem the hero; Scott the conflicted; Bunny the morose: it had promised an evening I could hardly wait to miss.

On my easel was a canvas, and on that canvas was the start of what would, I hoped, be a warm depiction of calla lilies, done in oils. I'd been dreaming of calla lilies, *Zantedeschia aethiopica,* fragrant, mudbound stems like ones I'd seen along old riverbeds so often in my girlhood. With January's icy hold on the house and the land here, I needed some warmth.

"You can go on to sleep," I told Scott. "I'm not tired yet, so I'll be a while."

In fact, sleep was becoming ever more fickle, refusing me when I needed it, demanding attention when I would have preferred to spend the afternoon with Scottie. At eleven, she was very much her own person, further from me than ever before. My minutes with her were precious. I tried hard not to interfere with her schedule or habits or friendships; she was getting more than enough direction from Scott, who advised her how to dress, walk, speak, wear her hair, study, eat, and laugh. ("Don't show your teeth so much, and be quieter about it; you don't want to draw so much attention to yourself. Boys prefer modest girls, girls they can respect and admire.")

Scott let go of the door frame and came into the room. Leaning against the wall, he studied me. Certainly I wasn't my glamorous best in one of his old shirts and a shapeless skirt—painting clothes. My hair needed washing. I had paint on my hands, could feel it on my chin, my ear, my forehead. I wore knitted green slippers that Mama had sent.

"Y'know," Scott said, "I *thought* we'd pick up girls."

"It's the middle of the night. The girls are in Scottie's room, sleeping," I said, assuming he'd gotten too drunk to keep her sleepover plans straight.

Scott gave a little bark of a laugh. "*Girls,*" he said. "*Prostitutes.* Christ, you really aren't right in your head, are you?"

My mouth opened but no words emerged.

He went on, "And I *know* that's true, and I should be a good Christian about it and forgive you and love you all the same, and I *do,* or I *did,* and I want to, but, Jesus, Zelda, I *don't.* I don't love you. I don't."

He slid to the floor and put his hands over his head as he cried, "You've ruined my life! I'm a goddamn eunuch compared to Ernest. *Three sons!* Bulls and blood . . ." He looked up at me. "Imagine this: I told him, 'I'm done, Ernest, I'm washed up, hang me out but I won't dry.' I said, 'Let's pick up some girls,' and Ernest said, 'You're in no shape for that.' A eunuch! No shape for girls, for writing—I'm good for *nothing* and it's *your fault.* I'm so tired of you."

I cleaned my brushes, covered the canvas, and without saying a word stepped over Scott and across the hall to a spare bedroom, where I managed to turn the lock before the tears came.

It's the liquor talking, I told myself, curled up on top of the quilt. *The liquor, the liquor, it's the liquor and Hemingway, damn him to hell, and damn Scott, and damn my weak, pitiful brain, damn everything. . . .*

After fitful sleep, I woke ahead of sunrise and found that a sheet of paper had been slipped beneath my door.

Darling, darling, what you must think of me now. . . . Too much bourbon turns me maudlin these days, but that's no excuse for mistreating you. You are brave and admirable, Zelda. I'd never survive what you've been through. Please forgive the wretch I can sometimes be. Say you still love me and I will be able to stand myself long enough, I hope, to find my way back to the path.

When I opened the door, he was there, waiting in the dim morning light. He'd changed his clothes, his hair was combed, his eyes looked bloodshot but alert.

I crossed my arms. "Decide what it is you want, Scott."

"Do you love me?"

I thought, *Do I? What does real love feel like, anyway?* I wasn't sure I knew anymore. And then I remembered Tootsie and me talking of this so many years before:

—I guess I ought to be aware of what to look for, is all. The signs of true love, I mean. Is it like in Shakespeare? You know, is it all heaving bosoms and fluttering hearts and mistaken identities and madness?

—Yes, yes, it is exactly *like that. Gird yourself, little sister.*

I would have needed iron ramparts, I thought—and even then it might not have been enough.

"I shouldn't," I told Scott, and saw him visibly relax. "I might not," I added. Why should he be able to relax when I still felt a wreck? "Don't count on it," I said.

He reached for me and wrapped me in his arms. "Then let's just have this for now."

Four months later, I had conceived and written and found a local playhouse to produce an original play I called *Scandalabra*. Scott, meantime, was still searching for that path he'd mentioned, searching one-handed while he held a highball in the other. He wasn't writing. The bills were coming in but not getting paid. Shopkeepers, suit makers, barkeepers were calling, all singing the same song: "Mr. F's account is past due; will you tell him that we inquired?" My patience was as brittle and thin as springtime ice.

I was brittle and thin. And icy sometimes, too, sure I was. He was never going to change, I would never be able to make him change, all my idealism had eroded away and now it was time to do what Tootsie and Sara Mayfield were urging: *Get out.* When *Scandalabra* flopped and closed after a one-week run, I wrote back to Sara, *Easier said than done— Ha, that ought to be my epitaph. Or Scott's.*

However, she knew, as I did, that there are many ways to leave a man if that is what one is determined to do. The easiest method is to snag a new man's devotion—a wealthier man is preferable, and I knew plenty of those. If I wanted to, I could seek the appropriate gentleman and turn his head sufficiently that I would never again worry about how, whether, and when the merchants got paid. What's more, the prospect of losing Scottie no longer terrified me; wasn't she lost to me as it was? Didn't she already distrust my stability, my judgment? Hadn't she become, during my absences, entirely Scott's child?

July 20th, 1933

Dearest Tootsie,

I know what you said in your last letter was right. Scott appears to be a hopeless case and I have too often felt pushed beyond my limits. We aren't either of us model spouses, though, are we? You know how I can get when I'm irritated—and even if I was once the darling of the social scene, I'm slightly less of a prize these days.

Who else would have stood by me so rigorously when I was the one who appeared hopeless? He must love me. This must be just another rough patch.

He's so brilliant, Tootsie, but so, so fragile. I want to swaddle him like we do all our finest Christmas ornaments before we store them away, protect him from even the most innocent-seeming hazards that can result from too much admiration.

I mean to try writing another novel. Max has said he'd be glad to see one from me. Scott will have a fit, as he's still a long way from being done with his. I am girding myself once again. If you think God is still listening to anyone on our dissipated behalves, say a prayer for Scott and me.

Best love to you, and Newman too—

Z~

All that summer we bloodied our knuckles, Scott and I did, neither of us giving an inch. I was fighting for my right to exist independently in the world, to realize myself, to steer my own boat if I felt like it. He wanted to control everything, to have it all turn out the way he'd once envisioned it would, the way he'd seen it when he'd first gone off to New York City and was going to find good work and send for me. He wanted his adoring flapper, his Jazz Age muse. He wanted to recapture a past that had never existed in the first place. He'd spent his life building what he'd seen as an impressive tower of stone and brick, and woken up to find it was only a little house of cards, sent tumbling now by the wind.

In August, on a day when Scott was upstairs working and my kitchen was aflutter with me, Scottie, and three of her friends attempting to make "gen-u-ine Southern biscuits," the telephone rang.

I hurried over to the nook and answered before the ringing could disturb Scott further. Tootsie was on the line. "Zelda, listen, honey, something's happened. It's Tony."

The girls were still chattering away, so I plugged my free ear. "What? What happened?"

"I know you and Mama have been corresponding about his treatment since he took ill last month; thank you so much for trying to help. . . . You spoke to him, didn't you?"

My heart was beating wildly. "Yes. God, he was a wreck." He'd been depressed about losing his job and was hearing voices, he said, or maybe they were waking dreams, what did I think? *Something* was urging him to kill Mama, he said, and he was desperate to make it stop. After seeing doctors in Charleston, Asheville, and finally Mobile, he'd checked into the sanitarium there.

"He was bad off," Tootsie said. "Baby, is anyone there with you? Is Scott home?"

"Just tell me," I said, choking out the words. The girls, all as flour-covered as I was, had gone silent and were watching me.

"He had a fever, he was delirious, he—God, Zelda, he climbed out his window and jumped. The fall killed him. He's gone."

I swallowed hard and blinked back my tears. Delirium? Had that really been the case, or was that the story Tootsie was telling in case the operator listened in? Had he just been desperate?

Then Scottie was next to me, saying, "What's the matter, Mama?"

"Oh. Aunt Tootsie has some awfully sad news."

"Is it Granny?"

"I'll call you later," I told Tootsie, then placed the handset in its cradle, saying, "Not Granny, no. Uncle Tony. He had an accident. He . . . he . . . He passed. Uncle Tony is dead."

What dread filled me then! It was as if my saying the words had turned my blood to a thick, cold fog. Gooseflesh covered my arms; I wrapped them tight around myself and thought, *Tony and I, aren't we two of a kind?* There was no escape for either of us, no escaping our bad blood, our bad fate, those moody ghosts that had followed one or another of us all our lives. No escape, except the ultimate one.

I looked at Scottie, her budding loveliness, her kind eyes, and before I could stop the words that were rising like a bubble in my chest, I said, "Oh, sweetness, we're doomed."

We both started at a noise from the corridor. Scott was there.

"No one is doomed," he said, his voice firm but soft, too, a salve for me, a raft for Scottie to climb onto. "But we will all be sad for a while. Girls, I'm sorry, I'll need you to wash up and get your things, and Scottie and I will drive you home."

They all got busy cleaning up. Only I saw in Scott's eyes the fear and dread that he'd managed to keep out of his voice. He'd understood what had happened without my having to tell him. That's how obvious it was, how easy for any thinking person to spot the rotten strain running through our family.

He caught me watching him. "Zelda," he said quietly, coming over to me. "No. His troubles were different from yours." He took my hands. "Look at you—having a perfect day in a perfect home with your charming, happy daughter. I could hear you all from upstairs; the girls were having a grand time. You were the life of the party."

I nodded and drew a deep breath; my heart felt heavy as a brick in my chest. "Yes, okay. Okay." In my ears, though, my pulse thumped away, *Doomed, doomed, doomed.*

52

I asked Scott, "Why do you suppose we haven't gotten divorced yet?"

It was Christmas Eve 1933, not long after we'd moved from La Paix to a cheaper residence, a redbrick row house in Baltimore. Scottie had fallen asleep during Scott's discussion—lecture, really—on *Ivanhoe* and was now in bed awaiting Santa Claus. Scott and I sat in wing chairs facing the fireplace, both of us with one glass of double-strength eggnog in hand and another already in our bellies—my first drink in ages, and it was having an effect.

Back in the fall, Scott had checked himself in for treatment at Johns Hopkins a few times, which would have impressed me greatly if he had admitted it was to get help with his drinking. What he *said* was that his old lung ailment—mild tuberculosis he claimed he'd caught in 1919—kept flaring up. Still, he managed to finish *Tender Is the Night,* his novel about the psychiatrist in love with a patient, and then sold the serialization to *Scribner's Magazine.* He had written Hemingway to share his news, and Hemingway had written back, *I'll bet you feel like you've shit a boulder finally.* Scott was disappointed; he'd hoped for something a little more congratulatory. He excused the slight, saying how Hemingway was occupied with his new baby, a new novel, and an African safari. (The new wife was yet to come.)

With Scott's book finished, I had again asserted my desire to write mine. I'd been reading every psychiatric tome I could find, learning all about the complex interplay of brain matter and chemistry and environment, trying to chase away *Doomed* by telling a story about it. Scott, though, insisted, "If you want to use anything about psychiatry, you've got to wait until my novel has carved its place into the American consciousness." He told my doctor that regardless of subject matter, he believed another attempt at a novel would only harm me. The doctor, not wanting to take any risk that might compromise his own reputation for success, agreed. We'd been fighting a lot about that.

Gazing at the fire, I continued, "I mean, I sure do hate you. You aren't anything like the man I thought I was marrying."

"I'm exactly the man I was. The real mystery is why I don't divorce you."

"Why would you want to? I'm smart and talented and I can be loving and devoted. I definitely have it in me."

"Remember the night we went riding down Park Avenue with you on the hood of that taxi and me on the running board, hanging on to the roof?"

I smiled. "Didn't we meet Dottie that night, at the Algonquin?"

"Mm. That dinner that Bunny arranged . . . New York sure was a blast."

"Lord, we had fun."

Scott reached for my hand. "Damn it all, you are the love of my life."

Warm words, though, are no panacea. Our ruts were now so deeply cut into the landscape, and we were so tired and worn, that neither Scott nor I could steer ourselves anyplace new.

In early February I trudged the six blocks over snow-crusted concrete to Sara Haardt Mencken's house, thinking, *Gray, cold day, gray, cold month, gray, cold life. Tony's body was gray and cold when I viewed it, same as Daddy's was when he left me behind. Gray cold awaits every living thing.* Even the light-falling snow appeared gray to my eyes. The wind whipped bits of paper trash about my feet. A delivery truck sputtered past, spewing oily smoke into the air in front of me. *God, why have you drained all the color from Baltimore? Isn't it enough to steal all the warmth?*

At Sara's stoop, I looked up at the dozen steps I'd have to climb to reach the door and sighed as if I'd come to the base of Mont Blanc. It might be easier to turn around and go home.

Except, inside one of those windows up there is Sara.

And I needed to see my darling good friend, my touchstone. It wasn't as if I had any particular complaint to share, no particular crisis, no event to fuss about. My list of Scott's offenses had grown so long that the devil himself would grow bored hearing it. But with Scottie gone all day at the Bryn Mawr School, our house was an inanimate space, lacking color, warmth, inspiration, purpose—or maybe that was just me.

"It's awfully cold and gray today," Sara said, after her maid had shown me into the parlor. She coughed, then said, "I shouldn't have asked you over when it's so raw out."

"No, I'm glad to see you."

"Goodness, you're so thin! Are you eating? Your hands are like ice! Here, sit by the fire. How about some hot broth?"

"Fine, sure," I said dully. Trying harder, I added, "Where's Henry today?"

"At the office. It's Tuesday."

"Of course." I stared into the grate. *Tuesday. Of course.*

"And Scott?"

"I haven't seen him since yesterday."

"Ah. Zelda . . . that's partly why I wanted to see you."

I turned toward her. "You know where he is?"

"No." She shook her head. "We saw him on Friday, though. Henry was having a couple of friends in. A quiet gathering—you know how he is." She paused to cough. "No liquor, no music, just a lot of book talk. There was a commotion downstairs, then next thing we knew, Scott was stumbling up the stairs and calling out to ask if they'd started without him."

"But he wasn't invited."

"Yes. So there was a bit of an argument. He's been coming by a lot—late at night, sometimes, long after we've turned in. Henry was losing patience. He said, 'Scott, can't you see this isn't your sort of gathering?' And Scott said, 'Right, right, *I* may have a new *novel* being serialized by *Scribner's Magazine,* but I haven't got the *exalted qualifications* to be a part of this esteemed group. What I do have, however'—and he undid his pants, then dropped them, saying—'is *this.*'"

"He *exposed* himself?"

Sara nodded. "I looked away, of course. We were all terribly embarrassed for him, and Henry hauled him out of the room. Later, Henry said there'd be no more socializing with either of you. He had steam coming from his ears, I swear to you, and that never happens."

I felt sick. "Who can blame him?"

"He eased up regarding you, though. Really, he has nothing against you. But Zelda, Scott has got to get help. How can you bear to stay with him?"

I shrugged.

"When did *you* last see a doctor?"

"It doesn't matter," I said. "They can't cure me, and Scott can't afford to pay them anyway, and I can't pay for myself." I glanced out the window. The view was of pale gray clouds and medium gray buildings and the dark gray water of the bay.

"Maybe you should go stay with Tootsie or Tilde."

I shrugged again.

"Are you writing at all?"

"I've been forbidden. The doctors agree with Scott that it's harmful for me. Maybe they're right."

Sara began to cough, a cough that seemed endless and left blood on her handkerchief.

"When did *you* last see a doctor?" I asked when the spell was past.

"Henry makes me go twice a month. Though of course there's nothing anyone can do."

Those words, that truth about her life and my life and all of life, seeped into my head and played themselves over and over and over. *There's nothing anyone can do.*

I used them as a mantra after reading the serialization of *Tender Is the Night,* which I'd expected to be a perhaps tragic but certainly romanticized, well-fictionalized story that used our experiences as a frame at most. But, no, no, Scott had used whole passages of tortured letters I'd written him from Prangins. He'd made his not-me into a half-homicidal incest victim whose eventual health comes only through the complete destruction of her once-exalted husband's life. I couldn't get any distance from it, couldn't separate myself from his Nicole.

I said nothing.

I poured a drink.

I poured another.

There's nothing anyone can do.

I guess the words showed up on my face and in my eyes, and at some point Scott noticed, and then somehow I found myself in a hospital room at Phipps.

—*Tell us what you're feeling.*

—*Tell us what you're thinking.*

—*Are you angry/hurting/fearful/sad?*

I told them nothing. I was blank.

Phipps wouldn't take on such an uncooperative patient. Scott consulted Dr. Forel, and then off I went to Craig House, an institution in Beacon, New York. *Another long train ride to nowhere,* I thought.

At first, all I could see—when I was alert enough to see anything at all— was a landscape of frozen, barren everything. I welcomed the slow, sucking haze of sedation. I lay prostrate for the team of nurses who prepped me for my insulin-shock therapy, anticipating the bliss of absence that would follow the convulsions. I didn't speak to anyone; what was there to say?

Spring was breaking, though, and soon the ground began to shiver with shocking-white snowdrops and agonizingly blue gentians that, the moment I noticed them, demanded I render them with watercolors.

"I'd like paper, paints, and brushes—and an easel," I told Dr. Slocum, my new dungeon master, when he came by on rounds one morning.

Startled, he said, "Beg pardon? You can speak?"

"You're a sharp one," I told him, and I even tried out a smile. "Those flowers outside are beautiful, see? I have an itch to put them in a picture."

He glanced out the window, then back at me. "Suppose you get dressed and come tell me more about this itch when I finish my rounds." So I did, and during that first session we struck a deal: painting supplies in return for the sort of conversational minutiae psychiatrists thrive on.

As the weeks went by, within those minutiae I tucked my requests for milder sedatives, and fewer insulin treatments, and biscuits with peach preserves. My days began to look like a lady of leisure's; Craig House was resort-like for patients who didn't have to spend their days sedated, or bound to their beds, or both. Plenty of new friends and recreation, little stimulation. I could only guess at what it was costing Scott to keep me there.

"I'd like permission to do some writing," I said one morning, when I'd been there for about a month. I told Dr. Slocum, "I have some short-story ideas nibbling at my brain."

He tented his fingers on his ample stomach. "It's important that you not overtire yourself."

"Maybe I could substitute golf and massage for writing, then."

He smiled wanly. "Here's my concern, Mrs. Fitzgerald: your illness was at its outset preceded by a rise in ambition—"

"That's not what this is," I said. "Probably my husband hasn't mentioned this, but he's heavily in debt. I was thinking I could sell some stories, maybe an essay or two, maybe some of my artwork—but only to help pay for my treatment. Think of it as the equivalent of a woman taking in sewing to help meet expenses. I can't sew worth a damn, but I can draw and paint—and write—well enough to earn what I would with piecework or alterations. I really need to be able to help out in what ways I can."

"Yes, well, admirable as that is, your husband was quite clear about his expectation that we continue the restriction. You yourself have told me that your greatest battles with him have been about your wish to write another book."

"Because he's wrong, and the other doctors were wrong; I feel *better* when I write."

"But inevitably you're disappointed in the outcome and feel *worse*. The drawing and painting are clearly therapeutic; pursue that as your economic contribution and all will be well."

"Will it?" I asked. And then I threw myself into the effort with all the determination I'd once put into my dancing.

"'Parfois la Folie Est la Sagesse,'" I said, reading from one of the brochures the gallery had printed for my exhibition. *Sometimes madness is wisdom.* Scott and I were alone in my room on an afternoon when most of my fellow residents were having massage. "It looks real good, Scott. Real professional."

"It does. This just might be everything you've waited for, darling. Finally you'll get all the recognition you've longed for and deserve."

The art gallery, a space in uptown Manhattan, would show my work for the entire month of April. We'd met the gallery's owner in Antibes years earlier; he'd been wild about my *Girl with Orange Dress* and always believed I ought to have a showing. Scott had seen to most of the details, as enthusiastic about this as he'd been about the Junior League production we'd done back in St. Paul.

I went to the window. All of winter's dun colors had given way to the brilliant, blissful green of new leaves and new grass. Cows dotted a distant hillside beneath wispy white clouds. "I don't know, Deo . . . I'd rather not get my hopes up."

"Hope is one thing you deserve to have more of," he said, coming up behind me. When I turned, he kissed me, kissed me tenderly, kissed me with all the passion and desire we'd used to take for granted.

Then he eased back, and I said, "Well then, I hope you'll kiss me like that again."

"Yes?"

"Yes."

He shut my door and complied. We made love then, with quick, sweet urgency, certain we'd get caught, laughing one moment, breathless and desperate the next.

"God, I miss you," he said when we'd finished and were buttoning up what we'd unbuttoned. "I miss us, *this* us—where do these two people live? Why is it so difficult to find them?"

I looked into those Irish Sea eyes. "I'm awfully sorry" was all I could think to say.

For the exhibit, I would show eighteen drawings and seventeen paintings in all. Some were whimsical expressions of the seventeenth-century French art I'd studied during our time at Ellerslie. Some were tortured-looking ballet dancers—I wanted to show the dancers' impressions of themselves, not the audience's impression of the dancers. Some were linear fantasies inspired by Braque and Pablo. I'd painted huge flowers, and lactating mothers. I'd painted Scott with feathers for eyelashes, his head encircled by a piercing crown of thorns.

For the opening, I was allowed to leave the hospital with a nurse as my travel companion; Scott made sure she had a separate room from us at the Plaza. He had invited every single person we'd ever met plus any and everyone he came across in his daily treks. The Murphys turned out, and Max, plus my doctors, Dos Passos, Dottie Parker, Gilbert Seldes, Bunny, and Henry—who brought the news that Sara was in the hospital with a lung infection, but sent her love.

Some members of the press were there, too, but few strangers came. The ones who did seemed unsure what to make of such a hodgepodge collection. "What is she?" they murmured, unable to figure out which label to apply. Six or eight things sold, most of them for almost no money at all, then I went back to Craig House.

Time magazine ran a review and had found a label for me: *Work of a*

Wife, read the headline, and despite the praise that followed in the body of the review, I felt myself deflating.

Work of a wife.

That was it, *W-I-F-E,* my entire identity defined by the four letters I'd been trying for five years to overcome.

Why was it that every time I finally *chose,* every time I *did,* my efforts failed—*I* failed—so miserably? Why was I so completely unable to take control of my own life? Was there any point to it, for me? I'd thought it was Scott I'd been fighting against, but now I wondered if it was Fate.

When I was young, I'd believed that it would be awful to try and try and try at something only to find that you could never succeed. Now I knew I'd been right: I was not a sufficient dancer, or writer, or painter, or wife, or mother. I was nothing at all.

Send me someplace cheaper, I wrote Scott. *I don't need all of this and only feel worse staying here knowing I will never be able to offset the expense. Didn't Hemingway tell you that I was worthless and you ought to save yourself? He was right.*

Upon swallowing this black, bitter truth, I began to shrink, and before long grew so tiny within the world that I

very . . .

nearly . . .

disappeared.

53

—

Blackness had poured into my head like hot tar. What came afterward is mostly lost to me, though here's what I've since been told:

Scott was out of money, so I moved to a grim sanitarium called Sheppard Pratt Hospital in May of '35. The doctors tried to thin that tar with insulin therapy, or scare it off with electroshock treatments, or blast it from me with pentylenetetrazol, a compound that provokes brain seizures. Still the blackness remained, and I began to see and converse with God.

Poor Scott had nothing but debt to show for all these efforts to get me well, yet the doctors insisted that the only way *out* was *through,* so he consented to more of the terror. He wrote stories when he was able to—but most got rejected or brought far less money than he used to command. He borrowed from the few friends who would still see him, and tried to find his own escape with a lot of liquor and a few women.

At some point someone told me that, unimaginably, Gerald and Sara had lost their oldest boy, Baoth, to meningitis. Then my sweet Sara Haardt got it, too, and between that and the tuberculosis, she'd given up her fight. Then poor Patrick Murphy succumbed to his tuberculosis two years later. Death was everywhere. Tootsie, bless her, saw that I had become eighty-nine pounds of incoherent despair, so she bullied Scott into breaking me out and moving me to a hospital in Asheville, North Carolina, where one of Newman's cousins had been treated with good results. Scott had been spending time in the area off and on—for lung treatments, that's what he said—but meantime hunting hounds with his friend James Boyd, or luxuriating in the rustic elegance of the Grove Park Inn. If North Carolina was a suitable escape for him, he'd reasoned, maybe it would do me good as well.

Highland Hospital was no luxury mountain resort. They had their regimens of drugs and shocks and reeducation. When I was finally capable of noticing my surroundings, I hated myself for being a burden to Scott, who insisted on living in the area in order to see me as often as he could, and too often still drank himself into oblivion in between times. He'd turned forty and, in his pathetic, diminished state, had given an interview to the *New York Post* that persuaded all who read it that he was absolutely ruined.

Highland did something right: in time, I gained back the weight I needed, played a great lot of volleyball, went hiking in the hills, and started painting again. When Scott got an offer to work in Hollywood once more, the money and I both persuaded him to go. "You can do this," I assured him, praying I was right.

By early '38, I was stable as ever, and I stayed that way. I also stayed there at Highland because the doctors insisted that the improvement was temporary. They told Scott I needed to stay put indefinitely—for careful monitoring and control, they said, while Tootsie and Mama were saying what I thought: that for Highland, just as it had been for Prangins, it was all about the money. Scott, though, was terrified by the prospect of having to tend me when he was barely in control of himself. He elected to believe the doctors.

With my ability to see and think and feel restored, what I saw was that even in Hollywood Scott was still stuck—and growing desperate. He was drinking often but working only intermittently, had no money at all, couldn't sell what little fiction he wrote, hardly saw Scottie, had few friends, little hope, and, during a catastrophic trip we took to Cuba in April last year—he got so sick and so drunk that I had to take him to the hospital in New York afterward—the saddest eyes I'd ever seen except in my mirror. "I'll never leave you, Zelda," he said.

What I thought when I saw him being wheeled off was *He's such an extraordinarily brilliant person that it would be terrible if he let himself do nothing in the end.*

What I felt was that same terrible lump in my throat that I'd felt in 1919 right before I'd cut him loose.

Knowing what I had to do, I found a way out of Highland myself. If it involved coercing a certain Dr. Carroll, whose own crimes against certain patients were far worse than my little blackmail plan, well, that was between the doctor and myself. For the first time in a decade, both Scott and I were free.

And now, I wait.

DECEMBER 21, 1940

Montgomery, Alabama

Tootsie is here for the holidays. She and Newman are staying at Marjorie's, so as to keep things simple for Mama and me. We sit together on the porch swing while Mama naps; this is the most pleasant time of day, we agree. I've just filled her in on what's happening with Scottie, and Scott. "I'm hoping he'll wire me money for a trip to see him," I say. "Maybe I'll move out there. Maybe I'll try my hand at scripts."

"Hmm" is her reply. "Well, I can't help noticing how relaxed you are. You sound good, you look good—though a decent haircut would improve the whole package. Do you feel as serene as you look?"

I knock my head with my fist. "Shock therapy. Calms the wild beast."

"It's more than that. Without Scott, you're—"

"Balanced?" Tootsie nods and I say, "I know. I figured that out a good while ago, at Highland."

"Then why ever would you want to change anything? Life here is just about perfect."

"Scott's remade, as much as I am. I think all the chemicals we've put through our systems have finally washed the devil out of us both. It'll be different from now on."

Tootsie looks skeptical. "If *you* believe that's true, I'll try to do the same. But I have to tell you, I've never forgiven him for abandoning you at

Sheppard Pratt. When I found you there"—she shudders—"you were nearly dead, Zelda. Do you remember any of that?"

"Not in any linear way, but I have impressions."

She takes my hand. "What was it like?"

"Do you recall the African river Aunt Julia used to talk about, the one she'd learned of from some tale her granddaddy told?"

Tootsie shakes her head, so I tell her what I remember from Aunt Julia's story, which she told like this:

"In the deep, wet, tangled, wild jungle where even natives won't go is a mystical, dangerous river. The river's got no name because naming it would make it real, and no one wants to believe that river be real. They say you get there only inside a dream—but don't you think of it at bedtime, now, 'cause not everyone who goes there be able to leave!

"That jungle canopy, it so leafy true daylight can never break in. The riverbank, it be wet muck thick with creatures that eat you alive if you stay still too long. To miss that fate, you gots to go into the black water. But the water be heavy as hot tar; once you in, it bind you and pull you along, bit by bit, 'til you come to the end of the land, and then over the water goes in a dark, slow cascade, the highest falls in the history of the world ever.

"There be demons in that cascading water, and snakes, and wraiths that whisper in your ears. They love you, they say. You should give yourself to them, stay with them, become one of them, they say. 'Isn't it good here?' they say. 'No pain, no trouble.' But also no light and no love and no joy and no ground. You tumble and tumble as you fall, and you try and choose, but your mind be topsy-turvy and maybe you can't think so well, and maybe you can't choose right, and maybe you never wake up."

"It felt like that," I tell Tootsie, "even after you got me out and Scott moved me to Highland. I couldn't choose. I couldn't shut out the wraiths. . . . But you would say, 'Hang on, sweetie,' and Scottie would say, 'I miss you, Mama,' and Scott would hold me, just hold me and say nothing at all."

Tootsie snorts. "Scott was useless the whole while."

"Scott was in the river, too."

———

362

Today is the winter solstice, the shortest day of the year. The light's already fading when I go to the closet for my coat. "I need some exercise," I tell Mama, who's got the radio on and is listening to news about the Germans bombing Liverpool again. This new war makes me heartsick. What is wrong with the world? Isn't there enough trouble, sadness, injury, death, in everyday life?

"Where will you go?" Mama asks. "It'll be dark soon."

"Just for a walk. I'll be back in time to help with supper."

My walks are my favorite part of being here in Montgomery. At first, they were my escape from Mama's too-watchful eye. If I so much as frowned, she worried that I was slipping back into depression. "I'm *fine*," I'd tell her, hiding my irritation because I know she worries that I'll end up like our poor Tony.

Now I go more for the pleasure of getting to revisit my past. *There* is the courthouse, so timeless in appearance that it's the most natural thing in the world to imagine my father inside, hard at work to understand and delineate some finer point of law before tidying his desk and shutting off the light, then catching the streetcar for home.

There is the building where the Red Cross had its office during the Great War, which everyone now calls the First World War. Not one of us, back in 1918, would have believed that only twenty years would pass before the Europeans would be at one another's throats again.

There is Eleanor's house, where I am a giddy girl who is unconcerned about women's rights and too concerned about romance.

And there is the corner where Scott proposed to me. Suppose I'd gone home that night and decided that, no, I stood to lose more than I might gain by taking such a risk? In that alternate world, there might be no *Paradise*, no *Gatsby*, none of the hundred or more published stories that readers so love. Ernest Hemingway might yet be poor and little known. And my life, it would look like Marjorie's: safe and predictable and unexceptional and dull. Even now, I wouldn't choose differently than I did.

Passing the post office, I think, again, of following yesterday's letter to Scott. I might miss Montgomery when I'm gone—it has become dear, after all—but I'm willing to sacrifice life here once more if it means I get a shiny new one with Scott. He's forty-four now, and I'm forty, which are not quite the unimaginably old ages we'd once believed they must be. We can start anew.

Finally I'm back at Mama's little house on Sayre Street, where she's lived for several years now. I'm just in time to make it inside before full dark. She worries if I'm not in by dark—which amuses me no end, since it never troubled her when I was young. She's scared of pretty much everything on my behalf. If it's cool out, she fears I'm going to catch cold; if it's hot out, she fears I'm going to get overcome with heat prostration; if it's raining, I'm risking pneumonia; if it's sunny, I'm risking a burn. Too much walking will tire me out, she says. "Why do you persist in going for miles and miles?" She keeps encouraging me to take up knitting; my modernist paintings trouble her.

Scottie, meantime, is at Vassar and doing quite well despite her up-bringing. To hear her tell it, her childhood was replete with wonderful nannies and terrific friends and fascinating teachers. She is a student of the world, as fluent in French as she is in English. Her voice is seasoned with Southern—my hope is that this is all she'll have inherited from me. No, I take that back: I hope she's got my capacity for forgiveness, and her father's, too. We sure don't have anything else of value to pass on to her.

She's staying with Harold Ober and his wife and son for her break from school, but she'll be here for Christmas. My sweet little lamb, all grown up; this feels somehow both so right and so wrong.

The smell of frying pork greets me when I enter the house. "Mama, I'm back!"

There's no reply, so I leave my sweater on the doorknob and go to the kitchen. Mama's sitting at the table with her folded hands pressed to her mouth. Her eyes are damp.

"What's the matter?" I ask. "More bad news? You should stop listening to the radio. There's nothing we can do and it's just so upsetting."

"A man phoned while you were out," she says. "A friend, he said . . . a friend of yours—"

"Harold? Was it Harold Ober? Is it Scottie?"

She shakes her head. "Not Harold."

"*Who,* Mama? Is Scottie all right? She was going to a dance in Poughkeepsie tonight—is it about the dance? Did something happen? It's icy there—"

"No, she's fine." Mama waves her hand, shooing away that particular worry. Then she says, "It's Scott."

"Scott phoned?"

"Scott *died,* Baby. A heart attack. Oh, honey, I'm so sorry."

See me sitting in Montgomery's empty Union Station on a cold, late-December morning, when most of the town's residents are home wrapping presents, baking pies, singing along to carols on the radio. I'm the woman alone on the long wooden bench, there in the middle of the waiting room. Pine garlands with glossy red ribbons make the balcony railings festive. High windows display a steely-gray sky. The arrivals platform is thirty feet away from me, through the stained-glass archway, right outside the doors.

My brothers-in-law Newman and Minor have stayed outside to keep the local reporters at bay. Those reporters, who've been calling the house and stopping by, want to see the weeping widow. They want newsworthy statements—something to supplement the lengthy obituary that ran yesterday, naming F. Scott Fitzgerald as Montgomery's favorite adopted son. Well, here's all I have to say, all that matters, a truth that's so simple but, for me, profound:

Scott is gone.

I've had two days with this truth. This truth and me, we're acquainted now, past the shock of our first unhappy meeting and into the uneasy-cohabitation stage. Its barbs are slightly duller than they were that first night, when even breathing felt agonizing and wrong. Tootsie and Marjorie hovered over me, waiting to see whether I'd collapse, while Mama looked on, white-faced, from her rocker by the fire. "Gone?" I would whisper, to no one in particular. I, too, waited for me to be overwhelmed—but all that happened was what happens to anyone who has lost their one love: my heart cleaved into two parts, *before* and *foreverafterward.* And then in the morning, I called my daughter and delivered the awful news.

Now I sit in the station remembering the suit I wore when I waited in this lobby twenty years and eight months ago, on a spring morning when the train would take Marjorie and me to the grandest city on the planet, to a young, prospering fella who'd imagined and arranged a romantic, imprudent existence for himself and his bride. Now I wear widow's black from the soles of my shoes to the crown of my simple wool hat. Now Scott—Scott's remains, I should say (oh *God*, that sounds so wrong), are traveling by train to Maryland for the funeral next week. Now the train will deliver my daughter, *our* daughter, a girl who's left with only her mother to depend upon.

"He said he was getting better," Scottie had protested when I called. "He sent me Sheilah's old fur coat, and we were— Oh, Mama," she whispered, and the whisper was swollen with tears. "I wasn't supposed to—"

"Shh," I said, tears filling my own eyes again. "It's all right. I knew. I didn't know her name is all. It didn't mean anything."

"He chided me about how I would write my thank-you note—before I'd even begun to think of writing it!"

I smiled a little. "Always looking ahead."

"How can he be *gone*?" she asked me. "It just feels impossible, doesn't it?"

It does. It feels as if, when the train pulls in this morning, Scott will step off it, then stride through the doors and wrap me in his arms. He'll kiss my wet cheeks and say, "What's this? Did you think I wasn't coming back?"

"Yes. Wasn't that silly of me?"

"Lingering side effects," he'll tell me, and tap my forehead gently. "Not to worry. I said I'd never leave you and I meant it. You know me, Zelda. I'm a man of my word."

And he was. Anything that didn't happen—for us, for him—turned out that way despite his best efforts.

Here's the train's whistle now, for the crossing at Court Street, and here's the rumbling that hails the train's approach. I know when I see Scottie, I'll see Scott's face in hers. The past lives in the present, just like he always said, like he always wrote. There's comfort in the thought.

And then when Christmas is done—a strange, somber event it's going to be—Scottie will board the train again, this time bound for Maryland. Again, she'll be traveling alone. All the worriers around me fear I'm too fragile to endure Scott's funeral, and I've chosen not to fight the current this time.

There's no need for me to be present; I'm not saying good-bye.

AFTERWORD

=========

Upon Scott's death, Zelda directed his lawyer to have Scott interred in the Fitzgerald family plot at St. Mary's Church in Rockville, Maryland, which he had said was his wish. The church, however, wouldn't allow this, as Scott was a lapsed Catholic at his death. He was buried instead at the Rockville Union Cemetery.

Together with Max Perkins, Zelda then put Scott's manuscript and notes for *The Love of the Last Tycoon* into Edmund "Bunny" Wilson's hands for editing. In late 1941, Scribner published it as part of a volume that included *The Great Gatsby* and the five short stories that Perkins felt were Scott's strongest works. Titled *The Last Tycoon*, the book was well regarded by critics, beginning an F. Scott Fitzgerald renaissance that would be helped along by paperback Armed Services Editions of *Gatsby* and "The Diamond as Big as the Ritz," which were distributed to servicemen during the Second World War. Soon after, Bunny Wilson compiled Scott's essays in a 1945 collection called *The Crack-Up*, and Dorothy Parker edited a collection titled *The Portable F. Scott Fitzgerald*. These efforts led to others, ensuring Scott's membership in the literary canon he always believed he should be part of, as well as sales of some twenty million copies of *The Great Gatsby* alone, to date.

Because Scott was in debt when he died and because it would be some time before his work would earn more than negligible royalties, Zelda and Scottie had only the thirty-five thousand dollars from his life insurance policy with which to fund Scottie's studies and support Zelda indefinitely. Her monthly income from the trust established by Scott's Princeton friend and lawyer John Biggs, who administered the estate, was not quite fifty dollars, which was supplemented by the thirty-five dollars a month she received for being a veteran's widow. Zelda, therefore, continued to live with her mother in Montgomery. She maintained relationships with a great many friends, including Sara Mayfield, the Murphys, the Obers, and Ludlow Fowler, traveling to visit them and others as often as her budget would permit.

Severed for good, however, was Zelda's connection to Ernest Hemingway, who was becoming increasingly dependent on alcohol and suffered worsening periods of depression. His opinion about the Fitzgeralds grew ever more critical in the years that followed, perhaps as if to push back against Scott's returning popularity. Though biographers and researchers have shown that the unflattering stories Hemingway wrote about the Fitzgeralds in *A Moveable Feast* consist of half-truths and outright fictions, they persist in popular culture as truth. Ernest Hemingway committed suicide in 1961.

In the 1940s, Zelda worked on a novel she called *Caesar's Things* and painted some of her most charming and whimsical works. She did a series of cityscapes depicting New York City and Paris locations, as well as scenes from fairy tales, and made a collection of intricately done, Arthurian-themed paper dolls. All these she exhibited at various galleries, and enjoyed genuine critical acclaim. Many of the paintings have since gone missing or been destroyed, but others have been preserved and are still sometimes exhibited publicly.

Scottie and Zelda's relationship following Scott's death was not always easy. Having been ill during Scottie's most formative years, Zelda was not as close to her daughter as Scott had been, and the two of them sometimes differed in their opinions on appropriate ways to ensure Scott's legacy. Zelda was delighted, though, with Scottie's 1943 marriage to a well-off tax attorney. The births of a grandson in 1946 and a granddaughter in early

1948 brought her real joy. Scottie, who would later have two more children, worked as a journalist, wrote musical comedies for charity events, struggled with alcoholism, and eventually returned to live in Montgomery, where she encouraged young women to get involved in politics.

While Zelda undoubtedly suffered from some type of mental illness, one of her physicians at Highland Hospital, Dr. Irving Pine, believed that Zelda had been largely misunderstood by her other doctors, as well as misdiagnosed as schizophrenic. According to more recent opinions of doctors who have reviewed her medical records, she had what's now called bipolar disorder, which was initially complicated by alcohol use and weakness from excessive physical activity. She suffered debilitating and permanent side effects from some of the very treatments that were supposed to make her well. The cumulative effect of years of "reeducation" and drug therapies may have contributed to her later infrequent episodes of depression and insecurity.

When these episodes occurred, she would go to Highland for brief periods of what she called "stabilization." It was her fourth such stay, begun in January 1948, that would be her last. During the night of March 10, Highland Hospital caught fire; Zelda, who had been out to a dance earlier that evening and then took her prescribed sedative before bed, was one of nine women who were trapped inside. All nine perished in the fire.

Zelda's remains were interred alongside Scott's at Rockville Union Cemetery. In 1975, however, Scottie prevailed in her efforts to have her parents' graves moved to the Fitzgerald family plot and had a marker engraved with the sentence that ends *The Great Gatsby:*

SO WE BEAT ON, BOATS AGAINST THE CURRENT, BORNE BACK CEASELESSLY INTO THE PAST

AUTHOR'S NOTE AND ACKNOWLEDGMENTS

This book is a work of fiction, but because it's based on the lives of real people, I have tried to adhere as much as possible to the established particulars of those people's lives.

It's impossible to find universal agreement, however, about many of those particulars. Where the Fitzgeralds are concerned, there is so much material with so many differing views and biases that I often felt as if I'd been dropped into a raging argument between what I came to call Team Zelda and Team Scott. For every biographer or scholar who believes Zelda derailed Scott's life, there is one who believes Scott ruined Zelda's. Further, popular culture has elevated certain aspects of the Fitzgeralds' lives to myth. (For example, there is steadfast belief but no apparent facts regarding Scott cavorting in the fountain outside the Plaza.) In my efforts to determine where fact gave way to opinion, and where gossip had grown into belief, I tracked differing accounts against established time lines and compared multiple sources, including ones compiled by the Fitzgeralds themselves.

The richest, and in many ways most reliable, resource was the collection of letters the two of them exchanged during their courtship, and then throughout the periods when Zelda was in the hospital and Scott was working in Hollywood. Invaluable, too, were the collections of letters Scott exchanged with his friends, his editor, his agent, and Ernest Hemingway.

While all the letters that appear within the novel are my creations, they are inspired by this amazing body of correspondence.

Fiction based on real people differs from nonfiction in that the emphasis is not on factual minutiae, but rather on the emotional journey of the characters. I've striven to create the most plausible story possible, based upon all the evidence at hand. Of particular interest to me was the exceptional animosity between Zelda and Ernest Hemingway. The animosity was real, yet I found no exploration of the issue, no explanation of *why* it began. Popular belief is that Hemingway simply knew Zelda was "crazy" and bad for Scott right away, but the record shows that he was uncritical and quite warm toward her for a while—until suddenly he was not. I approached the mystery of *why* much as a detective might, considering known motivations, character, and events, to arrive at the scenario I present in the novel.

I want to express my gratitude to the following biographers and editors, whose books and articles about Zelda, Scott, Hemingway, and the Murphys made it possible for me to envision the Fitzgeralds' journey so thoroughly: Linda Wagner-Martin, Nancy Milford, Sally Cline, Kendall Taylor, Amanda Vaill, Andrew Turnbull, John Kuehl, Jackson Bryer, Cathy W. Barks, Mary Jo Tate, Kenneth Schuyler Lynn, and Matthew J. Bruccoli. Special recognition goes to Frances Scott "Scottie" Fitzgerald for working with Scribner's to create *The Romantic Egoists*, a rich photographic representation of her parents' scrapbooks. I recommend it highly.

Also invaluable were Zelda's and Scott's creative works—their stories, novels, and articles, many of which are mentioned here in the novel. For an insightful look at Scott's early work, see the story collection *Before Gatsby*. All of Zelda's published work can be found in *The Collected Writings of Zelda Fitzgerald*. Both books (and many others about the Fitzgeralds) were edited by Matthew J. Bruccoli, whose high regard for them was lifelong and greatly informs my own.

My respect and affection for both Scott and Zelda inspired this book, which, again, is not a biography but a novelist's attempt to imagine what it was like to be Zelda Sayre Fitzgerald.

It's my good fortune to have the support of many friends and family members, including my colleagues from the Fiction Writers Co-op and beyond, members of the Hasenladies Book Club, Pam Litchfield, Sharon Kurtzman, Larry and Jean Lubliner, Michelle and Chuck Rubovits, Bryan and Susan Fowler, Earl Fowler, Pat and Bernie Clarke, Maggie Balistreri-Clarke, Ed Clarke, Jason and Linda Timmons, Adele Dellava, my husband, Andrew, and our boys.

Many thanks to the Weymouth Center for the Arts in Southern Pines, North Carolina, where I was writer-in-residence twice during the creation of this book. To work in what was once novelist James Boyd's home—a home visited by Thomas Wolfe and Scott Fitzgerald, among others—was a genuine privilege and pleasure.

I want to express my enduring appreciation and gratitude to Wendy Sherman, who has been coach and shepherd and friend these seven years, and to Jenny Meyer, for always telling it true.

I'm so pleased to have joined forces with Lisa Highton and the Two Roads team, who are bringing *Z* to readers in the UK and many points beyond.

I am honored by and grateful for the enthusiasm St. Martin's Press has shown for this book. In particular, I want to thank Dori Weintraub for her myriad contributions; Silissa Kenney, Laura Flavin, Laura Clark, Stephanie Hargadon, Steven Seighman, and Olga Grlic for their invaluable efforts; and Sally Richardson, whose faith and enthusiasm mean the world to me. Sally is purely a wonder. Finally, I give my forever-affection to the wise and brilliant Hope Dellon, editor extraordinaire.